BOUND BY LOVE

"I have to look at you," Nick said roughly as she lay curled into him in the dark, fitted to the curve of his body like a jewel in a perfect setting.

"No!" Justine whispered. Wary all at once, she felt him move away from her a little. She heard the scrape of a match in the dark and struck out, sending the box flying from his hands before there had been anything more than a faint blue spark. At once, she felt his arm about her waist, and, though she struggled, he managed somehow to secure her wrists to the bedpost with a soft sash.

"It's only a few hours 'til dawn," he said. "We'll wait."

Justine tugged at her bonds to test their strength, furious with herself for having been caught so easily and afraid of him now, of what he might do if he learned her identity.

"Please!" she whispered hoarsely, the single word freighted with such desperation that he freed her instantly, taking her in his arms.

"I'm sorry if I frightened you, love," he said, his voice softened by self-reproach. "But it wasn't so long, was it, that you were my prisoner?"

Justine almost answered, almost said, *Fool! I am your prisoner, now and forever, bound or free, with you or . . . apart* — and the thought of losing him that came to her then was so awful, she clung to him urgently and held fast, even when his deep breaths told her he'd fallen asleep. . . .

FIERY ROMANCE
From Zebra Books

AUTUMN'S FURY (1763, $3.95)
by Emma Merritt

Lone Wolf had known many women, but none had captured his heart the way Catherine had . . . with her he felt a hunger he hadn't experienced with any of the maidens of his own tribe. He would make Catherine his captive, his slave of love — until she would willingly surrender to the magic of AUTUMN'S FURY.

PASSION'S PARADISE (1618, $3.75)
by Sonya T. Pelton

When she is kidnapped by the cruel, captivating Captain Ty, fair-haired Angel Sherwood fears not for her life, but for her honor! Yet she can't help but be warmed by his manly touch, and secretly longs for PASSION'S PARADISE.

LOVE'S ELUSIVE FLAME (1836, $3.75)
by Phoebe Conn

Golden-haired Flame was determined to find the man of her dreams even if it took forever, but she didn't have long to wait once she met the handsome rogue Joaquin. He made her respond to his ardent kisses and caresses . . . but if he wanted her completely, she would have to be his only woman — she wouldn't settle for anything less. Joaquin had always taken women as he wanted . . . but none of them was Flame. Only one night of wanton ecstasy just wasn't enough — once he was touched by LOVE'S ELUSIVE FLAME.

SAVAGE SPLENDOR (1855, $3.95)
by Constance O'Banyon

By day Mara questioned her decision to remain in her husband's world. But by night, when Tajarez crushed her in his strong, muscular arms, taking her to the peaks of rapture, she knew she could never live without him.

SATIN SURRENDER (1861, $3.95)
by Carol Finch

Dante Folwer found innocent Erica Bennett in his bed in the most fashionable whorehouse in New Orleans. Expecting a woman of experience, Dante instead stole the innocence of the most magnificent creature he'd ever seen. He would forever make her succumb to . . . SATIN SURRENDER.

Available wherever paperbacks are sold, or order direct from the Publisher. Send cover price plus 50¢ per copy for mailing and handling to Zebra Books, Dept. 2525, 475 Park Avenue South, New York, N.Y. 10016. Residents of New York, New Jersey and Pennsylvania must include sales tax. DO NOT SEND CASH.

BEYOND SURRENDER
JOYCE MYRUS

ZEBRA BOOKS

KENSINGTON PUBLISHING CORP.

ZEBRA BOOKS

are published by

Kensington Publishing Corp.
475 Park Avenue South
New York, NY 10016

First printing: December, 1988

Printed in the United States of America

Chapter 1

"I've absolutely decided. I *will* not marry Walter de Peyster," Justine Hawkes said, sitting very erect, hands folded in front of her. Anticipating the uproar her pronouncement was certain to elicit, she tossed back her long, loose tiger-blond hair and let her unflinching clear green eyes travel the length of the suddenly silent dinner table.

Set with lace, cut crystal, and polished Tiffany silver, it was surrounded by relations and old family friends of the sort who were addressed as aunt, uncle, and cousin, whether or not there was an actual tie of blood. They were all gathered for a Sunday dinner at Silver Hill, the Hawkes estate on the East End of Long Island. Justine had chosen to speak at the end of the soup course, and when she did, even the serving girl clearing away the bowls and the impeccably correct houseman pouring wine, paused in astonishment. As she calmly folded her slender hands in her silken lap, Justine saw that her expectations of pandemonium were accurate.

"Oh, my dear! Not again! Your reputation will be ruined, simply ruined!" Brigida Hawkes exclaimed looking at her beautiful daughter with disbelief and consternation. "Are you sure you want to do this? An attack of nerves before a wedding is to be expected, darling."

"I *am* sorry, Mother. But I cannot marry Walter," Justine insisted with an apologetic little shrug. "I don't love him, and that's that."

"Why do you lead them on so?" Gray Hawkes asked his sister. "A little flirtation can be quite stirring, I've learned from experience, without going so far as to actually break hearts. You don't enjoy breaking hearts, do you, Justine?" Closest to her both in age and temperament of her four brothers, Gray was not really displeased at this turn of events. He'd always thought de Peyster something of a fop and no proper match for his exquisite sister.

"But . . . I thought I was in love with him, I did really, Gray," Justine insisted, looking adorably distressed, he thought, and he didn't miss the spark of mischief in her eyes.

"You were *really* in love with the one before Walter. And the one before that. For such a clever child, you're awfully foolish about this sort of thing." Jude, the eldest of the Hawkes sons, often took a paternal tone with Justine, the youngest in the family and the only girl. Reaching for a gilt-engraved card on the sideboard behind him, he read aloud with obvious if gentle sarcasm. " 'Mr. and Mrs. Slade Hawkes request the honor of your presence at the marriage of their daughter . . .' That's you." He glanced up at Justine who just smiled prettily. ". . . 'to Walter William de Peyster on Sunday, the twelfth of June, 1898, at half after two at Silver Hill.' That's barely three weeks off. Well, Justine?" he queried. Knowing every one of her kith and kin would have some comment to make, Justine determined to let them each have a say before offering any further explanations of her own.

"Fickle. Shallow Cruel." Roweena McGlory spat out the words with righteous disapproval. She and Justine were "courtesy cousins," and the two had, since childhood, shared a kind of intimate enmity. Roweena, a woman approaching thirty, was mean and divisive by nature and especially jealous of Justine's vibrant beauty, her Social Register standing, and the coterie of fashionable friends and admirers who surrounded the younger, prettier girl. "It's a family disgrace, Justine." Roweena was relishing this rare opportunity to openly attack her "dear little cousin" in front of everyone. Her eyes positively gleamed with malevolent satisfaction. Not an entirely unattractive woman, she had wide cheekbones and a clear high forehead, albeit a too-prominent nose. But her eerily pale eyes always looked on the world with malice or suspicion. Her small mouth was usually pinched in disapproval giving her face, that was framed by oddly thick, dark hair, the look of a clenched fist. "You know," she added, "it's not *done,* calling off a wedding three weeks before the date. You'll be a laughing-stock, shunned by all good society."

"Well, I've done it," Justine answered matter-of-factly, with a little frown. The servants were now moving about the table again, bearing heaping silver platters beautifully arranged.

"Judgment and character are to be valued, not the hollow forms of 'good society,'" Roweena's mother, Anne McGlory, commented, in a clear reference to her daughter's snobbery and to Roweena's lately vanished husband who'd absconded with a considerable quantity of cash and jewels. An elegantly dressed woman with canny eyes and a downturned mouth that gave her a jaded look, Anne brought a wine glass to her lips and shook her head in irritation. "I always thought," she said to Justine, "that your match with Walter de Peyster was a mésalliance. And I'm always right about these things, am I not, Roweena?"

"And what the bloody blazes is wrong with Walter I'd like to know?" Billy McGlory boomed across the table at his wife. "If your daughter had a chance at 'im, she'd be in seventh heaven and so would I, and here goes Justine runnin' off on another one," he added, as Roweena cringed with embarrassment at her father's crudity. She had always been unhappy with her own station in life. Her parents were, after all, "in trade," her mother a dressmaker, her father a saloon keeper, even if they called themselves a couturiere and a restaurateur. Billy McGlory, a big broad-shouldered man, now potbellied, had the battered look of the prize fighter he'd been as a young man. Before Justine's startling pronouncement, he'd been bemoaning, not for the first time, the downfall of John L. Sullivan after twenty-one rounds of bare-knuckled boxing, a disaster Billy had never been able to accept, though it had occurred nearly six years before.

"What? What Mulligan?" Justine's slightly deaf grandfather, Del, demanded, holding up an ivory ear trumpet. "I thought she was marrying a de Peyster. Good old stock, the de Peysters." A frail man well up in his eighties, Del had been loudly extolling the beneficial effect of vegetarianism to his old friend, the local doctor, Wade Burleigh, who had himself been half listening to the discussion at the far end of the table, at which Justine's father, Slade Hawkes, and her two middle brothers had been analyzing Commodore Dewey's victory over the Spanish in Manila Bay two weeks before. Near them, a tiny, thin, crusty old lady with expressive, blue-veined hands, Justine's grandmother, Elizabeth, had been expounding on the comparative merits of two new varieties of roses to another small, but very round, old woman, her dear friend, the former housekeeper at Silver Hill, Martha Phillips.

"It's well you're getting rid of that de Peyster boy," Elizabeth told Justine. "I've known the family for seventy years. Their babies are all colicky and their old men gouty. You'd have been bored into invalidism by the lot of them in no time."

"But her father should have arranged a match for the girl long ago," Martha complained. "I raised all the babies here—her father . . . her brothers . . . practically had to finish raising her mother, too, when Brigida came to this house a bride, not nearly as old as this baggage, not nineteen. With all the nannies and governesses and tutors Justine had, *I* know what's best for her. Get your daughter married to a man who can take her in hand," Martha ordered Slade Hawkes. "She's been given her head—freedom . . . education—and see the upshot? Scandal!"

Toying a bit nervously now with the cameo holding a deep lace collar at her throat, Justine glanced from beneath long, lowered lashes at her father at the head of the table. Slade Hawkes was a remarkably prepossessing man, of dark good looks, graying at the temples, with deep-set thoughtful eyes

9

and the strong chiseled features his sons had all inherited. His daughter, to his infinite delight, was the image of his wife, slender and fair and of a delicate beauty that, like her mother's, never ceased to surprise and amaze him, the one striking difference was the girl's lovely long slanting green eyes. Though Slade was pleased and proud and companionable with his sons, this girl-child, his youngest, coming as she had five years after the last boy, was an unexpected gift, his treasure. He'd always thought of her, and treated her, as a jewel to be kept safe in a velvet case, protected, and lavished with care. If it hadn't been for Brigida, so sensible and so understanding, he thought, glancing at his wife, the child would have been exquisitely spoiled. But her mother had kept Justine down to earth, passing on her own domestic skills and practical acumen—how to run a house and staff, but also how to do everything herself, if need be, to keep a family, a garden, a farm, going perfectly. The girl had been sent to school, then to Barnard College for two years. Inculcated with the responsibilities of the wealth and privilege to which she'd been born, Justine worked diligently as a volunteer, as did many young women of her position, for the Children's Aid Society in the settlement houses and tenements of New York City. All in all, he couldn't have been more delighted with the child who'd grown into an unusually sensible and independent young woman—sensible about everything but love. Now he knew she was waiting for him to champion her cause in this latest predicament. Slade casually sat back in his chair and offered her a barely perceptible, conspiratorial wink.

"I disagree with you, Martha," he said. "I think

Justine's young, at nineteen, for marriage. What do you think, Levi? What's to be done with my incorrigible daughter?" he turned to Levi Phillips, old Martha's son.

"The girl's got a mind quick as summer lightning. Stop worrying over her," Levi answered laconically, his tone implying tempests brewing in teapots, mole hills becoming mountains.

"But they're already gossiping in New York over her high-handedness with the others. They're saying she was rushing into this marriage before she could change her mind again," Jude's wife, Lucy, a Boston Ainsworth, reported.

"Justine always been in a hurry. She was even born two weeks before she was expected." Dr. Burleigh smiled.

"Well, I have changed my mind, so that proves them wrong, Lucy," Justine couldn't help interjecting. She was beginning to lose patience.

"A lady has got every right to change her mind but this impetuosity is getting ridiculous," the wife of Justine's brother Michael said in a soft New Orleans drawl. "She is being called a tease and a heartless flirt *now*. Imagine the talk there'll be in Saratoga and Newport this summer once the latest news gets out!"

"By the by, sister," Michael asked, "has the groom been told of the change in plans?" Justine only nodded. "And? . . ." he prompted, rolling his eyes skyward in mock frustration.

Justine pursed her lips and gazed off into the distance, through French doors that had been thrown wide on the beautiful May afternoon, offering a view of blue water and cloudless sky. A bevy of little girls in pastel smocks, her nieces, were settled like a flock of purling doves on the wide green lawn and she caught glimpses of noisy darting little boys, playing hoops and balls. After being fed earlier in the nursery, the younger children had been loosed into the bright sunshine like flower petals wafted on gentle breezes. Justine sighed deeply, all at once longing to be among them with a lovely, long Silver Hill summer, like all the summers of her childhood stretching endlessly before her, and with nothing so adult and tedious to worry over as broken engagements and broken hearts. She turned to Michael.

"Walter said," she began, " 'I just can't tell you, Justine, how much I love you.' He said that." She nodded. "He also said, 'I can only hope, Justine, that you'll love someone . . . someday . . . just this way.' " She looked about the table, her eyes green flickering with that hint of mischief that often lurked in them, close to the surface, even at the most serious moments. "And I told him, 'I hope I do, too, Walter,' and gave him a sweet kiss. He'll get over me and be all the happier with someone else who'll love him more. I told him that, too."

"You are an unrepentant little optimist, aren't you?" Philip Carpenter asked. An old family friend, he had recently returned home after years of travel and to Justine he was a stranger in their midst. "You know, I never got over your mother. That's what made me the wayward man I am, and sent me rambling half across the earth to the South Seas . . . to Australia.

"Oh, I didn't know about that," Justine said. With new interest, she seriously studied Philip's deeply lined and weathered face. Though she hardly knew him, she'd known about him all her

12

life, it seemed. It was this man who had sent her the magnificent black opals from Australia, a birth gift, her birth stone, her most prized possessions, her lucky charm. She'd worn them for the first time to her first ball though she'd known about them forever, too, it seemed. As a little girl, she had daydreamed about the mysterious Uncle Philip who'd sent her one of the rare and beautiful stones every October. Now she had a priceless collection of nineteen gems, magnificently set.

"You should have a care with young men's hearts. They're fragile, you know," Philip said with a sad smile, his words going straight to Justine's own heart, so that for a moment she couldn't speak, and was able to imagine, looking at him — to feel for the first time — how hurtful it was to be desolated by love.

"I will be careful from now on," she declared finally, "I promise."

"You might be the luckiest man in the world, Slade Hawkes," Philip said, though smiling broadly now at Justine. "You've got such a lovely family, and your wife . . . she's still as beautiful as the day you and I first laid eyes on her twenty-five years ago. Still dewy fresh and slim as a girl, and there's hardly a silver thread among the gold. Brigida," he said, turning to her, "you've been oddly silent on the subject of your daughter's future. What do you think should be done with her?"

"If she were a boy," Slade interjected, "she could be sent to sea for a stint as her brothers all were, as I was as a lad, but . . ."

"But she must be sent *somewhere*," Brigida finally spoke, having given the matter careful consideration. "There will be scandal and she must be

13

protected. In five or six months, when this has all blown over, Justine can come back and make a good match, one that—"

"Five or six months?" Justine echoed incredulously, glancing from mother to father and back again, aware of Roweena's smirk, of Gray's startled eyes and Levi's scowl. "I'll perish of homesickness."

"Darling girl, your mother's right," Slade shook his head, agreeing with Brigida as always when serious matters got down to particulars. "Don't forget, you are descended from solid seafaring stock—world wanderers—on both sides. You'll survive a little travel."

"Survive? Ha!" Elizabeth barked. "She'll do better than that." "Justine, you listen to me," the old woman ordered. "There's an excitement . . . a restlessness in the air now. The millennium is about to turn, the world is changing and you my dear are a courageous, modern young woman bred for the new century. Besides that, you're my granddaughter. You'll do splendidly wherever you go. Just don't be so quick to call every little flutter of the heart love."

"Yes, she will do fine," Grandfather Del agreed. "Who could resist that impudent charm of hers? No one, that's who!"

"She's flighty, but she's got her practical side, too; her mother and I saw to that," Martha interjected, taking credit where it was due. "But she needs settling down."

"She's wonderfully energetic." This from Anne.

"Impatient." From Gray.

"Willful." Roweena put in.

"Impetuous!" Michael declared.

"Needs a steadying hand." Jude said calmly.

"But she's got her mother's femininity and grace." Philip turned to positive attributes.

"And her father's taste for beauty and elegance," Doctor Burleigh commented.

"Slade's eye for horseflesh, too," Levi pronounced. "His passion for riding, for racing, for betting, and for winning. Leave the girl be."

"Also . . ." Billy stopped short when Justine suddenly stood, upsetting her chair. She covered her ears and closed eyes glazed over with furious tears and simply said, "Don't!" So loudly even Grandfather Del could hear her without his trumpet. In the ensuing silence, everyone, including the servants, stared, taken back. Then, resting her hands on the edge of the table Justine stood tensely, her tall, elegant, slim form quite atremble with anger as she tried to regain her composure though furious at everyone for meddling in her life.

"Please don't talk about me as if I weren't even here. I'll decide my own future," she declared, and then almost laughed aloud at realizing that moments before all she'd wanted was to be a child again.

"Justine, do you know what it is you really want?" Slade asked gently, and she nodded. "Well then, will you tell us?"

"I want . . . to be loved. Unequivocally . . . wildly, without reason or reserve. I want to be loved . . . madly, to complete distraction!"

"Oh, is that all?" her mother asked with a humorous little smile, directing a faintly worried glance at her father.

"No. I want to love unequivocally . . . wildly . . . madly . . . to complete distraction!" Justine answered, startled by her own words but knowing

15

even as she spoke them they were true. That *was* what she wanted and everything else be damned! She turned from the table, and the house dogs, three slumbering Pekingese, were instantly alert and scurrying about her ankles as she gathered up a kitten who'd wandered to the open French door. She inhaled the scent of pine and sand and sea in its fur. "Madly!" she called over her shoulder then.

Laughing with delight, she ran off to join the children at their games on the great lawn.

"She certainly has her father's determination," Brigida sighed.

"And her mother's lovely laugh," Slade added.

" 'Thou art thy mother's glass and she in thee/ Calls back the lovely April of her prime,' " Philip recited the lines from Shakespeare's sonnet. "She's also got quite a flair for the dramatic," he mused. "What's to be done?"

"I've a suggestion," Gray Hawkes said thoughtfully.

The others were still at the table sometime later when Justine, in a blur of silk and lace and golden curls, rode past the windows on her silver mare, headed for the shore.

Chapter Two

Low gray clouds dimmed dawn sunlight as Justine rode through a fine sea mist, along a curve of beach where ocean and land met at low tide. The wet sand was shiny and glistening, festooned with lacy bands of foam left by the receding water. Her mount, a four-year-old bright chestnut with a pale mane and tail, was, in equestrian parlance, a "daisy cutter," she was discovering. That meant he took long, low strides, his hoofs close to the ground, at least in the slower gaits at which she'd already tested him. Concentrating intently, she urged him into a slow gallop, the animal confidently surging forward at the slightest pressure of her knees and calves, his quick response enhancing her pleasure in the early morning ride and heightening her already high opinion of the horse, a French-bred polo pony she was seriously considering acquiring. At the fast gallop, the most natural gait for a properly trained thoroughbred of good conformation, he seemed almost to leave the earth and hang suspended with each stride, like the winged horse Pegasus, and she decided then and there she would have him. Whirling about into the mist, setting up a spray of foam, horse and rider turned in a wide, graceful arc to retrace their path along the sand, the hoofprints filling, as soon as they were laid down, with rushing sea water that would soon obliterate them completely.

On Deauville beach in Normandy at five in the morning, the dark-gleaming animal's legs stretched out fully at every long stride, his muscles rippling beneath the satin sheen of his coat. His slight, long-legged jockey, her long yellow hair streaming, was riding astride, using the short stirrup, sitting up high and forward, her fine flexible hands moving back and forth with every extension of her racing mount's neck. Both were enjoying themselves immensely, alone in the unpeopled morning world, the gulls just off the beach, riding the mist banks, disappearing and reemerging and letting out high shrieking calls as they fished the waves.

The stallion's speed diminished as he was eased through the slower gaits until, leaning to caress his neck, Justine dismounted, dropping the reins over his head. They were both breathing deeply as she extracted a pen knife and an apple from the pocket of her crimson riding jacket and, sharing the fruit with her equine companion, gazed over the long gray swells of the English Channel. She was thinking of home and the sands of the barrier beach at Silver Hill, once touched, perhaps, by these very same Atlantic waters though not yet this day by the ripening dawn. Sunrise was still hours away from the Montauk light on the eastern tip of Long Island and it surprised her a little to find herself so far from home particularly on what was to have been her wedding day, June 12th, 1898. With a wonderful sense of regained freedom, she sighed happily and reminded herself to thank Gray again for his brilliant solution to her problem.

Going down on her knees, she retrieved a small scallop shell offered up by a low wavelet. It was tiny

18

and perfect, the inner side a delicate pink, exactly like so many she'd found and discarded on her own side of the sea. This one she slipped into her pocket to take home to Silver Hill. Rather like carrying coals to Newcastle, she mused. Nonetheless she was charmed by the thought of a French scallop shell resting among the others in the vitrine in the library.

It was as she stood again that Justine saw the mounted rider emerge from the morning mist, already close and coming on so fast he'd have ridden her down if she hadn't hurled herself against her own horse, she and the animal moving out of the madman's path with inches to spare. At the last second he swerved off, his shouted words carried away on the wind and muted by the roil of the surf just as the sound of his approach had been. He shot past her, then whirled about and rode back, still at breakneck speed, for no other reason apparently than to repeat what he'd said. He sounded very angry, though Justine, not fluent in French, caught only a word or two, and those decidedly unpleasant—*imbécile* and *crétin* among them.

"Pardon, monsieur!" she began indignantly, lapsing at once into English, "but I must ask you to keep a civil tongue. You've no cause to berate *me* for *your* recklessness." She turned toward him, her face hidden until then against the side of her horse. "It was your fault, actually," she began, then hesitated, her eyes fixing on a very well made, well worn, and polished leather boot and a silver spur studded with turquoise. "You, sir, nearly rode over me," she concluded, looking up.

"Oh, an American," he said, not with pleasure, gazing off, looking at the sky, the sea, at his mount's lathered neck—everywhere but at her. "I suppose the place will soon be overrun with them, too, as it now is with English . . . and . . ."

"Yes?" Justine asked, meeting his eyes finally, knowing exactly why he'd gone silent. Confident as she was of the power of her beauty, she was anticipating with pleasure the effect her appearance would have on this short-tempered, impolite churl, but she'd have fled on the instant if he'd spoken his mind.

"Well"—he began again evenly, his voice darkening and deepening—"I'd wager there hasn't been anything like you since . . . the dawn of creation." The faintly exotic, stunning beauty of her exquisite, heart-shaped face, combined with her soap-scrubbed freshness, seemed to be affecting this man as it did every other who looked for the first time at Justine Hawkes. Her slanting, sea-foam green eyes, like aqueous jewels, were alive with laughter and beginning to dance with mischief, he saw. The first shaft of sun to pierce the morning mist flamed her golden hair, and the wind lifted it like a lover, tugged at her hem, and caressed her long legs and lithe body which was perfectly slender yet temptingly full, her waist so small he could encircle it, her breasts so rounded and thrusting, he could feel their weight in his hands, sense the tips firming in his fingers. He could imagine the taste of the sweet peony mouth that was both childlike and sensuous, and was curling now into a lovely schoolgirl smile as she placed a slim, half-gloved hand on the pommel of her saddle.

"But . . . you, too, are an American, are you not?" she asked as the man continued to stare down at her, fierce-eyed and imperious. His was an extraordinary face she thought, lean and narrow and brutally handsome, the expression almost cruel, certainly cold. Above a square cleft chin were hollowed cheeks and severe, angular bones. Dark eyes were set beneath strong brows, and his very black hair was worn unfashionably, yet attractively, long so that it brushed the collar of his hacking jacket.

"Yes, American. California," he said. "And not at all what you're looking for." His sudden, unexpected rascally grin didn't quite reach his eyes. Another Dollar Princess, but a beautiful brat, this one, he was thinking as she looked at him in confusion. One more silly little American heiress shopping for a European title and the great pile of old stones, the ancestral seat, that went with it.

"Looking for?" Justine queried, thinking Oh no, I'm surely not looking for you, *sir,* not for that hard handsome face. Nor for those fierce, melancholy Gypsy eyes, craving . . . rapacious . . . compelling eyes. Yet she was unable to turn away, though she was in fear all at once, not of him but of herself. I *promised* . . . I promised father I wouldn't do it again, fall in love, not so soon, no so . . . dangerously.

"You should take better care in the fog," he said not unkindly now, though with that same savage glare.

Justine said nothing more, just mounted up with easy grace, though her knees were atremble. Carefully, she took up the reins with unsteady hands, put the horse into a leaping gallop start from a dead standstill, and rode off without another word or backward glance, the words *I promise, I promise* repeating in her ears in cadence with the chestnut's hoofs.

"Promise one thing," Slade Hawkes had asked almost sternly before he'd granted permission for Justine's trip abroad. "That you'll not fall in love again for at least . . . oh, two weeks, but that if — when — you do" — he corrected himself with a smile — "you'll have the good sense to wait for it to prove true before you announce it from the rooftops." Justine had promised of course, flinging her arms about his neck, had promised from the bottom of her heart and had meant to keep her word no matter what.

"I shan't even look at a man, only at horses, I *swear*, Father," she'd bantered. They had been in the library at Silver Hill, the French doors open onto the great lawn and spring sky, blue and green reflected in the mirror over the fireplace at the opposite end of the room. Brigida, on the settee, was knitting a shawl for a grandchild due in the summer. Slade was beside her, puffing on his pipe and watching Justine pace the room with her usual exuberant energy. Gray leaned against the doorframe, clearly pleased with himself for having made so brilliant a suggestion. His sister had agreed, on the instant, to travel with him. She had in fact been so delighted with his idea she'd run up and down the stairs three times in an excess of exuberance.

Their passage, on a Cunard liner sailing the following week, had been booked immediately, Gray more than happy to move up the date of his long-planned departure for Europe, which was to have taken place soon after his sister's wedding. The purpose of his excursion to England, Ireland, and the Continent was the purchase of bloodstock for stud for Silver Hill's thoroughbred racehorses and the acquisition of additional mounts for his father's strings of polo ponies, already among the best in the Americas, North and South.

Fair as his sister and very tall, with a youthful lankiness about him still at twenty-four, Gray was a real horse trader, Slade knew, though in these modern days entrepreneur or financier were the preferred descriptions. The boy was shrewd and clever. His passion was profit, as Justine's was horses. The combination was unique and perfect for the purpose they all had in mind.

In very American form, mixing business with pleasure, there would be a good deal of socializing on the excursion, Gray had promised Justine. He had invitations already in hand to some of the grandest English country seats and French châteaux. Their hosts would be friends and acquaintances of the senior Hawkes, many of them members of the nobility that so fascinated certain Americans, those able to afford the hunting, racing, pig sticking, yachting, and other sports at which not a few of the European idle rich worked so hard. But between the house parties and hunt balls, Gray and Justine would do some real work, visiting stud farms and sale paddocks at race courses all over Europe. For both the work and play he had in mind, Gray had said, he could imagine no more delightful companion than his sister, Justine. Her eye for a superior horse was unmatched and her social instincts were superb. Open, charming, and startlingly beautiful, she relished every new experience, and her obvious enthusiasm attracted attention and invitations. She made new friends and she made things happen wherever she went.

"But you know, darling child," Brigida had said that day in the library, "no matter what you are looking at, men will concentrate on you. Great beauty can be a burden sometimes. It complicates life for a woman. I've told you that before."

"Who would know better than you, Mother?" Justine smiled, watching Brigida's clever hands, realizing she'd rarely seen them still, that she'd never known her mother to sit idle. "I will be cautious and sensible, really. I've learned from this mess with Walter that one must be."

"In that case," Brigida offered, "I'll tell you what my mother once told me—trust your instincts. They're sound, really, Justine, if you just take a moment to think before you leap."

"Or fall, as in 'fall in love.' Don't worry I'll keep an eye on the child," Gray nodded.

"Well, it's settled then and if you two leave in a few days, you'll reach England in time for Royal Ascot in early June. That's a horse event not to be missed," Slade said.

"But, Father, it's also the social event of the season there and I've absolutely nothing to wear!" Justine complained with such theatrical dismay they all had to laugh.

But of course she was packed and ready to leave on time, any little gaps there may have been in her wardrobe filled by Anne McGlory's busy seamstresses.

And so it happened that Justine Hawkes and her brother, Gray, made something of a stir at Ascot in the spring of 1898. In keeping with custom, he was dressed in a silk top hat and tails. Justine, on his arm, wore an amber satin and black lace gown, a bonnet streaming matching ribbons, and her black opals, like a captive rainbow, at her throat. And they both thoroughly enjoyed themselves.

"Dear Father and Mother," she had written some

days after the event, from Tramby Croft, the house at which she was a guest, "Ascot Race Week was a wonderful event, a great display, just as you promised. On the opening day, a very handsome man, a Lord Something or Other (they're *all* titled, it seems), wearing a gold belt and a bright green coat, led the royal procession down the turf that was very, very green. Fortunately, the sky was also very, very blue, at the Queen's command, one supposes.

"Gray and I were invited to occupy seats in the Royal Enclosure where the fashion display was wonderful. Before the Gold Cup was run, we dined on lobster, the Prince's favorite, in the Luncheon Hall, which has a glass conservatory roof that is kept cool by constantly flowing water that passes over it, a clever idea. The Prince of Wales, Edward the Caresser, as he is unkindly called—he's *that* interested in the ladies—is portly and balding, though regal enough in manner even with his pale, protruding eyes and receding hair. He seems to have taken notice of me. 'Divinely tall,' he said and, 'a beauty so dazzling it is almost unbelievable.' I am told this on the best authority, that of my hostess, Lady Glenmere, who accompanied us to Ascot.

"On the way into the park, we stopped, just for the fun of it, as many did, to have our fortunes told by a Gypsy woman who frequents the race tracks. You'll not believe what she said to me! 'You will win a bet on a horse and lose your heart to a tall, dark, handsome stranger.' Imagine! Gray and I had a good laugh about it, but she was partly right. I did win ten pounds, though I've kept my heart despite no end of dark, handsome strangers all about.

"Oh yes, I nearly forgot, Gray has purchased a very promising yearling filly, a chestnut with fine head

25

carriage. You'll never guess her name! She's Love Wisely, of all things, out of Slim Lady by Pendragon. We think you'll be pleased.

"I must end now as we are leaving in moments only for a country house party in Hertfordshire, north of London. The Prince, called Bertie by his intimates, of which there seem to be a great many, may be attending. The goings-on among the wild Marlborough House Set — that's the Prince's circle — are scandalous despite little old Queen Victoria's staid views. People here are fond of quoting a rather pretty actress, a Mrs. Campbell, who summed it up well, I think. 'It doesn't matter what you do,' she said, 'as long as you don't do it in the street and frighten the horses.'

"Oh now, Father, don't frown and don't be shocked by the frivolous ways of these supposedly respectable people. They are really delightful when one gets to know them. I am reluctant to leave England so soon, but Gray says we must, to see the stud farms of Normandy. We'll get the train at Charing Cross Station for Dover and take the boat to Calais. It won't be the peak of the racing season there at Deauville, but there will be polo! Gray says to tell you he has been playing your favorite game, Father, Scotch croquet as he calls golf.

"Well, I do miss you terribly." Justine concluded with kisses to all, deciding not to register her one complaint, the presence of Roweena McGlory.

The woman had accompanied them, in the role of chaperone to Justine, though she was really husband hunting for herself. Seasick during the entire Atlantic crossing, Roweena had done little but complain, and had found fault with everything since. The accommodations were too chilly, the servants too lax; even the food at Deauville was to "fancy" for her taste. Suffering dyspepsia, Roweena had kept to her room refusing Justine's dutiful invitations to morning outings at the beach.

And so it was that Justine found herself riding out alone early on the morning of June twelfth. In fashionable Deauville for only a few days, she and Gray had already acquired several excellent additions to the Hawkes stables. Normandy, particularly Calvados, the area of France in which the resort town was situated, had always been known for its fine stud farms, and Ormonde, the animal Justine was testing that day, was a prime product of centuries of breeding. It was when the horse had thrust his velvety nose against her pocket in search of more apple that a glint in the sand had caught Justine's eye.

She'd knelt to retrieve that sea shell and the wild rider had come out of the fog, his eyes fierce, arrogant, unforgettable.

The next morning, the very one after that unsettling encounter, Justine found herself in the very same place at the very same time. She was perfectly aware she shouldn't be there at all, but she had to test herself because she suspected she'd done it again, fallen in love, this time with a total and rather intimidating stranger.

Vehemently hoping her suspicions were wrong, she stared into the morning mist, hoping for a glimpse of the broad shoulders and brutally handsome face she hadn't been able to get out of her thoughts for the past twenty-four hours. But she *had* made a promise, one she fully intended to keep no matter what, no matter if . . .

He was there and her heart began to pound wildly at her first glimpse of him, tall and commanding, moving toward her obliquely as he put his well-schooled mount through a series of exercises—half-turns and reverses and pivots at varying gaits, horse and rider a pleasure, a joy to watch.

When they finally passed Justine, a dramatic sight in her white riding suit when mounted up on a small black Arabian mare, the man's rapacious eyes widened a little and he grudgingly offered his slow rakish grin as if gifting her with something rare and precious. She responded with her own bounteous, beautiful, unstinting dazzle of a smile but never slowed, not for a moment, though she did glance back over her shoulder. He caught her peeking and raised an inquisitive brow to which she responded with chilly hauteur, something not easy for so warm and spontaneous a girl as Justine Hawkes.

On the third morning, he lazily touched his hat as she approached, a wide-brimmed Stetson rolled on one side, and she found it difficult to break the hold of his black-velvet stare.

The next day as sunbeams were turning high cloud castles to gold, he overtook her as he went along at a canter, and some distance down the beach, he did a sharp reverse to come riding back toward her. Before he could pass again, Justine had wheeled about and fled, cutting short her ride. She would have to go out earlier, before full light, she told herself and be gone by the time he got there. This little flirtation had gone far enough. Retreat was the only way to avoid a situation she couldn't—wouldn't—allow to develop. Yet, despite herself, she wondered if he'd seen her turn away and hoped he'd miss her tomorrow when she wasn't there.

A quarter morning moon lit the beach just enough, through drifts of clouds, so that Justine could ride, the ocean's black swell to one side, the light-bleached sand to the other. In the near distance were the luxurious vacation villas of Deauville and beyond them the town, still drowsing in the hours before dawn.

She was taking the measure of yet another mount in which Gray had shown an interest, and she was less than enthusiastic about the animal. The French-bred bay was leggy. He had too much daylight under him, he was short gaited, and inclined to be fretful, obstinate, and mean. Going half her usual distance, Justine decided to take the shortest route in returning to the stables, which meant turning her back on the sea and crossing the beach, threading her way through the cluster of bathers' tents that were usually such a colorful sight in full sunshine, now just silhouettes in the half-darkness. The night was still when the wind dropped, the only sound the faint creaking of her leather saddle and the jingle of bridle fittings. The dome of the sky seemed low and weighted with stars, the moon so near, so large, she could almost reach up and touch it, Justine thought. Dismounting, caught in moon magic and starswirl, she heard the silent cry of her heart responding to the passion of the summer night. She was, all at once, weak limbed and aching with vague inarticulate longings that, as she stood moon-blind and dumb with wonder, began to take form in the hard handsome features of the nameless rider. There was such an irresistible dark glamour about him, such a romantic danger in his sardonic eyes.

"*He* could love me . . . madly," she whispered to herself as she sank slowly to her knees, feeling very small under the immensity of sky. "Oh, damn! I have gone and done it again." She sighed, cautioning herself to be sensible as she'd promised. It's probably nothing more than a physical attraction, a silly childish crush, and not at all love of the sort I want, she told herself. But the only way to be sure, to know for a certainty, was to see the man again, ride with him, talk with him, get to know him a little . . . if for no other reason than to dispel the allure of mystery about him or to discover he was everything she'd ever dreamed of.

She settled, cross-legged, in the the sand to wait, expecting him along soon if he was true to habit. As she leaned back on her elbows waiting, letting sand trickle through her fingers, that wretched horse, which had been nervously mouthing his bit, tossed up his head and, before she could do anything to prevent it, started off at a lively trot. Standing quickly, hands on her hips, Justine, not unhappy to be rid of the beast, just watched him go, knowing he was headed home to his comfortable stable and his morning serving of oats. As she stood there, a thick bank of clouds sailed across the face of the moon, plunging the beach into total darkness, and in the gloom, she was startled to hear a rustling sound, the flap of a beach tent opening, and a voice she recognized at once—*his* voice—calling.

"Boni? Is it you?" he questioned in a hoarse stage whisper. Her interest was aroused, but not wanting to be discovered like this, as though she'd been sneaking about and spying in the dark, Justine ducked into the tent nearest her. Holding her breath and crouching, she peeked out and there he was, the strong profile unmistakable in a slant of moonlight that illuminated more than just his handsome face.

He was stretching toward the sky, the muscles in his bare back rolling, his haunches and thighs flexing as if he were a model posing there before her. With his hands locked behind his head, he swung his wide shoulders from side to side and Justine, rooted in place, was speechless and wide-eyed, mesmerized by a sight she'd never seen before in her life—an entirely naked grown man. There were the Greek sculptures at the Metropolitan Museum of course, and the pictures in art books by Michelangelo and Leonardo, to which this man compared very favorably.

"All beauties, no faults," she whispered, falling into the terminology of a practiced horsewoman who had often appraised the conformation of a well-made stallion. Becoming aware of what she was doing, Justine felt a slow, hot blush rise from the tips of her breasts to her throat and then her cheeks. Drawing up her knees, she hid her face against them but when she glanced up again—she couldn't resist—she gasped, appalled to see him coming toward her.

"Boni! If it's hide and seek you want, you shall have it!" he laughed, the sound seductive, almost threatening as he ducked into one tent after another, relentlessly moving toward her as Justine, in swelling panic, withdrew as deep into her own shelter as she could, hoping she'd be missed in the thick darkness. Her heart was pounding as he came nearer and nearer. She heard him pause, then lift the flap of her tent and hesitate before he laughed again, low in his throat, a carnal, suggestive, lecherous laugh that made her gasp aloud and give herself away.

"You *had* to be here," he said, stepping inside, the darkness enveloping him, too. "There's only one other I haven't checked and I would have if . . . Come on, Boni, no more games now."

Justine, kneeling with her back to him, felt his hand on her shoulder, his lips at her nape as he knelt behind her to undo her hair ribbon before he turned her to him. When he took her lips, his mouth was hard and ravenous, his kiss unlike any Justine had ever experienced, no tentative, boyish exploration but a man's kiss. It took her by storm, piqued her curiosity and soon began to do more than that to her, more than Justine had ever imagined a mere kiss could do. It stirred sensations that swept over her like long, low waves, and she parted her own lips to meet the thrust of his tongue as it became increasingly urgent. When she brought her hands to his shoulders, his traveled, as they knelt face to face in the dark, from her slim waist to rest at the outer swells of her breasts. And his fingers played at their peaks in the most extraordinary way, making her pliant and needy of some more intense sensation that he could give her, if only he would. She *had* to have more—and more—of whatever it was he was doing to send such outrageous sensations flooding through her. It was more than her curiosity he'd aroused as he pressed her down and she felt the weight of him along her supine length.

Her hand played over his bare back, and as her mouth hungrily searched for his in the dark, she helped him undo the buttons of her blouse, then guided him to the sensitive bare tip of her breast, astounded with the wonder of it—the spread of intense pleasure from that single fine point beneath his hand. Darts of delight pierced deep in her body that was his now to manipulate as he chose, as he knew so well how to do. . . . She felt him slide the skirt of her riding suit to her thighs and, in one grasp, destroy the lace finery beneath it so that his wonderful hand could explore what had been hidden.

His breath rasped in her ear as she gave way to the delicious pleasure of it until . . . he parted her thighs. Only then, frightened at what she'd suddenly realized must follow, did Justine begin to struggle, to try to twist away from him and put a stop to what she'd so thoughtlessly allowed to begin. And let go so far. But by then, it was too late.

"More tricks, Boni? Want me to play ravisher to your innocent virgin, do you? Well, I'm always game, you know that." He laughed that same terrifying laugh and then he was prying, thrusting, as her nails raked his shoulders and Justine bit her lip, not wanting to cry out afraid he'd know her voice. She couldn't stop him, it was too late for that. She might as easily have fought against a tidal wave, she realized as she gave herself up to him again, totally, and began to accept the pleasure of what he was giving when . . . It was over. He was done.

"You surely could have fooled me, *ma petite*. That was quite a performance. Extraordinary," he said after a time, lifting himself away from her. Justine didn't answer, only caressed his shoulder that was damp with a fine mist of sweat. He went on speaking, raising her hand to his lips. "If I didn't know differently, I'd have sworn that I'd just deflowered a virgin, that it was your first time with a man." She heard him stand in the dark and grope for the tent opening "Swim?" he asked.

"Later," she whispered, in a French accent. She saw

him shrug as he lifted the tent flap, his muscled body gleaming in the moonlight before he disappeared.

Justine sat up. She smoothed her clothes, and redid her hair, still in a confused haze of wonder, both abashed and overjoyed at what she'd done. He could have sworn it was her first time, could he? Well, he was right, of course, even though, in the most literal sense, he probably hadn't actually deflowered a virgin. With all the riding she'd done, Justine realized that fragile secret shield had probably been torn long ago. That was why he had found no impediment and she had felt so little pain. So little, in fact, that all she wanted was to lie with him again, now, this instant, and tell him what she'd done, who she was—ask him to teach her everything he knew about love. Given the way she was feeling, that just might be everything there was to know.

When she stepped out of the tent, the sun's rim was at the horizon, and looking about for her magnificent marauder, Justine went pale with shock. He was poised, still naked, at the edge of the sea, and with him were *two* women, also completely unclothed, both laughing uproariously at something he'd said. Appalled, Justine watched as he plunged into the surf, his body flexed in the arc of a dive and embraced by golden sunlight before he disappeared into the curl of a wave. The women, more timid about dipping into the chill Channel waters, hesitated, and Justine studied them with a critical, jaundiced eye. He could have done better than that, she thought, finding one too tall and the other rather lumpy.

Wild with jealousy, knowing all the while she had absolutely no right to be, Justine turned and ran, frantically, as fast as she could, toward home, the beach villa she could glimpse in the distance. Before she reached its sanctuary, she came upon that dreadful runaway horse, cropping grass at the edge of the sand. Impulsively, she mounted up, dug her heels into its ribs and went tearing back in the direction from which she'd come, to race the animal right into the surf.

Not even glancing at the swimmer, she came between him and his companions, who shrieked in outrage as they were spattered with stinging sand and cold spray flung up by the horse's hoofs.

Justine didn't look back to see the man stand, waist-deep in water. His eyes narrowed as they followed her progress until she was out of sight, his curiosity keen even though at that moment he had no idea his morning lover had not been one of those indignant women standing and exclaiming at the water's edge.

Chapter Three

"*Coup de foudre,* the thunderbolt, Cupid's arrow . . . call it what you will, little Justine. It's love at first sight all the same, what happened to you, and that should not be a problem. Enjoy it!" Olympe d'Erlanger urged jovially.

The Duchess, Justine's hostess at Deauville and an old friend of Slade Hawkes, was a woman of ample proportions. Junoesque as her husband called her, but she was tall and weighty, top-heavy in fact, with a tendency to overflow her evening gowns. In day clothes, Olympe affected the pouter pigeon silhouette that was in style. Her bodice was one formless bulge from neck to waist, and was adorned with many brooches, pins, chains, ropes of pearls, and her ever-present magnifying glass, all bouncing and jiggling as she walked. Her stubby red-tipped fingers were beringed and her red hair, swept in waves to the top of her head, was frizzed into bangs that lay on her forehead above her puffy face. A generous, loud, outspoken woman who had never been a truly great beauty, Olympe d'Erlanger took vicarious pleasure in dabbling in the love lives of the charming young women who were her houseguests most of the summer season. As a former courtesan, one of the most famous and successful on the Continent, she felt uniquely qualified to do so. Her warmth and charm had always compensated for her lack of beauty, and she'd married into a very old, titled, landed, if slightly decadent, French family. She and Justine were taking breakfast at a tray table in one of the many guest rooms at the Villa d'Erlanger, this room done all in blues and greens, from the Chinese rug on the floor to the botanical studies on the walls and the floral print of the deeply swagged fourposter bed.

"The green room for your astounding eyes, darling," Olympe had told Justine on the day the girl had arrived. Now, a week later, double French doors were thrown open onto the balcony and the sea beyond, and her guest, just returned from a morning ride, was in a wild flush of anger and embarrassment.

Justine had peeled off her riding things, now scattered to the four corners of the room, and swathed herself in a white satin peignoir. Her hair pinned up, she was taking great gulps from her bowl of *café au lait* and swallowing quickly so that she could continue her tirade.

"No, Olympe, I don't want to be in love, not now, not with *him!*" Justine insisted, shaking her head vehemently. "I am the expert on love at first sight. It doesn't prove true. It's just a thing of the senses, not of the heart. Besides, the man's a scoundrel of the deepest die. He knows I ride along that way every morning and still he was flaunting himself and his *vivandières*—oh!" she exclaimed. Vexed beyond words, she stopped just short of telling Olympe everything that had happened.

"Camp followers? Really, Justine, you are inexpressibly adorable in your state of pique, but the man has only once or twice even laid his eyes on you, my dear!" Olympe laughed, a sound that seemed to begin at her toes and rumble up through her entire monumental form like a volcano erupting. "He had no way of knowing you or anyone would be on the beach at such an early hour—the middle of the night practically—to be so offended by a little flash of bare skin."

"Don't . . . just do not defend him to me, Olympe," Justine implored, striding across the room to test the temperature of her bath water. The servant girl, who had laboriously filled the portable copper tub, looked on skeptically. "Is something wrong?" Justine asked her.

"Will *mademoiselle* . . . get in there?" The girl pointed to the steaming water.

"Well, of course she will," Justine answered in bemusement. "What else would I be doing?" She glanced at Olympe for guidance.

"Americans and English are always bathing, but here, among the serving classes especially, most don't believe in it, darling, getting wet all over. Even wealthy provincials bathe perhaps once a month in summer, never in winter, and never totally undressed, not *tout nu*. Am I right, Agnes?" The girl nodded. "They soak through their bath shirts standing in two inches of water. My old cook has never seen her own navel, she tells me."

"But people do swim in the sea," Justin mused, meandering to the open doors, nibbling a brioche. She brought a small brass telescope to one eye and closed the other as she searched the shoreline that was now crowded with tourists and bathers and strings of polo ponies being exercised knee-deep in the surf.

"It's thought that the salt water is invigorating but dangerous if one is exposed to it too long. Five or ten minutes a day is enough. The same is said to be true of ocean air, which is why so many villas here are

38

built inland and facing away from the Channel. Looking for another glimpse of that splendid physique? Do you see him?"

"Who?" Justine smiled sheepishly, whirling about. "I wasn't looking for *him*. He's probably gone off anyway, to sleep all day after his very busy night. But, Olympe," she said hesitantly, "I was thinking . . ."

"Yes?" Olympe answered, smothering a smile.

"I was thinking that the only way I'll ever get him . . . out of my mind is . . ."

". . . is to see him again, *oui?* To flirt perhaps, just a little, just enough to get him wrapped about your finger and then keep him dangling awhile, not too long, just until you tire of him and grow bored with his company. Am I right?" Olympe teased affectionately.

"I don't want to be unkind," Justine nodded with a resigned, helpless little shrug. "But we've never . . . talked. I don't even know his name, and if I don't do something, I'll always wonder. I'm almost absolutely positively certain, but I want to prove that I didn't let true love pass me by."

"In matters of the heart, you know, things don't always go exactly as one might hope or expect," Olympe mused as she fished among the ornaments and jewels on her bosom for a watch hanging on a gold chain. "But . . . better remorse than regrets, I always say. We will find the fellow," she proclaimed, standing decisively and gliding toward the door with a fine grace for so imposing a figure, reminiscent, in her flowing morning gown, of a galleon under full sail in a good wind.

"There'll be neither remorse nor regrets, I assure you," Justine said a little indignantly. "The man's a scoundrel, lewd and vulgar and . . . and he's got a terrible temper besides."

"But you've told me he's an equestrian of considerable skill who rides only the finest mounts. Now, I've always thought close association with the horse, that splendid animal, enobles a man. Suppose, just suppose, my dear, this man is a more . . . substantial person than you'd expect?"

"Then I shall be pleasantly surprised."

"And what if he's not quite so easily managed as you anticipate?" Olympe queried as the serving girl left the room, passing Gray Hawkes in the doorway.

"I suspect there's not a man in the world my sister can't manage," he laughed.

"The self-confidence most of you Americans seem to share is admirable," Olympe said, offering him a meaty hand to kiss, "but you should both bear in mind that Deauville in summer is populated not only by the *haute monde* but by the higher priced *demi-mondaines,* as well, the courtesans, the *grandes horizontales,* whose survival depends upon their seductive charms. And these women have their male counterparts — mountebanks and gigolos, arrivistes with risqué pasts who are almost indistinguishable from the nobility and the millionaire industrialists who play here. Deauville is a very lively place, but one must take care."

"I've been hearing lots of hubbub and talk about this *fin de siècle* decadence in France, Olympe, about the immoral carryings-on," Gray said, taking a croissant from the table and settling into a tufted chair. "You think we're too naive to handle it, is that it?"

"Exactly, my charming friends. I'm afraid you'll be getting yourselves into impossible situations, and that's why I'm keeping an eye on all of you, though I must say that malcontent, Roweena McGlory, hasn't been a problem in *that* respect. Men don't flock to her in droves and those who have paid her some attention, because she is well turned out, flee once they learn she's not a Dollar Princess ripe for the picking but the well-dressed daughter of a modestly wealthy couturière just a mere shopkeeper."

"One could call Roweena a Half-Dollar Princess, wouldn't you agree, Gray?" Justine laughed with forced gaiety. "Her family is quite comfortable, Olympe. Her mother has a very lucrative boutique, though the McGlorys are not in a class with the Vanderbilts or Carnegies—"

"Or the Hawkes," Olympe said.

"Besides, Roweena's already been plucked and discarded by a true scoundrel. But has no one shown any interest in her?" Justine poured a quantity of fragrant rose oil into the steaming bath water. "Turn around, will you, Gray?" she requested as she started to undo her peignoir.

"I'm leaving. I'm to ride out to the stud at Victot to see a brood mare," he answered, following Olympe toward the door. "Will you come with me, Justine? It's in the very heart of French horse country, Calvados. I'd enjoy your company."

"She will accompany me this morning on a pleasure outing," Olympe insisted. "She's done nothing but work since you two arrived. Horses aren't that fascinating, really. It's time she saw the town of Deauville, the countryside about it, perhaps even the old port village of Honfleur, though that is a distance away. Some sightseeing is in order but of a different sort than she's been doing on her own."

"I didn't know you've been getting about," Gray commented. "When have you had a free moment, what with time spent at the stables, the races, the casino and—"

"You'd be amazed at the sights there are to see at the most unexpected moments, practically on the doorstep," Justine said, blushing a little as she exchanged glances with Olympe.

Chapter Four

The Duc d'Erlander, a member of the gratin, the very upper crust of French society, had awakened early by his standards, just before noon, and had deigned to accompany his duchess and her foreign friends on an outing. Usually, the duke had no interest in Americans. He found them too tediously energetic and direct, with no talent for subtlety. Worst of all, they were shockingly ignorant of the few subjects that were of keen interest to him: rank, position, and *le betting* — horse racing. Like many French of his station, the duke was an avid Anglophile. In imitation of all things English, he had his clothes made in London, was a member of the Jockey Club and frequented racetracks at Longchamps and Chantilly, as well as others. But like his old friend, the Prince of Wales, his favorite pastime was *le steeplechase*.

Amazingly, the lovely American, Justine Hawkes, shared his interest in equestrian sport and he actually *liked* her. Even though she made hardly any distinction between a horse trainer and a duke, her manner to both being completely open and friendly, she knew everything about horses and, most amazing, never lost a bet either at the racetrack *or* at the casino. Besides, her appearance was so extraordinary he had difficulty taking his eyes from her whenever she was about. In fact, he didn't even try, and so he found sitting opposite her in an open carriage on a golden summer day an appealing prospect. Best of all, looking only at Justine prevented his having to see the sour-faced traveling companion who always sat beside her.

"Pardon, mademoiselle?" the duke asked mildly as he became aware the lovely Justine was addressing him.

"Do you prefer Balzac or Zola, Duke?" Justine repeated a bit more loudly, wondering if the man might benefit from an ear trumpet like the one her grandfather used.

"But Aimery never *reads,* darling," Olympe, seated beside her husband, answered for him. "And if he did, it wouldn't be the works of socialist reformers preoccupied with the lower classes, would it, Aimery?"

"I've no interest in such things," the duke said mildly, leaving Justine to wonder exactly what did arouse his enthusiasm. He and Olympe were such an unlikely pair she could make no sense of the match. The man seemed to suffer from a peculiar malaise while his robust wife had energy for two. Very tall and thin, the duke had pink skin, red-rimmed blue eyes, and a perfectly waxed little mustache that he fingered now as he gazed at Justine, smiling blankly.

She looked away as their open landau, bright yellow and white, the duke's racing colors, made the turn at Deauville harbor and clattered over the cobbles of the town along a street of half-timbered Norman houses with steep mansard roofs and shops on street level. Waiting horses and carriages lined both sides of the narrow road as they approached the market place and pavilion where, later in the afternoon, the regimental band would play. The town square, the fountain at its center throwing arcs of water into the air, was filled with a mix of tourists and local people — young women in cycling bloomers and riding kits, well-dressed men in morning coats — sauntering, window shopping, or lounging in the bentwood chairs set about the marble-topped tables of the cafés that opened onto the sidewalks. There were laborers in heavy shoes, shopkeepers in aprons. The country women come to town to sell their produce or to shop with their egg money were dressed in dirndls and *coiffes,* the high, lace, beribboned Norman headdress nearly two feet tall.

"I must call in at the milliners to pick up a new bonnet," Olympe said. "I won't be a minute and when . . . Why, what is it, Justine? You look flushed." Olympe followed her young friend's glance to a pair of broad, linen-covered shoulders just disappearing around the corner of the street. "Well, this little milliner is very clever. Do come with me, Justine," Olympe ordered. "Aimery, be good enough to keep Miss McGlory entertained for a moment," she added, descending from the carriage that listed alarmingly as she stepped down. Seconds later, with a very agitated Justine at her side, Olympe hurried after the object of her curiosity and caught a glimpse of a tall, dark-haired man going through a doorway. *"Oh, mon Dieu!"* she muttered, coming to an abrupt standstill.

"What is the matter?" Justine asked, slipping an arm through Olympe's and trying to urge her on, which was rather like trying to move a mountain, she discovered.

"But, that's where *I'm* going. The hatmaker's shop. He's gone into the hatmaker's shop," she repeated. "Well, there's nothing for it. We must follow, or I must if you don't feel up to it, my dear. You look . . .

flustered."

As they reached the door, the man was already leaving, a banded hatbox in one hand and a sketch pad in the other. As he nearly collided with Olympe, he stopped and, with difficulty, juggling the objects he carried, managed to raise his hat.

"Pardon, madam," he said, stepping back inside the shop and politely holding the door ajar. Staring at him, Olympe passed through and turned, curious to see exactly what his response to Justine would be, to determine if he, too, had been a victim of the *coup de foudre,* the thunderbolt of love. He looked, did a double take, something not at all unusual where Justine was concerned, and half smiled with warm interest in that way young men will when an especially lovely girl comes into view. Though there was obvious interest on his part, there was no outward sign of recognition. Justine, nonplused by his response, hesitated, then smiled back engagingly, expectantly.

"Why, you could be a Gibson Girl, straight out of *Collier's* magazine," he said almost shyly and with an air of delighted surprise. She was dressed informally in a pleated, pale blue shirtwaist beneath a tailored jacket and a skirt that fitted smoothly over the hips then flared and dropped from the knee. She wore a red ribbon at her high white collar, a wide red leather belt buckled in brass at her tiny waist, and a straw boater with a red band atop her golden curls. "Do you know the work of Charles Dana Gibson, the illustrator I'm referring to, Miss . . . ?"

"Miss Hawkes," Justine answered, nodding. She was at a loss as to what else to say.

"The gentleman is absolutely correct, Justine. With your hourglass figure, you could be the original Gibson Girl," Olympe said, taking her young friend's arm and drawing her into the shop that was littered with ribbons and flowers and feathers and bolts of tulle and lace for veiling. Hat forms were stacked in the windows, where a tabby cat lay delicately, indifferently licking a paw.

"The cad! Playing the modest, polite innocent with me after I saw him steeped in scarlet depravity. He knows it, too," Justine hissed. The milliner looked up sharply, and Olympe glanced questioningly at her companion. "No, *she* wasn't one of his playmates," Justine responded, fanning her inflamed face with the hat she pulled from her head. She paid no attention to Olympe, who chatted animatedly in French as the milliner put a last flourish, an egret feather, on a bonnet already burdened with false flowers and fruits of every imaginable kind and color.

"Perfect, *mon chérie, et merci!*" Olympe exclaimed to the milliner as Justine, still in a state, followed her into the street.

Justine had always been inclined to trust her instincts and certainly her senses, but now they seemed to have led her astray. This man, this American, to whom she'd given herself with such reckless abandon only hours ago, was certainly most attractive, tall and broad-shouldered just as she remembered, and handsome, too, with his sculpted, angular face, but certainly no different from most other ordinary young men. He appeared pleasant, manageable and nice, not at all overwhelming, certainly not the mysterious, fierced-eyed rake he'd seemed on horseback at daybreak in the mist of morning.

"Jones!" Olympe proclaimed triumphantly. "The milliner told me his name is Jones and I will find him."

"How?" Justine asked skeptically.

"How will I find him?" Olympe repeated. "Easily, my dear. How many tall, dark, handsome, and I must add charming, young Americans named Jones do you expect there are in the vicinity of Deauville? I shall have inquiries made. He will be invited to the house party and ball we are having next week."

"At home in America there are a great many Joneses, so many in fact," Justine explained, "that if one wanted to be elusive, to travel incognito and never be found, one might affect the name Jones, either that or Smith." She watched a man cross in front of them with a long loaf of bread under his arm and a net bag over his shoulder. The bag contained a wheel of cheese and a bottle of red wine. Strapped to the man's back was an easel and palette.

"The neighborhood has been overrun with artists every since Boudin did his first seascape here years ago. It's the light. It has a special quality, they say. Do you suspect this Jones of being a card sharper or gigolo here to bilk some heiress out of her inheritance?" Olympe asked, getting back to the subject that really interested them both.

"Oh, he's up to something. He is easily the coolest customer I've ever come upon. And he has a lot of nerve . . . or no nerves at all, to act so . . . so sweet tempered and mild, and so friendly, as if he'd never laid eyes on me before or glowered at me, as if he didn't know what I saw."

"A Napoleonic pulse rate, we call it, about fifty-four I think. Darling child, remember where you are. Deauville is an international bacchanal for these few summer weeks. Every liberty is permitted. It is not unusual, my dear *naïf*, for a man, even in daylight, wearing only a sheet of toweling, to simply throw it off and plunge into the sea. You know, there are some among the French, and even among the English, who believe that Americans are so caught up in *pruderie* they put trousers even on their piano legs.

Now, I must say that Mr. Jones despite his having allowed you to get a look at him in a state of nature, seemed to me not a wicked, wild man at all but an entirely pleasant person no matter what you saw or think you did. But you are right about one thing. He is deliciously good-looking, isn't he?" Olympe linked her arm through Justine's as the two moved more quickly toward the carriage in which the Duke and Roweena sat in stiff silence. "I can't wait to see your handsome Mr. Jones at our next hunt ball. And we're giving one of Aimery's English house parties soon; Jones will surely stir things up. It will be like setting the cat among the pigeons, seeing *him* in the drawing room with the bored, fashionable ladies of the French nobility. Now, my Gibson Girl"—Olympe giggled like a girl herself—"I'm starving. I shall take you to a fine little bistro for a wonderful meal. You'll enjoy it, I promise. And then, you must take Aimery off to the afternoon polo matches and let me get to work."

Chapter Five

By the time they had left Deauville that day and driven back to the villa to change for the afternoon, Justine was growing used to the Duke's peculiar attentions, his unwavering, adoring gaze, and his distracted smile. She smiled back at him from time to time during the drive to La Toques polo field as she puzzled over Mr. Jones. She was dreadfully disappointed, she had to admit, that in the full bright light of day, he lacked the fire and passion with which she'd endowed him in fantasy. Expert seductive aggressor that he'd been in the dark, he now seemed in awe of her like so many others before, so taken with her appearance he'd never seen beyond it to her heart and passionate spirit. Justine just sighed aloud and the duke regarded her even more fixedly.

"It must be an *affaire de coeur, mademoiselle,* that makes you pensive, *oui?*" he asked.

"Oh no, Duke!" Justine insisted a bit too quickly. "I'm not in love at all, I've decided."

"Well, no wonder you sigh, my dear. To be young and not loved — *that* is tragic." He pulled at his mustache and frowned a little. "Perhaps at our next soirée there will be someone to interest you. Did Olympe tell you, my dear, that His Royal Highness Bertie, will be among our guests? When he learned *you* were here, he specifically asked for an invitation. The Prince of

Wales has taken an interest in our pretty American horse trader. Did you know, *mademoiselle?*" The yellow landau clattered past the rail station at Deauville, where the regimental band was practicing for the late afternoon concert.

"We met briefly at Ascot," Justine explained. "The Prince seemed an affable man."

"Bertie and I have long been great friends, since his first visit here to France as a boy of thirteen. Over the years, he has often slipped away from his watchful and disapproving mamma, the Queen, for a bit of 'a rip' as he calls his risqué escapades. He's nearly sixty years old now and still Bertie does love the ladies," the duke said with a wan smile.

"But how can a prince slip away?" Justine asked, particularly one of Bertie's bulk and girth, she thought.

"Usually he travels incognito using one of his lesser known titles—Lord Renfreu . . . Earl of Chester. That's who we shall be hosting at our little castle five kilometers from Deauville. The beach villa isn't grand enough for Bertie or for the sort of very British weekend I simply adore." The duke sighed as though already exhausted by pleasure. "There will be croquet, high teas, pigeon shoots, a hunt, a hunt ball, and then"—his lashes drifted closed over blue eyes—"a discreetly arranged liaison with the lucky lady of the Prince's choice. Actually, there will be many little love affairs begun or continued after the ball. It's de rigueur at these parties. Did you know, *mademoiselle?* You mustn't be shocked." The duke, nearly fainting with enthusiasm, look pointedly at Justine.

"Yes, I had heard something of the sort. Also that divorce is considered a disgrace in good society here, but to be . . ." she hesitated, uncomfortable with the turn the conversation had taken, relieved that they had reached their destination.

"... but to be the chosen object of the Prince's attention is considered an honor," duke d'Erlanger completed her sentence as he handed her down from the carriage with a limp, soft manicured hand. "That's quite true, my dear."

"Americans play polo like madmen . . . like cowboys, all speed and daredevil recklessness, practically pitching themselves out of the saddle to make a shot. Just look at that one. *Do* look." The tall, pencil-thin duke, perched like a crow on his shooting stick that was driven into the turf, fluttered his eyelids at a particularly aggressive player on a very fine pony. The animal had just stopped short and turned in a very tight circle, making it possible for his rider to get control of the ball.

"I am watching, Duke," Justine responded with a hint of impatience. Though Aimery d'Erlanger had a certain neurasthenic charm she was discovering that he did nothing with any noticeable zest , a characteristic that made him a less than ideal companion, particularly at an exciting event like a good polo match. Because of his nonchalance, they had missed the first two chukkers—rounds of seven and a half minutes each—and the players, who had just changed their horses, were into the third. They were at the far end of the field, more than three hundred yards off, and the one dubbed the "wild man" by the duke rode head down, his face hidden beneath a brimmed white polo helmet as he stood forward in the saddle, reaching across his pony's neck with his right hand to make a magnificent backswing. As the other players thundered after him, horses' hooves throwing up turf, he sent the little white ball rolling at speed halfway down the field toward the goal and looked up for the first time.

"Why . . . it's Jones!" Justine said in astonishment.

"Yes, Jones. One of your countrymen. A hot-tempered fellow I hear, a contentious competitor, a prodigious drinker, heavy gambler, and heavier womanizer. He bothers with none of the usual refinements and niceties in his pursuit of the gentler sex, it's said, but then he doesn't have to bother, I've heard. Women find him irresistible."

"What?" Justine asked, concentrating on the play yet listening to the duke who tended to babble, partly in French. She watched intently as a player came up on Jones's left and pulled slightly ahead, getting into position for a ride-off. The pursuer's horse leaned into the shoulder of Jones's mount; usually that was all it took to deflect an animal from the line of the ball.

Then it was permissible, according to the rules of the game, for a player to cross that line and get into position for a shot. But Jones's mount didn't veer off as most did. It not only held its position, but lunged—bumped the opposing horse so hard he and his rider went down, putting Jones now to the right of the ball and making it easier for him to swing the long-handled mallet with greater accuracy. He did, and scored a goal. His concentration was intense throughout the rest of the chukker, his fierce eyes fixed on the ball from the second of the toss-in until the first half of the match ended three minutes later.

"If I were a referee, Duke," Justine commented, "I'd call a penalty on Jones for rough riding, but that is the finest pony I have ever seen play," she added with admiration, gathering up her gloves and parasol. "Now, about this Jones," she said, "what more can you tell me?"

"I met him last fall in England at Tattersall's horse sale. He's a notorious so-called 'gentleman rider.' He threatened to throw Lord Roseberry over the rails during a race on the flat there. He's barred for two years from English tracks, from riding anyway. He likes to hang about with the underclasses of the sporting crowd—jockeys, grooms, trainers, exercise boys, those sorts of persons. He's friends with Jim Mace, the old bare-knuckle boxer. But were are you going? Don't desert me, *chérie*."

"It's the half, Duke. That gives me ten minutes to buy that pony!" She laughed and hurried toward the players' enclosure.

Jones was there, leaning against the white fence, breathing deeply, a look of triumph and exhilaration on his handsome face. The brimmed polo helmet was pushed back, and a shaft of dark hair fell across his brow. When, with a shock of recognition, Justine's clear green eyes met his, they were as she remembered them in dawn light, dark velvet, alluring Gypsy eyes.

"You look . . . different," she said, smokey-voiced, thinking it must be the riding, the racing, the competition that brought out those qualities in him, the fierceness and confident power he was radiating now. He was obviously in his element though he hadn't been earlier that morning at the milliner's. In full daylight, and at her leisure for the first time, she could study him more carefully. His shoulders were wide, and the muscles of his forearms, left bare by a short-sleeved red polo shirt, stood out prominently. There were large turquoise nuggets set in his silver belt buckle, and his close-fitting white jodhpurs were tucked into knee boots decorated with turquoise and silver studs.

"We meet again," Justine said in response to his silent glare.

"Bound to happen." He shrugged. "I hear someone was making inquiries about me at the stable a little while ago. Was it you?" he asked as he continued to lounge casually against the fence, flexing the long handle of the mallet he dangled in one hand. Other players were milling about and grooms were walking the overheated ponies that had just finished the round while others were saddling fresh mounts for the next chukker.

"No. It was my friend, the Duchess d'Erlanger, who was asking about you," Justine answered.

"Why?" he demanded with blunt irritation.

"To invite you to a ball." Justine smiled, "But she needn't have bothered. The duke, it seems, knows all about you."

"Knows what exactly?" Jones scowled, his eyes going over her slowly.

"That you're something of a rake who fancies himself a connoisseur of potables . . . of horses . . . of women," Justine teased, suppressing a laugh. "In other words, a brawler, a gambler, a drunkard and womanizer. *That* I saw for myself," she added, blushing and wishing she had bitten her tongue.

"Something of a rake?" he asked with mock indignation. "Your informant doesn't do me justice," he added, aware of the faint blush that had risen on her cheeks, making him suddenly think of a delicate watercolor sketch, an Impressionist painting. Her beauty seemed illusory and elusive like a work of art so perfect, so delicate one could only gaze upon it with wonder, never really possess it, never tire of looking. Yet he knew that the controlled wild grace with which he'd seen her ride took some physical strength and even more skill and courage. Dwelling for a moment on the rare combination of tomboy recklessness and ladylike fragility, he couldn't help

55

but imagine the abandoned voluptuousness she might offer a lover, the *right* lover, one who could handle her. Such women could be dangerous unless one kept aloof from them, kept the upper hand, and kept one's heart untouched. They had to be handled like fine thoroughbreds, expertly, and slowly broken, carefully trained to willing submission.

Jones took a step toward Justine who stood perfectly still and lovely as a picture in her pale yellow dress, the short train spread behind her on the very green grass of the turf. Her face was shaded by a white linen sun bonnet, its untied strings falling over the full soft swell of breasts that he was more than a little tempted to trace with his fingertips as he was already doing with his eyes. One more step and she was within his reach, his hands encircling her slim waist as he drew her toward him. His mouth was hard as it came down on hers in what was at first more a bruising assault than a kiss until he'd forced her lips open and felt her body go soft and pliant as it molded to his and her tongue began to respond to the thrust of his. Then, instantly, he released her. He'd learned what he wanted to know and he glared down, awaiting her response.

Isolated together in the aftermath of that kiss, they were oblivious to everything but each other—to the horses and riders, the stable boy applauding and whistling, even to the duke who, though disinclined to exert himself, had risen from his perch and slowly started toward them. Justine didn't—couldn't—move. She said nothing for what seemed to Jones an interminable time, just stared at him with a storm in her eyes, those extraordinary sea-foam green eyes, so defiant now, so audacious, it seemed to him she was flinging down a gauntlet, offering an unspoken challenge. She was silently daring him to bet his life on a lethal game from which only one of them could emerge unscathed, he reasoned, the other likely to be left humbled and broken by unrequited love. With this exquisite creature, though, the game would be worth the candle. Besides, he'd never been burned before and didn't expect to be now.

"Why didn't you join us for a swim this morning?" he asked, the flash of his rascally grin telling her he'd play, that he was in her game, whatever it was. His dark eyes were aglow now as if banked fired burned behind them. "I'm sure you'd have enjoyed yourself, I'd have seen to that."

"You are so vain, Mr. Jones, you must watch your own shadow go by, but I don't share your high opinion of yourself and I don't cavort naked in the surf with uncouth savages," she answered, having rediscovered her voice. Her eyes now, he was both confounded and delighted to see, were merry and positively dancing with mischief.

"With whom then *do* you cavort naked in the surf?" he demanded.

"You twist my words. I didn't mean . . ." That brush stroke of pink again appeared on her cheeks and he almost laughed.

"Well, what do you want of me, little girl? The play's about to begin again." A groom had brought up a fresh pony and he mounted, glaring down at her.

"The animal you rode in the last chukker. Will you sell him to me?"

"No," he answered shortly.

"Not for love *or* money?" she goaded, teasing him.

"Not for any amount. But I will give him to you. What do you want him for anyway? Polo is no lady's game. It's too rough and tumble."

"You'd be surprised by this lady," she answered proudly, "but I want him for my father. The pony's

57

agile, well balanced, fast, and best of all, bold. But . . . why do you make me a gift of him?" She raised a lace-gloved hand to shield her eyes from the sun as she looked up.

"I've two excellent strings, a dozen good ponies and though I never ride any animal more than one chukker a game I can spare you one. If you accept, you'll be forever in my debt. One day—who knows—I may have cause to call in that debt. Besides," he said, removing his helmet and drawing his wrist band across his brow, "you've a perfectly lovely seat. You sit a horse as well as any woman I've ever seen." He grinned. "I'll enjoy seeing you on one of mine. I'm sure he'll be very responsive to those soft, subtle hands of yours . . . those long legs, Miss? . . ."

"Hawkes, I told you. Justine Hawkes," she said icily, at pains, for all her bravado, to hide her embarrassment at his suggestive talk and the double entendres he made in front of all these people. She became aware of where his eyes went, following her bonnet strings to the tips of her breasts that began to tighten and tingle as if touched. Blushing furiously, she tied the ribbons under her chin, and this time he did laugh.

"If you want to go a chukker or two with me, I'll be here tomorrow afternoon. There's no match scheduled and we'll have the field to ourselves. Or better yet, join me for a morning swim." He brought a finger to his hat brim, his bejewelled boots flashing sunspots as he moved off onto the field. Justine watched, not wanting to take her eyes off him, feeling weaklimbed and soft and exquisitely terrified at what she had gotten herself into. Go a chukker or two alone with him? Not very likely when it was all she could do, in the midst of a crowd, to extricate herself from his arms. And in the dark, she hadn't even wanted to

58

try. Oh, he was a dangerous man as she'd thought from the first, perhaps too dangerous to toy with. If she'd really lost her heart to him as she seriously suspected, and if she didn't play at this game of love with the same consummate skill she brought to other games, why, she could very well lose everything.

Chapter Six

"What shall I do with my hair?" Roweena McGlory asked unhappily. She was leaning over a deep basin in Justine's room submitting to the rubbing and scrubbing of Olympe, whose arms were elbow-deep in suds. The Duke d'Erlanger's entire establishment had been moved, several days before, from the French Gothic beach house in Deauville to the country château, set at the edge of a deep Norman forest.

The Prince of Wales, Bertie, was due momentarily. The ball in his honor would take place that evening. Entertaining a future king placed great demands on a hostess and her staff, in the Duchesse d'Erlanger's case about a hundred servants including a steward, a butler, a wine butler, bakers, chefs, chambermaids and parlor maids, kitchen maids, scullery maids, vegetable maids, porters, valets, gardeners, drivers, and grounds keepers, all rushing about frantically to carry out Olympe's orders as she calmly washed Roweena's hair.

Looking at Olympe, a simple woman of humble origins, a farm girl, it seemed remarkable to Justine that she managed such a staff without a hitch and took the great delight in doing so.

"*Il faut souffrir pour être belle,* Roweena. It is necessary to suffer for beauty unless, of course, one is Justine Hawkes," Olympe said, continuing her task with energy.

"Have you ever tried rinsing with dead champagne, Roweena?" Justine asked. "I do and it works wonderfully." She sat in the window seat, looking out on the countryside beyond the moat of Château d'Erlanger to gloriously green fields in the distance, dotted, as every field in France seemed to be, with slow-moving brown and white cows and clouds of fluffy sheep, all endlessly grazing. The result was superb cream, butter, milk, cheese, omelets, and roasts.

While listening to Olympe, Justine watched rain fall in sheets as a mist hovered at the tops of distant trees. The castle, of about two hundred rooms, Olympe thought—she had never counted—had a steep mansard roof, dormered and flanked by two spherical, conically topped towers that were right out of a fairy-tale picture book. Justine's high round room provided a view of fifty acres of gardens in which lime trees arched over long walkways and flowers bloomed in shades of pink and mauve. Le Miroir, a small lake, was framed by formal box-hedge mazes. In her tower perch, she was pretending to be a princess waiting for her knight to come riding over the drawbridge.

With knees drawn up, she was also writing a letter on note paper swagged with flowers, describing her accommodations to her eldest niece, Jude's daughter, Maud.

". . . a jewel box of a room, one so simply, yet daintily decorated that the plasterwork on the walls is not interfered with. The color here is pale almond green, suitable for my eyes, the duchess said, and the bed has a pink scalloped valance and a pink spread. It's all like a storybook, and tonight a real Prince will be coming

61

to dine. I wonder if I'll discover my shining knight this night. I think I might have already met him, but this time I am being sensible and having second thoughts. I'll let you know."

"No one but you, Justine Hawkes, would wash her hair in champagne," Roweena interrupted her thoughts, standing and wrapping a towel about her dripping dark head as she spoke. "It sounds sticky," she added, her inclination to find fault asserting itself as usual.

"Not at all. Champagne adds body and glimmer. I don't know why you must always find something critical to say." Justine paused, looked up, and decided not to go on. "What are you wearing tonight, Roweena?" she asked instead.

"The flounced primrose muslin Mother made for me, with my pearls. I'm not so fortunate as you, Justine, to have jewels like those opals to help me bedazzle my admirers, but I shall do my best. Olympe says there will be several desirable unattached men in attendance, of the right class, of course. I live in hope that it's not too late for me to find love. But how will my hair ever dry in such damp weather as this? It needs sun."

"The rain will not last past noon." Olympe sighed to suppress her exasperation. "But, for now, go down to the kitchens, Roweena, and sit beside the oven if the head baker will let you. You must be tactful and stay out of the way. On the day of a large dinner, it's all chaos and bustle down there. Off with you!" she urged.

Relieved to see Roweena's back disappearing down the hallway, Olympe turned excitedly to Justine. "I've news, but in front of her I did not want to speak. Jones will attend. My invitation has been accepted and you, *ma petite,* should be delighted." She was purring like a satisfied cat.

Justine instantly put aside her gold-tooled leather stationery caddy, a parting gift from her father. It had been filled with fine Florentine writing sheets, and the presentation had been accompanied by an admonition to keep up a steady stream of letters, which she'd done.

"What else have you heard about him?" she asked.

"Such conflicting reports, my dear." Olympe got well settled in a tapestry-upholstered gilt armchair as though she meant to stay awhile. "From Adelaide de Courance, who has met him but once, I hear he is part gentleman, part American savage, wild, reckless, and—imagine—generous to a fault." She gestured with her left hand. "From Madame Manière, I hear he is a mild, sensitive, humorous fellow who fancies himself an artist but lacks much talent." She turned up her right hand. "I am told that he is a man of action who likes racing, boxing, billiards, and cards." She shrugged. *"But* also that he is content to sit by the fire and read and sketch, that he does most things with competence, but nothing with brilliance." She raised a brow.

"Nonsense," Justine bristled. "He rides like a god and kisses—" But Olympe would not be stopped.

"When in England, it is said, he associates with the most dissolute youngbloods of the nobility and with the lowlife of the docks and the night haunts of St. Giles." She frowned. "But here in Normandy, my coachman's informants say, he's often to be found sketching and in the company of artists and intellectuals in their simple, austere cottages along the beach. On the other hand"—Olympe clapped hers once—"Baronne de Belbouf, who has entertained Jones, says he does everything with the easy mastery

of a true aristocrat. She insists the man is a connoisseur of horseflesh, fine cookery, noble vintages, old
editions — "

"And women?" Justine asked.

"Well . . . yes. The *baronne* says that his true self-
indulgence is women and that they find him irresistibly fascinating. My dear" — Olympe hesitated, closing
her eyes for a moment — "men of . . . experience have
always held a certain fascination for ardent, innocent
young girls who know little of love. You will have a
care?"

"I promised my father I'd not break any hearts, but
with this Jones, I'd better worry about my own." Justine nodded.

"You've seen the man in both his guises, as sensitive artist and wild rake. How do you explain all these
conflicting stories one hears?" There was a bemused
expression on Olympe's large, mobile face.

"Have you ever read the story by Mr. Stevenson, the
poet, 'The Strange Case of Dr. Jekyll and Mr. Hyde'?
Perhaps it's something of that sort."

"Oh! You suspect a drug that affects the mind?
Morphia . . . opium? . . ."

"Coca. That's being advertised everywhere now as
a 'brain tonic' and cure for nervous afflictions, neu-
ralgia, even melancholy," Justine conjectured.

"How evil. How mysterious." Olympe blinked.
"I'm consumed by curiosity!"

"We've only a few hours to wait before we can begin to solve the mystery for ourselves," Justine said,
with admirable calm considering she too was consumed by curiosity, and more, was haunted by a resplendent memory still vivid. Though it had
happened days ago, she could still taste his lips and
feel his muscled arms enfolding her. This Jones had
taken her, not knowing who she was. Then, knowing

exactly, he had wanted her, the fierceness of that public kiss on the polo field, the low intake of his breath that had followed, had told her as much. And when she'd challenged him with her eyes to try to win her, he'd accepted, she was sure. But this Jones was no innocent and no gentleman either. And so she'd avoided him ever since that day at the polo field, steeling herself to do romantic battle with a dangerous changeling, a demon lover. She would take him on. She'd play the game, but in her own time and on a field of her own choosing. It would really begin, their contest, at tonight's soirée, where she'd shine to best advantage, glow in her fabulous jewels, her lucky opals, and where she was certain to be the recipient of attention from, among others, the man who would one day be King of England.

"You will wear one of your Worth gowns this evening, Justine?" Olympe asked, now bustling about the room like a mother hen, picking up a dropped hair ribbon here, a fan there. "Jean-Philippe and Gaston, the couturier's sons, will be among our guests. There will also be Colonel North, the nitrate king. He went out to South America broke and made his fortune in Chile saltpeter; that's used in fireworks and gunpowder. What with all the little wars in the world these days, he's done very well. And Barney Barnato will come. He's the diamond king, a former English musical hall comic who got rich in South Africa. And some Americans, too. Bet-A-Million Gates, the barbed-wire king. Poor Bertie! Still a Prince after all these years and always surrounded by 'kings' of one sort or another."

"Does he enjoy socializing with ordinary people?" Justine asked, sitting at the dressing table and vigorously brushing her glistening hair.

"Oh yes. Princes, knowing themselves to be royal,

need not be snobs. You must be kind to the poor man. He's been playing this social game for almost forty years now, and poor Bertie keeps at it with undiminished vigor. He loves loud company, amusing women, hunting, shooting, racing—fun." Olympe giggled. "Truth to tell, he seems to me a bit sad now and then, bored perhaps. Your smile will cheer him, my dear. And Justine? . . ."

"Yes?" Justine replied as she browsed through her open armoire.

"Aimery is determined that this house party will be more British than the Prince. The duke insists that we follow English custom to the letter, even to the placing of name cards in brass holders on each bedroom door so that liaisons may be consummated with the greatest ease. A good English hostess, you know, is expected to situate known lovers near, but not adjacent to, each other, and with the name cards, any new arrangements, usually made during the course of the ball, may be carried to the desired end with no one but the involved parties ever the wiser. Once the beds are turned down and sandwiches are left at bedside tables, the servants retire and one may do as one pleases. You musn't be shocked, dear. Most Americans think the British very proper because Queen Victoria is so prudish, but the crowd around the Prince plays very fast and loose indeed, as you may already have discovered."

"But why are you telling me this, Olympe?" Justine asked. "I saw at Hertfordshire how this game goes. You didn't think the duke expects *me* to participate?" She looked up startled.

"Just lock your door, my dear. And Justine, don't mind Aimery following you about like a poodle dog. He always chooses the prettiest creature in sight and does exactly that, follows her about. He's quite harmless." Justine paused in the perusal of her wardrobe.

"Don't you mind?" she asked sympathetically.

"That he's harmless or that he follows girls about like a poodle dog?" Olympe asked with a sad laugh. "I mind neither because I know he loves me, in his way. He has been very kind to me. He secured my future when most ladies of my former profession are reaching the end of their careers and must go off to live out lonely, dull autumn years. Some do so quite comfortably if they've been frugal, unpleasantly if they haven't; but it's dull either way. I was not frugal. I was one of the most influential courtesans of my day, like Blanche d'Artigny in hers. For women like us, love is an art and one thinks it will all go on forever. It doesn't. For me, it was any nobleman in a storm as they·say, darling, and Aimery has been all that I could ask for. Well," she said, drawing up to her full height, "I must choose my jewels for the ball. I'll send in my maid to help you dress."

Chapter Seven

Mr. Jones was late. Guests had been arriving at Erlanger Castle for hours, since before teatime, in fleets of carriages with mountains of luggage watched over by valets and ladies' maids, and Justine had grown increasingly agitated as she waited for a glimpse of the man who had preoccupied her thoughts for days.

Lord This and Lady That were announced incessantly. Italian counts, Russian dukes, barons, and baronesses, and Middle European princesses arrived. There was a marquess or two, and many of the untitled, a few Americans among them, were members of the elite circle that included the Prince of Wales. They had collected to drink champagne before dinner in the long gallery of the castle — it was one hundred feet long to be exact — beneath a gold-leaf ceiling, supported by intricately carved walls hung with Brussels tapestry. The gentlemen's tailoring was English; the women wore costly gowns. None, though, was so splendid as Justine in her golden confection of moiré silk and her flashing opals.

When everyone had arrived and still Jones failed to materialize, Olympe delayed seating her guests as long as it was politely possible to do so, but she warned Justine that the Prince of Wales, a man of an enormous appetite which bordered on the gluttonous, was growing restive. It was when he sought out Justine to escort her in to dinner that she realized the depth of her disappointment. This whole evening, for her, had revolved about that truant Jones. She had dressed for him, done her hair, put on her jewels, touched rose perfume to her wrists and brows only for him, anticipating through all her preparations the look in those fierce, melancholy eyes when he saw her resplendent and glowing. She had wanted to flirt and tease him a little to make him smile, really smile, as she began to discover what sort of man he was — one who would love her to distraction or just another disenchantment.

But, if he'd stood her up, well then, damn him, she decided. She'd not let that spoil her evening. She'd use his absence as an opportunity to observe the nobility at play and to gather enough chit-chat and gossip for ten letters home to Silver Hill, she supposed.

As Justine rested her hand on the Prince's proffered arm, the footman called out the name Jones. And there he was in waistcoat and evening clothes, black hair slicked back, dark eyes . . . But his eyes were different, Justine thought, observing the man carefully as he was greeted by his hostess, Olympe, who began guiding him toward her. And his smile was almost . . . shy. As the Prince, Bertie, looked on, Justine offered Jones her hand and then waited expectantly, for what, she wasn't quite sure.

"Miss . . . Hawkes, I believe? I'm Anthony Jones. We're slightly acquainted, very slightly. We exchanged a few words at the milliners in Deauville and then—"

"Exchanged a few words?" Justine laughed incredulously. "Your talent for understatement is prodigious, I must say." Jones looked at her with some confusion until understanding lit his eyes.

"Do let me explain. You see, I have—"

"Mr. Jones!" the footman sang out again, and Justine looked up, appalled, amazed, and *elated* to see the perfect double of the man standing at her side. The other Mr. Jones waited at the threshold with that supremely self-confident look she recalled so well, flashing his devastating smile, and exuding a wonderful devil-may-care rascality as he started toward her. The perfectly cut black evening clothes and snowy linen were set off by flashes of turquoise, silver, and gold at cuffs and watch fob, and by a bright red silk handkerchief in his breast pocket, the effect, one of smoldering elegance, heightening his dark glamour and turning every head in the room in his direction.

"Ah, the lady with the subtle hands and perfect seat," he grinned, delighted to see Justine taken so off guard, a blush coloring her checks.

"Don't, Nick, she's embarrassed by such talk," Anthony Jones said. "Miss Hawkes, may I present my brother, my twin, Nicholas Jones."

"*Your* Jekyll and Hyde?" Olympe whispered as Justine's tinkling laughter bubbled up and spilled over in wave after wave, so charmingly contagious the Prince joined in with a few hesitant chuckles at first, then more heartily, until the whole company had paused in its progress toward the dining salon and was laughing at what must have been, they were all certain, the most wonderful joke whether they'd actually heard it or not.

What madness took hold of her that festive, fateful night Justine would never be quite sure, but far from home as she was, all her restraints simply fell away and all promises were forgotten. Before dawn, she had committed another impulsive act of abandon, had taken one more immutable step that would change her life forever.

70

It could have been the wine or the music that affected her overly much, or the misted, soft summer night, so fraught with promise. Probably her fever pitch of excitement over the bet she had entered into at dinner, the stakes astronomical, her lucky opals pledged against millions, made her reckless, she would realize later. Certainly the sensual, hothouse atmosphere at Castle Erlanger and the jaded nobility at play there, so flamboyantly displaying their wayward intentions, influenced her judgement. In the heat of the moment, it seemed that all things were permitted and that love was all that really mattered.

Surely, Nicholas Jones played his part in the events, there was no doubt of that, though Justine never would—never could—blame him for her own failing. Because, far from acting the seducer that night, he had, after their first waltz together, ignored her almost completely.

She had felt so right in his arms she could have remained there forever and he had felt it too, she had been sure, that lovely mysterious perfection, that aptness, that harmony of love. There had been a gentleness in his touch that was protective and possessive. They'd hardly spoken as they'd danced—they didn't have to—and they'd separated reluctantly, slowly, when the music stopped and he passed her hand to his brother, Anthony.

Nicholas hadn't danced the next waltz. He'd just stood alone, his back against the wall, his hands in his pockets in a pose of exaggerated nonchalance, watching Justine and Anthony whirl through the "Blue Danube" by Strauss. And all the while she'd pondered the marvel of it, looking with each sweeping turn from one twin to the other, from her partner's face to his brother's. They were exactly the same in every feature—in the long, lean line of the jaw and

71

the cleft chin, in the configuration of the dark velvet eyes. Identical, yet so different in mood and manner, in gesture and expression, she would have no difficulty at all telling them apart anywhere, anytime. When her dance with Anthony ended, smiling and eager, Justine had turned back to Nicholas only to find him paying rapt attention to the pretty young English widow who'd been seated beside him at dinner, Lady Caroline, viscountess of Lenster.

Hours later, after the dancing had long been over, after the billiards and baccarat had ended and the late repast of sandwiches and deviled beef bones and scotch and soda was finished and just a few stragglers were left, Justine had come upon that Lady Caroline at the bottom of the stairs, still loitering about the great hall. The woman was chattering to the duke in what Justine had come to think of as her ridiculous British upper-crust nasal twang, and was obviously waiting for Nicholas Jones to come along and take her to bed.

Of course, the torment of jealousy, abetted by injured pride, was a strong influence on Justine's behavior that night—or misbehavior as she would later come to think of it in a more rational and much more sorrowful moment. But at the time, she'd had no choice, really. The decision hadn't been hers to make. It was already too late to be sensible because, of course, she was desperately in love, and in the unfathomable, mystical, irrational way of love, she had claimed Nicholas Jones as her own.

So, when she saw Lady Caroline follow him upstairs, Justine, keeping her distance, was compelled to follow, too. Staying to the shadows, she observed the woman zigzagging down the long, dimly lit corridor and nearsightedly squinting at the name cards on each bedroom door. When Caroline found the one she'd been looking for, she paused, glanced about to get her bearings, and hurried on to her own room five doors away.

Confirming her suspicions, Justine furtively read the name that had put an end to Lady Caroline's search: Nicholas Jones. It was written in the perfect cartographic script of Olympe's personal secretary. Without even so much as a quick peek over her shoulder, Justine removed the card and replaced it with the one she had taken from her own door as she'd come along the corridor. Then, with a mischievous secret smile, she, too, hurried off.

Chapter Eight

In the rain-scented hush of predawn darkness, Nicholas Jones lay back on his bed, hands clasped behind his head, waiting for one woman and thinking of another. There was just one small lamp burning in the room, and in its dancing shadows and the waves of blue smoke from the hand-rolled cigarette he pulled on from time to time, Nicholas saw Justine Hawkes animated with shining excitement and pleasure, felt her swaying in his arms with all the willowy grace of a ballerina. Her arresting beauty was vivid in his mind's eye—the almost childlike softness in the curve of her cheek, the sensual womanly promise of pink rosebud lips always so inclined to smile, that halo of golden hair, and the laughing green eyes. He had felt the fragile strength in her pliant body as it had molded to his, so fleetingly; the promise in its supple warmth. And then . . . he had watched his own brother fall in love with her right before his very eyes. He'd seen it happen as Anthony and Justine had whirled in each other's arms and he'd wondered, each time she'd smiled over at him as he'd stood stunned, as if pinned to the wall, if she knew, if she could tell, if she could feel what was happening.

She must, he'd decided, and then and there he'd withdrawn any claim of his own, any thought of a dalliance he might have contemplated. Because, of course, careful man that he was, what he felt certainly wasn't love, merely lust, and for a man of his own intemperate habits and wayward pleasures, that wouldn't have lasted very long.

Besides, he'd never in his life taken anything away from his brother. He never would. But could Tony, inexperienced as he was, handle such a woman? Could he attempt to woo her and win her and not be devastated in the process? One could never tell about love. Nicholas shrugged as a tap sounded at his bedroom door. He glanced quickly about at the Beauvais tapestry chairs and old-rose walls, at dull green velvet hangings and draperies lush and warm and sensually pleasing. This was a room well suited to seduction, with champagne and caviar waiting on the bedside table for later, after . . .

"Come," he answered, standing as the door opened but only a little and Caroline, looking down, stepped into the room, her face hidden by the tasseled hood of her velvet wrapper.

"No lights," she whispered in an oddly strangled, almost frightened, voice, and surprised as he was, Nicholas immediately extinguished the only lamp plunging the room into thick, nearly total darkness.

There was no moonlight, only the sound of rain against half-opened windows and the rustle of footsteps as he stood still and extended his hand, pleasantly surprised than Caroline was more imaginative about these things that he'd expected. Both her soft hands tentatively touched his. They rode up his arms to his bare shoulders and met at the nape of his neck as she drew him toward her. Her mouth was wonderfully sweet when he tested it, tasted it, lightly at first, more hungrily very soon, drawing her against him, her velvet robe like butter under his practiced hands as he explored her with delighted surprise. He hadn't realized, seeing her in the yards and yards of her richly draped gown, how tall and slender she was and how prominent the outcurvings above and below her amazingly little waist.

"I want to see you," he said hoarsely, turning away toward the lamp stand.

"No!" It was that same odd whisper as he felt her arms enfold him from behind, and her hands began to play over his smooth chest as though she were a sculptress, molding each protrusion of hard muscle. Disentwining her arms, he found his way to a satin wing chair and sank into it, positioning her to kneel over him, his hand exploring again, riding her flanks, tracing up her thigh, delving beneath the loosened robe to cup a hard-tipped breast of superb firmness. He slid off her hood to find her hair softly coiled in a braided plait. Pulling open the robe, he exposed the other breast and tasted it, his tongue working first at one, then the other as he heard the catch of her breath in the dark.

In absolute astonishment at what he was doing to her, what he was making her feel as he had once before, Justine had gone perfectly still, her

76

back arched slightly, as if to concentrate totally on those two points of intense sensation until her mouth searched for his again and she felt his hands on her hips before he enfolded her waist with one arm. He traced the long line of her back, molded the swell of her *derrière,* then followed the inside of a firm and satin-smooth thigh to the apex of sensation, his first, faint grazing touch eliciting a shuddering tremble, his delving exploration a stifled moan. Again, his tongue and teeth were delicately devouring the taut budded tips of her swollen breasts, and she didn't move for a long time, afraid he might stop what he was doing, afraid it might end. But, after a while, her lips found his neck, and small teeth carefully caught at his ear as her lithe body began to undulate in rhythm with his stroking caress.

"I have to see you," he insisted, but she didn't answer, just placed a fingertip on his lips to silence him. He stood, her arms enfolding his neck, her legs about his hips as he found the bed and settled her there, a trembling shadow against the faint whiteness of the sheets.

Free of his clothes, he stretched out beside her. He felt her hand again explore his face and chest, and then, with his guidance, glide lower over the flat of his stomach, hesitating as if with the hint of shyness or fear he might have expected in a younger, far less experienced woman than he thought the once-married Lady Caroline to be.

There was that expectant stillness about her again as he shifted over her, parted her thighs, and lowered himself between them. His lips found hers warm and welcoming; his hands slid beneath her hips lifting her toward him and then he pressed into her, moving with unrestrained purpose, his repeated thrusts delving deeper and deeper, the tight, smooth encompassing flesh parting slowly . . . as she remained quiet and still, cautious, and expectant, he thought, even fearful, perhaps, as if she didn't really know how to behave, what to expect. Free and giving as she'd been when they'd played kiss and touch in the dark, she was now leaving it all up to him almost as if . . . he couldn't be absolutely certain . . . but almost as if she'd had little experience with a man. She was no virgin, he knew, he could tell that, and certainly, she'd shown an enticing aptitude for the activity, but there was a lack of . . . craft . . . skill . . . of worldly wisdom that was at once appealing and puzzling.

But the puzzle was something he could do nothing about at the moment. It was too late for that, for polite inquiries and childlike explorations and so he continued with unstinting strength, deciding to get it over and done with and to ask questions later.

When the storm shook him, he heard, through his own low moans, her smothered cry, surely one of pleasure but also, he was certain, of something else, perhaps bafflement and, astoundingly, regret.

"Sorry to disappoint," he said with a sharp edge of anger, reaching for the lamp until she captured his hand and kissed him, over and over, then clung to him, trembling and sighing in his arms, without words making her loving feelings clear.

"I thought," he began, kissing her eyelids, then the smooth curve of her ear, "Lord Lenster? . . ."

78

"Not . . . really right," she whispered so softly he barely heard.

"And you don't want me to see you, to look at you because you're shy and unpracticed?" She burrowed her face against his throat, gentle as a kitten, not at all what he'd expected of Caroline who was so briskly flirtatious. He kissed her lips and felt her nod in agreement, then move against him, still clinging. "I understand," he said, smiling, and hearing the smile in his voice, she wondered if, this time, it had touched his velvet Gypsy eyes. "We'll do it again . . . and again. And even again if we must, until we get it absolutely right. You'll know. We both will," he said huskily, astounded by the sensual warmth and loveliness of this delightful creature in his arms, whom he couldn't even see, could only feel like air and sunshine. He began to explore her again, much more slowly and thoroughly this time, his lips and his fine, sensitive fingers leaving no inch of her untouched, uncaressed, unexplored. When he mounted her again her body moved to him, her hands guided him unerringly, and when, to her surprise and delight, he rolled so that she rode him, she almost laughed aloud with the pleasure of it. He must have felt that gleeful, suppressed exultation and the playfulness in her now, because he told her it was all right to say anything, do anything, even laugh if she wanted to, but she only kissed his lips instead.

Nicholas was asleep when the first pale light of a rainy dawn showed Justine his handsome face.

He was breathing deeply, evenly, one arm flung over his head. In repose, the fiery eyes closed, the sardonic smile gone, he was more like his brother, exactly like him, she thought but studying Nicholas with caressing eyes, Justine decided she would always know this man to whom she had given herself so freely, who had ravished her so wonderfully and completely. She shivered, recalling the night past, tempted to kiss his lips, yearning to, but rising instead, carefully so as not to wake him.

As she slipped into her wrapper, she realized that her velvet belt was caught beneath him, one tassled end dangling a little over the edge of the bed. Going down on her knees, she very slowly and gently, and with great trepidation, began to work it free, little by little, inch by inch, concentrating hard, catching her lower lip between her teeth.

A full five minutes later, she still hadn't managed to reclaim the belt and he moaned in his sleep, his eyelids fluttering. Pulling up her hood and holding the robe closed with crossed arms, she fled.

Safe in her own room, Justine was free to savor the memory of her first night of love and to plot the next step in her plan to conquer and ensnare Nicholas Jones. She had to decide when and how to let him know who it was he'd made love to so passionately, who it was that had gifted him with her innocence and her passion, and had lost her heart to him completely.

Timing would be everything with a man like Nicholas. Tell him too soon, before she'd won his heart, and she could lose him. Wait too long and he might feel foolish and deceived. Women were always flinging themselves at him as she had done. The duke had told her that, as Nick himself had. Probably, he was the sort of man who threw a woman over and ran as soon as he had made his conquest. Pondering the problem, Justine decided that the bet they had made at dinner the night before would be no end of help to her on that score. He couldn't get away from her now even if, after last night, he might actually want to. But that was something the optimistic, naïve and love-blind Justine couldn't begin to conceive of as, in her mind's eye, she re-created every minute of the evening and night that had just passed.

Chapter Nine

At dinner Justine had been seated to Bertie's right, Olympe on his left, Nicholas beside his hostess. The dining salon was an extraordinary sight, like something out of the palace of the Sun King, Louis XIV. Done all in pinks, yellows and gold, with flocked wallpaper, its gilt-framed mirrors reflected light from crystal sconces and a massive shimmering chandelier.

The female guests were attired in lavish and costly gowns of watered silk and embroidered satin, of velvet, taffeta, and grenadine, creations of the elite couturiers of the day. On display were jeweled tiaras, and ropes of pearls, and reams of diamonds decorated throats, wrists, and waists, or were caught in curls or dripped from scented earlobes. Faceted diamond-cut Waterford crystal candlesticks caught and threw off the flickering lights that danced down the center of the damask-covered table. Footmen in the duke's yellow silk livery stood behind each diner's chair to assist as platters containing course after course were passed by an army of servants. The whole event was a production of such opulence and extravagance that Justine wasn't quite sure if she fully approved, but keen observer that she was, she took it all in, determined to learn what she could.

* * *

"French chefs are the cleverest of all, I think, sir," she said, bestowing her smile on the Prince. He was being helped to the sixth course of the evening, pheasant stuffed with woodcock stuffed with lark stuffed with truffles, served in a rich, dark sauce. This had been preceded by, among other things, caviar and ortolans, grilled oysters, foie gras in aspic, and the Prince's favorite, lobster.

"Yes, my dear," he said quietly, "I have always regretted that I was born too late to have enjoyed the magnificent preparations of the greatest chef of all, Antonïn Carême." He cleared his throat. "But your smile, my dear is compensation this evening. It would dim the moon, if there was a moon tonight." As the Prince cut into his pheasant, Justine dipped her head to acknowledge the compliment.

"Carême cooked for some of the most distinguished nobility of his day—Czar Alexander, Prince Talleyrand, the Baron de Rothschild. The chef would have appreciated your Majesty's exquisite taste and healthy appetite, Wales," Nicholas Jones said, addressing the Prince with an easy familiarity.

"Very clever, the French chef. And the French designer is the equal of the French chef," Justine said, inviting Jean-Philippe Worth into the conversation.

"Oh, yes," the Prince had agreed, raising his glass. "To Jean-Philippe and Gaston, carrying on the grand tradition of their papa, Charles Frederick Worth, a dressmaker famous on four continents, who was, after all, Englishman!"

"We have always been very proud, sir, of the cross-Channel connection," Gaston Worth smiled. A pleasant-seeming man with his father's receding hair and unfortunate weak chin, he had, since the elder Worth's passing, taken over design at the fashion house, while his brother dealt with the ledger books.

"French women are universally acknowledged to be the best dressed in the world, but you, Mademoiselle Hawkes"—Gaston smiled—"wear our gown superbly. You make it a living work of art." Justine's favorite Worth was her gold gown with the taut waist above a swept-back skirt. The décolletage was deep, and at her throat, her opals flashed red and blue and green against their own field of black. She was a spectacular sight.

"Miss Hawkes proves out your father's philosophy, that woman is merely man's creation," Nicholas Jones said, directing a teasing half-smile at Justine. "Charles Frederick alone was the arbiter of taste for the women he dressed."

"Exactement," Jean-Philippe agreed. "And, we continue in his tradition. But, Miss Hawkes, I am compelled to say, needs no arbiter. Her fashion sense is pure perfection."

"I am compelled to agree," Nicholas said in an offhand way, raising a brow at Justine, "but it must be very beneficial to your business, sir, that Frenchman, among others of course, like to advertise their virility, shall we say, by dressing their wives and their mistresses with the greatest possible display of expense."

"Exactement again!" Gaston said this time, laughing. "Our father's creations have always been seen at Longchamps, at Chantilly and so forth, on opposite sides of the racetrack. It's hard to say whether it is high society women or the demimondes who appear more dashing."

"But appear they all do!" Bertie laughed. "You know, it's often said that if French women are the best-dressed, English women are the most naturally beautiful, but you"—he turned to Justine—"win that superlative description for the Americans." The Prince had eaten through his pheasant and woodcock and was now making quick work of his lark.

"French couture is one thing," a gentleman seated down the table from Nicholas Jones put in, "but French art, when not frivolous, is obscene." There was a disconcerting silence until Olympe filled the void.

"Surely, Sir Eustace, you can't be serious. The problem is, I think, that some art critics and journalists don't understand what they are looking at. We French are very proud of our contribution to elegant couture *and* to art."

"I've come to Normandy just to draw," Anthony Jones, seated to Justine's right, interjected. "The seascapes of Boudin, Monet's Rouen Cathedral in its ethereal light — masterpieces."

"Besides," Nicholas Jones added, "Turner and Constable, who were English, were Impressionists before the word had been applied to French painters."

"Well, what would you expect of journalism, Duchess. It is merely a branch of commerce," Sir Eustace replied with distaste, ignoring the Joneses. Roweena, seated beside him, looked up at the Englishman with interest, her sharp expression softening with admiration, as she studied the very tall, stooped, ungainly-looking man. He had a full, soft, pouched face, wet lips, and moist pale eyes. "Journalists make their money stirring up the rabble," he continued, "Anarchists, laborites, Bohemians . . . all that riffraff. Government should be left to those fit to govern, landowning gentlemen, natural rulers."

"That's the trouble in America, of course," Roweena offered. "We have no aristocracy of the blood, just a rabble. Self-made men make me uneasy."

"Exactly so," Sir Eustace agreed, looking down his long nose at her. "There are natural leaders . . . and others."

"Who is he?" Justine softly asked the Prince, leaning toward him.

"Eustace Molesworth, a man of a large fortune and small passion," Bertie answered, sotto voce, patting the hand that rested on the arm of her chair. "He's a man wanting in vigor, shall we say? And inclined to fuss with his china and antiques. Eustace diligently, but unsuccessfully, tries to avoid the mental excitement of reading and conversation, which, he is certain, causes irritation of the brain."

"But such a tactless haughty man must often find himself in dispute," Justine commented, withdrawing her hand and placing it on her lap as she felt Nick Jones's eyes on her. Beside her, Anthony Jones cleared his throat pointedly as Bertie went on whispering in Justine's ear.

"Eustace cares nothing for the opinion of others. He cares only for sport and he does love his stud, his race horses. He likes them to win."

"Really?" Justine coughed a little behind her napkin. "Tell me, Bertie, who are the women opposite him?"

"The two Miss Percivals, dear child. Rubenesque, are they not, with that fine red hair and pale skin and those ample proportions?"

"You do have an eye for the ladies, sir," she said with feigned surprise. "And the angry fellow seated between them? Who's he?"

"He's one of ours," Anthony Jones said, moving his chair closer to Justine's and regarding Bertie with an almost unfriendly expression. "That's James Gordon Bennett, an American expatriate. He's publisher of the Herald newspapers, the New York and the International editions."

"Sir," Bennett bristled at Eustace Molesworth. "Watch your tongue. This is France. Here I still can

86

call you out to avenge my honor in a duel. Journalism is more than mere commerce."

"You're a journalist, I take it?" Molesworth asked with obvious distaste. Then, informed of the speaker's identity, he added with even more obvious sarcasm, "You, sir, are an exception, of *course.*"

"Why so?" Bennett demanded somewhat less aggressively, not yet mollified, but willing to moderate his stance.

"Why, any man who would drive stark naked up the Champs Elysées to deliver newspapers as you have done as a publicity stunt, is certainly a responsible, serious journalist. Any man who would send that maniac Stanley off to Africa to find Dr. Livingston, is of course a great journalist, even if Livingston wasn't lost, didn't want to be found, and remained exactly where he was after *he* found that fool Stanley thrashing about in the bush, lost himself."

"What a blasted snob you are," Bennett blustered, his voice rising as he stood. "I'd punch you in the snout, sir, if not for the ladies. Care to step outside?"

"This is not a pub and I will not engage in a brawl." Eustace sniffed. "Of course I'm a snob. I've a right to be. Lineage always tells. Your manners, Bennett, prove me right. You're a mongrel." There was a stir and a murmur around the table.

"It's not unknown, Eustace," Nicholas said, "for a real maverick, a man with no roots and no past—no lineage, to use your word—to rise to power and wealth like cream to the top of a milk pitcher." His commanding tone silenced Eustace, who had been about to interrupt, and captured the attention of everyone at the table. "A mongrel dog can possess great dignity, beauty, loyalty, and strength. The same is true of a horse. From out of nowhere, a mixed-breed foal grows into a magnificent animal that can put up a fine race against any thoroughbred on any track in the world—and *win*."

"Not so," Eustace insisted, his twiglike fingers drumming the tabletop nervously. "I'm getting a headache," he whined.

"How is this to be settled?" the Duke d'Erlanger asked with lethargic interest.

"Settled? There's nothing to be settled," Gray Hawkes said, "not for us. Americans have done very well, thanks, for more than a hundred years without a so-called aristocracy, and without—excuse me, sir," he said to Bertie—"a King, no insult intended. We're looking forward to a new century in which new discoveries and new inventions will mean a better life for all, we—"

"Americans!" the duke sighed. "Such optimists. In France, before the last millennium turned, before the year one thousand, it was predicted that the world would come to an end. A kind of madness was in the air, the historians say. Now, as this second millennium draws to a close, doom looms again and there is lassitude, decadence, anarchy, labor strikes—"

"Boredom!" the Prince pronounced. "There's *boredom,* and that's the terror of mankind. What is the least boring thing you can think of?" he asked Justine with a suggestive wink.

"A horse race," she answered without hesitation. "And that's the way to settle this argument."

"With a horse race?" Anthony Jones asked a bit skeptically.

"Yes, with a horse race," his brother agreed. Nick's eyes met Justine's and lingered on them with restrained curiosity, almost, she thought, as if he were seeing her for the first time.

"A horse race of what sort?" Eustace said slowly, the clicking of his brain almost audible as he began at once to plot a victory. "No horseflesh out of my stud can be beaten by any American-bred beast, thoroughbred or maverick. Nor could a French or an Italian animal compete." He glanced across the table at Count Mauro Zenga.

"What terms?" the count asked with a lethal smile, his aquiline features and deeply lined face recalling the patrician rulers of ancient Rome.

"Anyone here tonight can play. Mr. Bennett, will you agree to hold the sums put up?" Justine suggested eagerly.

"If I get an exclusive story on this," Bennett responded. "What are the rules? Who will run and where and when and how will it be done?"

"The Grand National Steeplechase at Aintree, England," Sir Eustace said. "A mongrel sport for this rabble, your majesty excepted."

"The toughest race in the world," Bertie said. "I'm in."

"Agreed," Zenga nodded.

"We'll play," Gaston Worth nodded.

"I'm in, too," Barney Barnato, the diamond king, said, his heavily beringed fingers flashing, his face florid beneath tufts of white hair.

"Me, too." Colonel North, the nitrate king, joined the others. "I'm a mongrel myself, Eustace. I left England broke, and came back from Chile very well off indeed. There's nothing I'd rather do than watch your face when a horse of mine puts your whole stud to shame." A little gnome of a man with a gristled beard, North grinned broadly, resembling nothing so much as a happy gargoyle.

"I'd like to take your money, too, Eustace," Aimery d'Erlanger shrugged. "My, this has been a taxing dinner. Usually there's nothing but men's business talk and women's complaints."

"I bet a million," Bet-A-Million Gates, the barbed-wire king, said, bringing his massive fists down on the tabletop, "a horse of mine will walk away with it all."

"Is that pounds or dollars?" Nicholas Jones asked, exchanging glances with Anthony.

"Whatever," Gates said amiably. "Are you going to play, sir?"

"Well. . . ." Nicholas sat back as if considering the matter, never for an instant really doubting he'd compete but taking time to think out a strategy. "The stakes are very high," he said with a skeptical look, aware of the disappointment appearing in Justine's eyes. "What do you think, brother?"

"We can't begin to match these gentlemen with cash," Anthony mused, "pounds or dollars, but if they'd consider property or—"

"The castle we inherited from Mother in Wales?" Nick asked. "The newspaper Grandfather Jones left to us, the ones in Florida? Would you chance it, Tony?"

"No good," Eustace shook his head. "Wales isn't really England, even though the Prince of Wales has a castle there. They even speak a different language. Who would want some run-down old pile full of bearskins or a tabloid rag in the Colonies?"

"I would," Gordon Bennett said. "I'll hold the deed on the castle and a lean on the papers and put up a half-million for the Jones brothers. Miss Hawkes, will you play?" he asked.

"I've nothing to bet, nothing of my own. Gray, do you think Father would be party to this?" she asked.

"Your opals," Nick Jones said simply while Gray was still considering. Jones's eyes were challenging, goading Justine as they held hers across the dinner table, over the flickering candles. He was challenging her, she knew, and she never could refuse a dare.

Gambler that she was, she, too, stalled for time now, her expression thoughtful.

"My godfather gave me the opals, Mr. Jones," she said, fingering the largest of the stones set in gold adorned with sapphires, garnets, and smaller black opals. "It might be unlucky to chance a wager on such a gift, do you suppose?"

"There are people who think opals themselves are unlucky, who won't have them, who are afraid to wear them." He shrugged. "For a horsewoman of your skill and experience, you seem strangely lacking in confidence. Pity not to have you participate since this was your idea."

"Mr. Gordon Bennett," Justine said, her long slanting green eyes flashing fire like her opals, "would you be willing to put up another half-million on this race, secured by my opals?" Bennett nodded, looking from Justine to Nicholas, aware of the fire between them, the only one at the table, besides Olympe, who seemed to be. "They're priceless, your stones, full of red flashes. The best."

"Done," she said. "The Jones brothers and I have a million together." She turned to Anthony and smiled. "We'll make a single entry, one superb piece of horse-flesh, American bred, schooled and conditioned. And we will put all your nags to shame." She laughed.

"The details will be worked out after dessert, after brandy and cigars, after dancing," Bertie said. "Now, tell us about your opals, your spectacular opals," he urged Justine. "I've never seen any as fine, or as dark. Her Highness, the Queen, has added opals to the crown jewel collection, but none are so magnificent as yours."

"They're my birthstone. My Uncle Philip, whom I met for the first time only several months ago, has been sending them to me since I was born. He finds these opals in some desolate place in Australia that he calls the 'Never Never,' the Outback. But he won't say exactly where it is, I suppose because he wants to keep his discovery to himself. These black opals are unique. No other mine produces such dark stones as Philip's."

"Opals bring bad luck, it's thought," Roweena said, finding something negative to voice.

"Do you think I've been unlucky, Roweena?" Justine asked. "Only the timid fear to wear them. There's superstition and magic associated with all precious stones. For example, carnelian is thought to protect the wearer against envy," she said pointedly. "And turquoise, as you certainly know"—she turned to Nicholas Jones—"is the horseman's talisman. It's supposed to protect mount and rider from injury and falls."

"The Apache Indians say that if you go to the end of the rainbow after a storm, and search the damp earth, you'll find a turquoise there," Nicholas told her. "Would you like to go to the end of a rainbow, Miss Hawkes?" he asked.

"I have my own rainbow," she answered, gesturing at her opals, "but if that's an invitation, how could any woman resist?" she added flirtatiously.

"Pendants of glittering stones and rare, brilliant metal distract the Evil Eye as a lightning rod does the electricity of a storm," Count Zenga offered, his own hooded eyes the color of gray slate as he studied Justine. "Now, your green starry orbs are sometimes the color of jade, sometimes of copper verdigris, which can be beautiful but dangerous—a poison." He smiled. "Are *you* dangerous, Miss Hawkes?"

"Oh, really, Count! Do I appear to be?" She laughed, the center of attention as usual and enjoying herself. "Did you know that in the Orient emeralds are prized as an antidote to poison? You, being of the same blood as the Borgias, the greatest poisoners in history, should remember that."

"I shall, of course, remember every word that comes from so pretty a mouth and so wise a head as yours, you may be sure," the count responded, charmed by the spontaneity of the girl. "How do you come to know so much about gems?" he asked.

"My opals started it. They roused my curiosity, so I learned about other stones, diamonds for instance, and I'd like to ask Mr. Barnato a question. Sir, you're an expert on the subject. Do you believe, as I have heard, that diamonds can duplicate themselves by turning air to drops of water that then harden into unblemished icy pure gems?"

"Listen, dear"—Barnato guffawed—"do you think I, or anyone else, would be diggin' down into the blue earth—that's real deep—if we could pull diamonds out of the air? Just wishful thinkin' by some lazy slug, that sort of thing. Now, I got one for you, darlin'. What the pearl fishers of Borneo do. They put every ninth one they find into a bottle along with two grains of rice expecting to get two more pearls, free of work," he croaked in a gravelly baritone.

"But that's only if they stopper the bottle with a dead man's finger," Justine said.

"Ghastly, hey?" Bernato nodded. "You do know it all, don't you?"

"When Satan saw the brilliant colors of the flowers in the Garden of Eden, he imitated their bright beauty in the precious stones that have spawned so much covetousness among men," Nick Jones told Justine. "But I suppose, know-it-all that you are, you've heard that before."

"I think that magnificent gems on a beautiful

woman bear eloquent witness to the power of love," Aimery d'Erlanger said, looking at Olympe who, if not exactly beautiful, was heavily adorned with weighty, costly jewels. She blew Aimery a kiss and blushed.

"Oh, how very lovely a thought," Justine sighed, touched by the Duke's affection for his wife, so simply expressed in an unguarded moment. It gave her a new view, and changed her opinion of the man whom she had thought, until then, too jaded and self-centered to love anyone but himself.

Anthony Jones was affected at that moment, too, though by Justine's response, not by the display of affection between two maturing lovers. Whether it was her little intake of breath, the look of wonder and revelation in her eyes, or, a bit later, the first touch of her hand as he claimed his dance, Anthony would never be absolutely certain, but at some instant between the sigh and the touch, he fell helplessly, hopelessly, in love with Justine Hawkes.

He sat through the rest of the meal, all the chitchat and small talk and laughter, oblivious to everything but the beautiful girl beside him, aware only of her throaty voice, her golden hair, her exotic, lovely eyes.

"Mr. Bennett," she said, "I'm told that you will soon be offering a cup for balloon racing as you do already for yachting. Is it so?" she inquired.

"It is," Gordon Bennett answered. Delighted to be asked, he enthusiastically launched off into a description of the new sport of ballooning, calling it the most exciting thing he'd tried since he had first introduced polo to the United States twenty years before.

"I must ask you, Miss Hawkes, is your father, Slade, one of the founders of the Meadowbrook Polo Club?"

"He is," Justine replied, and the talk continued as

94

Tony listened in silence.

"Sir Eustace," he had heard that pretentious lump of a woman, Roweena McGlory, ask in her strident voice, "what are your spiritual beliefs?" Several other conversations began and continued simultaneously, talk of Kitchener, the British soldier, the Boers in South Africa, and of Commodore, soon to be Admiral, Dewey.

"The best kind of war is one that's waged far away in some picturesque locale against some barbarous foe," Tony heard someone remark. And then, "The favorite sport of cuckolds is fishing." The speaker was one of those appalling Englishwomen who, for all their airs, seemed to him rather coarse and frivolous. This one, who was not unattractive, was talking to his brother, Nicky, who seemed to be giving her his full, lecherous attention. Anthony glanced at Justine then, but apparently she had not heard the tasteless remark, involved as she was in a *tête-à-tête* with that fat, old Prince of Wales.

Damn him! Justine had been thinking at that moment, for she'd glanced obliquely across the table at Nicholas Jones. Damn him. He is practically drooling over that insipid creature. It was just then she felt the Prince's first tentative touch at her knee. The rotund royal had hardly paused in his eating, his plate having been repeatedly cleared, his wine glass drained and refilled again and again, as he'd rambled and ruminated in his deep voice about this and that—of his trip to America, of his fondness for the American West and Buffalo Bill dime novels, and for Buffalo Bill Cody himself who had brought his whole Wild West Show to the Queen's Golden Jubilee twenty-five years ago. Only last year, in 1897, Her Highness had celebrated her Diamond Jubilee, seventy-five years on the throne of England and he, Bertie, was still only a

Prince, and not a favored one at that.

"Do you know what the Queen, my mama, calls the Maharaja Gaekwar of Baroda?" he asked, his protuberant eyes on Justine's face as she shifted her knee out of his reach. "She calls him her favorite son. Now, what am I to make of that?" he opined.

"I'm sure she doesn't mean it, Bertie," Justine smiled sympathetically but distantly.

"My dear," he said very softly after devouring the last bit of meat on his plate, his stockinged foot searching for hers and climbing her leg beneath the table, "usually my amorous attentions are greeted with a more positive response than yours. My interest is taken as a sign of favor, actually. It is Mama's coldness to me that has made me crave the company of . . . gorgeous, generous women."

"I *am* flattered, Bertie," Justine said very seriously. "But in America we don't . . . we still believe in love and I—"

"Say no more, dear child." He beamed. "You've a young man! I remember love, I do indeed. Well now, where's dessert?" Bertie asked, looking about though he had already devoured an enormous quantity of food. "If we don't start the dancing soon, it may be too late for me to make tonight's arrangements with an enthusiastic partner, and that, little American romantic, is unthinkable."

It was with a certain sense of relief that soon after Justine watched the Prince waddle away from the table, leading the other gentlemen to the Duke's billiard room for cigars and brandy before the party reassembled again in the ballroom.

Justine had had her first and only dance with Nicholas Jones, who then avoided her for the rest of the evening, and, in fact, handed her over to Anthony, as though making his brother a gift of her, though she was in no way his to give, while he himself went off in very obvious pursuit of Lady Caroline. It wasn't until the early hours of the next morning that he took any notice of Justine again.

"Wales certainly does enjoy the sport of kings, doesn't he?" Nicholas, on his way to bed, had stopped to ask her.

"Horse racing?" she had responded in a frosty tone. "I suppose."

"No," Nicholas interrupted, "I meant bedding women. It's as much a sport for him as watching his ponies run. And will His Royal Highness be exercising his *droit de seigneur* with you tonight?"

"His what?" she had queried innocently, somewhat taken aback by his answser to her question.

"His *droit de seigneur*," Nicholas repeated. "The right of the ruling lord, in feudal times, to bed his vassal's virgin bride on her wedding night, before her new husband did. Of course, in Bertie's case and yours, it isn't exactly the same, is it?"

"That's absolutely no concern of yours, sir," Justine countered, stung by Nick's angry attack and not about to explain anything to him. His manner was so cold and cutting, his words so hurtful, and the loitering presence of that ridiculous Englishwoman was so galling, Justine almost struck out at Nicholas but managed, by standing rigidly still, to control herself.

"Why don't you just take your aristocratic doxy there, Lady Caroline, who's been waiting with such impatience, off to bed and leave me alone," she'd hissed furiously and he'd almost laughed, she thought, as he leaned toward her. She'd raised hurt questioning eyes to his, almost expecting him to kiss her as he'd done before, but he'd only whispered in her ear.

"I don't discuss my women, especially not with innocent little girls like you." To Justine's outrage, he'd patted her patronizingly on the top of the head and turned away toward the great staircase that rose to the bedrooms above. Lady Caroline, who'd witnessed the whispered scene from a little distance, had gone up after him almost at once, her expectations high. But, she was to be sorely disappointed.

Chapter Ten

"Can you tell them apart? For the life of me I surely cannot!"

Olympe and Justine were sitting together the next morning over an English breakfast, so unlike its light French counterpart of *café au lait* and croissants. On the laden sideboards, were porridge and cream, scones and marmalades, eggs, deviled kidneys, hams and sausages, pressed beef, tongue, and cold roast ptarmigan — a kind of grouse. On a separate table were great mounds of fruit, pots of coffee, and several teas of both the China and India varieties. Guests had been drifting in and out, helping themselves for some time before Justine had arrived, filled her plate with mounds of food, and gone to sit beside her hostess.

"Oh, yes," Justine responded with a tremulous little smile, "I most certainly can tell them apart. This gentleman just arriving for breakfast, looking so . . . attractive? That's Nicholas." She sipped her coffee and gazed at him over the gold rim of her Sèvres cup. He paused on the doorsill to look around the room, found what he was seeking and moved to help himself to breakfast, barely nodding at Justine as he passed her on his purposeful way to Lady Caroline who was sitting a few places down the table.

Justine watched him pull up his chair and move it closer to Lady Caroline's. She saw the viscountess glance up at Nick with the cool hauteur of a jilted lover; it was obvious to her, though to no one else, least of all to the enamored Nicholas himself. When he lowered his head to whisper in her ear, Lady Caroline jumped as though pricked by a pin. Then she flushed to the roots of her hair, her color deepening to a vivid scarlet as Nicholas continued speaking, unaware of her reaction. Suddenly Caroline began to sputter and cough, and her eyes widened and Olympe leaped up to thump the woman on the back and offer sips of tea, afraid she was choking on a bit of kidney. It wasn't until Lady Caroline actually left the room in a huff that Nicholas realized his error. He frowned, glanced about bemusedly for a moment, then ate heartily, obviously deep in thought. As he strode past her on his way from the room, he paused at Justine's chair.

"Will you be chasing the fox today? You should," he said.

"Oh?" She gave him a dazzling smile, aglow with pleasure at his attention.

"The lady with the best seat in Deauville should show it off," he pronounced, wondering how it could be that she seemed even lovelier than he remembered, lovelier today than yesterday. He supposed a good night's sleep had enhanced her freshness and inner glow.

"And imagine how absolutely devastating she'll look in hunt pink," Anthony Jones said, slipping into the place beside her. "Will you ride today?" he asked. Justine noded.

"But you *will* be careful?" Olympe said, a worried frown on her face. "Aimery insisted on a hunt, ever so British, so un-French. He even borrowed a pack of hounds from an English cousin but I have had danger signs put up at all the jumps and—"

"Olympe, really!" Justine laughed. "Danger signs?"

"Nicky's right, you know. Someone will have to show them how it's really done, Virginia style," Anthony said when his brother had left the room. "For the first time, I'm a little sorry I don't hunt. But later, when it's over, will you sit for me and let me sketch you? You've inspired me to get back to work."

Justine agreed reluctantly, and only at Olympe's urging, put off as she was by the look in Anthony's eyes, one she'd seen so often before, shy hope bordering on adoration. She was aware that any encouragement from her could send his hopes soaring. And the next thing one knew . . . But that would be intolerable, impossible, she told herself. He *can't* fall in love with me, she told herself, it just wouldn't be fair!

"Olympe!" Justine called, dancing down the center of the grand staircase in breeches and knee boots, equestrian hard hat pushed up, red jacket caught over her shoulders. "Wait, Olympe! I must tell you something . . . extraordinary, but"—she caught up with the older woman and drew her into the library off the great hall, away from the scurrying maids and boot boys and valets with breakfast trays—"you must promise not to repeat one word I will say to you now, not ever to anyone no matter what. Will you promise?"

"Ladies don't ride astride in pants here, Justine. You will shock them all," Oylmpe answered.

"They are all seen about in bicycle bloomers, aren't they? Oh, let them be shocked. Will you promise?"

"Oh, of course. What can possibly require such secrecy? Tell me quickly, Justine, because they are all waiting for you, all those barking dogs and everyone."

"I did a terrible . . . *wonderful* thing last night," Justine began her story eagerly, and as she talked, Olympe's eyes grew wide and round and worried, then softened into a warm glow and she made little clucking sounds with her tongue and clasped her hands in front of her chin.

"Such a deception!" she crowed. "How will you make it all come right with this fierce American? What if? . . ."

"No 'what ifs.' It will be right, I can feel it. It was already right last night." Justine laughed with exhilaration. "Not a word to anyone, remember. You promised," she called over her shoulder as she rushed out into a sparkling, rain-washed, brightening day, leaving her befuddled friend bemused and completely enchanted.

"You are such a delightfully energetic little optimist, you make my head spin!" Olympe called after her. She then gathered up her gloves and parasol. Wearing her new bonnet, weighted with flowers and fruit, and a day dress the color of the red wax cherries on the hat brim, she readied herself to watch what she could of the hunt with Roweena, who didn't ride, from the safety and comfort of her well-appointed yellow barouche. It was then that one of the Joneses prevented her from quitting the house.

"Duchess d' Erlanger, I need your help," he declared earnestly. "I had a very unusual—indeed, an extraordinary—experience last night that I mention to you only because my, ah . . . curiosity has been whetted and you may be able to shed some light on the mystery."

"Oh, my!" Olympe responded with false concern. "Was something lost or? . . ."

"Lost?" he repeated. "No, something's been given away, to be more precise, given to me with the most amazing largess. Nothing for you to worry over, Duchess," he hurriedly assured her. "It's just that . . . well, there's a young woman among your house guests I must identify."

"Identify, Mr. Jones?" Olympe smiled with puzzlement. Knowing full well what he was about to ask, she quickly pulled on a glove. "But I must be off or I shall miss the start of the hunt. Can't we chat at teatime?"

"No," he said bluntly, not a man to be put off when he considered his vital interests to be at stake. "I hope what I have to say won't embarrass you, but we're neither of us innocents, are we?" he asked, standing in her path and offering the most compelling smile she'd ever seen. "Will you listen, please?" he implored.

"Has any woman *ever* been able to say 'no' to

103

you, Mr. Jones?" she responded with a sigh and a nod, resigning herself to endure whatever the perversities of fate and the whims of love had in store for them all.

And so Olympe heard from Nicholas Jones very much the same story that had been told her by Justine Hawkes moments before, both versions heavy with superlatives though discreetly sketchy and imprecise in detail, and when he'd done, she stood to her full height and fluttered her lashes as if in disbelief.

"Really, Mr. Jones, I am a woman of the world as you've noted and you are not an April Fool. Do you really expect me to believe that you spent an entire night with a woman whose identity is a total mystery to you?" He nodded reluctantly, his expression almost sheepish. "You mean you haven't a clue?" Olympe pressed. "The sound of her voice, the length of her hair . . . her laugh, a hint of fragrance . . . nothing?"

"Hair fine as . . . cornsilk," he said softly, his eyes distant. "But coiled in a braid so . . . so I couldn't tell." He recalled himself to the moment as if snapping out of a mesmeric trance. "I have a belt, of hunter green velvet with passementerie tassels, lost from a velvet robe. That's all I have besides a lovely memory. Can you — will you — help me find her?" Jones asked, so intensely, so urgently, Olympe was tempted to do just that. All that prevented her was the promise she'd made to Justine.

"I am so sorry, Mr. Jones" — she smiled with the greatest sincerity — "but I cannot. Perhaps the person you're seeking will reveal herself in time. I advise you to be patient and stay on with us awhile. Will you?"

"I must, mustn't I"—he grinned—"if I'm to try to unmask my nocturnal nymph on my own? Because that *is* what I intend to do. Oh, I'll give her a little slack but not very much, not for long. Your advice, Duchess, is appreciated, but I'm not a particularly patient man." He tipped his hat and left Olympe standing in the great hall, wondering what on earth to expect next.

Chapter Eleven

"Ah, the prettiest seat in town," Nicholas couldn't resist commenting as he passed Justine, already up on a white-faced chestnut, to mount his own horse that was being held by a groom in red livery. "Do you think you'll last the course?" he asked, riding beside her down the drive and across the drawbridge.

There was a trace of medieval pageantry in the atmosphere of the hunt, with the band and flags and balloons, the hounds baying, terriers yapping, riders eager to get on with it, and the chattering, cheering spectators in carriages lining the way.

"We'll see, won't we, who stays the course?" Justine laughed happily, again imbued with a sense of the rightness of things, this time because she was riding beside Nicholas, knee to knee.

Then the hounds caught a scent. The hunt was off, unhampered by the inappropriateness of the season or anything else.

Three hours later, there were only a few survivors still up at the finish. Nicholas had stayed with Justine, who set the pace as she hurtled across the Norman countryside with abandon, ignoring Olympe's danger signs and never even drawing rein at any hazard. To the baying of the hounds, the pair had negotiated the stone walls and ditches that gradually winnowed out most of the others until, at the end, they found themselves alone with the few whippers-in who were in charge of collecting the hounds, and Eustace Molesworth.

"Oh, well done. For Americans," he said grudgingly as the three turned back toward Castle Erlanger. "You do ride with pluck, Miss Hawkes. I hope you'll accept an invitation in the fall to visit my country estate at Scrapcroft in Quorn. It offers some of the best hunt country in England."

"We'll have to be getting back home by September, to prepare for our steeplechase, Sir Eustace, but thank you all the same," Justine answered, wishing the man gone.

"You took a fall, I see, Eustace," Nicholas noted dryly. He, too, wished the man were elsewhere.

"Even the best do, you know. I've seen the Prince in the mud going over a very nasty bogey with a wide drain," he sniffed. "That's a hidden ditch for your information, Miss Hawkes," he added condescendingly. "You do sit a horse rather well. Have you done this sort of thing before or are you one of those Wild West Show entertainers like . . . what's his name . . . Cody?"

"How did you guess?" Justine asked. "I usually wear a Stetson hat with a rattlesnake band, but I'm trying to be less conspicuous here in France."

"Really?" Eustace responded stretching out the word so that it had several extra syllables. He regretted that so beautiful a woman should be engaged in so indecorous an activity, but if plans he'd been hatching since he'd first seen her last night at dinner came to fruition, as he expected they would, he'd put an end to such things for her forever. These rich American girls were all shopping titles. Members of the nobility like himself, with costly residences and large staffs to keep up, strapped for cash, maintaining appearances on credit, had done splendidly by marrying them. When that Mabel Swift, the meatpacker's daughter from Chicago, was wed she brought her impoverished Danish count a guaranteed three hundred thousand pounds a year. The Duke of Marlborough got more than two million the day he took that Vanderbilt girl to wife. Eustace himself was no duke, of course. His lesser title was not as impressive, and he was well aware of that. But he *did* have his accent, his gardens, some very old family silver, and impeccable manners to offer. What more could any colonial want, he wondered, overvaluing himself in the extreme. Now that he'd found this exceptionally pretty one, he'd cancel the advertisement his solicitor had been running in the *Daily Telegraph,* where there were many others like it: "A lady who is willing to purchase a rank of peeress for twenty-five thousand pounds sterling, paid in cash to her future husband, should communicate with . . ."

That amount would hardly pay his haberdasher's bills but it was a start, Sir Eustace thought. It would be enough to tide him over until the race, the steeplechase, that would put more than a million pounds in his pocket and would take care of all his difficulties. He couldn't lose, he wouldn't, no matter what he had to do to win. Now, though, he'd concentrate on securing this rich American beauty. But looking sideways at Justine, her long yellow braid bouncing down her back, he had a troubling thought.

"You don't shoot fox in your country, do you?" he asked with a worried frown. "In Spain, they shoot foxes. Appalling, really, though I did get a fine ten-point buck at Jerez. We drank Solera wine like water, smoked cigars from their colony, Havana, that were big as spinnaker booms and . . . Have you hunted Spain, Jones?" he asked.

"My brother and I have been almost everywhere in Europe in the last year or so. We've just come back from Albania."

"Went for the wild boar, did you? They're tough, Albanian wild boar," Eustace commented.

"My brother sketches," Nicholas said cryptically. Then he seemed to become distracted and preoccupied, Justine thought. When they came to a narrow place in the road, he gestured her ahead, and they rode side by side again, ignoring Eustace. The temptation was great to reach out and touch his hand, to smile, to say I hope its me you're thinking of because I want you to take me in your arms here and now and do all those things you did last night.

When Nicholas, also lost in thoughts of the night past, finally glanced at Justine, there was that delicate hint of pink in her cheeks, and her eyes, under fluttering lashes, were dreamy and soft when they met his.

"Shoot snipe, do you, Jones?" Eustace called out. "Pigeon? I was quite successful at the Grand International Pigeon Shoot at Brighton a few years back."

"Were you?" Jones responded in an offhand manner, tempted to ask Justine what thought had brought that blush to her cheek. She was entirely too appealing, too dangerously beautiful for Tony who approached all of these pretty tidbits seriously, heart in hand. He'd have to keep an eye on them, his brother and this girl, and find out all he could about her before it went too far. Perhaps she was just what Tony needed, just what the direct green eyes proclaimed her to be, what that open encompassing smile promised. But Nicholas was skeptical, distrustful of all women, especially the very, very pretty ones.

He was scowling, Justine noticed as they rode out from under an overhang of trees and skirted a meadow that was waist high in pastel wildflowers, then clattered over the Castle d'Erlanger moat bridge, where they came upon Olympe and Roweena posing for Anthony. He'd already done several studies of each woman in profile and full face.

"Will you sit for me?" he said to Justine. "Right now, just as you are, mud-spattered and flushed and . . . perfect?" She nodded and reined in. "No, don't get down. I want to do a full figure of you mounted on the mare," he said eagerly, flipping over the pages of his pad to a blank sheet, the outline form of horse and rider

110

quickly appearing on it, the details accumulating more slowly.

Justine found his enthusiasm charming, his concentration amidst the chaos of the returning hunt — riders, hounds, and the crush of carriages — admirable. When he'd gotten what he needed, for the moment at least, he smiled with a boyish warmth. "You're so remarkably pretty," he said in a dreamy voice. "I want to do you in pastels. You should always be surrounded by garden colors — lemon yellows and dusty pinks, periwinkle, and most of all jade green. I want to capture you in oils, standing in a field of poppies near a farmhouse. You should be wearing a high-waisted Renaissance gown . . . all that lovely golden hair will be loose, a fillet of velvet will band your brow and . . ." He hesitated self-consciously realizing everyone was listening and staring. "I think I found my inspiration at last," he told his brother who had been observing the scene with imperious, impassive eyes.

"You're the center of attention as always," Gray Hawkes teased, falling in beside Justine as she turned her horse toward the stable. "And Roweena is stewing in jealousy, as always. I must say" — he looked at his sister intently — "you do look especially luminous just now. You haven't . . . done it again?" he asked.

"Heaven help me, Gray" — she laughed — "I think I have. I have fallen in love again, but this time — "

"This time you may have chosen well for a change. I think he's a fine fellow."

"Do you? Oh, I'm so glad you think so, so

relieved because—"

"Yes, and judging by the way Anthony Jones was looking at you, I'm sure he shares your feelings. He seems a good-humored man of decent character. Everybody here seems to like him immensely and so do I."

"But, Gray . . ." Justine began as they pulled over to the side of the road to let the large pack of hounds pass.

"Of course, his brother, Nicholas, is another matter, I'm told, not remarkable for his consistent good nature. He's a man of dark moods, yet despite that, he's irresistibly fascinating to women, you should know, and wickedly clever with them. He takes advantage," Gray said with pointed emphasis. "Amazing, isn't it, that two brothers—twins—could be so different, one a gentleman, the other a scoundrel, by reputation at least?" he asked and Justine turned away.

"What else did you hear about the Jones brothers and from whom?"

"I heard it all from Anthony. He'd like to go home to California, but he feels responsible for Nicholas. He won't leave his brother. Such a wastrel needs watching, Tony says."

"Anthony Jones said *that* to you about his own brother?" she asked.

"Yes. I thought that unpolitic myself but I decided he spoke so that I would warn you, so you wouldn't . . . well, be taken in by Nicholas."

"You must thank Anthony for me," she said shortly, and tell him his warning's come too late, she thought.

"Thank him yourself." Gray smiled, tipping his

hat as they passed Lady Caroline trotting in on a white hunter of very elegant lines. "You'll be riding out with Tony this afternoon," he said. "By the way"—Gray dropped his voice—"I found her," he tilted his head at Caroline, "wandering the halls in the wee hours, obviously disappointed in love. Or lost. One or the other. Her eyes lit up when she saw me, but the games these decadents play are not to my taste. They all commit blazing indiscretions all the time it seems. You will have a care, little sister, not to get caught up in it? Justine didn't answer, just handed her mount over to a stableboy and strode off toward the castle to change for her afternoon drive with Anthony Jones.

Chapter Twelve

Erlanger Castle
Deauville, France
June 26, 1898
2 A.M.

Dear Father,

The busy pace of life here leaves little time for correspondence but we've just come back from the casino and I'm stealing a moment to pen a few lines.

Justine and I have done very well in Normandy for the Hawkes stables. She's found you a very fine polo pony of the best first-string quality. I've acquired, with her expert assistance, a brood mare of impressive lineage and a stud stallion of great beauty, promise, *and* cost, but worth every cent, I'm convinced. He's already sired several French champions so I've reason to be optimistic.

Justine and I will be leaving the Erlangers in just a few days for the Tully Stud in Ireland where I expect we'll do as well, if not better, Irish horseflesh being what it is. Justine has been of inestimable help to me in this enterprise. She's a hard worker, very dedicated, and brings to these endeavors all her delightful terrier tenacity, her quick intelligence, and her almost uncanny horse sense, all three of which she possesses in no small measure as you know. Of course, she causes a sensation wherever we go and attracts admirers that range from the future King of England, whom she has handled with the charming dexterity of a much older, more experienced woman, to the youngest stableboys who fall over themselves and each other in their haste to be of service to her. And of course, your daughter has an admirer. She's spent all her free time this past week or so with an American guest of the Erlangers, an artist who has been showing her the countryside and sketching our darling child against every conceivable background in all weathers and at all times of night and day—in fields of flowers, on cliffs above the sea, in gardens, in the great halls of noble houses, in cafés, on horseback, even at the casino wearing her opals and, of course, winning.

I do believe she is being sensible about this little *amour* as she promised she would be but should it develop into something more serious, I think you'd not be displeased. This Jones seems an exemplary fellow in every way, though I can't say the same for his twin brother, a man of intemperate extremes who, fortunately, is not our concern. What is our concern though, is a million-dollar bet Justine has gotten herself into before I could stop her. Now, she refuses to go back on her word. It's the one impetuous thing she's done on this whole trip, but she's so confident of winning

115

she has even pledged her lucky opals on a steeplechase to be run a year from now on a course built for the occasion at the estate of the Prince of Wales, Sandringham. The Grand National course at Aintree will be duplicated in every detail, including the fifteen fences, ditches, water jumps, and all. This way, horses who don't qualify under English Jockey Club rules for the real thing at Aintree—American mixed-breed mustangs, for instance—can run against each other. The competitors are an impressive international lot of millionaires, except for the Jones brothers and Justine who are in this thing together representing the United States. There's also the American Bet-A-Million Gates; you know him. His entry won't be bred in the United States necessarily. Do keep your eye out, Father, for an outstanding American jumper. If Justine's going to win this thing, she'll need one!

> Love to all,
> Your son,
> Gray

Erlanger Castle, half after two in the morning
June 26, 1898
Dear Mother,

We are having a splendid time! The Erlangers have been the most wonderful and attentive hosts and have anticipated our every need and desire, though the extravagant self-indulgence of life here does begin to pall and I look forward to our departure for Ireland.

When Gray and I are not hard at work, as he calls what we do, though for me it is more like play—appraising and riding horses—we have been wined and dined and driven about and feasted and fêted in every imaginable way. Normandy is a beautiful place with its orchards of pear and apple trees and its green pastures of magnificent horses and ordinary bovines, although the Norman butter, cheese, cream, and milk are unmatched. We have seen innumerable, quaint fishing villages and country markets, and I have acquired some extraordinarily beautiful lace in Alençon. We also visited the school of lace-making at Bayeux, and saw the famous tapestry that is kept in that city. It's really an embroidery showing the Norman conquest of England in 1066. It is told that for months the forests of Normandy rang with ax blows as trees were felled and William's fleet was assembled at Dives. He scanned the sea from the beautiful, rough Norman cliffs before setting forth to claim the throne of England and get himself crowned King at Westminster Abbey on Christmas Day in that year. In the city of Caen, here in Normandy, we visited William's tomb, though whose bones are there now isn't at all clear since his own were torn up by French revolutionaries and hurled into the sea centuries after he'd passed on.

So much for immortality. I'm off now for a moonlight ride despite the late hour, just as at home, but I must add that we have encountered several people here whom you and father know. One is James Gordon Bennett, the publisher and also a William Gates, called Bet-A-Million, whom you met in Saratoga years ago, he says. He keeps a racing stable in England, where it's reliably reported he actually dopes his horses and rakes in millions in winnings with mediocre animals. I've gotten into a wager with Mr. Gates, and a few others, that I will describe to you in detail when I see you next.

And, oh yes, Mama, I have met two brothers, Americans named Jones, with whom I have spent some pleasant afternoons and evenings. Perhaps you will meet them, too, one day.

Kiss everyone for me, especially Maude.

Au revoir for now.

Justine

This pair of letters reached Silver Hill by the same post and were placed side by side on the library table. What was said by Gray and what was left unsaid by Justine set off resonant alarm bells in Brigida Hawkes. Knowing her daughter as she did, she read far more between the lines than pleased her, and her concern about Justine's bet and about the Jones brothers, so casually mentioned, prompted a conversation with her husband.

"Twins," Brigida said. "Billy McGlory's niece, Caitlin, married a Jones."

"Yes. What a tragedy befell that lovely girl, passing so young, leaving . . . *twins?*" Slade Hawkes looked up at his wife over his morning *Tribune.*

"It would be odd, wouldn't it, if these twins were Caitlin's? I'll talk to Billy at once, but whoever they are, it sounds to me as if Justine must now be extricated from more than one of the complications she appears to have gotten herself into. Perhaps if she returns home at once I can—"

"Too soon," Slade said, shaking his head. "There's still too much gossip and talk about the canceled wedding. No, not home . . . but somewhere away from that Marlborough House Set she and Gray have fallen in with." Slade rattled his newspaper. "Gates, Bennett, that Prince of Wales . . . He's a cross between Priapus and John Bull I've heard, not fit company for a lovely child like my daughter. I'll think of something that will be sure to please her and serve our purposes at the same time."

How best to do that, though, was something of a puzzle, and by the time a plan was worked out and set in motion—indeed, even at the time Justine had penned her cheery little note—her position had become difficult, impossible really, her deception harder and harder to maintain. She had spent all her days, every day for the past week, with Anthony Jones, of whom she was growing very fond, and all her nights, every one, with Nicholas whom she loved . . . *madly,* that was the only word that described it. Digging herself in ever deeper, Justine was at a loss as to how to bring matters out into the open without devastating Tony, losing Nicholas, and finding herself with a broken heart.

Chapter Thirteen

"I knew you'd come, that you'd have to come to me again," Nicholas said. Returning to his room the evening after their first encounter, he sensed Justine's presence there, like the fragrant exhalations of flowers in the dark.

The bed lamp, always left on by the servants at these house parties, had been extinguished, and as his eyes adjusted to the dimness, he became aware of the faint pearly glow of the moon behind drawn drapes and of a shadow at the window, a figure silhouetted in vague outline. He locked the door behind him and crossed swiftly to her, coiling an arm about her slim waist as though he expected her to vanish like mist or smoke. As her long, bared body locked firmly back against him, Nicholas explored it with his free hand, rediscovering her loveliness, substantiating the accuracy of tactile memories that he'd begun, during the long day, to doubt. He found the fine, high, hard-tipped breasts he remembered and the sleek curve of flank, as his lips played at the soft joining of neck and shoulder, then at her nape. He was staggered by the invisible loveliness he perceived by every sense but sight, those other senses overcoming his imposed blindness as he took her precise and intimate measure, recreating her by hand from memory in the darkness.

As he did, Justine became acutely aware of her own delineations, of an exquisitely heightened sensitivity, a glow of carnal delight that he was burnishing to a high luster; and she was wondrously still at first in that way he remembered, as if the intensity of her pleasure demanded total concentration. Suddenly, she raised her arms to reach back, her vibrant body pressing urgently to him, the aroused memory of their encounter of the night before throbbing in her blood. She slipped from his embrace and turned to face him; her lips parted when they met his. She slipped his jacket from his shoulders, hurriedly undid his starched collar and shirtfront, his tie tack and stays, turquoise and silver, falling in the dark unnoticed.

"You're an impatient little beauty tonight, aren't you?" he asked with a throaty laugh. "This time you know what to do . . . how to move . . . what's to come, don't you?" His mouth was at her lips, her brow, the curve of her ear. Going down on one knee as she tried to lead him to the bed, he persisted in his tracing and sculpting, taking the measure of thigh and long, finely muscled calf, completing an image of her in his mind's eye that was pure perfection. Then, restrained desire in both brought them together with unbridled, desperate urgency as she found the bed and drew him to her, over her. He plunged hard, sheathed completely with the first thrust, her moist depths taking all of him; and it was as if scarlet inundations of light pulsed through her with each stroke. And shooting stars, it seemed, fell . . . and fell.

Long after, she lifted her head, slowly, like a fragile reed that had been buffeted by a violent storm and her hands, he thought, in his half-dreaming state, were like flower petals, caressing him everywhere, her lips following, so that he wanted her again, and took her, but more slowly, at his leisure this time, and hers.

He caressed her smooth, sleek expanses, and sometimes with a fine delicacy, sometimes with knowing strength, grazed, stroked, *invaded* all her soft interstices and silken joinings. Her slightest intake of breath, her faintest movement, guided him as he prolonged the delicious agony of desire, drawing it out with loving cruelty and precision until she was undulating and sighing under his hands.

And yet, as he so gently, generously tortured, she never spoke a single word. Even when he relented finally, and gave what her sinuous, expressive body inarticulately but so clearly demanded she was silent, speechless, dumb, swallowing the cries of pleasure and words of love that surely, he reasoned, must have risen in her throat. Unbridled and abandoned as she was, given over completely, it seemed, she still retained a vestige of control, and her holding back, not letting him see her or even hear the caressing sound of her voice, rankled intolerably.

"I have to look at you," he said roughly as she

later lay curled into him in the dark, fitted to the curve of his body like a jewel in a perfect setting.

"No!" she whispered.

"Making love this way . . . it's like exhaling in the dark. You lose some pleasure if you can't see the smoke turn and coil and drift."

Justine, wary all at once, felt him move away from her a little and reach out, and she realized, when he spoke again, he'd put a cigarette in his mouth.

"Fine as it is with us, it will be even better if we *see* each other, if I can watch you," he said insistently. She heard the scrape of the match in the dark and struck out, sending the box flying from his hands before there had been anything more than a faint blue spark. At once, she felt his arm about her waist, hauling her from the bed, and though she struggled, still in silence, he managed somehow, in the darkness, to secure her wrists to the bedpost with a soft belt or tieback that had come quickly to his hand.

"It's only a few hours to dawn," he said. "We'll wait."

Justine, in silent rage, tugged at her bonds to test their strength, frantic and not knowing what to do, furious at herself for having been caught so easily, and afraid of him now, of what he might do if he found her out.

She waited for what seemed an eternity though it wasn't more than a few minutes, and his remote tenderness almost broke her resolve. But it wasn't time yet for him to know. And if he found out this way . . . well, that could ruin it all completely. In the end, Justine's self-control and self-interest prevailed. When she did speak, it was in a concealing whisper and in an accent he couldn't quite place. It might have been Italian or French or anything. He decided, as the minutes passed, to collect clues rather than expose her by force and chance ruining the game, perhaps losing her altogether.

"Please!" she said. The single word was freighted with such desperation that he was drawn to her at once, and she felt his lips at her nape and his arms enfolding her. Her wrists were still secured when his hands at her hips drew her poised body back toward him. He made love to her again, this time with an almost punishing ferocity that was a fusion of rampant passion and anger. Then he freed her and took her in his arms.

"I'm sorry, I am, if I frightened you, love," he said, his abrasive voice softened by self-reproach. "But, it wasn't so long, was it, you were my prisoner?" Justine almost answered, almost said, Fool! I *am* your prisoner, now and forever, bound or free, with you or . . . apart. The thought of losing him was so awful, she clung to him urgently and held fast even when his deep breaths told her he'd dropped off to sleep.

Such a dangerous game she thought later, as she was about to slip away with first light. She had dozed off and awakened with a start, relieved to find him still asleep beside her. At the door she paused, her back to the room, her hood pulled up. She was about to turn and reclaim her velvet sash, still dangling from the bedpost. He had used it to tie her wrists.

"I'll be waiting for you tonight," Nicholas said just then, and at the sound of his voice, she darted away like a frightened rabbit wondering if he'd been awake all along and if he'd seen who it was lying beside him.

Some hours later, he found a note slipped under his door.

" 'All human wisdom is summed up in the words, *wait and hope*,' Alexander Dumas said that. If you will agree not to press me to reveal myself before the moment is right, leave my tasseled belt dangling from your door. If you do not agree, I may never come to you again."

The tasseled belt had been there that night and every night for the past week, and Justine, aware with each visit to his darkened room of some new augmenting pleasure, discovered fresh delights in Nick's arms and indulged her flowering passion to its farthest limits. She never tried to resist him, to hold back or deny him anything but that one thing he wanted so urgently, a glimpse of her face.

She left him each dawn and then observed him each day as he tried to find her out, to discover who she was. As Anthony danced attendance upon her, Nicholas took breakfast with one woman, tea with another, and pursued yet a third during the course of the evening, once even giving Roweena McGlory the benefit of a doubt.

Gradually, the number of guests at Castle d'Erlanger dwindled away until, one morning, Justine realized she must not go to his room again unless—until—she was ready to confess her trickery. And her love.

She had almost decided to do just that when Anthony Jones made a confession of his own that appalled her. She'd tried so hard to warn him, had even said it outright. "Have a care, my friend. Whatever you do, don't fall in love with me!" she'd admonished more than once, and Anthony had laughed and winked and said, every time, "Aw, shucks, too late," in a broad Western twang that made her laugh, every time. It was their own private little joke she'd thought, until today.

She'd been leaning back as he'd requested, posing against a wind-twisted tree on a cliff above the Channel. There was a cool off-shore breeze, salt spray flying. Her wind-whipped skirt revealed flashes of white lace petticoat. The sun was warm, the water blue and dotted with sailboats, and farm fields were a green and yellow patchwork in the distance. It was a perfect summer afternoon.

"I love you, Justine," Anthony said, not looking at her, fussing with his beautiful Italian drawing pencils in their marbleized paper casings. His

126

hand, she saw, was unsteady.

"But I love someone else," she had answered, without hesitation about to start toward him when he said, "Don't move, please." His hand now gripped a pencil, white-knuckled. He began to work again, and was silent for a long time until he cleared his throat.

"I had counted on you," he said. "What am I to do now?"

"I'm so sorry! But I warned you. Oh, Tony, I never meant this to happen!" There was a catch in her voice.

"I know," he said reasonably, "but I couldn't help it. Is there any hope for me?" Tempted to soothe him, to say Perhaps . . . one day, she simply answered "No," then added, "Oh, how can one ever say about such things?"

"And the person you love, does he love you?" Tony carefully replaced a pencil in its teakwood box.

"No," Justine answered, "Not yet. Oh, I don't know!"

"Well . . ." Anthony smiled so sadly she couldn't bear to see him and looked away across the meadow. "Well, then we can commiserate and comfort each other, can't we? We can be friends for now? I haven't anything else."

"You have your work," Justine had offered desperately.

"Oh, sketching," he had answered in an offhand deprecating manner. "It's just my way of making a little order in the chaos of things. My drawings are really slight efforts, an excuse for doing nothing in life and appearing busy, a way to keep the hands occupied and the eyes—the mind—focused in the middle distance, never looking too far ahead or delving too deeply."

"Someone will love you," Justine said with passion, aware of an echo, a sense of déjà vu. She'd said exactly the same thing to heartsick young men before and more than once.

"Tomorrow we'll go to Honfleur," he stated as if nothing untoward had passed between them, as if nothing had changed, but, of course, things would never be the same again. Perhaps that was best, Justine thought. All her cards—almost all—were out on the table now. She breathed a sigh of relief.

"Friends then?" she had asked Anthony, and he had nodded and gone on working. That was all there was to it, she had foolishly thought.

But by two-thirty in the morning when she sat down to pen a note to her mother, Justine was no longer sure the problem of Anthony Jones had been so easily managed. She was truly glad, as she'd written, that she and Gray were leaving for Ireland in a few days' time. She needed a respite from the Jones brothers, to sort out her feelings and decide what to do and where to turn. With a troubled sigh, she sealed her letter and, on her way to the stable at three in the morning, left it on a silver tray in the great hall for the morning post.

* * *

An hour later, the sky already whitening at about four o'clock, Gray Hawkes was bidding a long adieu to the girl he'd been entertaining. The tall, rangy American, unencumbered by old-world snobbery, suspected he'd fallen in love with Marie-Laure, the sloe-eyed beauty who was a third assistant baker in the duke's kitchen. Though not ready to commit themselves—they'd known each other for only a week and both were prudent and sensible by nature—they'd decided that Marie-Laure would come to Silver Hill for a visit in the fall. Relieved to have this commitment from her, Gray had finally let the girl slip away from him and then he'd been drawn to the window by the sound of a horse clattering over the drawbridge below.

Extinguishing his light, Gray looked out in time to see the rider, Justine, rein in and dismount to stand like a garden nymph in the pearly light of a low morning moon to which she lifted her face, raised her arms, and stretched upward on tiptoe as though welcoming the embrace of a lover. She reminded him sometimes of a beautiful butterfly kite he'd had as a boy. It had soared and then plunged dangerously, as if with a will of its own. When it fought, tugging against his hold, he'd always given it more slack and it had always come up right in the end to fly with verve and style. He was doing the same thing, in a way, with his sister, letting her fly free even though she worried him sometimes. His parents, he knew, wouldn't approve, but nonetheless, Gray was purposely turning a blind eye to Justine's intrigues and flirtations, fully expecting that everything would come right for her as it always had before, in the end. She came and went very much as she pleased and did as she wished, even to the point of indulging in moonlight rides alone in the French countryside at all hours of the day and night.

"That girl's probably got more energy than's good for her." Gray smiled to himself as Justine led her horse away toward the stable.

Chapter Fourteen

Someone else awake in the small hours also observed Justine, though not with the same affection and admiration as Gray. Nicholas, deserted by his mysterious lover, missing her as he had never missed any woman before, his body aching for her, was unable to sleep. There were other reasons, too, for his unease as he gazed out his window, a glass of brandy in one hand, a cigarette in the other, deep in thought.

"Speak of the she-devil," he muttered under his breath as he watched Justine do her little seduction of the moon. She was so very beautiful and so wicked, just as he'd been told by a mutual acquaintance he'd chanced onto today, and by that woman, Roweena, several days ago when he'd followed her into the music room. Almost desperate, he'd done so on the off chance that she was the one he was seeking, but Roweena had talked of nothing but Justine.

"I see your poor brother has fallen victim to my little 'cousin,'" she had said with what was meant to be a look of sympathy in her eyes, and Nicholas couldn't imagine, once she'd opened her venomous mouth, how he could have thought even for a moment that such a graceless and charmless female might have been his midnight lover. He hadn't wanted to believe a word she'd said, had thought her merely jealous and destructive to run down her more attractive friend; but her words were disturbing, given Anthony's nature, his inexperience, and his habit of taking women far too seriously. Just to be on the safe side, Nick had encouraged Roweena to talk on.

"Well," she had said with nasty pleasure, laying a hand on his arm, "Justine has a history of this sort of thing. I think you should know that. She delights in having devastated young men grovel at her feet."

"Why are you telling me?" Nicholas had asked suspiciously, withdrawing from her touch.

"Just so that you can protect yourself," Roweena had insisted. "I mean, twins would be such a coup for a girl like Justine. She'd never stop crowing over a double conquest. Everyone would know about it from here to New York, and beyond. Self-dramatizing as she is, I can just hear her now."

"Your concern is unnecessary, thanks all the same. I've no interest in her at all," Nicholas had said coldly, but for his brother's sake he was disinclined to believe what he was hearing. For his brother's sake, too, he put out of his mind the thought that Justine might be the elu-

sive woman he was seeking. Not even a true
Jezebel could be so heartless as to make passionate love with one brother by night and then
by day so charm the other he had no thought
for anything but her.

"If you'll excuse me?" he'd added, turning his
back on Roweena and stalking off after Count
Zenga's mistress, Monica Matti, who, he conjectured, could be the woman he was trying to
find.

Nick had been wrong about Monica and
wrong, too, not to have paid more attention to
Roweena McGlory. After what he'd learned today, after what had occurred, her words certainly rang true, he thought angrily as he
watched Justine lead her horse away toward the
stables.

She had walked the horse to cool him down
and then, in the animal's box stall, had worked
him over vigorously, grooming his coat to a fine
luster with a stiff-bristled brush. Justine liked
the warm, redolent stable at night, when the
only sounds were the snorts and snuffles of the
resting animals, the scrape of mice in the raft-
ers, and a barn owl outside, calling. Moonlight
fell through the open shutters and she needed
no lantern as she worked with purpose until the
animal's dark coat, so soft and silky under her
hands, was brought to a high bloom. Only then
did she secure the stall gate and start for the
door, feeling her way along the dark interior of

the stable where moonlight did not penetrate.

Just as she released the latch and was about to step outside, she was roughly gripped from behind and spun about, her shoulders pinned back hard against the stone surface of the stable wall. But terrified as she was, her gasping scream died in her throat when she looked up at the profile silhouetted in the door frame.

"Tony?" she whispered. "What are you doing?" Then, as he turned into a flood of moonlight, she recognized the fierce countenance, dark with anger.

"What is it?" she managed, despite her confusion, to ask as Nicholas Jones's daunting eyes raked over her wild hair and parted lips. The top buttons of her shirt had given way as he'd held her shoulders back, and her breasts were thrust high and forward.

"You tell me," he demanded, his savage eyes raking over her. "What the devil did you say to my brother?" Justine was dumbfounded, silent, awed by the fury she felt and saw at work in Nicholas, afraid to speak and afraid not to. "You told him you were in love with someone else." His voice was thin and cold as a knife blade. She nodded. "Why did you have to say that?" Feeling the rage building in him, she began to tremble a little.

"Because it's true," she answered, and was about to say more when he pulled her, not gently, into his arms, enfolding her waist, crushing her to him, his mouth bruising her lips as they parted to his. Her arms, which had hung limply at her sides, slowly rose to rest on his shoulders, then to enfold his neck, the length of her body by instinct and habit and desire curving to his.

"A little terror puts an edge on delight, doesn't it, liar?" he rasped, pulling away.

"No, I—"

"No woman in love kisses a near stranger the way you just kissed me." He towered over her in the doorway, his hands resting on the wall to either side of her, trapping her there. "I know all about you, everything." He laughed coldly. "Your history, shall we say? The broken engagements, the broken hearts casually discarded, all the suitors . . . the flirtations? I ran into an old schoolfriend today. He was supposed to have attended a wedding recently, Walter de Peyster's wedding. It was called off by the bride, you, at the last moment." He stepped away from her, his manner now withdrawn but still menacing. "My brother is in love with you and in despair. Leave him alone. Stay away so he can get over you."

"But I promised to be his friend always, to take care of him, help him," she answered. "He said no one ever had."

"Tony said that? To you?" Nicholas looked doubtful at first, then pained. His eyes were softened for a moment by that touch of melancholy Justine had seen in him before.

"You've already called me a liar so I don't

expect you to believe that I really like your brother, that I can be his friend, that—"

"Just stay away, damn you!" Nicholas repeated raking back his hair then plunging clenched fists into his jacket pockets.

"I never break a promise to a friend," Justine responded defiantly, beginning to do up her silk-covered buttons. "Besides, he wants to finish his sketches of me and . . ." When Nicholas kissed her again, stopping the flow of her words, she managed to stand rigid in his embrace before pushing him away. A sardonic smile played at his mouth.

"You'll never be alone with my brother again, I warn you," he said in a low voice. "I'll always be there, every second, never out of your sight, watching you, making sure you don't tempt him . . . lead him on . . . do him any more damage than you have already. I know your kind, you see, a jilt who uses men like chess pieces; playing them, moving them about—to her own advantage. Be warned, Miss Hawkes. You won't get away with it this time." He turned on his heel and strode off, his turquoise-studded boots grinding gravel then ringing on stone as he crossed the stable yard.

Justine, freed but still atremble, was aghast at the turn things had taken. She sank wearily on to a stone bench, wondering how she had made such an impossible mess so *quickly*. A week ago, she had been all high hopes and optimistic expectations. Now, for the first time in her life, perhaps for the last, she was truly in love and truly in despair. Oh, poor, poor Tony, she thought, sighing deeply.

Chapter Fifteen

"But why love a man who doesn't love you when you have his perfect double in the palm of your hand?" Olympe asked, a hint of humor in her voice though she wasn't entirely joking. "From what you've told me, Justine, Anthony is the true gentleman anyway." The two women were taking tea in the shade of Castle d'Erlanger's turrets. The Georgian silver pot that was set on the flowered linen cloth was reflecting sky and intermittent flashes of the duke who was lazily playing croquet by himself on a wide lawn he'd had installed just for that purpose.

"Love's not as rational as that, so please don't tease me. Help me!" Justine implored. The Jones twins had left the castle that morning without ceremony or farewell, though Anthony had penned a brief note saying he'd return to escort Justine to the casino late that evening.

"But how can I help, *ma petite* Justine?" Olympe asked pouring a thin amber stream of tea into a fine porcelain cup. Justine sighed grandly and shook her head.

"I don't suppose you can. No one can. I've lost my heart to a man who has no interest in me at all, who absolutely hates me, actually."

"Ah, but you are wrong about that," Olympe

smiled smugly. "Heavens, I'm glad Bertie's gone. Now one can simply have a nice cup of tea without the other seven courses he demands." There was only one cake on the table, concocted of strawberries and *frais des bois* mousse.

"What do you mean I'm wrong? Oh, tell me, Olympe!" Justine implored, sitting up very straight and flinging back her hair.

"Nicholas came to see me early this morning as he was preparing to leave our company. He wanted to know the names of the young women—all the women to be more precise—who'd attended the hunt ball the first night you so graciously bestowed your favors upon him. He wanted to know who had stayed on, who had left the next day, and the day after and so on, and so on. He intends to track her—*you*—down. There! You should just go to him at once and announce yourself and let fate and love do the rest." Olympe tasted the cake and closed her eyes in ecstasy. "Oh, my dear, it's heaven. That new baker's helper, Marie-Laure, is a jewel."

"But how can I go to him?" Justine asked, taking a tiny taste of the cake then a larger bite. "As it is, he thinks me a tease and a flirt and worse. If he knows I've been so bold as to . . . as to . . ." She blushed a little. "He'll think me a terribly wicked wanton if he knows. No, he must be made to love *me,* not the fantasy woman he thinks I am. It must be arranged for him to seduce Justine Hawkes in the full light of day while he is permitted to think it's all his own doing, his very own idea." She passed her plate for another slice of cake, beginning to feel better now that she had the rudiments of a plan. "You know, I've never had this problem before. Usually, it is just the opposite one, getting someone not to fall in love with me. This is a challenge."

"Oh, but how will you do it?" Olympe asked doubtfully. "What with his brother and all—"

"Nick threatened never to leave Tony alone with me again. If I spend as much time with him as I have been doing—"

"And if Nichols carries out his threat . . ." Olympe smiled. "Why, he is bound to fall in love with you just a little bit, as any young man often in your company would, delightful as you are. Aimery agrees, don't you Aimery?" The duke, who'd wearied of his game and had meandered over to listen to their talk, folded his long frame into a wrought-iron garden chair and breathed deeply two or three times.

"Exhausting, croquet," he sighed, tugging at his mustache. "Of course, I agree," he added, smiling his thin smile at Justine. "But that way madness may lie, dear child. Just think how difficult it will be, loving one, loved by the other, and always the three of you together, a triangle fraught with all the possibilities for tragedy."

"I can manage the Jones brothers, I know I can. I must," Justine insisted confidently. "And there's no other way, is there, to make Nicholas fall in love with me?"

Nicholas was cold as polished marble, elegant

distant, and absolutely correct when he arrived with Tony, as threatened, to escort Justine that evening. Both men were in black and white evening attire. With Justine between them in a jade green gown, her hair upswept and coiled, her opals at her throat, their entrance to the casino was greeted by a flurry of interest and comment as even the most intense gamblers glanced up.

Tony sketched Justine through most of the evening as she and Nicholas played roulette and baccarat, her obvious, though controlled, excitement and pleasure heightening the drama of her appearance. Nicholas was impassive, expressionless, and silent. Justine always won, Nicholas usually did and always split his earnings, as he called them, with his brother after each game or round. Later, they danced in the ballroom, Justine finding herself in the arms first of one, then the other Jones, the envy of every woman there to have two such extraordinarily attractive men at her beck and call, or so it appeared. She, though, was beginning to feel the strain by the time the evening ended, of Nick's savage glare and of Tony's brave front that didn't mask his lovelorn glances. And, through it all, the differences between the brothers seemed to her to grow more stark and more obvious—Nick's arm at her waist commanding as he drew her to him, Tony touching her as though she were fragile as lace.

As the days passed, the gap widened. One twin, her lover, was a formidable man whose heart harbored heaven-only-knew-what dark passions and secrets. He glared out at the world with barely restrained ferocity as if love had been dammed up in him somehow, love that would flow like a river if only she could free it in him.

His double, on the other hand, was a mild, usually charming boy especially when he was a bit tipsy as he often was. But for all his manly good looks, Tony had about him the tentative manner of a hurt animal. He reminded Justine of injured birds she'd nursed to health, of trapped rabbits freed, of unwanted pups saved from drowning. Even as her passion for Nicholas grew, her platonic affection for Anthony did, too; and she came to feel responsible for him in a way that was new to her. While his brother was always remote, correct and cold, Anthony tried so hard to be cheerful it almost broke Justine's heart. The duke was probably right, she decided after a particularly difficult outing, this way madness very well could lie.

One day, in desperation, Justine invited Roweena to join them for luncheon, and so four, instead of the usual threesome, drove along the river to Trouville past fishermen selling live shrimp and crabs and flounders and the tiny lobsters called *lanqoustines* that the French so favored. They had borrowed the duke's yellow landau because Roweena would not drive in the Jones's light, fast phaeton.

When they stopped at the edge of a quay in

front of a small bistro with sprays of purple columbine set on each white-linen-covered table, the woman glanced about with unconcealed disdain.

"Not very distinguished, this *auberge*." She sniffed. "What are those dreadful children doing there?" She dipped her parasol toward the river's edge, where four boys were leaning, gesticulating, and chattering excitedly as one of them tossed a great ball into the water and a second snapped open a large black umbrella. A few minutes later they scooped something from the water, closed up the umbrella, and ran into the café only to return almost immediately and repeat the whole process again.

"They were catching our lunch," Anthony explained pleasantly, snaring the boy with the umbrella as he passed again. "In the dark of the night, these young fellows dig worms from some fertile ground, and when they have a pailful, they stitch them together with thread and needle into long strings, roll them into the pink balls you see there and drop them into the river. The worms soon attract conger eels by the dozens that are then trapped in the big umbrella and sold to Monsieur Lesufleur in the tavern." At a gesture from Anthony, the child, who had been shifting restlessly from foot to foot, opened the umbrella to display his catch, an energetically wriggling mass of dark snakelike creatures, a sight that caused Rowenna to go pale as she backed away.

"How simply revolting," she gasped, covering her mouth with a scented handkerchief and averting her eyes. "With all the good things there are to eat in this world, why would anyone ingest those?"

"They're just babies. The longest of them is not more than two or three feet," Nicholas said with something like pleasure. "They'll grow to seven feet and weigh twenty-five pounds eventually. Will you join us, madam, for one of the world's great delicacies?" He leered, offering Roweena his arm. But she declined. In fact, she retreated to the safety of the carriage, where she sat under her parasol with her eyes closed while the others ate baby conger eels served in rich, thick Normam cream.

"What's the matter with your friend?" Nicholas asked, breaking a long silence. "More to the point, why did you bring her? She resembles nothing so much as a Halloween crone, with her nose and her chin and her scowl."

"Poor Roweena. She does always manage to put her worst foot forward, but she has had a difficult kind of life," Justine answered. "She's been through four husbands and she just passed thirty."

"Who'd want to marry her?" Tony asked, genuinely bemused.

"There's no accounting for taste, it's said. In Roweena's case, it's very true. She married up the social ladder each time. It was the next to last husband, a childless lawyer, who left her quite well off. Then she made the mistake of marrying once more, trying to rise to the exalted social sphere to which she feels she belongs."

"And?" Nicholas asked, as the table was cleared and three glasses were brought for calvados, the strong apple brandy that follows most meals in Normandy and is sometimes taken, in quick gulps, between courses to create what is called the "Norman Hole," room in the stomach for more food.

"Calvados *vieux,* it is a full fifteen years aged, mademoiselle," the chef-proprietor of the bistro told Justine proudly as he poured out his precious brandy. "Here in the north of France, the climate is too chill for wine grapes so we have our apple orchards—Binet Rouge, Bisquets, Rouge Mulot—and other varieties that are crushed together, each lending its distinctive flavor to our favorite drink, calvados. Taste, *s'il vous plaît,*" he encouraged and when she did Justine felt a warm afterburn and her eyes watered.

"The Reinette is my favorite apple." Tony smiled, offering her a handkerchief. "It's russet and yellow, and meant to be eaten right off the trees, not fermented for cider or aged to calvados. Oh, Justine," he sighed, "you must be here in the Augue Valley, this green garden of Normandy, in late summer when the air is filled with the fragrance of ripening apples. If only I could show you . . ." He stopped abruptly and shrugged. "Well, tell us more about this McGlory woman and her fourth husband."

"The man was nothing but an Eastern European adventurer in New York, posing as royalty. Soon after the wedding, he absconded with Roweena's hard-earned, if modest, fortune."

"Oh, my," Anthony couldn't help suppress a laugh. "What happened to all the other husbands?" He downed his Calvados and signaled the waiter for another.

"Well, the first husband," Justine began, sipping

at her drink, "was a bank clerk, run down by a dray on Fifth Avenue one snowy afternoon. The second, a merchant, expired after eating a spoiled oyster, and the lawyer died of apoplexy caused by vexation, though what over, we've never been told. Very sad."

"Married to her," Nicholas said, standing and putting an end to the meal, "one can easily imagine expiring of apoplexy."

"Sounds like foul play to me," Anthony joked. "Did anyone else ever wonder? I mean *four* is a bit of a coincidence, don't you think?" he questioned, but by then, Nicholas had stalked off and Justine was looking distracted. He got no answer to his question that day.

Chapter Sixteen

On the next day, Roweena wasn't invited, and when Anthony came to call, alone apparently, at Erlanger Castle, Justine thought that perhaps Nicholas had finally been deflected from his purpose. But when she left the castle on Tony's arm, Nicholas was there, lounging casually up on the front seat of his phaeton. He had a big cigar clutched in his teeth, a straw boater tipped forward shadowing his eyes, and his long legs, in white flannel trousers, were propped on the carriage panel. When he grinned at her, the raffish glint in his eye went straight to her heart and she was swept by a wave of longing that almost made her lose her balance on the bottom step. She clung to Tony more urgently than she'd meant to, and in that brief moment of vertigo, she doubted she could keep up the charade through yet another afternoon. Besides, she didn't want to pretend indifference to the man in whose arms she had lain night after night, whose touch and caress and kiss she'd been longing for constantly since they'd last been together. It had begun as a yearning ache that first night he was gone. Then the tormenting dreams of him began, of his touch, so intense and so real. She was caught in a conflagration of unfulfilled desire that burned night and day with no promise of relief.

"Are you all right?" Anthony asked, concern in his voice, as she clutched his arm.

"Are you?" Justine responded a bit breathily, really looking at him for the first time that day and finding the change in him disturbing. His eyes, that seemed deeper set than they'd been yesterday, were dark rimmed, and his face was pale and gaunt as if the skin had been stretched taut over his forehead and high cheekbones.

"Well . . . you see Nicky's driving today," he answered. "He doesn't think I can handle a horse or anything else for that matter. You especially."

"Perhaps we shouldn't go at all. You look ill," Justine said, hesitating, toying with her parasol, and glancing at Nicholas.

"Merely the result of intemperance, my condition." Tony's attempt at a smile was more like a grimace. "I went on a bit of a spree with a bottle of the local poison, that apple jack they call calvados. Powerful stuff. The air will do me good," he added, handing her up into the carriage with a shrug.

An awkward silence enwrapped them like a chilling fog as they drove across the drawbridge and turned down toward the shore. In silence, they emerged from the shaded cool hills to drive through a rolling land of farms and orchards, pastures of horses grazing, colts agambol. Gloom thickened about Justine's heart as the silence weighed on her, and her anger began to swell until she decided she'd just about had enough. Despite Nicholas Jones, she would have a fine time and see to it that Anthony did, too. She began to point out things that pleased her as they drove along a narrow, now overhung, road that soon emerged to parallel the curving shoreline. Two children, a boy and a girl, saw the carriage pass and tried to pace it but soon gave up to collapse in laughter while their large dog barked with excitement, seeming to laugh, too.

"They remind me of Gray and I and the others when we were growing up at Silver Hill. I've told you about Silver Hill, Anthony," Justine said, turning toward him, "how we ran wild in the woods and along the shore in those lovely childhood summers?"

"Tell me more," he answered, smiling weakly.

"Life was always full of dogs and ponies, lambing in the barns in spring . . . I had rabbits . . . kittens . . . I still have quite a few of them at home now, waiting for me. You must visit Silver Hill one day," she announced excitedly as though the idea was the best one she'd ever had. "You must come at Christmas, you and Nicholas," she said to an indifferent back. The driver of the phaeton never so much as glanced over his shoulder.

"Tell me more," Anthony said again, letting his head loll against the seat and closing his eyes. "Silver Hill sounds like a picture-book place."

"There are trellises of lilacs and laburnum in spring, and scented peonies," Justine said softly, her voice remote and dreamy now. "The fragrance of cut hay and roses wafts through the house that's open all summer long to the air and the sky. We had a screened sleeping porch, and we'd wake

149

in the morning to the cries of gulls over the water and the sound of waves, and our eyes would open on endless shadings of blue water and sky, on tan reeds and long green fields. On summer nights, the waves curl with phosphorescent flickers like millions and millions of stars. Oh, I'm getting homesick!" Justine said, and the catch in her voice actually made Nicholas glance back at her quickly. Realizing that she'd been speaking for his benefit all along and that she'd caught his interest at last, she went on.

"In winter, too, it's beautiful at Silver Hill. My grandmother used to paint, Anthony, up in her cupola at the top of the house, and I liked to go there to watch the snow fall, all day sometimes, silent and steady. Then later, with a big shawl wrapped close about me, it seemed I could actually *feel* winter moonlight touching my skin through the long windows. I could hear the faint distant crash of the surf, and I'd think about all the animals in the barns and stables, the wild things in their nests and warrens, all tucked in, safe and warm, like me. All of us safe—home." She smiled. "And I thought about the others, too, the ones caught in the storm and floundering in the snow with no safe haven." She wasn't smiling anymore. "Now, you tell me—"

"Ours wasn't so lovely a childhood. We hardly had a home. After Mother died, Father traveled. He left our upbringing to servants and then to boarding schools when we were older. We raised each other more or less, wouldn't you say, Nicky?"

"Yes," Nicholas answered tersely.

"Father was — *is* — a collector. We did have his Impressionists and his old masters to look at, our very own museum."

"Mausoleum," Nick interjected. "A memorial to *her.*"

"He means our mother," Nicholas explained to Justine. "They were so in love, she and Father, it seemed sometimes they hardly noticed us at all. We were shut out of their private world, and when she died, he . . ."

Anthony said no more as Nicholas turned the carriage very sharply off the main road onto a shaded wagon track that led eventually to an inn set above the sea in a lush, small garden.

At the Ferme Saint Simeon, a farm turned inn, one could dine and look off into the distance at the estuary of the Seine which is exactly what Justine did, faced as she was by the now all but silent Joneses, one suffering the aftereffects of overindulgence, the other merely taciturn by choice. After giving the waiter his order, Nicholas left the table, and his companions saw him a few moments later pacing the garden and glancing toward them now and again as they sat at an open window sipping wine.

"Restless, Nicky," Tony shrugged. "Talking of home — about *them* — mother and father — affects him that way. I think he's always been terrified, after seeing what happened to Father, of finding love, and even more frightened of losing it. I'm just the opposite. I've always been afraid of never finding love at all . . . but now, there's you." He drank down a glass of wine and poured himself

151

another. "Look, I didn't mean to upset you the other day, talking about love and all that, but I couldn't help myself. I can't help myself now."

"I think it would be best if we said goodbye *now*—today—for a while. Gray and I are leaving soon for Ireland." Justine looked away.

"No! You musn't," Anthony whispered desperately. "I'm sorry I'm dull and tedious. I promise I won't be ever again. One more glass of wine and we'll go out and join Nick. See him? He's playing a game of ball with that little boy. You'd like that. It's more fun than sitting here with me." He pushed back his chair and staggered to his feet, then sat heavily. "You go out and play with Nick, Justine, I insist," he added weakly, his words slightly slurred.

"So much wine won't help your condition, you know," Justine said, wanting nothing more than to join Nick out in the sun. She was feeling constrained after the carriage ride and even more so sitting at this little table in a dim room while a glorious day went to waste outside.

"I'll have them call you when the food's served. I'll watch you. You know how I love watching you, Justine," Anthony smiled.

Through the window, he saw her cross the garden, her dress of white *broderie anglais* whispering over the grass, an onyx-handled parasol in one hand, a tiny purse in the other. She was dressed formally today, for her, with a high, boned collar and a straw bonnet with lace and flowers decorating its wide brim. She stopped before Nick saw her, and stood hesitating, not like herself it seemed to Anthony. But all at once, there was her smile, like a ray of sunshine piercing a cloud. She dropped the parasol in time to catch the ball the child sent flying through the air toward her. No sooner was it in her hands than she hurled it away again, obviously trying to catch Nick off guard. "Impossible," Tony laughed, sipping and watching.

Nick extended a hand and the ball, as if by choice, dropped into it. He was down on one knee, on a level with the little boy but stood at Justine's approach, almost smiling, Tony observed, feeling uncomfortable suddenly and not knowing why. There was something in the way his brother's eyes narrowed as Justine drew closer, a tension in Nick's arms as if . . . as if he would enfold her. And Justine . . . There was a faint inclination of her head, a sway in her hips Tony had never seen before. Puzzled but not really wanting to be enlightened, he quickly finished yet another glass of wine and poured himself more as Justine and Nicholas turned away from him and sauntered to the edge of the garden.

Nicholas hefted the ball from hand to hand. Justine took off her bonnet and shook out her hair, gold cascading to her shoulders. She was gnawing her lower lip a few minutes later when she whirled about and came quickly back across the lawn to reclaim her parasol, leaving Nick to study the horizon alone.

* * *

"Proud of yourself?" Nicholas had asked her. "You've got yourself another conquest to add to your grand total. But Tony's such a walkover, how can it give you pleasure to see him this way?" The words were hurled like daggers.

"People are always falling in love alone. I didn't mean it to happen. Won't you believe me?" It was then Justine had taken off the bonnet and let her hair fall. The gesture, the flood of gold, her sunlit features were so lovely and sincere, compelling, Nicholas had a nearly irresistible urge to kiss her, to taste her lips again as he had once or twice before. And he would have, too, if Tony hadn't been watching.

"I don't believe you," he said, "because I kissed you. And you kissed me, remember? With intent to . . ." He looked off into the distance as if searching for a word, and found it. "With clear intent to entrap. And with a reputation like yours, as a false beguiler, why should I believe you? How could I?"

"Because whatever you have been told about me is wrong. I am not suited to deception. It is not in my nature to wound. I have faults enough, heaven knows, without adding what I can't rightfully claim to the list." Justine spoke with emotion, quickly, and her urgent tone drew his now-puzzled eyes down from the sky to meet hers. "I know I'm willful and impetuous and perhaps . . . too easy in my friendships with gentlemen, but I was easy always with my brothers and a habit of openness is a hard one to break. I am trying, though, since it was explained to me about young men's hearts,

154

how easily they are broken. I warned Anthony, I did!" Her direct green eyes shone with such clear candor Nicholas wavered for a moment in his opinion of her.

"My brother . . . he's in love and he thinks you are perfection," Nick said. "I told him love can be lethal. I also told him there's no such thing in the world as a flawless woman. I said that some females are gifted with one attribute, some with another — you, for example, with an uncommonly pleasing appearance, but your character . . ."

She had turned away in a fury and strode off then, leaving him feeling oddly lonely. After spending these past days with her, he had grown used to having her about and he realized, all at once, to having her in his thoughts when she wasn't. Her sudden withdrawal affected him like a desertion. Hell, he thought, starting after her, I need some distraction from this girl, forced by circumstance as I am to be always in her company. The solution, of course, would be to find his mystery *amoureuse,* the one who'd come to him under cover of darkness, "chaste as unsunned snow," to gift him with everything and ask nothing in return, the perfect lover.

But it was more than loneliness Nicholas was feeling at that moment, more a yearning as sudden and sharp and clear as the cut of a crystal dagger. He had to find her. He would, he knew, if only Justine Hawkes would leave him — leave Tony — alone long enough for him to do anything else at all.

* * *

By the time Justine and Nick returned to the table, Tony had finished the first bottle of wine and was well into a second. In the manner of a man whose tongue is loosened by drink, he talked on uninterrupted, in a low oddly angry undertone, throughout the meal, unaware apparently that Nicholas and Justine were exchanging daggered looks.

"I think we should go to Paris, the three of us, sail down the Seine to Paris, like we did that time, Nicky, remember? Justine, you must come to Paris with us. You'll see Nicky at his best there, up to his usual seductions. Wherever he goes, his reputation precedes him," Anthony said sarcastically, "and little innocents are always captivated by such . . . such a man of the world as my brother. Am I right, Nick? You know I am." Nicholas put a hand on Anthony's shoulder for a moment to calm him, but said nothing. "Always in popular demand is Nick, by fashionable hostesses and in Bohemian Paris, too, you'll see, Justine. You'll meet a fascinating crowd. Who was that woman, Nicky, who came to a soirée that time with two tame rats on her shoulders instead of a fur? I think—"

"I must leave now," Justine interrupted.

"Fine," Nick agreed at once. "If you'll escort the lady out, brother, I'll see to the addition." He helped Tony to his feet and practically carried him to the carriage where his brother fell asleep at once.

Anthony was still asleep when the phaeton

reached Erlanger Castle. Nicholas reined in and jumped down. Justine declined his help and, holding parasol, purse, and bonnet in one hand, she gathered her skirts in the other preparing to descend unaided. But he encircled her waist and lifted her to the ground.

"Mr. Jones," she said, her green eyes ablaze, cheeks bright, "I will thank you to keep your hands off me, but I will not thank you for a lovely time because it has been one of the worst afternoons of my life. I have been insulted, ignored, and accused, by you, of high crimes and deceptions. If you will persist in guarding your brother from my evil influence, I'm afraid I will have to decline ever to see him again. I hope you will be good enough to convey that message to him when his condition is sufficiently improved to allow comprehension. Goodbye, Mr. Jones." she extended a gloved hand imperiously, eyes lowered.

"One day your exquisitely spoilt air is going to provoke some man beyond his control. And yours," Nicholas said, his grip so strong she looked up almost fearfully into dark eyes. There was a flash of that rascally grin. "I don't suppose we'll meet again, not if it can be avoided," he said. "Now I can get on with . . . other things. Have a good life, Miss Hawkes," he added, dismissing her, it seemed, for good and always. She watched him climb up into the carriage, push the straw boater to the back of his dark head and set a cigar between his teeth, grinning. Holding the reins carelessly in one hand, he waved to her with the other and drove off.

"And that's that," she said to herself, her anger already fading and a gnawing despair beginning to take its place.

Chapter Seventeen

"Darling!" Olympe waved and called to Justine who was crossing the lawn, her arms laden with flowers. Setting them alongside her straw garden hat on a bench, the girl removed her gloves and pinned a rosebud in the Duke's lapel. "Darling," Olympe repeated, "it's been three whole days now that we have been devouring your culinary creations. We are all getting fat, even Aimery. You must cheer up and stop cooking." The garden table at which they sat was piled with food—a terrine of rabbit, a mussel and cheese tart, loaves of bread, crêpes calvados ready for flaming, a sweet custard flan and more.

"When I was little, the cook at Silver Hill, Martha, always took me under her wing and set me to baking cookies whenever I was upset. It was usually over the boys going off on some adventure without me, because I was too young or of the wrong gender. Don't worry, Olympe, I'll soon have it out of my system," Justine explained as Eustace Molesworth and Roweena joined them.

"We've missed you at the casino," Eustace said with his toothsome smile. "Bertie's been asking after you, dear girl."

"And how is he?" Justine responded with mild interest, smoothing her lace-trimmed apron.

"Fine, fine. He invites you . . . all of you" —
Eustace glanced about — "to his country estate,
Sandringham, for a Saturday-to-Monday. Formal
invitations will follow, of course. After that,
there'll be the Goodwood and Newmarket Race
Weeks, yachting at Clowes and so on. His Majesty
would like you to be included in all the events of
the summer social season in England, Miss
Hawkes. I do hope you'll accept," Molesworth
pressed, anxious for Justine's response. If she accepted, he'd have all summer to woo her, even if
he did have to put up with Olympe d'Erlanger's
genial vulgarity and Roweena McGlory's incurable
dullness.

"Well, really, Eustace!" Roweena sang out. "You
hadn't told *me* about all these invitations. Of
course, we'll come. It's no small honor, Justine, to
be included in the Prince's circle. Besides, you
must be feeling dull here now that your suitors
have deserted you and you've taken to the scullery."

"I'm never dull, Roweena, you know that," Justine said coolly. "I'll have to ask Gray what our
plans are before I accept any invitations."

"I've heard that Nicholas and Anthony Jones
will be at Sandringham," Olympe said very pointedly to Justine. "Nicholas has gone to some pains
to be asked. He's planning to spend all his time
this summer in England at these very same house
parties, darling, to which you've just been asked.
Lovely mussel tart, by the way," she added.

"I doubt those Americans will be going to England at all. One of them's had a fall from a

horse. He's laid up with something broken," Aimery said, nibbling at a crust of bread. He turned away from the table to avoid looking at Roweena and watched a groundsman rolling his croquet court.

"Was it serious, the fall?" Justine asked, feigning disinterest. "How did you hear of this, Duke?"

"In these little towns, there's not much else to do besides gossip. I overheard some of Olympe's chambermaids chatting. Seems whichever one of the twins it was, he's ensconced at their place on the sea near Dives. Champagne?" Aimery asked as the butler approached them from across the lawn. Justine stood.

"I must go. I have some sweets baking."

"But what shall I tell Bertie?" Eustace called after her. Apparently, she didn't hear him. He got no answer at all.

"What is this with your Bertie?" Olympe asked suspiciously.

"You know Bertie, Duchess, he likes pretty women about him wherever he goes." Molesworth's damp eyes blinked.

"And I know what sort of woman he likes— hard, witty, experienced ones, not dewy girls like my houseguest. I smell a rat," Olympe declared and Eustace's full soft face disintegrated into what passed for a smile.

"Royalty has its privileges," he answered. "It was your own Napoleon III who demanded, and got, a cigar and a woman after every meal. Bertie's more discreet than that."

"I suspect, Sir Eustace, you are yourself taken

161

with the pretty child. Is that so?" As Olympe challenged him, Eustace felt Roweena's pale-eyed stare and it unnerved him.

"No, no, dear Duchess," he corrected. "You misread me. My interest lies elsewhere. In fact, though I cannot name the lucky lady at this moment, I promise you'll be among the first to learn the happy news of our betrothal."

"Of our marriage," Roweena interjected, ignoring Molesworth's murderous frown.

The silly creature has given the whole game away, he thought, glancing from Olympe to the duke. Of course, he had agreed to marry her, but he'd no real intention of ever doing so. When Roweena had made her proposal to him soon after they'd met, luring him into the boxwood maze to make her offer, Eustace's thin-lipped slit of a mouth had curled in a disbelieving smile. She hadn't gone at it directly, not at first. She'd used the steeplechase as a pretext for their conversation, offering to become his silent partner. She'd helped him win in return for a share of the prize.

"I'd have expected you, madame, to be rooting for your countrymen in this event, yet you offer to help me. Why?" Eustace had demanded, guiding Roweena deeper into the maze. A hissing sound had escaped her small, tight mouth as she'd dabbed at her nose with a handkerchief.

"Because I want those opals. I have always wanted them. I deserve them."

"And what exactly do you propose?" Eustace

had asked, gazing with wonder on Roweena's pale face and on eyes that brimmed with malice. Naturally inclined to intrigue and treachery, she was at a fever-pitch of excitement that seemed to affect her sinuses he noticed.

"Doping!" she'd spat out, after blowing her nose.

"Have you Americans no sense of honor?" he had responded haughtily. "That loudmouth Gates dopes the horses he runs in England, everyone knows that, and since the Jockey Club hasn't yet forbidden it, it's a perfectly legal practice if a low one." He'd spoke then in a modulated voice, leaning toward Roweena. "I have, I admit, done it a time or two myself, but only with poor horses, of course."

"Oh, of course," Roweena had said. "I know you wouldn't stoop to such a thing, not as a rule."

"Well, Roweena—may I call you Roweena?—thank you for the suggestion but it's hardly original. I don't see how it makes us partners."

"I could also keep you secretly informed of how the American training is going once we return to the United States."

"Besides doping and spying, what else have you to offer?" he'd asked wearily.

"Money," she'd snapped, angry that she had been pressed to play her high card when she'd been hoping she wouldn't have to go that far.

"That's different," Eustace had nodded. "How much?"

"I secreted away ten thousand dollars of what my third husband left me. No one, not even my fourth husband, had any idea it existed. I'll invest in training your horse if . . ." Her terrible eyes had narrowed.

"Yes?" Eustace had encouraged her, keenly interested. His own eyes rolling heavenward with delight.

"If you'll marry me," Roweena had said with a defensive glare.

"My dear, this is so sudden!" he'd laughed, the sound high and mocking.

"You needn't make any pretense of affection, not yet. But we will grow to care for each other and . . ." Roweena had hesitated as he'd brought her hand to his damp lips, his larcenous mind already working out the details of a plot that had begun to form as soon as she'd said the word 'money.' He'd had no intention of marrying this witch of a woman. It was the other American he'd wanted, but now he'd found a way to have the money he needed at once and a beautiful wife . . . later.

"My dear, you flatter me with such a proposal and I accept." He had kept hold of Roweena's hand, his quivering fingers, like thin twigs enfolding hers. "But," he had said, and felt her begin to pull away, "I think we must wait to announce this betrothal until after the race. Otherwise, you'll not be made privy to inside information of the most important sort. Don't you agree?" Roweena had nodded, her suspicions somewhat blunted by visions of herself as Lady Molesworth with a castle and carriages and servants. This time she'd be married to a real nobleman and they'd be invited, on their infrequent visits to America, to all the best houses in New York.

"Where is the money?" Molesworth had asked, clearing his throat, his prominent Adam's apple bobbing. "When can we get it?"

"It's banked in New York. I'll write first thing," Roweena had smiled, baring small pointy teeth and plotting now herself to secure this man and his title before a single cent changed hands. A marriage could be kept secret as well as a betrothal, and Eustace Molesworth would be made to understand that. Roweena had vowed as they'd stood hand in hand in the boxwood maze.

"Yes, marriage," she repeated for the benefit of the Duke and Duchess, meeting Eustace's scowl. Furious that he was still dragging his feet, she'd decided it was time to force his hand. And if her stratagems did not work? Well, she was hedging her bets, as the sporting crowd would put it. She'd already planted seeds of dissension among the American racing partners in order to make them far less likely to win the steeplechase. When Nicholas Jones had followed her into the music room that day, she'd told him all about Justine's treacherous games. Now the twins weren't even speaking to Miss Hawkes, and that served Roweena's purposes in more ways than one. Just because she was going to marry Eustace she didn't intend to deny herself a little pleasure in the meantime with the very handsome young Nicholas Jones whom she had already charmed, she was certain. He, after all, had approached her that day in the music room with something on his mind. Oh, enjoy herself she would with that superb specimen of a man, and make Molesworth jealous to boot, an added incentive that made Roweena smile until she noticed where Eustace's gaze had strayed.

"Now where is she off to in such a rush, do you suppose?" Roweena asked, as they all turned to watch Justine, driving a light runabout, take the stable turn on one wheel, throwing up a spray of gravel before she clattered over the drawbridge and was gone.

Chapter Eighteen

It was late afternoon when Justine drove her carriage into the brick-walled farmyard to which she'd been directed some miles back by an itinerant laborer. The place appeared to be deserted by human inhabitants, though there were a few chickens standing about and a large spotted cat asleep in the sun.

She climbed down and walked around to the front of the house that faced the sea. It was a plain, gray stone structure, two stories tall, with a black tiled roof and yellow shutters. It's lower garden was bordered by hedgerows that deflected offshore winds. The upper garden was reached by steep stone stairs and was charmingly framed by wisteria and begonias. Justine pushed open lace-hung French doors and stepped into a dim parlor to look about, and as her eyes grew accustomed to the gloom they took in a scene of absolute chaos. Chairs were overturned, soiled dishes were piled on the mantel and windowsills, and odd items of clothing were scattered over the wide-planked floor and the rug. There were empty wine bottles everywhere, even in the fireplace where shards of broken glass glinted among cold ashes. Asleep in a chair was the very scruffy-looking Anthony Jones, dressed in rumpled clothes, one ankle in a cast, a crutch beside him on the floor. As Justine went quickly about, opening all the long windows and shutters and letting light and sea air pour into the room, he came awake slowly, hiding his eyes and rubbing a hand over a stubble of dark beard.

"I thought you weren't coming back until tonight or tomorrow," he said, not looking up and holding his head in his hands.

"I wasn't coming at all after my last talk with your brother, but I heard there'd been an accident. I see I'm needed. What happened? Where is Nick?" Tony sat up, grimacing and blinking against the light.

"I . . . we . . . had a bit of festivity, a real debauche actually and now he's gone off and left me," Tony said, then gave her a shame-faced pathetic smile. "I'm so glad you've come. You are needed, more than you can imagine. I wrote to tell you I wasn't getting about very well, but Nicky kept forgetting to deliver my letter." He pointed to an envelope on the mantel.

"Forgot? Gone off?" Justine planted her hands on her hips and looked about with disgust. "But you need him."

"I know," Tony agreed with melting soulfulness. There was that vulnerable, injured-animal quality about him that immediately aroused her sympathy and she began to move about the disordered room, stacking dishes on a heavy wooden farm table.

"But how could Nicholas help you make such . . . such a shambles and then leave you in your condition? How irresponsible. Where's he gone off to anyway?" she asked with false indifference.

168

"He's on one of his quests, something about a woman, but then, with Nicky, it usually is something about a woman. He's chronically promiscuous you know. He never lets a female get really close to him, goes through them too fast. But his latest, it seems, is different. She's elusive. That's probably the reason he isn't bored with her yet. He's quickly bored, Nicky, always looking for some new sensation. My brother exists in a permanent state of refined depravity, I've decided," Anthony said, shaking his head in disapproval.

"That must make things very difficult for you," Justine commented, both elated and horrified by what she was hearing. Nick was actually looking for her, but the more she learned about him the more certain she became she shouldn't be pleased about that at all.

"Yes, it is difficult for me because I'm not like him. We may look alike, but there it ends. All his hunting and whoring and brawling. I mean, can you imagine Nicholas Jones taking a fall from a horse as I did and fracturing his ankle bone? It's unthinkable. But I don't want to talk about him anymore. I want to talk about you. What have you been doing?" Tony struggled to his feet and, leaning on his crutch, went from chair to table to mantel, draining the dregs of flat champagne from glasses as he went.

"When's he coming back?" Justine persisted, starting to collect empty wine bottles. "Got a broom?"

"If he's managed to avoid the moneylenders and the bookmaker's shops on Henrietta Street, he

169

could be back anytime."

"Has he gone to London in search of . . . his latest paramour?" she asked in surprise and Tony nodded.

She found the kitchen was in even worse condition than the parlor, though it was well equipped and provisioned. Glass-fronted cupboards displayed yellow and white faience plates and simple stemmed glassware. There were copper pans hanging above an enormous enameled, cast-iron stove, nested wooden bowls on the window sills, and fruit baskets filled with peaches, apples, and pears. Bins were stocked with potatoes and onions and there were bags of sugar and flour in the pantry. A lace cloth, trailing on the floor, half covered a round, marble-topped table. Just outside the door, Justine discovered the kitchen garden, the *potager*, that would provide almost anything the most demanding cook could ask for — little cornichon cucumbers, carrots, leeks, ripe tomatoes, even the plump pink French melons she liked so. "How perfectly lovely it is," Justine said to Anthony who, hobbling, had followed her out.

"Yes. Well, it's Nicky's garden. And his kitchen," Tony said with an irritable edge in his voice, Justine thought. "Yes, gone to London. He's got a velvet sash and he's searching for the slender waist it's meant to encircle, like the prince with the glass slipper looking for Cinderella." Tony motioned to his head with a forefinger, indicating Nick was slightly mad.

"Oh my, how romantic." Justine sighed, wanting to say, Oh, I'm here, right here, waiting . . . and wanting and . . . Instead, she smiled at Anthony. "Well, we do have our work cut out for us, don't we?" she asked.

Hours later the house, perfectly set to rights, was filled with the spicy fragrance of a roasting duck and the scent of baking bread. The lamps were lit, a small fire had been kindled in the parlor against the evening damp, and there were cut flowers everywhere, even in the billiard room with its leather chairs and sporting prints. It was a very comfortable cottage, Justine decided, and pleasing. Everywhere the eye fell on simple furnishings of dark carved woods, soft shapes, and warm colors.

"I adore this old farmhouse," she told Anthony as they settled down in the parlor with glasses of cider. "Perched here this way, between the sea and the sky, with its rose garden and the beach below, it reminds me of home, of Silver Hill. I had a lovely afternoon!"

"Lovely?" Anthony laughed. "Working like a chambermaid? Well, I'm glad you like the place. It's Nicky's. He found it and he's bought it and . . . I want you to stay. I want to tell you—"

"Now that everything else is so neat, you need some sprucing up, my friend," she interrupted before he could go on. "Where's your razor? And, by the way, where are all your paintings? There's not one hanging here anywhere."

"I burned them all," Tony answered, "all but my sketches of you." There was a sad, soulful look in his eyes.

"But why?" she asked slowly, terribly disturbed.

"I told you. It was all slight stuff until you. Before you, there was only one other subject I ever wanted to paint, the mountains, our Western mountains, but I couldn't even begin to face the vastness and beauty of it all as Frederick Church did and Whittridge, not with my small—tiny—talent." His smile was bittersweet. "That's what I thought then, anyway, but with you, Justine, with your American-bred beauty in that wild setting, I think I could capture it or at least try to. If you'd come home with me, I'd go now, today, to try and paint seriously, and who knows? If I do something great and grand and become famous for my work and praised, why, you might even learn to love me and—" He was half smiling, gazing into the distance.

"Stop," she said softly, unnerved by his rambling flight of fancy, thinking how like a child he was, full of impossible dreams and so needy of affection, of reassurance, and much more.

In the strained silence that fell between them, they heard voices approaching, one masculine, going on at length, telling a joke or story that was frequently interrupted by staccato bursts of feminine laughter. And then, there was the sound of footsteps on the garden stairs.

Chapter Nineteen

"Tony!" Nicholas called out. "Come see who I've found on the road on the way to visit you, a fine pair of models, all the inspiration any artist could need!" With an arm about the neck of one woman, a hand on the other's hip, Nicholas made a raucous entrance and then stopped, still, his smile fading as he saw Justine.

"Look who's come, Nicky," Tony said. "She's practically cured me already."

With the barest civility, Nicholas greeted Justine and begrudgingly introduced his companions, none other than the two women she'd seen cavorting with him in the surf.

"Meet Zou and Boni," he said, nodding curtly. They were, Justine had to admit, nodding curtly herself, not as unattractive as she'd thought them in her state of outraged propriety and pique on that shocking morning. The plumper girl, Zou, was actually more voluptuous than fat, very full bosomed and short, with her hair cut in a Bohemian boyish bob. The other, Boni, was a strawberry blond with immense eyes and a slightly receding chin, an imperfection that prevented her being a truly great beauty. She was wearing Nick's Western hat tipped back and a skirt so short it exposed her stockings and high-topped lace-up boots.

"I'm just going," Justine answered, cold with jealousy.

"I'll walk you out," Nicholas snapped.

"She's staying for dinner at least. She's already prepared it," Anthony insisted as the two French women hovered over him, one exclaiming at his injury, the other planting a kiss on his cheek.

"Ah, the morning rider," Zou said of Justine.

"Oh, and I thought we had been splashed by a viscountess at least" — Boni feigned disappointment — "but I see she is only a chambermaid."

Justine had left Castle d'Erlanger without bothering to change from her work dress, a striped cambric gown with eyelet-trimmed cuffs and collar, and her matching pinafore apron. Her hair, which she'd pinned up, was escaping its clasps now in strands that suggested the intimacy of the boudoir, while a smudge of ash on her cheek lent her a charmingly comic touch. Nicholas was finding this new incarnation of Justine very different from the tomboy rider and bejeweled belle of the ball he'd seen before. Such a calculating, insinuating creature, he thought, to take over here this way, spend a whole day with Anthony, baking and cooking and cleaning. She was flaunting her talent for domesticity in a way that was . . . captivating, he admitted to himself with surprise.

"Well, let's get it done with, this dinner of yours," he said grasping her wrist and unceremoniously leading her off to the kitchen. "I thought we'd seen the last of you," he whispered fiercely as soon as the door swung to behind them.

174

"Not by a long chalk," she hissed back, her fists clenched at her sides. "We have a bet to win, remember? Besides, I heard that someone—Tony—was hurt. It's a damned good thing I arrived when I did. You'd abandoned him here in his condition, the whole place looking like a tempest had come in off the Channel after your little debauche."

"Did it look that bad?" Nicholas asked, speaking aloud in a normal voice now and looking bothered.

"Don't dissemble." Justine stamped her foot. "You know it did, or were you too much under the influence to recall? Little elves didn't repair the damage you left. I did. Tony and I worked all day." Turning her back to him, she took up a heavy knife and began chopping parsley.

"An indulged child like you engage in such dull domestic chores? It's hard to believe," he said, teasing her now.

"Believe it. And we had a very pleasant afternoon while we were about it. Anthony is a very nice . . . young man." She had been about to say boy.

"My brother has a quiet gift of friendship when he's . . . feeling well," Nicholas answered simply. "That's why I want you to leave him alone. Stop leading him on so he can get over this crush and get back to work. Why do you have to bother with him?" Nicholas asked as Justine finished tearing watercress and began slicing pears for a salad. "Haven't you been enjoying yourself among all those bloated aristocrats and their torpid waspish women? I'm really surprised you haven't found

175

yourself an English title to marry, complete with a staff of bowing liveried lackeys to do your bidding. Of course, there are hordes of Roman aristocrats, too, with their gloomy palaces and—"

"Why don't you go home to California, Mr. Jones? You don't seem to approve of these people at all," Justine declared.

"My brother likes the light here. Anthony sometimes paints and draws, you know," Nick replied sarcastically.

"Are you his keeper?" Justine asked and turned to see his eyes go opaque like cool, dark stones.

"In a manner of speaking," he answered laconically.

"But you left him alone to indulge in a little rat-baiting and cock-fighting and Mayfair-whoring across the Channel with your dissipated friends. I couldn't help but notice you were gone when I got here."

"That's not exactly why I went," he said, going to the window. Justine glanced at him over her shoulder.

"Oh, that's right. I heard something about a glass slipper. Have you met the girl of your dreams?" she asked with a secret smile. He shrugged and said nothing, just looked out over the water. Banks of thick fog were massed offshore, where a storm was brewing. The sky was a roiling gray mass of clouds, though the air below was almost still as if with expectation, only the leaves of the very tops of the trees fluttering. When the rain began to fall, Nicholas lit another lamp and in its flickering light, she studied his handsome face, etched by heaven-only-knew how many squandered nights and lover's dawns.

"Girl of my dreams? I don't know," he mused, and Justine looked away not knowing whether to laugh or cry over the irony of it all. "She is a very daring woman, vibrant . . . mysterious . . . a generous warm woman. Even an inveterate tease like you could learn a lot from her."

"Oh, could I?" Justine asked archly, furiously whisking the salad dressing while Nicholas, unknowingly and longingly, envisioned her in the clouds, conjured up that perfect image he'd constructed in the dark . . . high breasts that filled his hands . . . a waist so narrow he could encircle it . . . a body of such sinuous grace and unrestrained passion—"

"She has no faults, then?" Justine asked very, very softly.

"Only beauties, I think," he answered, using the horseman's phrase as Justine did.

"You think?" She pretended to laugh at him. "Don't you know?"

"She is rather . . . quiet. Some might consider that a fault, but I consider it an attribute in a lover." He had begun to uncork a bottle of wine.

"And in a wife?" Justine raised the lid of a saucepan and let a great cloud of fragrant steam into the air.

"Wife?" Now it was his turn to laugh. "You're in the marriage market, not me, Miss Hawkes. All I'm after is a certain gratification—pure sensual pleasure. These house-party affairs are just a form of sport for the participants," he said, lecturing himself as much as he was instructing Justine in the ways of the jaded, sophisticated world.

"Sport? For your lover, too?" Justine's voice was a bit brittle. "Then why are you searching her out with such diligence?"

"She brings a certain . . . imagination to the game, a dramatic flair that makes her desirable, for the moment at least, until it palls, as these things always will," he insisted. "But you're blushing, Miss Hawkes. Do I shock you, speaking so bluntly? I'm not used to Dollar Princesses who trade on their innocent naïveté as well as on their money. This is 1898 remember, almost the twentieth century, and I've spent most of my time of late with rather freer spirits." Nicholas took a chair at the kitchen table, stretched out his long legs, and clasped his hands behind his head.

It was raining harder now, a high wind hurling drops at the windows, torrents gushing down the roof spout; and it was pleasantly warm and cozy in the kitchen that was softly lighted. Justine, he observed with growing surprise, went about her business with such efficient pleasure, he actually enjoyed watching her cook in his kitchen almost as much as watching her ride his polo pony.

"Freer spirits like your Bohemian companions in there?" Justine asked smiling, turning to face him, words forming in her mind — you fool, it's me you're looking for. I'm the one you want, and not just for now, not just for sport, for always. "Taste?" she queried, proffering a wooden spoon coated with yellow batter.

"What is it?" he asked almost warily, feeling

178

that temptation, as he often did with this sprite of a girl, to simply reach out and take her, not just the sweet mouth this time.

"Butter cake." She laughed as his tongue snaked out to touch the tip of the spoon tentatively. Then, as she turned it this way and that, very slowly in front of him, he licked it quite clean, her laughing green eyes holding his and never wavering.

"Who taught you to cook?" He half smiled.

"My mother." Justine smiled now, too. "She taught me to cook and to sew a fine seam and to tend a garden and to . . . care for a man." They were still studying each other when the kitchen door opened, then Justine guiltily moved away from Nick.

"She thinks you're a Bohemian, Zou," he said, licking his lips with pleasure.

"*C'est vrai,* it's true. Perhaps we *should* go to Paris as Tony is saying and show her wicked Bohemian Montmartre . . . the Moulin Rouge and all that. Lautrec, the artist, will certainly want to sketch her, I'm sure. *Elle est jolie comme un tableau,* pretty as a picture, *oui?* What do you say, Nick? Will you come?" He shook his head no.

"Neither will Tony," he added sharply as Zou, standing behind his chair, rested her hands on his shoulders, the gesture at once possessive and challenging as her eyes met Justine's.

"You are quite right, Nick. Tony's not up to it, and neither is this little American. She's far too wholesome for the depravities of *fin de siècle* Paris where sin and vice are so much in fashion. Bored

179

voluptés de luxe and even erotic dilettantes are playing at all sorts of deviant games, you know."

"What do you mean exactly?" Justine asked, her head tilted to one side, arms folded in front of her defensively.

"Oh, don't look so worried, little one! I won't say anything really shocking, not to *you*." Zou laughed. "I'm talking about occultists, Satanists, anarchists, and so on, and so on. Various prurient preoccupations I wouldn't began to describe. There is also the artificial paradise that certain substances — drugs — provide." Zou's fingers, as she'd kept her eyes on Justine, had been kneading Nick's shoulders and now moved to the back of his neck. He glanced up at her for a moment but said nothing, and Justine found it difficult to control her growing anger and jealousy without giving everything away. As far as anyone knew, she had no claim at all on this infuriating man.

"The duke told me that Parisian jewelers do a thriving trade these days in gold-plated syringes for fashionable ladies. I may look wholesome," Justine added archly, "but I'm not completely . . . inexperienced."

"Oh?" Zou laughed. "A woman of the world, are you? Come, little girl, have you ever tried laudanum as an aperitif before dinner? Perhaps strawberries soaked in ether for dessert? Both are quite the fashion these days, though Anthony and I prefer Vin Coca Mariani. It's a medicinal wine infused with coca leaves, very . . . effective." Justine was genuinely shocked now and she sought Nicholas's eyes, but they were half-lidded as he leaned back, apparently enjoying the massage that Zou was working at so diligently. "Perhaps after dinner you'd like to try some of our Mariani?" the woman persisted, scenting the air like a rabbit as Justine slammed open the oven. "Mm, *caneton* Rouennais seasoned with calvados and pepper. It's Normandy's gift to the world, that half-wild duck. It's so *good* of you to come and cook for us. Isn't it good of her, Nick?" Zou challenged. "I always said to them, to the twins"—she pointedly addressed Justine again, her eyes more than challenging now, sullen and angry though her bantering tone didn't change—"I always said 'You two bachelor lone wolves need a woman's touch about the place, eh, Nick?' "

"I wouldn't know about that," he said with a frown as Zou rolled her eyes heavenward.

"Well, while the pretty cook here offers one sort of woman's touch, I'll provide another," she said with a forced laugh, sinking to his lap, her arms encircling his neck before she kissed him, long and hard.

"Oh, Nicky," she pouted, coming up for air a good half-minute later, "you didn't even kiss me back! You must really be in love for good this time, *oui?*"

"*Peut-être,*" he answered turning, for some reason he didn't understand, to look at Justine. But by then, to his great irritation, she was gone.

Nicholas got a horse saddled as quickly as he could and rode after her, but she was nowhere to be found. She'd simply vanished into the storm, it seemed, though he covered more than five miles and got soaked to the skin before he gave up the futile effort and turned back to the cottage.

Next morning, still angry that she'd bolted off without a word, he went to inquire after her, for Tony's sake, of course. At Castle d'Erlanger, he was told that she'd gone only hours before, both she and Gray.

"To Ireland and England?" Nicholas asked with some annoyance.

"No, *monsieur*," the duke's valet replied.

"Where, then?" Nick was just barely controlling an overwhelming urge to shake the man who looked at him with bored indifference, his high-domed head gleaming in the morning sunlight.

"To Italy, *monsieur*."

"Italy?" Nicholas repeated. "Then to Ireland?"

"No, *monsieur*," the valet replied.

"Where then, you liveried fop?" he demanded, fists clenched, eyes slitted. "To India, *monsieur*," the man stated as though he was simply saying Paris or London or New York, which of course he wasn't. He was naming no accessible, sensible place, but referring to a vast country, an entire subcontinent, halfway around the world.

"India," Nicholas repeated, thinking he should be relieved to be really rid of the girl this time and wondering why he wasn't. He just stood there in the doorway at Castle d'Erlanger a full minute or more before he turned on his heel and strode off.

Chapter Twenty

"The first really dedicated, profligate gambler of modern times was a fourteenth-century Italian, Franceschetto Cybo," Count Zenga told Justine with a certain pride. Seated beside him, Monica Matti, tall and titian haired, a cool elegant beauty, poured out tiny cups of very black, very thick coffee that she passed to her guests, Justine and Gray, with slender hands, pale as doves. "That should especially interest you, Justine, about Cybo. I watched you more than once at Deauville Casino. You gamble with superb concentration." Zenga smiled, his profile multiplied infinitely in the large gilt-framed mirrors that hung on opposite walls of the airy drawing room in his palace in central Italy.

"I do like to gamble and I like to win," Justine returned the smile, sipping her coffee and exchanging glances with Gray.

Brother and sister were both still a bit dazed to find themselves in Sienna after a hasty departure and very long train ride from Deauville. And they were both decidedly put out by the sudden change in plans executed at the explicit instructions of Slade Hawkes. They'd had to get themselves to Sienna in time for the July Palio, a street horse race unlike any other in the world, their father had written, and, though Justine and Gray both had certain serious interests in France, it would never have occurred to either of them to go against their father's wishes. These had been conveyed in a letter hand-delivered by the purser of one of Slade's merchant ships. The vessel had apparently made the Atlantic crossing from New York in record time and had carried, beside Slade's message, his ocean-going yacht, the ketch *Whitehawk,* that was to be put at the disposal of his son and daughter.

"Now I know where it comes from," Gray had grumbled, "your flair for the dramatic gesture. It's the same as Father's." He was hurriedly packing a few things into a carpet bag and pormanteau when Justine, greatly agitated, rushed into his room at Castle Erlanger. "Where have you been all night?" he asked, hands on his hips, looking at her and shaking his head.

"I don't want to leave here any more than you do," she'd answered carefully scrutinizing the letter from home. "I got caught in a storm and took shelter in a barn until it was over and—Oh! Meet father in . . . India?" She read on with a sinking heart. "Good heavens!"

"Yes. Olympe will have our steamer trunks packed and sent on directly to Bombay while we tour Italy. The *Whitehawk* will meet us at the boot heel and we'll cruise the Mediterranean before we go through the canal at Suez and on to the subcontinent." Gray sounded like a dutiful child reciting his lessons. "But if we're going to see this

Palio race, you'd better get moving. Oh, Justine
. . ."

She'd heard no more, just raced down the hall
and slammed her door and began furiously flinging about open boxes and trunks, realizing all too
clearly that she'd wasted a night, one that might
have been her last with Nicholas . . . and her last
chance to tell him the truth. Like a child playing
at hide-and-seek, she'd concealed herself in a barn,
in the loft. Her horse and cart had been pulled in,
too, and the doors shut. She'd watched Nick, hat
pulled low and water pouring down his collar, ride
by in the rain. She'd said nothing, thinking it better there in the barn than watching that reprobate
flaunt his cocotte right in front of her. Oh, she'd
renounced him this time, washed her hands of him
completely, decided it could never come to anything more with such a man than it already had, a
few nights of lustful pleasure that would never
lead to love or marriage . . . or to anything else.
Then, after a long ride home in the early morning,
she'd found the letter Gray had left propped on
her dressing table among her satin traveling cases
and scent bottles. And all her resolve had evapo-
rated on the instant. At the mere thought of being
torn away from Nicholas, she began to miss him
awfully, and she knew at once that all her silent
raging in the dark, all her resolve, had counted for
nothing.

"I won't go, I absolutely won't," she said aloud
to no one but herself, "I refuse."

Twenty-four hours later, Justine was in Mauro Zenga's palace. As she was shown from one vast room to the next, its history and his ancient lineage were evident in the soaring ceilings, in Renaissance *trompe l'oeil* illusions of bookshelves and cupboards, all in perfect perspective down to the least dovetail. The convoluted scrollwork and cartouches on engraved chests of walnut polished to the luster of bronze were also creations of Renaissance craftsman. In other rooms, Roman baroque burgeoned in virtuoso carvings of nude figures, of tritons, of foliage and shells; the style carried to greater extravagance two centuries later in the sensuous elegance and linear curves of the rococo. There were Oriental woods, etched ivories, gilded moldings and gadroons, Genoese velvet cushions, Lucchese silk draperies, all evidencing an opulence beyond anything Justine had ever seen. As their footsteps rang on marble floors, she and Gray were graciously entertained by the courtly Count Zenga who himself called to mind the Roman Caesars with his strong, aquiline features and patrician manner. All the while Justine smiled and admired and questioned and commented, she wished only to be back in a small simple Norman farmhouse at the edge of the sea.

"Like you, Justine, so did Cybo like to win," the count continued, his heavily beringed hand enfolding his tiny cup. "And when he lost fourteen thousand ducats at cards to a Cardinal Rosaria, he complained to the Pope about his emissary's cheating."

"You will see much of that today, cheating,

when the Palio is run," Monica said. "It is expected. This is a race to be won by any means at all. Contrivance, sabotage, bribery, poisoning, nothing is forbidden today — only one jockey seizing hold of another or the reins of another's horse. Riders are permitted to strike each other though, and certainly to unseat each other if they can."

"But a horse is allowed to win anyway, without his rider, and sometimes an animal actually does better for the lack of weight," the count interjected with a laugh.

Dressed, as always, in an elegantly cut, black vested suit, his silvered hair receding slightly from a high brow, heavy rings flashing, the count was an imposing figure, his manner that of a man used to privilege and control. He led Justine to the palladian window of his drawing room that overlooked the Campo of Sienna, the village square where the race would be run at dusk. The piazza was already filling with people and had been since eight in the morning, most of them keyed to a fever pitch of excitement as the culmination of a year's preparation and three days of preliminary runs was now only hours away. The pageant that always preceded the Palio had begun with ox-cart floats, pages in Renaissance dress and knights in armor, and drums and silver trumpets and cymbals sounding. Standard bearers and mace bearers milled with the crowd, hawkers selling toy horses and dolls called out incessantly, and there were flowers everywhere.

"The Palio is an ancient ritual that goes back

into antiquity. It's a tournament. It's a bloody war game. It's a religious rite, it's a—"

"And it's all about a piece of cloth?" Justine asked the count.

"Once that piece of cloth was a cloak of brocade and gold, trimmed in ermine and of great value. Now, it's a painted banner to be won only for the glory of winning. But to understand the race, you should know that, as much as anything else, the Palio is an almost pagan celebration of Fortune, of Chance, of Lady Luck as you Americans call her, because anybody can win the Palio—any way he can."

"Mauro, you must explain better than that. The glory is not for one's self but for the *contrada,*" Monica said, folding her hands in her lap. "To explain the *contrada,* that is not an easy task. It is like one's family but more . . . one's neighborhood . . . one's tribe . . . it's hard to explain. There's nothing else quite like it anywhere, you see. Every Siennese, rich, poor or middling, is born into a *contrada* and it is for the glory of that group that this race is run today as it had been for so long, since before the Medicis even. When the horses are brought to the starting line, each draped in the color of his *contrada,* each has already been taken right into the church of his *contrada,* for good luck, of course. Then he is brought to his place on the starting line, which has been assigned by lot as the animal himself was assigned by lot to his *contrada.* So much is left to pure chance, you understand, though the animals have been guarded twenty-four hours a day since their arrival in Si-

enna because foul play is part of the Palio and
. . . Oh, my, it is so difficult to explain, really!"
Monica clasped her lovely hands beneath her chin,
looking confused and fluttery.

"Even more to the point than all that, by the
time the horses are brought out this evening, many
deals will have been made. Some *contradas* have
been enemies for two hundred years and the ri-
valry is wicked. Others, to influence the outcome,
join forces. There is much contrivance. Cunning
counts for a lot today," Zenga added.

"And the quality of the horses and the skill of
the jockeys? What of that?" Justine asked. "To
ride in such a race must be glorious!"

"The animals used were once nags, the city's
worst. Now they are thoroughbreds and the riders
are experienced competitors hired by the *contradas,*
but not above taking bribes. It's all part of the
game." The count smiled happily. "Some horses
and men have been in this race more than once or
twice, but even a good horse can be destroyed by
one Palio, it's so grueling."

"Look there! What's that?" Justine said, suddenly pointing as she leaned over the balcony rail,
waves of excitement rising, with the noise, from
below.

"The entry of the *drago contrada—drago* . . . it
means in English dragon—took a fall yesterday
during a practice run. He had to be destroyed.
Today, his hoofs and tail will be carried through
the procession on that black cushion."

"Oh, I'm sorry," Justine said.

"Well, we all know it's a dangerous course even

with the dirt packed down over the flagstones of the Campo. The animal that wins isn't so much fast as he is a survivor. Now, would you care to venture out into the crowd?" Zenga asked. "Sienna on Palio day is worth seeing."

Chapter Twenty-one

The steep, narrow streets of the town, not much more than alleyways in many places, opened into lovely medieval courtyards that were thronged with celebrants and tourists drawn to Sienna by the event that would take place later in the day. Justine, on Mauro Zenga's arm, followed by Gray and Monica, was completely caught up in the air of tension and expectation, the mood of festivity, as she imagined with pleasure putting up her hair and pretending to be a boy so that she could ride to victory in the extraordinary race.

"Our race, Justine, we must discuss it," Zenga said abruptly, interrupting her thoughts. "William Gates will cheat. Everyone knows that he drugs his horses. What is not so generally known is that Molesworth will cheat as well. You must have a care."

"Sir Eustace? He's so arrogant and stiff upper lipped, so superior. It's hard to believe."

"He's in dire financial straits. I've looked into his situation. He has unpaid bills all over London and his staff had gone without remuneration for some time now. The man may be desperate enough to do something rash."

"Why are you warning me, Count? We're competing with each other, after all," Justine asked, almost flirtatiously. She'd been buying toys for her nieces and nephews and hard candies in little parcels wrapped in paper of the *contrada's* colors. She juggled these from hand to hand.

"To win an important race, one must have allies. I learned that from the Palio long ago." Justine stared up at him then, and his face, angular and hard, was serious, that of a great deadly bird of prey, she thought.

"Are you offering to help me win?" she asked, no longer flirting at all, deadly serious herself and taken aback though she tried not to show it.

"No. But I don't want you to lose to anyone but me. I want your opals," he went on, "I've never seen their like, and to own what no other man possesses or ever can, *that* appeals to me. I've everything a man could desire. I lack for nothing, so, of course, the great frivolous rarity — a costly painting, a fine horse, a jewel — has special attraction for me." His voice had grown very soft and warm and almost caressing.

"You're right. There are no other opals like mine for sale anywhere in the world," Justine nodded. "But I've no intention of giving them up to you or anyone. I've also no intention of letting our steeplechase be tampered with. It's going to be a fair race. I'll share your information and concerns with my teammates," she said firmly, though she wondered if she'd ever see either of the Joneses again.

As Justine strolled on the count's arm, both of them silent now, she thought about Nicholas Jones. And when they reached the outskirts of Sienna and climbed a high jutting rock to look over the countryside, she was thinking of him still. In her mind, she borrowed the vantage of a falcon that soared along a slant of a Tuscan hill, and saw herself, very far from Nicholas, saw him in the north of France at the edge of the sea, saw the distance between them growing wider and wider as he crossed the Channel to England on a fruitless search for a woman he wouldn't find while she was carried ever farther in the opposite direction.

The Palio was a spectacle, a minute and a half of pure mayhem, a shared madness of the multitudes gathered around the Campo that second day of July in 1898. There were six false starts. Horses bolted and bucked. Women screamed and fainted. A jockey was rolled from his mount and almost trampled, but managed to get up again; and the race finally began to the roar of the crowd that echoed against the ramparts of medieval palaces and churches surrounding the square.

At the second turn, the treacherous San Martino curve, five horses crashed and went down, and one, a fine thoroughbred that had three times before won the Palio, got up screaming with pain and awash in blood only to be shot, his pastern broken. It was then that Justine turned away unwilling to watch anymore.

"A sentimental one, aren't you?" the count questioned, his gray eyes amused.

"Not at all," Justine said coolly. "I know a great deal about horses. Anyone who does can't be sentimental about them, but this . . . is barbaric cruelty." There was a flash of anger in Zenga's face, but he only laughed.

"Does an outlander like you tell us, whose ancestors civilized the western world, that we are barbaric? Imagine."

"She is not so wrong, Mauro," Monica said. "This race is intense, passionate, violent, primitive. See now." She pointed. The frenzied race had ended, and in the hysterical aftermath, the winning jockey was being lifted shoulder-high and carried off to trumpet blares and drum rolls. Men let tears flow without shame, women held up their infants to see the banner pass, girls fell weeping into each other's arms in an excess of joy or misery, and the parties, the carousing, began. In the palaces, as in the streets of Sienna, wine flowed like water.

"Trompe l'oeil, meaning to 'fool the eye,' " Zenga smiled, gesturing at what appeared to be a curtained wall, but was not, in the small salon of his palace where he, his mistress, and guests had dined. "It is a very old art form. Pliny the Elder wrote of the Athenian artist whose painted grapes were so temptingly real, birds came down to peck at them. It's an art form that I find particularly engaging. The line between what is and what merely seems to be is almost invisible."

"It's purposeful deception, not to my taste," Gray Hawkes said, reaching out to touch a table on which coins, bits of cheese, and a hand of playing cards were painted with such perfection they appeared to be three dimensional.

Zenga offered him a cigar from an inlaid humidor.

"I wouldn't really expect you new-world young people to be comfortable with this subtle sort of thing." He shrugged. "Horses are more to your interest, are they not? Yours and your charming sister's?" he nodded at Justine who tilted her head in agreement and brought a hand to the opals at her throat.

That little gesture of hers, the aristocratic slender hand resting at the daring décolletage just covering the full swell of her creamy bosom, seemed to Zenga at once provocative and defiant, now that she knew of his passion for the stones. She knew because he had told her himself, and probably she knew, too, without having to be told, of that other passion that had possessed him since her arrival earlier in the day. Of course, he had been acutely aware of her at Deauville as every man there had been, a woman of such beauty electrifying the resort town. But he'd never gotten this close. She'd always been surrounded by admirers and escorted by one young man or another, usually one of those Jones twins.

But today, having her almost to himself, what had been Zenga's merely paternal interest had given way to a far more compelling emotion.

"I own a seven-year-old stallion. He's half brother to the thoroughbred that won the Palio today, a magnificent animal, aggressive, and a beautiful fencer. I thought you should know what

195

you'll be up against," Zenga told Justine. He stood behind her chair, his hand resting on her bare shoulder as their eyes met in a smoked-glass mirror. "Tomorrow, if you like, I'll take you to see him. He's stabled near Sienna."

"But tomorrow we're leaving," she answered, "so I shall have to see you again and meet your stallion at Sandringham before the race."

Zenga took her soft hand and brought it to his lips. "I regret that you must leave us so soon," he said, the expression of warmth on his angular face softening its harshness a little. "Is there nothing we can do to convince you to stay?"

"What? Not leaving!" Monica sighed. "You Americans, always so busy, so rushed, never taking time to sit in a café and watch the world go by, never stopping even for a pleasant dalliance among friends." She looked petulantly at Gray.

"We've business in Jodhpur," Gray said with a distant disapproving look that only Justine was aware of.

"I think business is the religion of Americans. Don't you think so, Mauro?" Monica sighed again.

"We're just hard working, is all," Justine corrected. "We've such a big country, you see, and there's so much to do . . . to build . . ."

"And you haven't a languishing aristocracy to slow you down," the count commented. "That's been said before, but I wonder. Some of you do quite well at languishing decadently, the Jones gentlemen for example, your teammates."

"Oh, there's gossip about those two," Monica reported, "fingering a very large ruby earring that dropped almost to her shoulder. "But, of course, one never can tell which of them is doing what, can one?"

One certainly can, Justine wanted to say but of course she didn't. She focused instead on her most secret, private image of Nicholas, one that stayed with her during her travels over the next several weeks as she and Gray moved south through Italy, in the waxing heat of summer, to the dazzlingly clear Mediterranean Sea. There they found the *Whitehawk* waiting, a curved sliver of sickle moon, as their mother always described the craft, a familiar and welcome bit of home in this distant place. The ketch was all fine mahogany and teak and polished brass within, and her three-man crew was waiting to welcome them aboard.

Chapter Twenty-two

Justine awoke often in the night to the sound of the yacht's creakings and shifting, to the tapping of fittings against the mast, the sound like wind chimes of the deep. It was then the yearnings of her body flooded her mind with such sharp memories of Nicholas that she seemed to feel his presence close all about her. Her need was so desperate and encompassing she often got up to sit on deck, sometimes alone, sometimes with Gray who was also restless and ruminative, both of them silent for hours on end, thinking and dreaming.

And sitting there with her brother under the Mediterranean sky, Justine kept imagining the world as it looks in geography books, the bright blues of oceans, the yellows and greens and browns of the vast continents, separating her from Nicholas who, for all she knew, might have gone home by now to the California mountains.

She imagined him there in his natural setting and the picture that came so easily to her was a familiar one of desert-haunted, fierce dark eyes and a lean, lank frame—the Western horseman in leather leggings and duster coat, his deep-brimmed hat pulled low, turquoise and silver spurs catching light.

On their leisurely way to Bombay from the bootheel of Italy, Justine and Gray visited the palaces of Malta before the *Whitehawk* called at Suez and Port Said, all heat and dust, and later at Aden where great protrusions of volcanic mountains reminded Justine of some other-worldly moon fantasy.

By the time the boat was moving along the north shore of the Arabian sea, Justine had decided what it was she must do—simply find Nicholas Jones wherever in the world he was. It was as simple as that. She'd return to France, go to England, even to California, anywhere, no matter how long it took . . . and she'd tell him everything.

Justine slept wonderfully once she'd come to that decision. Her self-confidence restored, she was radiant with excitement as the *Whitehawk* reach its destination. The harbor at Bombay was filled with sailboats, barges, and steamers as they approached the green, tropic-island city that lay beneath distant, light-tinted hills at sunset. Slade Hawkes would be there waiting for them, and her father, Justine knew, would understand why it was she had to go away at once, why she wouldn't travel inland with him to Jodhpur. He'd know her very life depended on her following her heart.

Their craft anchored offshore and Justine and Gray were taken landward in a barge sent out to meet them. They stood in the prow as the sights and sounds of an exotic city grew larger and became more distinct. After a time they could discern, on the teeming docks, Indian natives moving about, some in long fragile flowing robes and others hardly clothed at all, merely swaddled in bits of cloth. At one harbor berth, a merchant ship was unloading a live cargo and Justine exclaimed in wonder at an elephant in a canvas sling dangling high in the air as it was shifted from deck to dock by a powerful crane. The huge creature, waving its legs and trunk, bellowed in panic but calmed at once when it was set down and its handler, its mahout, came to its side.

Justine herself, an even more unusual sight in that place than a flying elephant, attracted a great deal of attention as she stepped ashore. Fair and slim in a pale green traveling suit and spotless white gloves, her eager eyes dancing, going everywhere, she took in the sights until she saw a barouche and four, with a turbaned driver up top. She started toward it at a run through the crowd that parted for her, and soon she was in her father's arms, laughing and nearly crying, too, as he hugged her and held her close for a long moment before he raised her chin and scrutinized her shining face.

"I missed you, you know. We all did, especially Maud," he added, passing an arm about her shoulders as he extended his hand to Gray. Then he hugged his son, too, and began to help Justine into the carriage, "I must say you look none the worse for wear, either of you."

"Father . . . I must tell you something now," Justine began, hanging back as he pulled off his wide-brimmed hat and fanned at his face. As Gray went off to oversee the handling of the baggage, he looked about him with interest, his tie now loosened, his linen jacket undone.

"Come, Justine, get in. It's too hot to be standing about, and the dusk doesn't last long here in Bombay. It will be full dark before you know it. Don't you want to see some of the sights on the way? We're expected at the home of the British Governor here for the evening meal."

"But, Father," she began, only to be interrupted by Gray.

"I'm ready," he said climbing up beside the driver as their two postilions on fine Arabian stallions, came to attention.

"Well, I suppose what I must tell you can wait . . . a little," Justine agreed, settling herself beside her father as the carriage started off and a pair of servants, *saises,* much to her skeptical concern, ran alongside keeping up with the carriage, flapping horsehair fly whisks.

She asked for, and was immediately supplied with, all the talk and gossip from home as they moved away from the shore and toward Government House, passing through groves of palms and mangoes in flower. There were parrots in the tamarinds, fields of lilies, and the fragrance of jasmine was thick in the evening air.

Justine was still asking questions of Slade when a very large country mansion surrounded by wide verandas came into sight. All its many arched doors were thrown open to capture any passing breeze in the heat of the Bombay summer. Every window was lit in greeting, and there were rows and rows of servants, draped and turbaned and sashed in crimson and white, lined up in honor of their arrival.

"I'm sorry you didn't get to Ireland," Slade was saying as they moved up the drive, "but the Palio—"

"A brutal affair, destroying fine horses as if they were mere flies," Justine said very seriously.

"And our host, Mauro Zenga"—Gray turned in his seat—"is not a simple straightforward man, not an easy man to know. He seemed to have the moral cunning of a Machiavelli and the murderous instincts of a Nero. Don't you agree, Justine?" he asked, but never did get an answer. He looked on with confused amusement as his sister stood before the carriage had come to a full stop and, not waiting for the salaaming, turbaned *saise* to open the door, flung it aside herself and jumped down, passing the governor and his wife and daughter, who were poised to greet her, leaving them all openmouthed until her lovely, infectious, shimmering laugh brought smiles to everyone within hearing. Justine ran to the steps of the mansion, where she paused, but only for an instant before hurling herself into the arms of Nicholas Jones.

"How? . . ." She managed to say that one word, no more, as she anticipated his kiss, yearned for it, willed him in her heart to crush her to him in front of everyone, as he had that day on the polo field at Deauville, not caring about these proper Englishmen and startled Indians, or about her father or Gray or anyone. And he almost did, she was certain, almost kissed her but . . . didn't, just looked into her smiling eyes, his own eyes savage and sultry, until he produced his wonderful smile that was all rakish charm and seductive invitation.

Then, encircling her waist, he simply set her aside. He stepped *away* from her, and when he looked at Anthony standing tensely behind him, the message in Nicholas's eyes, in the angle of his body, the gesture of his hand, was clear to Justine. As he'd done before, he was handing her over to his brother without even a by your leave. Furious, wanting to wound him or at least spark a *hint* of jealousy in Nicholas, Justine greeted Anthony with the same passionate warmth and smile, the same long, clasping embrace, even with the brush of a kiss, something she would never have done if not for the flare of anger she felt, like the leap of a match flame in the dark and as quickly extinguished. She glanced quickly, guiltily, at Nicholas over her shoulder, aware of the danger of her act, knowing Anthony's feelings for her, his hopes and desires. She hadn't meant to encourage him at all. She'd simply used him in a silly, selfish, thoughtless moment, to taunt his brother. It was a near-fatal mistake though Justine wouldn't know it for a long while, not until she'd lost them both, lover and friend, perhaps forever.

"How did you get here?" She finally finished

her question.

"I was so afraid you wouldn't be glad to see me." Anthony grinned. "I'm so glad I was wrong." And then Slade Hawkes was at his daughter's elbow, clearing his throat, reminding her of the propriety of this very formal moment. Justine, suddenly all decorous charm, turned her smile on the governor and his wife and daughter and on their aides-de-camp, Captains Cavendish and Duff, all of whom were quite smitten by this exuberant and uninhibited young guest.

"How *did* you get here? You never have said," Justine asked again, much later, after the dinner that had been served on the veranda, beneath a tent of muslin mosquito netting, was done and the dancing, too. There was moonlight in the palms surrounding them as she strolled the pathways near Government House alone with Anthony and Nicholas. The others had all retired early, anticipating a morning excursion. Justine had been too agitated and excited to sleep, and so elated she could hardly contain herself. Nicholas, it seemed, was showing some interest in her after all. He'd been not only civil but actually attentive all evening, and contrary to her expectations, he wasn't giving Anthony any advantage as the two vied for her attention.

"Olympe d'Erlanger made no secret of your destination. I couldn't live without you," Anthony said, trying to make light of his words though his voice broke. "You are my favorite model, after all." He drew her arm through his as they walked. "You and Gray certainly took your good time getting here. We came on directly."

So very directly, Nicholas thought, watching the play of light and shadow in Justine's hair, noting that her gown rustled faintly as she moved and the opals at her throat, fired by moonlight, glinted.

Chapter Twenty-three

"I can't live without her," Tony had said. Nicholas had just returned from Erlanger Castle with the news of Justine's precipitous departure from France. The color had drained from Tony's face and his hand had been unsteady as he'd reached for his glass, spilling amber liquid as he'd brought it to his lips.

"She doesn't love you. She loves another," Nicholas had said in a voice thick with anger. "Forget her. Try to. We'll go home. I've had enough of this life, and so have you."

"I need to be where she is, to be with her wherever she is. I'll be content just to hear her voice, to hear her pretty laugh, to see her . . . smile," Tony had responded. "And who can tell? She may someday learn to love me. I'm going after her. You go home." Anthony had struggled clumsily to his feet, the effects of his injured ankle and drink apparent in his poor balance and slurred speech.

Nicholas had helped his brother to bed that night and, for a time had stood looking down at the face so like his own, the same and yet not. Though both had been molded by the same accidents of fate, Nicholas had been forged by life's blows to a self-reliant steely hardness. Tony, a tentative, self-effacing boy, had grown into a man weak-willed and pliant. They'd practically raised each other, growing up half-wild in the Western mountains, isolated in the mysterious country of the heart; his brother desperate for the love they'd both been denied, Nicholas wanting no part of it. "Better to be needed than need," he'd always said, but Tony couldn't stand on his own so Nicholas had taken care of him, defended him, pulled his brother, drunk and raving from his "nerve storms," out of the low dives he favored. Later he'd paid his debts and kept the exploiters, like Boni and Zou, in line. Nick had always been able to protect Tony from everything, until now, until this bewitchingly beautiful bit of skirt, Justine Hawkes, had come along to plant false hopes and evoke dangerous dreams that could never come true. Couldn't because she was just like all the rest—capricious, faithless, and hurtful.

As he'd walked along the shore that night in Normandy after he'd put his brother to bed, the image of Justine as he'd last seen her was still clear in Nick's mind. There had been such an uncontrived beauty about her as she'd worked in the kitchen, an artful simplicity of manner that seemed to belie everything he'd been told about her. Her dress and apron, the long golden braid down her back, had all enhanced his impression of open, sweet innocence. But she took delight in breaking hearts, that woman Roweena and others had said, and she had left a man distraught, standing alone at the altar.

It was already dawn by the time Nicholas had decided what to do, that mysterious, magical time when he himself had first laid eyes on the girl, standing like a sea sprite at the edge of the waves — so very, *very* lovely. He would give her the benefit of a doubt, for Tony's sake. If his brother, on a sober awakening, was still determined to follow her halfway across the globe, he too, would have to go to India. If she treated Tony well and fairly, he'd accept that and hope for the best. But if there was even a hint of manipulation and teasing, of toying with his brother's affections, Nick was determined to take matters into his own hands and force Tony to see her for what she really was. The surest, quickest, way to do that was simply to seduce the creature himself. To ruin her reputation once and for all and let everyone, especially Tony, know how weak and frivolous she really was. It would be hurtful of course but better a fast clean break, a sharp, short-lived pain than a lingering agony.

And so it was that Nick's course of action and Justine's fate were decided in those first moments when she'd come into his arms and parted those tempting lips in readiness for his kiss. Then, she'd turned and actually kissed his brother right there in front of everyone. Her act just might have been a bold proclamation of affection he'd conjectured until she'd glanced at him over her shoulder. Right then, Nicholas knew without doubt that Justine was playing Tony false.

* * *

"We're to make a very early start," he said as the three returned to the veranda of Government House, where silent, turbaned equerries stood to either side of the door. "You'll ride with us tomorrow, of course," he added, offering Justine his smile. "That way, Tony can sketch you and I can . . . entertain you."

"I'll see you both then, in the morning," Justine answered. With a smile, she turned away toward the stairs, mulling over the miraculous change in Nicholas. Too elated to think of sleep, she wandered about her room. It was large and airy and high ceilinged, and had several doors and windows, all latticed, all opening onto a colonnaded balcony.

The bed, beneath its tent of white gauze, was turned back, and the flowers and fruits that had been left for her pleasure seemed amazingly exotic especially with décor that was English country style—striped rose-chintz chairs and little round tables. Justine had been followed, as everyone in the whole country seemed to be, by a trail of servants; one attached himself to the cord of the ceiling fan in the center of her room, another readied a bath of cool water, a third poured iced tea. Her things had already been unpacked, and a cotton lawn bed gown and peignoir laid out on a chair. Finding herself at a loss as to how to proceed with all these people hovering about her, Justine sauntered onto the balcony and out into night air that was still hot at three in the morning, to find Nicholas Jones a few doors from her, leaning at the balustrade and smoking a cigarette.

He didn't notice her at first but then, slowly, as if drawn by an invisible strand, he turned in her direction and his smile flickered.

"Can't sleep?" he questioned in a loud whisper, starting toward her, aware that she was lovely awash in moonbeams. "Guilty conscience?" he asked.

Her heart began to pound as she thought, of course I can't sleep, because of you, because I want you so terribly. I've missed you so desperately, imagined everything again and again.

"It's rather . . . crowded in there," she answered, gesturing at her door, her head a little to one side, watching him, the hard grace of his stride pleasing to see.

"I'll help you out," he said, stepping into her room and, with a word, clearing it of servants. Left together, they stood a moment in restrained silence, neither quite sure how to proceed, he not wanting to tip his hand by moving on her too abruptly, she determined to win him, heart and soul, this time before giving in to the impetuosity of passion that was making her weak as she looked up at him. What she saw in his face was a bit terrifying. His eyes were fierce, his sensual lips were parted alluringly. Alone with him for the first time since she'd last left his bed, Justine felt, all at once, blushingly timid and shy. They both looked away at the same instant, she to her wrist as she undid a bracelet clasp, he about her room; the unexpected intimacy was charming but disconcerting. There was a beribboned sheer bed gown and peignoir draped suggestively over a chair. The sheets, invitingly turned back, were embroidered with tiny sprays of rosebuds, and there were mauve ribbons and roses on the lace fan that peeked from a half-opened drawer. The dressing table displayed a silver-backed brush and hand mirror, a silver-lidded butterfly-shaped box, and several monogrammed pink satin bags, some ribbon tied, that held lingerie and jewelry. Here, in this room among all her soft and pretty things, Justine seemed somehow a less formidable opponent than Nicholas had supposed.

"This little silver bottle," he said, lifting it from a table and caressing its fluted narrow throat, "is very old. It was made in Rajasthan, probably two hundred years ago, to hold *asha*. It's a liqueur flavored with saffron."

"Yes," she answered with a slight smile, "saffron from Kashmir, the costliest spice in the world." She hesitated to move, not trusting herself any nearer to him than she already was. "We are going to Rajasthan, you know, to Jaipur and then to Jodhpur, for the polo."

"Your father told me," he responded, sauntering about the room, running a finger along the edge of a little table, taking up a silk scarf. "I'm going to ride for him . . . with him. The best polo in the world is played there now." When he came to the armoire, the mirrored doors of which were a bit ajar, Justine flew across the room. Standing before it as though guarding a fortress, she reached behind her to fasten the catch. Her tasseled velvet robe had been hung there, even though it was far too warm for the Indian summer, and she'd been terrified that he'd see it.

"Just flimsies and such, personal things," she said by way of explanation as he'd looked at her perplexed. "I'd be embarrassed for a man to see them. You understand." She appealed with that little blush that so affected him. She was very close to him now, within his reach. Nicholas was acutely aware of it. The temptation of her tiny waist, the swell of bosom above it, the curve of hip below, was more than he could resist; and he did what he'd not planned on doing, reached out and drew her toward him, very gently, gazing into eyes that were fearful and curious both before he kissed her on the lips, slowly and deeply.

With a restraint she'd not ever imagined her self capable of, Justine held her body away from his this time and just rested her hands on his shoulders, then broke free and crossed the room to stand against the door and stare at him with the oddest look he'd ever seen.

"You better go," she said in a voice that was little more than a whisper, one that he found vaguely familiar as it teased his memory.

"Don't look so terror smitten, little girl." He shrugged, his own voice sultry and low. "I'm not in the habit of forcing virgin innocents, not unless they ask me to." He strode across the room, her scarf, she noticed, still twined about his hand, and was gone. When Justine sank weakly into a chair, she noticed something else and wondered if he had a little flag of hunter green velvet — the hem of her wrapper caught in the closet door.

* * *

When Nicholas reached his own room and placed the rose-scented scarf beside the velvet belt in one of his travel cases, memory stirred again, and unwittingly, unwillingly, he began to fall in love again with Justine Hawkes.

But of course he wouldn't admit to any such thing and by the time he stopped fighting it, three hearts had been broken, and he was sure he'd lost her forever.

Chapter Twenty-four

"Roweena McGlory has done it again, married for the *fifth* time," Anthony Jones reported. "Lady Molesworth and her groom, she asked us to tell you, will be joining us at Jodhpur. Message delivered." He and his brother were lunching with a large party in the ancient Buddhist caves of Bombay where a very elaborate meal had awaited them along with furniture, plates, silver, even carpets — everything needed to assure their comfort.

"Oh my! I don't look forward to seeing Eustace at all, and Roweena . . . she's something of a complainer," Justine explained to Daisy Havelock, the governor's daughter, a girl of about her own age. "But Anthony," she asked, with a hopeful smile, "perhaps they're really happy and in love. Molesworth can't have married her for her money. She hasn't any and neither has he; Count Zenga told us."

"That must be a bit of misinformation. Eustace is spending wildly, mostly on himself, though this little honeymoon jaunt to India is costing him a pretty penny," Anthony commented as he sketched the scene around him, with Justine, as usual, at the center of the picture.

"Well, I hope your friends expect the extraordinary heat and all the crawly things." Daisy giggled. "Spiders, earwigs, centipedes—all of extraordinary size, actually. I've grown used to it, the heat and all, but some never do." A pretty, baby-faced girl, Daisy enjoyed guiding her father's many visitors about the country she had grown to love.

"It seems that most of the English in India live far more extravagantly here than they possibly could at home." Gray Hawkes smiled at her. "Servants have servants, I see. Even horses and dogs have their own valets de chambre.

"I understand that when we travel to Rajasthan there will be a sizable entourage." Slade Hawkes finished a serving of tamarind chutney and bananas, aware of the flirtatious byplay between his daughter and, it appeared, both Jones brothers.

"Yes, yes, jolly right," Governor Havelock assured him. "Fifty elephants, each with a mahout, easily a hundred camels, too, and as many horses, plus the messengers, tent pitchers, cooks, water carriers . . . a sizable contingent, indeed. But if you will go for tiger, you must be attended properly."

"Our ultimate destination is Jodhpur of course," Nicholas said. Seated between Daisy and Justine, he was sleekly handsome, captivating, and undeniably charming. He knew a great deal about India, something that very favorably impressed his hosts and Justine and her father as well.

"You must see at least one elephant hunt. It's rather like a roundup of horses in your American

215

West, I'm told," Captain Duff said, wiping his brow in the damp intense heat. "The wild tuskers are driven into a stockade and later tamed with the help of domesticated elephants. It's quite a remarkable process."

"I work with horses the same way," Nicholas commented. "I use a calm, older animal to help soothe the wild ones, at the start."

"I didn't know you tamed wild horses," Justine said with interest. "I've always wanted to see them running free as they were meant to, our mustangs, untouched and untamed."

"If you'll come home with us as I've asked you to before"—Tony smiled—"Nicholas will take you into the hills after the herds. I'll come, too, though I don't like to see them being run in, they're so terrified."

"I'll come! I accept your invitation, Anthony," Justine promptly responded.

"But first you must accept mine," Captain Cavendish insisted, "to hunt black buck with cheetahs. The cats are hooded like falcons. Close to the prey, their blindfolds are pulled off and their speed is astounding. You must also see elephants fight, against each other, and rhinos, buffalos. To come to India and not see the Bengal Cavalry, among the best riders in the world, do their pig sticking and tent pegging is to miss a great deal."

"What I *really* want to see is the Paradise Garden, Shalimar. And, also the Taj Mahal. It's an edifice of love, it's said." Justine felt Nick's eyes on her then.

"Twenty thousand men worked twenty years to build the Taj," he said. "Of course, Shah Jehan's memorial to his beloved wife bankrupted the Mughal Empire. Eventually, he was imprisoned by his son and died incarcerated, of an overdose of aphrodisiac. Love," Nicholas added, "can be dangerous."

"I'll try to remember that, Mr. Jones," Justine answered. His expression at that moment was so dark and threatening, she was more than a little inclined to believe exactly what he said.

She stood then as everyone prepared to explore the ____ before the return trip to Government H___se, but her father's hand on her arm held her back for a moment. Nicholas and Anthony waited also neither, apparently, willing to be parted from her even briefly.

"I've discovered something that will interest all three of you, I think," Slade said. "I knew your father, gentlemen, years ago. Quinn Jones and I fought together during the War Between the States, and later, he met his wife, your mother, at Silver Hill one lovely summer day. Caitlin McGlory Jones was Billy's niece," he told Justine.

"The one who died so young and left—" She clasped a hand over her mouth.

"Left my father so desolate he was never the same again. I think he'd have built her the Taj Mahal if it hadn't already been done," Nicholas said before he stalked off.

"Nicky's always felt it was Mother's fault somehow, what happened to our father, to all of us after . . ." Anthony paused with a helpless look.

217

"Well, but . . . that makes us some sort of relatives of Roweena, then. Seconds cousins, is it?" he asked with a comic grimace.

"Afraid so." Slade couldn't help but laugh. "But think of the bright side. Your newfound great-uncle, Billy McGlory, is a man in a million, and so eager to meet you he almost joined me on this trip. Now you and your brother will *have* to visit Silver Hill just in case you weren't planning to already." He winked at Justine.

"They've been invited for Christmas," she said, slipping her arm through Anthony's, but really wanting to go after Nicholas whose pained expression had gone straight to her heart.

"Have a care, Justine. Those caves are . . . dangerous," Slade said with concern as she hurriedly turned away.

She found Nicholas leaning under a great outcropping of rock, looking over the plains far below, the hot air shimmering over them, a hot wind rising from them. Anthony immediately set up an easel some distance from his brother and went to work.

"I'm sorry about . . . everything," Justine said to Nick, undoing the top button of her blouse and patting her temples with a handkerchief.

"Why should you be?" he asked, turning to her, his voice low, his rapacious eyes devouring her, the need in him so apparent, so terrible, a little cry escaped her, the sound carried off by the wind. "It's nothing to do with you."

"I'd want to comfort anything as hurt as you seem," she said, and he almost believed her for the briefest moment. He wanted to but . . . wouldn't.

"We're going exploring," he called. With a quick wave to Anthony, he grabbed her wrist and led her off toward the caves. They plunged into a cool dark cavern, followed a steep incline until it turned a corner and they were out of sight of the entrance. Justine felt herself pressed back against the wall; his mouth met hers, and she responded instantly to his desperation. Her arms went about him, drawing him to her, her body arching. His hands were at her throat, her breasts, then delving beneath her skirt, parting her thighs before his knee came between them.

"There's only one way any woman will ever comfort me," he rasped, and she said, "Yes," and drew his mouth down to hers again and again, all the while thinking, No! Not here, not in the dark again, but in sunlight with no secrets or deceptions, with everything open between us, for better or worse . . . forever or for just one perfect moment.

"Let me comfort you . . . any way . . . at all," she added very softly, and he held her to him for an instant longer before he straightened up and stepped away.

He glowered at her in the gloom, puzzled, and then, when he strode off, Nicholas wondered at how their positions seemed to have changed, reversed completely. She, the great tease, had offered herself up to him without resistance, and he, the rake who prided himself on his invulnerability to sentiment, had declined her generous offer, as if he'd been held back by some antiquated chivalrous restraint. She'd played right into his hands and he'd let her get away. Well, she'd have been cold comfort anyway, that type always were, he insisted to himself, deciding to take up his seduction again later in more propitious surroundings.

When they all left Bombay the next morning in a huge caravan, Nicholas had again become his charming, attentive self. He seemed always to be near Justine whenever she looked about, offering his cupped hands when she was ready to mount her Arabian mare, lifting her down at each stop, holding her chair at table, spreading his jacket at the base of a tree when the caravan paused for rest.

Anthony was close also but remote and dreamy as he filled pad after pad with sketches of the countryside, of the flowers and plants and birds all about them, capturing color and fine line as his work grew more precise and more perfectly detailed. All the while he worked he puffed on an ivory-bowled pipe and smiled at Nicholas and Justine who both were captured in almost every drawing he did.

"Where did you find that flower?" he asked one afternoon, a week into their excursion, when Nicholas and Justine, resting their horses in the late-day heat, joined him in a covered camel cart that had just been cooled down with a rose-water wash.

"Oh . . . Nicholas gave it to me," Justine answered self-consciously. "Pink powder puff it's called," she added, handing it to Tony as though it meant little to her, the gesture a lie.

"It will soon wilt in this heat," Daisy Havelock said. "Everything here does. One feels boiled to rags, doesn't one?" The girl, who did some sketching herself, had taken up a friendship with Anthony, who often lent her the tools of his trade—the soft pastel chalks he kept in a finely polished wood box, and his sable brushes and watercolor paints from Sennelier in Paris, who also mixed colors for Cézanne.

"I've never been bothered by the heat overly much," Justine said, looking down at Daisy's pad on which a poor likeness of Anthony was drawn, only his shoulder-length hair and the long mustache he'd recently grown making him identifiable at all.

"This climate's been the destruction of more than one Englishwoman. Lady Dalhousie, whose husband was governor here some time ago, was sent home in shattered health and died on shipboard within sight of England. So tragic. Char Canning, the first Vicereine, had been here nearly six years when she succumbed to Purnea fever after a trip through the forest in the wet season. She was to go home the next month. Lady Canning also sketched," Daisy added in a very funereal tone as Anthony and Justine exchanged glances and he began to draw her yet again, this

221

time in miniature.

"Got any other happy stories for us, Daisy?" Nicholas asked, his head lolling back, his half-lidded eyes on Justine opposite him.

"Oh, indeed!" Daisy answered with the greatest seriousness. "There was Lady Alice, marchioness of . . ."

Justine heard no more, just sat back, languid and longing, furtively glancing at Nicholas and wondering how much longer she'd be able to hold herself from him when he was there, so close, always, night and day. Her thoughts turned passionate as she sank into voluptuous imaginings, and Anthony, not realizing what he did, captured that quality in her, the soft yearning that was in her face for anyone to see, if he chose to. But Tony, with deliberate, obstinate blindness, didn't choose to acknowledge it, not yet anyway. And Nick? He didn't choose to, either.

Chapter Twenty-five

Things changed drastically between Nicholas and Justine in the tiger jungles of Baroda. It was after the first hunt, after she'd saved his life and decided he owed her something for her trouble, if not love, then it's approximation or a moment's pretense of it anyway. That was the least he could do, she told him.

"I was planning to seduce you anyway," he said gruffly when she came to his tent late at night and found him smoking in the half-dark, still booted though shirtless, his head thrown back, his legs stretched out in front of him. He tossed away the cigarette and offered her his hand. She took it and brought it to her lips, then guided it to her breast, hard-tipped and firm beneath her fragile muslin bed gown. He stood and drew her to him, his eyes closed, as her hands played over his chest and drifted along his muscled arms . . . to the silver buckle at his waist.

"Wait," he said, sinking back into the camp chair and watching her hungrily, what he could see of her, mostly flowing tiger-blond hair caught in the single shaft of moonlight that penetrated their enclosure. She knelt to pull off his boots, and when she rose, he drew her over him to straddle his hips and then touched her, cautiously at first, gathering her breasts in his hands, tracing the long line of her elegant neck, the curve of ear, the swell of cheek. By the time his long sure hands encircled her waist there was an urgency in his every gesture as an image took shape in his mind, and, astoundingly, it was his midnight lover there with him in the flesh—such beautiful flesh. And he *knew*.

"You!" he said, then cursed quietly until her kiss silenced him and his hands traced over her again, following each swell and turning, her exquisite sensitivity heightened beyond control by his masterful manipulations and her own long-checked passions. "Deceiver!" He laughed a low, mean sound, as he stood and let her slide from his lap, catching her up before she fell and setting her on her feet in the shaft of moonlight, then prowling around her like a jungle animal, a wild tiger, before he moved away. She heard him rummaging about out of her sight.

"What are you doing?" she asked, almost afraid of him now but wanting him too, not knowing whether to search him out in the dark or run while she still could. He stepped out of the shadows with something in his hand, and before she was aware of it, he'd tied her tasseled velvet belt about her wrists.

"Don't move," he hissed, tucking a pistol into his belt and an ivory-handled riding crop into one of the boots that he'd pulled on again. In one fast motion, he swept off her feet and strode from the tent.

"What are you doing?" she repeated.

"Tormentor! You should be thrashed for what you've done," was his answer.

"You wouldn't," she said.

"Wouldn't I?" he asked, and his icy laugh silenced her. She buried her face against his throat, slipped her bound wrists over his head, encircling his neck. Wanting never to let go, wanting him desperately, she gave herself up to whatever would come, whatever in his awesome anger he might do. She had deceived him and she had no choice, now. She couldn't fight him and win. She didn't want to.

They had left the camp and entered the tiger woods, where moonlight fell in silvery pools between the wavering palms and where every shadow was a lurking menace, every sound a threat. He walked a long way before he set her down, and in the steamy heat of the night, she trembled at his frosty, threatening grin.

"Up," he said, gesturing with the riding crop at a rope ladder. It led, Justine knew, to a *machan*, a platform, set in a treetop high above the ground. From it, that hunting animal, man, had the advantage over that other great hunting animal, the tiger. She climbed, catching her bare foot once in the hem of her gown, and when she reached the top he was right behind her.

"Well?" she said bravely, looking directly at him. "Now what do you intend?"

"Beguiler," he whispered. "You ask me that, do you? Don't you know?" She moved away from him a step, as far as she could in the small space, and shook her head, terrified now, the look in his dark eyes so rapacious, so cruel, she was stunned. "Take off the gown," he ordered and she did at once, lifting it over her head and letting it fall. Then she stood in moonlight, not trembling any longer, her long lithe limbs still. At his gesture, she turned, feeling his eyes touch her

225

now as his hands had so often before, tracing each line and curve and swell of her lovely body. And when she'd come full circle, he opened his arms to her, and, sighing, she stepped into their enfolding circle, his bare body smooth and hard against hers, the muscle swells familiar now beneath her exploring fingers.

"I'm going to make love to you in full moonlight, bright as day, and again in dawnlight and at high noon, one day soon. In the shadowless glare of the midday sun, I'm going to watch you every minute," he said, "look into your eyes . . . see all the sinuous twistings and turnings that responsive body can be made to endure. The curl of your shoulder, the roll of your hip, all the undulations here . . . and there." He kept talking and touching as if polishing a marble sculpture as he moved all around her, his lips at her nape, then at her throat, at her breasts. "And I'm going to hear your voice while I'm doing that . . . while I'm making love to you. Out here, where no one else can hear you, you're going to say every word you didn't speak on all those nights, my silent lover. You'll make every sigh and cry and plea you never made, utter every love word you never said before. Or else I will use the crop, I swear," he growled, sinking into the softly mounded bamboo leaves and pulling her after him.

And then, embowered in the rustling tree, drenched in jasmine-scented moonlight, he made love to her, and she to him, uninhibitedly with primordial carnality and fierce tenderness and all the while her soft voice caressed him, whispering in his ear, saying all he wanted to hear, and her lovely tinkling silvery laugh rose triumphantly on the hot night air.

* * *

Nicholas wasn't in love, far from it, he insisted to himself. What he'd done, and would certainly do again, was all for his brother's sake. Back in his tent in the early morning, as the camp began to come alive, he sank into a canvas tub of water and carefully peeled an orange with a razor-sharp bayonet, the skin unwinding in a single long curl, the sections of the sweet, moist fruit parting as he thought of Justine, of how she'd come to him virgin-pure that first time, as dewy fresh as a spring day, as sweet as any nectar.

The girl was even more devious than he'd suspected, offering herself to him in the dark all those . . . extraordinary nights in France, all the while leading Tony on and proclaiming her love for yet a third man who, somewhat unbelievably Nicholas had to admit, didn't love her at all. But then, when it came to Justine, he shared his brother's deliberate blindness. Nicholas wouldn't allow himself to even suppose that he might be the errant lover who owned her heart. So, how then did he explain her behavior? Clearly, she was trying, as Roweena had predicted she would, to chalk up a double victory. Justine wanted twins, brothers, both groveling in the dust at her feet. That must be it.

Nicholas rose from the tub, sending a wash of water over the edge, and his man handed him a thick long cotton towel. Scowling, he twisted it about his waist as he sat at the table that had been laid at the center of the tent and gulped down a yogurt drink flavored with cumin that was served in a large brass beaker.

But, she had saved his life and surely he owed

227

her something more than the one night of love she'd asked for and gotten, even if that one night had been beyond anything they had experienced before the tiger hunt had changed his plans.

They'd gone out onto the plain beyond the woods just before sunset, riding high in an elaborate *howdah* atop an elephant, swinging a trunk that was painted saffron yellow, its great flapping ears a pale green. The mahout had urged the great beast forward to keep up with a long chain, a hundred or more elephants, moving in pincer formation through a sea of tall grass deep into tiger territory. Rifles were spitting incessantly from the *howdahs* at any movement in the teeming grass as the hunt, accompanied by the clanging of cymbals and the thunder of drums, followed the beaters who drove every living thing before them out into the open—deer and antelope, rhinoceros and buffalo, cheetahs and other small cats, hundreds of terrified creatures all running for there lives.

"*Kubudar! Kubudar!* Take care!" someone called and then they heard the peacock's call, too, its tiger cry that warned them, though not quite soon enough, that one of the great hunting cats was close, too close, in fact rising from the grass with a roar, jaws wide, magnificent paws reaching out to swipe at their *mahout* who froze in terror.

Nicholas came to the man's aid without even thinking, sliding to the ground and then turning to catch the rifle Justine tossed down to him, not having to be asked, knowing exactly what was needed. Before he could take aim, the raging animal turned on him crouching to spring, and it was then Justine fired her first barrel, rolling the cat over. Her second barrel went off at the same instant as Nick's gun, the two shots finishing the magnificent beast just as it rose to its feet again.

It was the only time Justine had lifted her weapon that day, or any day, and it all happened so quickly, neither she nor Nicholas had time to do anything but react. But in the aftermath, Justine trembled violently as he stood over the tiger, still as a statue, cradling his rifle, his legs, partially covered by tall gaiters, planted far apart, his tan field shirt, opened to the waist and sweat-soaked.

"Thanks," he had said, nothing more, not then.

"Ever at your service, sir," she had answered, removing her pith helmet and wiping her brow. "Pity we had to kill the tiger, I think. He is so beautiful."

"Count Zenga accused you of being overly sentimental about animals and I think he was right," Gray told her. "These creatures terrorize the countryside here, raking at elephants, clawing mahouts, even pulling riflemen out of their howdahs. These aren't the stray kittens you're always picking up in New York, you know."

"That's Justine," Slade Hawkes said, resting a steadying hand on his daughter's shaking shoulder, "all cool courage and tough enough to ride the hair off a thousand-pound polo pony, but she'll burst into tears over an injured robin. Good shot." He smiled.

"The trophy's yours," Justine told Nicholas. "I don't want it."

"Thanks again." He smiled.

And that night she'd come to him and the next one as well, because he'd left her tasseled velvet belt dangling from his tent pole. They'd dressed for dinner in the jungle, as usual, British officers in uniform, the other men in light flannels, the ladies elegantly gowned and jeweled; and that was how she appeared to him, stepping quickly through his tent flap to stand still, taking the time on her second visit to look about. The tent contained a table and chairs, a wash stand, the canvas tub, large leather pouches of water, and a bed piled with pillows.

"Undress me," she said, and he moved toward her as she loosened her hair, shaking out a fall of gold.

"Now you astonish me," he said, when he'd done as she asked and she stood before him in the lamplight wearing only her opals that flashed green and blue and red. And she did astonish him as no woman ever had before.

The night after he went to her. It was nearly moonset when he roused her from sleep, stepping beneath the veil of mosquito gauze about her bed.

"I'm on fire," he said hoarsely, striking a light and looking into her dream-sodden eyes that began to glow like molten emeralds.

He took pleasure, and gave it, quickly, then lay back to watch her when she rose to get him some refreshment. "Don't," he said as she leaned over, on her way back to him, to extinguish the candle. "Never in the dark, not again, not after your wily tricks. I want to see who's sharing my bed."

"It's *my* bed. But wouldn't you know me in the

dark?" she asked archly, with false indignation.

"I'd know you anywhere," he said roughly, raising a hand so that she stood still where she was. "You know, a mare is considered beautiful when all her parts are like yours, and when they are proportioned, one to the other . . ." He rose and crossed the small space between them. "Proportioned one to the other so that"—he enfolded her waist—"so that they are perfectly suited to her work, like yours. You *are* perfectly beautiful."

"And . . . what is the work"—she led him toward the bed again—"that I'm so perfectly proportioned for?"

"I'll have to show you again," he said, "if you really don't know by now."

Nicholas himself would never really know the exact moment he fell everlastingly in love with Justine, when it was precisely that she became more than a transient, pleasant distraction for him. It had already happened when they broke camp next morning on the last leg of their trip to Jodhpur. But he wouldn't really admit he was in love until all the damage had been done.

Justine though, was giddy with love, so drunk with happiness that anyone who cared to look could see. Anthony became vaguely aware of something different about her when she threw her arms about his neck in an excess of exuberance that morning and then slipped her hand into his for a moment when she asked to see his latest sketches. She took her place at the breakfast table, around which the whole safari was gathered, some of the men already drinking whiskey and soda, Tony one of them.

"There's more money spent on hunting and racing and shooting in Britain than on the Royal Navy. In my opinion," Governor Havelock pronounced, "that's a mistake, what with all the fuss in the world these days, the Boers in South Africa and all the rest. Bumpers," he added, raising his glass in a toast.

"There are better uses for wealth than sport or war," Gray said, pulling uncomfortably at his tie. "There's that fellow Diesel with his new engine, and this wireless sound box that talks and the new art . . . Gaugin and Van Gogh and—"

"And Anthony," Justine smiled as she kept looking over her shoulder for Nicholas who hadn't yet appeared.

"Wireless or not my dear," Lady Havelock interjected, "in some states of India, one steps off the train and back into a positively medieval world where a prince controls the lives of his people entirely."

"And if he is a self-indulgent prince," Captain Duff said, "it goes hard with everyone. The Maharaja of Patiala has a passion for pearls and pedigreed dogs. Those animals eat better than his subjects do. In Hyderabad, the prince has forty wives, kept in strict purdah—that's veiled in a harem, you know, very costly to maintain."

"But that's not true in Jodhpur," Nicholas interrupted, taking the place beside Justine vacated by his brother, who'd gone off to get his drawings. "The Rajputs, feudal princes of northern India, with jewels beyond number and imaginings, are of the Hindu military caste. They practiced the kingly sport of war for centuries. Their history traces back fourteen hundred years to a warrior desert tribe that claimed direct descent from

232

the Moon and the Sun. The Maharajas of these city kingdoms are still beyond all rules but their own."

"Fascinating as their history is, it's their legendary equestrian brilliance that's brought us here — and their magnificently bred horses," Slade Hawkes said. "By the way, I've heard the state of Jodhpur referred to as the Sparta of India. Is it a fitting description?"

"The Regent King of Jodhpur, Pratrap Singh, sleeps on a plank bed and always has," Captain Cavendish said. "At one time, after he'd broken both legs in a fall, and had difficulty mounting his horse, the man spent thirty-six hours straight in the saddle on march. He's the best horseman in the world, an outstanding person, not called the Lion of Glory for nothing. You will all meet him quite soon now."

Chapter Twenty-six

More than a hundred elephants, carrying glittering golden howdahs, swayed with lumbering grace across the amber plains of Rajasthan traveling north, upcountry toward Jodhpur.

From her high vantage, Justine could see the whole caravan—elephants, camels, horses, servants and bearers—spread out behind them like a mobile city passing through the desert. She shared her perch with Tony and Nick. The twins, it seemed to her, had expanded their exclusive group of two to include her, and that boded well, she thought, for the future. In return, in appreciation, in her intense blinding happiness, she showered Tony with what she meant to be friendly, sisterly affection.

But he, too, was blinded by love, and read something altogether different in her easy manner. Basking in her smiles, he began again to secretly plan a future very different from the one she was envisioning.

It was Nicholas, of course, who filled Justine's dreams, though he'd never so much as whispered the words 'future' or 'love.' He just concentrated, with a kind of moon-blind absorption, on her. Justine. She so dazzled him that, he was aware of little but the delectable, lustful cravings they shared. And so, benighted by love as they were, all three, the stage on which they would play out their parts was set for a tragedy none of them anticipated.

Through long seething days in the desert heat, Justine and Nicholas stoked their own inner heat with flashing glances and secret, stolen kisses, the unavoidable brushing of hands and grazing of knees and thighs as they traveled, always side by side, on horseback or in the confines of carriage or howdah. In sheltering darkness, they came together in a near-violent conflagration, and renewed desire curled in them both again and again all night long. They slept little, but neither suffered in the least until the caravan began to travel by night because of the desert heat. Camped in daylight, no secure assignation could be arranged, and as they approached Jodhpur, both were in a melting fever of thwarted passion.

"There," Nicholas said, pointing into the distance and glancing at Justine beside him, smiling at her with unabashed lechery. "Look."

Rising before them in the heat-shimmering dawn light were the white houses and temples of the city clustered at the base of a walled stronghold fortress, a seven-gated medieval bastion perched on a pinnacle of rock that rose four hundred feet above the plains, its towers silhouetted against the morning sky.

Soon after their first sight of Jodhpur, the travelers were ceremoniously greeted by Sir Pratrap Singh, the Regent King who came out into the desert to meet them, at the head of a troop of cavalry, the prancing horses in silver harness, he himself attired in an embroidered white silk jacket and leggings, a jeweled turban, and ropes of huge pearls. With him came the bearers of the state umbrellas and of the peacock fans, and fifty elephants panoplied in gold-embroidered velvet, their trunks studded with rubies, their tusks encased in silver sheaths. The faces of the great creatures were painted in shades of yellow and green, their huge earrings dangled almost to the ground, their necklaces of silver bells jingled, and their anklets of gold flashed in sunlight.

"Such lordly splendor," Justine whispered with awe.

Nicholas nodded as they rode forward to the sound of beating drums and the blare of trumpets. "But it makes me almost long for a simple cottage in Normandy or . . . somewhere."

The procession passed through the lower city, sun-drenched now, where preparations for a festival were underway. The streets and bazaars of Jodhpur were a carnival of sight and sound. Women moved hurriedly about in long flowing dresses of rainbow colors — vermilion and cerise and turquoise — many carrying burnished brass bowls and pitchers, their rows of metal bracelets clicking. Dogs and children, and free-roaming chickens were everywhere, as were camels with heavy-lidded eyes, their turbaned drivers wearing long curving jeweled swords.

The travelers dismounted from the elephants, using silver ladders set against the sides of the huge creatures that had, with great heavings and lurchings, dropped to their knees. The ascent to the fortress of Jodhpur was continued on foot or in litters and gilded palanquins, up along a narrow steep path that climbed past eight stories of the fabled royal palace with its fretted jalousies, carved balconies, and thousands of windows.

The main gates of the fortress itself swung wide as the Regent's guests neared them, their path now softened by what seemed an endless carpet of royal blue that stopped at last at an open balcony jutting out into the air as if it were hung in space on invisible threads. Warm wind whistled, hawks circled above, calling, as the Regent finished his official speech of welcome and Nick leaned to Justine.

"Here . . . later," he whispered, and she smiled.

"Your daughter and her young man, they are an enchanted couple, are they not?" Sir Pratrap Singh said to Slade Hawkes when the speeches were done and his guests had been greeted, one by one. The Regent was a man of middle height, slim and erect, with sharply etched features and dark, observant eyes. His natural reserve had softened once the ceremonies had ended, and he had smiled warmly at Justine and Nicholas before they'd been escorted away to their rooms in the palace below. "I have a daughter of my own," Singh went on, "and if only she could be so happily in love, a great sadness would be lifted from my heart."

"Oh?" Slade queried, saying nothing of his

concerns for his own daughter's happiness, but fully aware, as she seemed not to be, of the difficult situation she'd gotten herself into this time, having a pair of brothers—twins at that—both helplessly in love with her.

"Yes, my Indira is a rebellious girl, betrothed to one man and in love with another who is . . . unacceptable."

"Justine was to be married in the spring but she broke it off," Slade commented.

"Indira blames me for her predicament, because I did not arrange a marriage for her at sixteen but instead let her live the life of a modern young woman."

"I, too, have been told that I am at fault, that I should have persuaded Justine to marry long ago." Slade nodded with understanding.

"Ah, but we will not talk all day of the difficulties of daughters. We will talk of polo. After you've had a rest, will you join us on the field below, sir? We have been eagerly awaiting the arrival of the notorious American 'cowboys' who have so changed our ancient game. It's the oldest game in the world as you know." Singh smiled warmly. "We shall see if all your speed and recklessness have really changed it for the better as I've been told."

As the women of the visiting party followed a guide up and down twisting stairs, past room after room, through a disorienting mazelike complexity of chambers and halls, Justine's heart sank as she wondered how Nick would ever find her in such a place.

"Rather like Theseus in the labyrinth," Daisy said. "We should have brought a ball of twine so that we could find our way back."

"These Rajput palaces are all asymmetrical and warrenlike, with their secret rooms and blind turnings. It's not accidental at all, though. It's part of a complex Hindu view of life. There's a wonderful lavish exuberance in all the decorative detail," Lady Havelock explained as they turned a corner and paused before a pair of tall doors of hammered gold elaborately embellished, as were all the columns and ceilings and walls of the palace, with detailed reliefs and carvings; these of tigers in all poses and moods, regally reclining, hunting, kittenish.

"Lady Singh and her daughter will greet you now and offer some refreshment," they were told as the doors swung inward. They passed through a series of antechambers before reaching a vaulted hall with windows and balcony that looked out over hundreds of miles of amber desert.

The room was decorated with rosewood and satinwood and calamander, the carved furnishings surrounded by piles of pillows, exquisitely engraved tea chests, and round tea tables. At one end of the room was a circle of ivory-framed chairs and footstools with slender reedlike legs, and waiting there were Lady Singh and Indira. The mother was a plain woman and gravely sweet in manner, the daughter a beauty with golden olive skin and immense dark eyes. Beside them, as if enthroned on her tall ebony chair, was Roweena, who actually seemed to be offering a suggestion of a smile. There was a flurry of introductions and greetings and kisses in the air and exclamations over the sudden surprising Molesworth marriage, and then, as teas were carried in on round brass trays, the ladies settled comfortably and began making those first somewhat formal explorations and exchanges that led to friendships, but their reticence quickly disappeared for, as diverse a group as they were, they found much in common.

"I shall never, never leave India," Daisy Havelock said with impassioned warmth. "I adore India, everything from the paradise of Kashmir nestled in the Himalayas all the way to the Cape, Land's End at Comorin in the south," she told Justine and Roweena. "That's where three oceans meet with much foam and thunder. There's a simplicity in the wildness of nature one finds that soothes the soul."

"Don't you miss England?" Indira asked.

"I could never fit in again with all those girls raised in country houses, adoring their ponies and dogs and despising their governesses and their brothers." Daisy laughed. "Besides, I never really saw the sun until I left there. One doesn't in England, you know, not *real* sun. This is home for me, really."

"There are many such English as you, Daisy, who prefer our country"—Indira smiled—"while I long so for England. There, I was free to live as I liked and I enjoyed the garden parties, the

240

dancing, and the cross-country rides. I sit a horse as well as any Irish girl, I must tell you that myself." She laughed.

"Ah, but what my daughter did not understand on her travels, I'm afraid," Lady Singh said, shaking her head, "is that freedom involves risk. Now she does not understand that a broken heart is of no greater consequence than the fall of an acorn to the ground. She will flounder on the rock of parental authority if she goes against custom and defies her father's command.

"But, understand, we are modern here in Jodhpur," Lady Singh quickly added. "For the most part we have given up purdah. Indira and I do not keep to a harem though tonight, in the Thousand-Columned Hall of the palace, we will watch the festivities of the Durbar from behind our screens on the balcony. Only men are allowed to attend."

"Only men?" Justine asked with dismay.

"But will we get to see the jewels?" Roweena asked, for the first time showing real interest in the conversation. "I've been told, Justine," she went on eagerly, "that up in the Royal Treasury in the fortress above are heaps of gold and silver, thousands upon thousands of immense pearls, daggers with jade handles, ancient shields encrusted with rubies. I understand" — Roweena coughed with agitated excitement — "that there is a pair of dancing slippers cased in diamonds. The secreted wealth of centuries is there and yet there's nothing to equal your lucky black opals."

"Do you know that we Hindus also endow

jewels with magical powers?" Indira asked Justine. "Tell me, why are your opals so incomparable and so lucky?"

"Because there are no others like them," Roweena answered with pride, as if the opals belonged to her.

"For every great stone there is a legend of power or love or treachery," Indira said. "Some gems can be used to foretell the future, some to protect against lightning and thunder and other natural disasters. Jasper stems bleeding. The agate, placed on the eye, will aid those who find difficulty in welcoming sleep, the bright red ruby banishes dark forebodings and brings joy. In the past some warriors have thought that embedding blood red rubies in their flesh would protect them against wounds from swords or spears or guns, and would keep their blood from flowing. Would you like to know our legend of the opal?"

Indira turned to Justine, who nodded.

"It is said that one day a poor musician went into the woods and heard a melody of unearthly beauty. The singer, he discovered, was a golden bird with emerald eyes who told the poor, gentle man to cut a reed in those woods and make a flute and he, too, would be able to warble melodies of unearthly beauty." Indira's eyes had become vacant as she sat cross-legged, hands on her knees, her melodic voice the only sound in the room. "The musician cut his reed and made a flute, and when he put the instrument to his lips, divine music issued forth, soft as moonbeams on a lake . . . dripping sweet as honey . . . so sad it

242

caused tears to flow in all who heard. The musician went from village to village and his fame grew and spread far and wide. One day, he was summoned by a Maharaja to vie against the court musicians who sang and drummed and played their harps and cymbals, ignoring the poor man but only until he began to play. And when he did, what came from his flute was the song of songs in the language of love, like cascades of rubies and diamonds and pears falling into golden bowls. When he had done, the Maharaja offered the poor man a kingdom and his daughter and riches uncounted. 'Sire,' was the answer, 'I am poor, but by divine grace I am a musician, no beggar. I gratefully decline thy gifts and thy daughter.' 'Surely you are richer than I,' said the Maharaja, 'for thou art freed of all desire.'

"Soon the gods themselves sent for the musician and when he played for them they encircled him as cobras surround a snake charmer, and this time, when the musician had done, the gods placed in his hands a gem that held all the harmonies and melodies of his music in clear color that was ever changing, beautiful, imperishable— the opal, beautiful and luminous as a perfect song."

"Indira! Such a lovely story!" Justine sighed. "Have you one about the turquoise, perhaps?"

"The god of storms and clouds fell in love with a beautiful mortal, and when he lifted her to the heavens, he left behind, as consolation for the girl's father, a blue stone the color of sky in springtime, vivid and flawless, the turquoise. I have many such legends that I will tell you, Justine, but soon it will be time for polo. I don't know about you, but I wouldn't miss this match for anything."

Chapter Twenty-seven

"Polo is no woman's game, damn it!" Nick whispered furiously. "You'd consider riding in a rodeo, too, I suppose. A little bronc busting and barrel racing should be just to your taste." Justine, in jodhpurs, knee boots, and helmet, a mallet in one hand, pulled away from him as they left the stable to cross a field green as a magic carpet in the midst of the desert.

"I'm sure I'd love rodeo riding as much as I do polo. I didn't come all this way to watch, damn it!" she hissed back at him, her blunted spurs jingling as she walked. "Besides, I always play. And besides that, there're only three of you. You can't use Eustace. His hands are so hard he was damaging his pony's mouth. Sir Singh had to ask him to dismount. These horses are the best trained and bred anywhere in the world, too fine for Molesworth. I'm sure he's terrible at the game anyway."

"They have rules in this country, I'm sure. Women don't play games in public. Besides, you don't know the horses and . . . well, I want to win fair and square. You'll inhibit the opposition. They'll hold back because you're . . . smaller."

"That's their concern and none of mine, I assure you. My greatest talent is that I can ride any horse," Justine insisted as the ponies for the first chukker were led out, their tails tightly braided and their ankles bound. "Father," she said huffily, her face charmingly flushed as she went over to Slade, hands on her hips. "I am playing, am I not?" He didn't answer, not wanting to get into this particular confrontation. If Nicholas Jones had serious intentions about Justine, he'd best learn now how headstrong she could be.

"She's too good a rider for this rough-and-tumble. No one can sit a horse properly in this game." Nick set his helmet on his head and glared at her. "She couldn't ride badly if she wanted to."

"But she's been at this game most of her life. You should have seen her, up on a wooden practice horse, swinging a mallet, almost before she could walk," Gray smiled.

"I trained on a bicycle, too," Justine told Nick proudly. "One Father had specially built for me. And then he bought the bicycle factory, but that's another story."

"Justine has the eye and all the aggressive instincts anyone needs for polo." Slade smiled. "She always does just fine, and it appears Singh's daughter is going to play, so . . ." Indira, in jodhpurs and knee pads, her hair dangling in a long black braid from beneath her helmet, waved from the opposite side of the field.

"That settles it," Justine said with a self-congratulatory smile, running off to talk to her friend. "You didn't tell me you were playing," she exclaimed to Indira.

"You didn't tell me, either, but I knew you would. I used you as an excuse to Father."

"And I used you, too," Justine said looking

over at Nick. "So we're even."

"Justine rides short. She stands in the stirrups, almost the whole time and she's very feisty," Slade told Nick.

"That's to be expected, of course." Nick shrugged, feeling he'd been manipulated but not sure exactly how it had been done.

"She's very competitive and . . . well, reckless, but best of all," Gray commented, "she's awfully high-spirited. Even so, she never gets hurt. I've had plenty of broken ribs and one pretty serious concussion, but not Justine with her luck."

About a half an hour later, when Nicholas knelt over the motionless form of Justine, so small and fragile-seeming in the middle of that vast green carpet, his eyes would meet Gray's and they'd both recall those words with perfect clarity.

Justine had done very well, just as Gray and her father had said she would, through most of the first half, her endurance making up for her lack of sheer strength. She was fast, clever and agile, her upper body twisting and turning as she repeatedly reached for the ball. She was a fine sight, Nick had to agree, a beautiful hundred-pound woman atop a magnificent thousand pounds of horseflesh running, more often than not, at full gallop. Both these superb examples of their respective species were having a wonderful time when Justine, trying to score for the second time, leaned out of the saddle, racing downfield, her right arm fully extended back and up for an offside forehand drive. It was then that an opposing player, the one guarding her, came galloping up for a ride-off. As she made contact with the ball, he got his knee under hers and did what he'd been trying to do since the game began. He unseated her and she went down hard and lay very very still.

As the incident was happening, Nick's back was turned. Not wanting to waste even a second in a fast game that allowed no time-outs, he was in the process of switching from an injured horse to a sound one without even bothering to dismount. As he swung about to reenter the fray, the first thing he saw was the deathly still form of Justine at midfield. With a terrible roar, he raced to her and reached her before anyone else had moved, the silent observers all frozen in place, the other players pulling offside as a trumpet blast signaled the end of the chukker.

Nick's hands went all over that still body he knew so well, working slowly and carefully, searching for an injury, a break, a swelling — anything that would hint at what was wrong — and as he searched, his anger increased, waxing and building unbearably until, in those transforming seconds of devastating fear, just before he lifted her in his arms, all the fury he was feeling turned to love so desperate and overwhelming even he knew exactly what it was.

And finally, he admitted as much, to himself at least. When he stood holding her delicate, damaged form so gently against him, Nicholas Jones was proclaiming his love to all the world. He made public claim to Justine Hawkes there and then. There was no doubt in his mind, or in anyone else's after that moment, that the woman in his arms was his.

248

It was apparent to Justine's brother, Gray, who recognized Nick's expression of anguished tenderness for what it was — nothing less than love. Her father saw it, too. Slade let Nick take her off the field, following after.

The only one who didn't see — because he wasn't there, but should have been — was Anthony Jones.

Chapter Twenty-eight

The chamber women undressed Justine. They bathed her and placed her lightly gowned body at the center of an immense carved-ivory bed, then draped her with silken sheets. While one cooled her brow again and again, another waved a peacock-feather fan and a third flourished a fly whisk.

It wasn't until after the palace physicians had attended her and departed with puzzled, worried looks, until after her father and Gray had left her room, grim-faced with concern, that Nicholas could force himself to look again on the sight he so dreaded.

Justine's beautiful face was ghostly pale, he saw, even before he crossed the room to her bedside. Her lips were faintly blue-tinged and her breathing shallow as he approached hesitantly. And her eyes, those lovely laughing eyes, were closed and unmoving. As he leaned for a while at the tall bedpost, tracing its intricate carvings and staring at Justine, love and anger overwhelmed him, anger at himself for letting her play in a game that was always rough, but especially so when the competitors were the best in the world. Standing there, helpless to do anything for her,

Nicholas inwardly raged at the perversity of fate, at the cruel whims of the gods that had offered him an unexpected gift of love with one hand and seemed to be withdrawing it now with the other, before he'd even been able to tell Justine what he felt, how strong his feeling was.

All at once, it seemed to Nicholas the most important thing in the world that she know every fine shading and nuance of his love, that she hear every thought in his head, feel every emotion in his heart. He had to share his love with her, he who had always kept a shell about him, who had kept women, in one sense at least, at arm's length because, he'd thought, if one ever got through his defenses he was lost. Now, he didn't care. He wanted to be lost . . . and found, by Justine.

But if her eyes never opened? . . She'd never know and he'd never get over it, never forgive himself for having been so blind so long. Because, thinking back over the past months, he knew he'd loved her from that first morning he'd seen her, Triton's daughter riding the horses of the sea out of the dawn mist.

Hers was such an arresting beauty—that child-like softness in the curve of her cheek and in the tilt of her nose, but the invitation of her full lips was womanly warm. She was sensuality incarnate; timeless, elemental woman. Her mouth, always inclined to smile, her eyes bright with eager pleasure, she responded to air and sunlight like a flower; to the sky and the wind like a sea bird, free and soaring. And, like the natural and spontaneous creature she was, she'd known at once, at first sight what he'd just recognized. He recalled every kiss then, lived again through every night she'd loved him concealed by the cloak of darkness, as well as every moonlit, starlit, candlelit joining they'd had since she'd revealed herself. And all along, he'd been blind to what was shining before him, clear as crystal.

"For Tony's sake," he said aloud, startling the women at the bedside as he began to pace the room. But not just for Tony, he admitted. His own stubbornness and his distrustful nature had held him away from her, making him deny he felt anything at all beyond a temporary lustful appetite.

He struck the marble wall with such force he heard the crack of bone in his right hand, but he paid no attention, just dismissed the frightened women and took up a post at Justine's bedside, standing statuesque and unmoving through the long, hot afternoon.

Others tiptoed in and out—doctors taking her pulse, women wiping her brow, Lady Singh offering him teas and little cakes that he refused. He just stood at his post as if somehow he could rouse Justine by the sheer force of his formidable will.

The sky was pink-tinged with sunset, falcons still wheeling and circling about the palace and shrieking into the desert sky when Nick saw Justine's lids flicker, and then she looked right at him with those perfectly wonderful, long, slanting sea-foam eyes.

"What's wrong?" she asked.

"I think . . . I love you," he answered, his voice burred and rough timbred.

"Well . . . But that's nothing to look so grim about." She smiled.

"I never expected to say that to anyone and— How are you?"

"Fine," she said, laughter in her eyes, and jubilation.

"How do you know?" he asked.

"Because you love me," she said.

Neither of them moved. They just smiled at each other until she lifted her arms and then he was gathering her in his with immense gentleness.

"I love you," he said again, as if testing words that were foreign to his tongue, "and I thought I'd lost you before I could ever tell you so."

"Not a chance. You know what Gray always says about me." She brushed back the coil of dark hair that had fallen over his brow, a possessive gesture and an affectionate one.

"Terrier tenacity." He grinned.

Probably Justine had been winded by her fall, and perhaps she had struck the back of her head on the edge of a mallet, the physicians concluded. There was a swelling but no symptoms of concussion. The flush soon returned to her cheeks and her appetite returned with it, and after she'd eaten and drunk and celebrated her recovery with everyone, it was time to dress for the Durbar, the festival party, that would take place in the Thousand-Columned Hall of the Palace of Jodhpur.

"Let me tell Tony about . . . us," Nick said when he was about to quit Justine's room. "It'll be better if I do it in my own way." Relieved of what she had foreseen as a difficult duty, Justine agreed, and Nick went off in search of his brother, whom he hadn't seen since early that morning.

Once he'd been ensconced in his rooms, Anthony had, at his leisure, bathed and smoked three pipes of opium. His personal servant in Bombay had introduced him to the drug, and Anthony had come to appreciate its effect. It offered him a drowsy, furry calm and a softened, narrowed vision of the world. He'd taken interest suddenly in small details like birds' wings, finding their subtle variations pleasing. He'd filled pad after pad, when he wasn't concentrating on Justine, with accurate drawings of flower petals and leaf shapes and of the myriad finials, crenellations, and carvings in wood and stone that was so profuse in this country, especially in this Royal Palace of Jodhpur. Now, dressed and ready to get to work, Anthony stopped to go over the sketches he'd done since they'd all left Bombay, and when he had them spread out across the bed and over the woven tapestry carpet on the floor, he grouped the works by subject. He smiled to himself, studying Justine, whom he'd captured more perfectly and in finer detail these last days than ever before, his portraits of her at play and in repose becoming smaller in size so that they began to remind him of the Indian miniature pictures he admired for their precision and detail. He gazed with increasing interest at Justine, more often than not sketched with Nick beside her, and concentrated most intently on the series he'd done in the camel cart on those blistering days crossing the desert. It was then Tony began to see something wonderful. Justine was in love. There was a languorous sensuality about her. Her eyes were softly yearning and her lips were parted as if inviting his kiss. He'd been so intent on the work at hand, perhaps a bit befuddled by the opium, he'd missed that quality of warm readiness in her. But now that he recognized it as love, he would act at once, this very night after the Durbar. Blinded by his own love for Justine, Tony failed to notice the expression on Nick's face. But of course, and even more to the point, Anthony Jones trusted his brother implicitly.

Arranging for a palanquin, he left the palace for the city below.

Chapter Twenty-nine

The Durbar hall with its soaring, domed ceiling and crenellated columns, was ablaze with thousands of candles, their light falling on jewels beyond counting.

Sheltered in the balcony, wearing silks and satins, saris or bright trousers and long diaphanous veils, the women had dressed for each other, not for men, who would not see them. They looked down through small holes in the sheltering screens at the scene below. Food fragrant with spices — clove and cinnamon and cardamom and garlic-tasting asafetida — was served them on jewel-studded gold plates. Pipes and flutes and sitars played incessantly and repetitively, their volume and tempo increasing as the meal progressed.

Before dinner had begun, there were elephant-wrestling matches in the open court of the palace, ostrich races, jugglers, and snake charmers. Then attar of roses had been sprinkled about as the guests presented gifts to the Regent — brocades and shawls and clocks and pistols — and he, in turn, draped his male guests — women were excluded — with ropes of pearls to be worn throughout the banquet. Justine had seen this as she'd looked down at Nick who kept glancing up impatiently at the screened balcony. It was an agony for them to be apart. They'd been kept from each other's arms through most of the long desert crossing, and now, the custom of this country prevented them from sharing each other's company on a night when they had so much to talk about. Well, only one or two things, really. Justine smiled to herself. Love and the future.

Later, when the Regent gave a small private supper in his inner rooms, men and women were allowed to mingle, and Justine and Nick sat close to each other, only vaguely aware of the conversation going on about them.

"I have been to Paris," Sir Singh told his guests, the diamond plume on his turban wavering each time he turned his head. "I did not like it at all. The moral atmosphere is noxious. Only pleasure seekers resort there. It is improper for men of good birth and high breeding to stay in such a city."

"I couldn't agree with you more," Eustace Molesworth nodded, his pouched cheeks quivering with righteous arrogance. "No Frenchman, in my opinion, can be said to be well bred, no matter how high born."

"European life," Lady Singh said very softly, "ruins many of our men for life here. They will not find at home in India the sort of women they meet there."

"The problem in India, madame," said one of the young Princes of Jaipur, a guest at the banquet, "is not with its men, but with its high-born women giving up the veil as you and your daughter have done. That is the trouble. That is why Indira resists an appropriate marriage and would rather go off with her British cavalry officer."

"But surely you don't advocate complete return to the veil for these charming ladies?" Daisy Havelock asked, as her father, an experienced diplomat, inwardly cringed at his daughter's directness.

"I do indeed," was the response from the affronted Prince. "Secluded women are thoroughly feminine beyond all else. Their very remoteness gives them their charm. They know that it is really women veiled and separate that men crave. The cloistered wife is not a casual companion of her husband's every walk and game, but that object of delight always awaiting his pleasure with smiles and flowers. They are captives of passion, and the better for it."

"Would you be my captive of passion?" Nicholas whispered to Justine, leaning toward her.

"I already am," she said, her expression never changing though she instantly felt an uncoiling of desire. Her hand fluttered to the opals at her throat, the only jewels she wore, both she and they attracting the admiring eye of every gem-encrusted nobleman and woman in the room. "But I'd be very lonely, I think, in a harem. I'd have to be the only woman there," she added, and Nick threw his head back and laughed aloud.

"As soon as you can, slave, get up and slip away. I'll follow," he said. She nodded.

"Have you told him?" she asked as she returned Tony's dreamy smile from across the table.

258

"He was off sketching in the city and . . . now I might as well wait until morning," Nick answered. "He's enjoying himself I think. But then your father is always an interesting companion."

"A lot of the Britons who came out here for the East India Company tried to re-create what they found when they went home to Europe," Slade Hawkes was saying, and Anthony was listening very attentively to the man who, he was certain, would soon be his father-in-law. "There was a Colonel Robert Smith," Slade went on, "an architect and artist like yourself son. He spent his time out here restoring the ancient buildings of Delhi and Calcutta and when he retired to Nice as so many English have, he built Redcliffe for himself, modeled after the Red Fort at Delhi. When I met the man some years ago, he was living there in solitary splendor, alone with the lions and tigers who roamed his gardens. Uncaged, I should add."

"You know, Mr. Hawkes," Lady Havelock interjected, "the Royal Stables and Pavilion at Brighton were the earliest examples in England of what's now being called the Indo-Gothic style."

"Yes, and then the American P. T. Barnum, the circus showman, visited Brighton and had some details of the Pavilion copied in the lavish home he built in Connecticut. It, too, had verandas and domes and cusped arches," Slade said. "Unfortunately, the place burned to the ground a few years after it was completed."

"More recently, Lockwood de Forest, a New Yorker, I believe, associated with Mr. Louis Tiffany came here to visit our wood-carving workshops. He sent back to America beautifully wrought panels with details copied from our balconies and windows and mosques," Indira said. "Mr. de Forest bought some of the patterns used in the tinfoil that decorates our homes during festivals and weddings. I am told he copied them in thin brass and that it now lines the ceiling of the East Room in your White House. You see, in a world so large and varied, we are all connected, one to another, in various ways, are we not?"

"I want to be connected to you in every way you can imagine," Nicholas whispered to Justine, and he saw a lovely blush stroke of pink color her cheeks as she looked at him with a combination of cautioning sternness and melting affection. "Leave now," he went on in a low, intimate whisper.

"Do you remember how to find my room?" she whispered with very real concern, but when he grinned, she quickly slipped from her chair and withdrew.

Only moments later, as she hurried through a deserted hall, Justine heard footsteps behind her and she turned with a loving, welcoming, eager smile to find not Nicholas but Anthony returning it.

"Where were you all day?" she asked casually, slipping her arm through his. They walked along together a little way, chatting about the Durbar and the palace and her upset during the polo match—he'd not seen it but had been told if it— and then, with a hand at her elbow, he stopped her and turned her toward him.

"Justine," he began almost somberly, "I think I

know now what your feelings are and I want to tell you . . ."

"Yes?" she encouraged, positive he was going to say how happy he was for her and Nicholas, certain he'd realized at last where her affections really lay and was going to gracefully bow out and wish them well. But she was wrong.

"I want to tell you I'm the happiest man in the world. It was looking at the drawings earlier today that made me really see you and see how in love with me you are."

"Anthony . . ." Dread took hold of her, a chill forming about her heart. "Don't—"

"I bought this for you today from a dealer in the city." He slipped a ring on the third finger of her left hand. "It's from the diamond troves of Golconda. It's the largest stone I've ever seen. I intend to talk to your father first thing in the morning, if you agree."

"Oh, Anthony," Justine said very gently, taking the ring from her finger and returning it to his hand. "Don't you remember what I told you? My heart is given to . . . another." About to say more, she recalled Nick's command—*"Let me tell Tony about us"*—and, at a complete loss for words, she fled, leaving Anthony hurt and confused, the sound of her footsteps echoing in his ears long after she was out of sight.

Justine flew to her door at the first knock and threw it open to find Nicholas before her, as magnificent as any desert-bred spare-living Indian

Prince in a yellow silk jacket with upstanding collar, narrow leggings, and a white turban hung with rubies.

"Aren't you in splendid plumage!" she exclaimed, and before she could breathe another word or tell him about Tony, he swept her off her feet and into his arms, his mouth possessing hers, taking her breath away, and erasing all thoughts but one. He helped her with her gown, deftly unlaced her bustière, stripped away layers of petticoats with an impatient, purposeful tear, and when she stood completely unclothed, slender and perfect, he watched her take the pins from her hair, her upraised arms lifting her full breasts, the tips tight and hard in anticipation of what she knew was about to follow.

But he surprised her. He unfurled a long gold-embroidered banner of silk that he wound about her waist, then tucked and twisted before he brought it up across her bosom and over her shoulder, the end left dangling like a lovely scarf.

He smiled. "Such an ingenious bit of cloth, the sari, so graceful and fluid and flattering, with not a seam . . . a hook . . . a button. So very easy to get into. And out of," he added, keenly aware of her sleek body, fluid and tremulous beneath the form-following silk. When he took her hand and led her from the room, she asked no questions, just followed him through the maze of the palace, from hall to courtyard to twisting, secret narrowing staircase, climbing higher and higher until, passing through what had been a hidden door until he pushed it open, they emerged inside the locked gates of the now-deserted fortress above. The night sky was filled with the flares and explosions of fireworks rising from the plain below, and when they began to climb again, Justine finally asked Nicholas where he was taking her.

"To the stars," he answered, leading her on, "to the magic moon that's waiting just for us."

And when they'd gone as far and as high as she thought possible, after they'd followed the blue carpet right up to the marble and carnelian terrace suspended over the desert, he took her farther, up into a watch tower of the fortress where great piles of pillows and fruits and nectars were waiting for them. Then, finally, he stopped and kissed her, and it was as if they had touched the sky.

"No one will find us here. They're all at the Durbar." He smiled, his dark velvet eyes glowing like coals. "And everything has been made ready for our own celebration of the moon. Did you know," he asked, beginning to undo the sari, letting the silk slide slowly through his fingers, "that long ago in this country"—his voice was very low and caressing—"long ago, love was . . . perhaps is still . . . considered a sacred duty?" He brought his mouth to each breast and as he bared it, and his hands were at her waist, her hips; caressing, molding, until the silk sari lay pooled at her feet. And while he undid his own clothing, he talked on in a low smoky voice. "Some temples"—he smiled—"were decorated with the most astounding sculptures . . . demonstrating love in all its . . . varieties. Standing, for instance," he said, moving toward Justine, who'd never taken her eyes off

263

him, and lifting her, her arms enfolding his neck, her legs his hips. "And . . . in ways . . . you never ever dreamed of."

"Oh . . . I have dreamed . . . quite a lot" — she gasped as he sank to his knees — "since I met you."

"It's all been like a dream — Deauville . . . Sienna . . . here — fairy tales and moats and castles and noblemen — but now that I've found my prince, I'm ready for real life. I want to go home," Justine said. She and Nick were looking up at the sky, hearing shrieks and the explosions of fireworks still going off. Content, during a pause in their own fireworks, to be alone together, they naturally turned their thoughts to the future.

"Soon, the silver linden tree at him will be flaming in fall, and the geese will be passing overhead and then it'll be Christmas and— Will you come to Silver Hill with me?" she asked. He nodded, his eyes closed, his hand behind his head. "I want you to be there in May when the lilacs bloom . . . and under the Sprouting Grass moon, as it's called, in April, when the roads are all mired but—"

"Come home with me to the mountains," he said emphatically.

"All I want is an ordinary life," Justine declared very seriously, sitting up and leaning on her elbow. "You know, screen doors slamming on summer afternoons, Sunday suppers cooking, babies cooing—

"They're depthless royal green," he said, looking into her eyes then and toying with her hair.

"There's no such color as royal green." She laughed.

"Then there should be," he insisted, before his expression, too, became serious. "I never had any such thing as an ordinary life nor expected to, but then, I never expected you either. I'll give it a try. One thing we'll do every day of our extraordinary ordinary lives is ride at dawn and see the sunrise together in my mountains that are more awesome than anything you've ever seen, than any cathedral or temple or fortress anywhere."

"The stars are going out. Let's ride now," she insisted, standing and reaching for his hand.

"Only if you wear this," he answered, slipping on her finger a ring of silver with turquoise and ebony stones.

"After your spill today I think you can use a little turquoise for rider's luck." Holding up her hand to admire his gift, Justine thought suddenly of Tony's offer earlier in the evening, and she was about to tell Nick. But she held her tongue. If sad news had waited this long, it could wait a few hours longer, she decided, reluctant to dispel the magic of this night, one she'd always remember as her moontide surrender. She'd given herself so completely, so totally, she felt there could never be another night like it for her with anyone but Nicholas Jones.

Twenty-four hours later, she knew there'd never be another like it. By then, she'd lost him. He'd gone.

Chapter Thirty

"It's almost dawn," Roweena said in a harsh whisper, poking Eustace with the tip of her parasol. "If we will do this thing, it must be done now." He opened a bleared, pale eye and sat up in bed.

"Of course we will do it," he agreed. "Such an opportunity presents itself once in a lifetime. It's not to be missed."

"Must you always reek of patchouli?" Roweena complained some moments later as Eustace, fully dressed, splashed on his favorite cologne. He glowered at her but said nothing, thinking with what pleasure he'd see the last of this dreadful creature once the foray they'd plotted was over.

As Nicholas and Justine had hours before, though with very different purpose, they moved with quiet stealth through the palace, taking several wrong turnings, retracing their steps, bickering and complaining, each blaming the other for every mistake until, finally, they found themselves at the top of the palace standing before the vaulted doors of the fabled treasury of Jodhpur.

Setting a stick of dynamite in a high, grilled window, Eustace waited until a flare of fireworks went off and then exploded his own charge. When, after considerable grunting, he managed to pull his long, stoop-shouldered frame through the narrow opening, he reached out to Roweena. She struggled and groaned with the effort, lost her grip once and her voluminous skirt rode up nearly to her waist, but finally they stood side by side, she holding a candle, both of them awed into silence as they looked about at piles of silver and gold—mountains of it—and open jewel cases, like flower beds of uncut rubies, polished emeralds, agates and sapphires, jade and topaz; the stones, set and unset, lying on black velvet and satin dark as rich soil.

"There it is!" Roweena was so affected by the massed wealth before her, she spoke with difficulty. "The Star of the East, the fifth largest diamond in the world."

"Don't touch it, you fool! It's more than a hundred carats and world renowned. Take only what won't be so easily identified." In the manner of a man beside himself with joy, Eustace stuffed his pockets with gold coins and links of silver, with handfuls of pearls, some of immense size, while Roweena poured large trays of gems into the carpet bag she'd brought, until the receptacle was filled to overflowing. And still her greedy eyes searched about for more. She and

267

Eustace both trembled with excitement, their hands shook, their mouths hung slackly open as greed, for the first time since their wedding, struck a little spark of passion in them for each other.

"Roweena"—Eustace leered at her—"perhaps, if you would recline there . . ." He gestured at an open chest filled with gold coins.

"Yes, yes." She quickly obliged, unfastening the buttons on her gown.

"No. Don't bother. No time," he said heaving himself above her with a groan and fumbling at her petticoats, not looking at her but at a jeweled object on the shelf above her head.

"Oh, Eustace!" she cried, clutching handfuls of cool gold coins. "Eustace . . . why . . . didn't I bring another . . . satchel?"

"There are no black opals here like Justine's, only gray ones," Roweena said when Eustace helped her to her feet, causing coins to cascade from the chest, and she at once began stuffing her pockets with diamonds. "But soon I'll have Justine's opals. And compared to them, everything here is ordinary."

"Just look at this!" Eustace reached for the object that had held his attention earlier. Licking his heavy lips he hefted a massive gold tiger-head finial with diamond eyes, a ruby tongue, and a collar of emeralds. The gems glinted in the light of the single candle. "Call this ordinary, do you?"

"Don't take it. We'll never be able to sell it, as you said of the Star of the East," Roweena said sternly.

"I *want* it," Eustace snarled, "for myself, a secret treasure I can look at whenever the mood strikes me."

"You mean a treasure to drool over, you silly fool. Let's go before we're found out. Hurry!" Roweena set her carpetbag high on the window ledge and waited for a hand up from her husband.

"I'll go first to be certain the coast it clear," Eustace said, at that moment seriously considering leaving her behind but deciding it would be too much of a risk. She'd certainly talk if she was discovered while she still could. No, there were better ways of ridding himself of this detestable woman who'd given him no peace since the day they'd been married, doling out the money she'd promised him, almost literally in pence and half-pence.

"Yes, you go first, Eustace dear. I'll bring the jewels once you've looked about," Roweena said, clutching the heavy bag to her chest jealously and fixing him with her pale-eyed witchy stare.

Once they'd both climbed out of the treasury and stood side by side, Eustace reached for the jewels. "*I'll* carry the bag," he said.

"No, *I'll* keep it, *and* its contents, thank you," Roweena retorted. "Now that you've spent all my money, I need these gems more than you do. You have your inherited wealth, of course, and your houses and all."

269

"But, my dear, it is time you knew. I haven't any money of my own." Eustace smiled wickedly, his soft lips twisting. "I only married you for your pittance. Now that's it's gone, I intend to seek a divorce once I'm back in England. I've other plans, dear wife. I need the money these jewels will bring to carry them out."

"Other . . . plans?" Roweena asked, as they walked back in the direction from which they'd come.

"Yes, precious spouse. I've always fancied Justine Hawkes, you see, *and* her opals."

"Oh?" Roweena turned to follow the royal blue carpet, not toward the fortress gate but in the direction of the marble and carnelian terrace. "Yes, I see. Most men do fancy Justine, and it's understandable, what with her beauty and wealth and luck. Shall we just part amicably, husband dear? Share this bag of jewels and call it quits?"

"I'm not sharing. I want it all." Eustace had begun to laugh peculiarly.

"Of course, I'm in no position to lodge a complaint against you if you steal stolen good from me, am I?"

"Quite right," he snapped gleefully, glancing about. "Where are we? Idiot! You've taken a wrong turn again. I'm in no mood to gaze at the sunrise from the edge of a precipice with you, madame, and . . . Well," he said, squinting off into the distance, "look out there, will you? It's Justine and one of those twins heading into the desert for a morning ride." He pointed.

270

"Now a sunrise with her would be an altogether different matter and . . ."

Eustace Molesworth never did finish his sentence, the very last one he would ever utter in his life. His wife, Roweena, with a bloodcurdling shriek of rage, swung the heavy carpetbag, catching him at the small of his stooped back and sending him hurtling from the terrace, out into the great red abyss of the Indian dawn.

Eustace Molesworth made no cry, but Roweena did hear glass shattering many floors below. By the time the body was discovered much later that day, she had sewn all the gems into the linings and seams and hems of her gowns though not into the black widow's weeds she'd thought to bring with her when she'd left England some weeks before—on her honeymoon.

As Roweena was slipping back to her room that morning, satisfied with a night's work well done, she came upon Anthony Jones. The man was staggering along the hallway, lost and drifting it appeared, and as she opened her door, she invited him, with a gesture, to follow her.

"Is something wrong?" she asked, sliding the carpetbag under the bed and beginning to undo her buttons. "Perhaps I could comfort you in some way?"

"You?" he half laughed, then stared at her incredulously. "But you're not Justine. She's the only one who can help me now. Here, you might as well have this," he said, thrusting a diamond ring into Roweena's hands. She looked at it, at him, at the ring again, and she, too, began to laugh, very low at first and then almost uncontrollably until he grasped her shoulders and shook her. "Don't laugh at me, don't!" Tony implored wildly.

"You bought this diamond for her, did you?" Roweena questioned. He nodded, covering his eyes with a hand. "And she turned you down?" He nodded again. "Do you know *why* she did that? Do you know where she is right now? Who she's with and who she's been with for months?" Anthony stared at Roweena, suddenly fearful of what she was going to say but not knowing how to stop her. "Justine Hawkes is with your precious brother, Nicholas, and if you don't believe me, look in her room. Then look in his. You won't find either of them because they've gone off — together. They've been *together* in every sense of the word, probably since our very first day in Deauville. If you didn't hear about that notorious kiss, you must have been the only person in town who didn't." Roweena's eyes glinted with malicious delight as she watched the man virtually crumbling before her.

"What kiss?" Anthony asked in a barely audible voice.

"Their kiss in the middle of the polo field. It was quite something, I was told, and . . . Where are you going?" she called.

"As far as I can go from here," Anthony answered, running along the deserted corridor toward his room. Looking down at the diamond ring in her hand, enjoying her sudden embarrassment of riches, Roweena decided not to add it to the collection of gems in the carpetbag. She had just thought of an immediate use for the object, and she could hardly wait to put her latest plot into action.

"Your brother's gone," Roweena told Nicholas. She'd been waiting for him in his room when he'd come back from his morning ride with Justine.

"Gone where?" he asked, irritated to find the woman there, wanting his bath and shave and a good meal before the next polo match.

"Gone away was all he would tell me," she said. "Probably to Delhi or Bombay, I'd suppose. He seemed . . . disturbed, unsteady in his mind." Nicholas stopped what he was doing and listened to her now. "You see, he tried to give this beautiful ring to Justine yesterday and she told him about you."

"About me?" Nicholas asked in a voice gone cold.

"Yes, that you and she were . . . well, you *know*. Isn't it true?" When he didn't answer, Roweena clucked disapprovingly. "Some women just seem to have an ability to bring on disaster, not for themselves, of course, but for others. Justine is one of those women, Mr. Jones. I did try to warn you but . . ."

With one sweep of his arm, Nicholas cleared

the low table that had been laid for his breakfast, the dishes and glassware flying against the
wall and then falling to the floor with a clatter
and crash before he strode from the room with
an oath.

When he burst in on Justine, she had just
stepped out of her cool bath, and at the intimidating sight of him, she reached for her silk
sari and held it before her protectively, for the
first time feeling vulnerable and exposed and
self-conscious under his stare. He crossed the
room and, with a gesture, sent the chambermaids fleeing, then stripped the silk away from
Justine before he trapped her wrists behind her
and then took her lips with a bruising ferocity.

"I didn't come to make love to you," he
growled, aware that her body was already responding, bending to his, those fine breasts
hard-tipped; a smile, like a butterfly, fluttering
at the corners of her mouth.

"Why did you come, then?" she asked with
that flash of mischief in her eyes he'd seen so
often before.

"To beat you," he said with a fast cool grin,
still holding her helpless. "Women like you . . .
so beautiful . . . so wicked . . . should be kept
imprisoned in harems and beaten every day, if
only for the way you're looking at me right
now." He reached behind her with his free hand
and brought it sharply against bare flesh.
"That's better," he growled as her expression
changed from teasing arrogance to surprise and
she began to struggle against his hold. "But not

good enough." He slapped her again, still holding her bold, unwavering gaze, and though her eyes glazed, the look in them became more stubborn and defiant. He was tempted to continue what he hadn't meant to start, to make her cry out, as he had not done on all those secretive nights when she'd come to him like a thief, a thief of love in the dark. Her silence rankled now as it had then, and the set of her mouth, her eyes, *so* determined and arrogant, were provoking. But instead of giving sway to his rage, Nicholas swept her off her feet and set her back in the tub with a great splash. Then, arms folded over his chest, he paced in silence like a caged tiger.

Justine hid her real fear of him behind an expression that was audacious and challenging. "Well, is that what you came for, you brute?" she demanded furiously, and then, in a gentler tone asked, "Nick, what's wrong . . . what's happened?"

"I came to say goodbye and you provoked me. How can you ask what's wrong after you refused Tony's ring and never breathed a word of it to me?"

"Goodbye?" she echoed, aware of the quaver in her voice, afraid that the dam was about to break and the tears she'd been holding back would flow in torrents.

"Before I go, I want you to know that what happened between us meant nothing," he said with icy detachment. "I wanted a distraction during this safari, and you offered me a way to kill two birds with one stone."

"Yes?" she said, raising a brow and sinking back languidly in the tub. "What do you mean, exactly?"

"I only wanted to show my brother what a duplicitous female you are. I had to ruin you in his eyes so that he could get you out of his heart. I did. Or, rather, you did that yourself better than I ever could have. What are you laughing about?" he demanded with a furious look.

"About how alike we are, you and I," she answered, locking her hands behind her head, the pink tips of her breasts temptingly raised just above the level of the water, the air fragrant with the scent of her rose oil. "But I've beaten you at your own game. You see, all I wanted was to have you *and* Anthony craving my . . . favors, eating out of my hand, in my thrall. And I had that. Or thought I did. But our little interlude was a double deception, it seems. You're a good actor, Mr. Jones. You had me fooled."

Though shaken by what she said, Nicholas showed no emotion. He just touched a finger to his brow in a kind of offhand salute.

"Well then, you won't miss me even a little, will you, Justine?" He grinned.

"Nicholas"—she grinned back at him though she knew her heart was breaking—"you're already a memory."

"Well . . . have a nice life," he said, his own heart riven. Not wanting to go, he filled his eyes with the sight of her, so lovely. He knew beyond a shadow of a doubt he'd never forget her.

But it had to be this way, a sharp pain, a fast break and no looking back, not for his brother, not for him. It could never have worked anyway, with Tony feeling as he did, and not with the way he himself had always felt about love. True or false, the odds were against it lasting. With Justine, he would have taken the gamble but now it was too late.

"You don't really much like women, do you, Mr. Jones?" she asked with an aloof smile.

"On the contrary, Miss Hawkes, I adore them," he answered, his tone cruel. "In the *dark*."

Her wounded look struck right to his heart, and he turned and left without glancing back.

"It is sad that your friend, Roweena, is going home a widow," Indira told Justine. Sitting cross-legged in the middle of a very beautiful rug, she was brushing out the blue-black hair that fell below her waist.

"It's a state Roweena's had considerable experience of. She handles bereavement well. Such a staunch woman," Justine said with an ironic smile. "I'm sorry that she is going home the widow of a thief. What a dreadful way Eustace chose to repay your gracious hospitality. In his haste, he took a wrong turning, it appears. Has everything that was stolen been found?"

"Just a tiger-head finial of great value and a few old coins in his pocket. Far more is missing than has been retrieved." Indira stood and picked up a small bundle of envelopes that she tied with a pink ribbon, then buried deep beneath the scarves in an ebony chest. "Love letters crumble, you know, if they aren't read again and again. I read mine every day." Indira looked sadly at Justine who had come to her rooms to say goodbye. "I'm sorry you are unhappy, my friend," she said.

"Your letters are more than I have or ever will," Justine answered, taking Indira's hand in hers. She was dressed in her pale green traveling suit and white gloves, her hair put up under a small neat bonnet, she was about to entrain in the Regent's private railcar for Karachi, where one of Slade's ships lay at anchor waiting to take them home.

"Have I ever told you about Tommy Gordon?" Indira said. "He was a wonderful merry boy. I was already betrothed, at twelve, when Tommy and I met. He was sent out here to be attached to the Viceroy's staff and he was so handsome— fair and tall, with a full mustache; one of those men, like your Nicholas, with whom women are always falling in love. I was no exception. It was just an innocent, childish love at first, until we met some years later in England. Then what we shared could not be called childish or innocent." Indira sighed and began to braid her hair.

Justine removed her gloves and took up the braiding. "If I were you, I'd run off with him, far off, where no one in the world would ever find you," she said.

"But we would be outcasts in two worlds, his and mine. How would we live? I am a Princess, used to certain comforts and . . . I did tell the Prince of Baroda that I would be marrying him, but only to satisfy my parents' wishes. He wants me for love. He already has one wife whom he does not love, and so our marriage may not come to pass. It has been deferred in the expectation that I will learn to love this Prince.

"Will you, do you suppose?" Justine asked, concentrating on the thick, dark braid taking shape in her quick hands.

"Perhaps. In a way. There may be many loves in a woman's life, but only one is true—warm as the ruby and pure as the pearl—such as mine for Tommy Gordon, and yours."

"If you had one wish, what would it be?" Justine asked, hesitating.

"To be free of all desire like the musician in the legend of the opal. I will love Tommy Gordon all my life, but we are already strangers."

"I think you will marry your Prince of Baroda."

"Yes I think I will do my duty. Sometimes, in the search for happiness, that is best."

"And if you marry him, would it also be your duty to throw yourself on his funeral pyre should he die before you?"

"It would be my duty, yes," Indira answered. "I know it is hard, perhaps impossible, for someone like you to understand, but it is as if we bathe in fire as you do in water."

"But sati is against the law." Justine looked stunned.

"No matter. The custom is still strong, particularly here in Rajasthan. It is an ancient ritual and such things cannot be so easily changed by the passing of a law. In the ancient time, when a warrior was killed, his wife would commit sati rather than be taken by the invader. It is a most sacred act, the highest achievement here for a woman brought up to revere her husband as something very like a god. Ah, but Justine! Don't look so shocked. No matter what we do, our lives are ruled by fate, I think." Indira offered a resigned, helpless smile.

"And luck. But I think what we do does matter," Justine insisted, pulling on a glove. "What happened with Nicholas was my fault. I was being too clever by half, careless . . . blind." She shook her head sadly.

"My friend, do not berate yourself so. It was not meant to be, you and Nicholas, but if luck and fate decree, perhaps there'll be another love for you one day."

"I won't look for love again, but I won't turn away from it either." Justine smiled. "And if ever you do decide to take charge of your life — just throw it all up — you and your handsome Tommy Gordon will always be welcome at Silver Hill."

Chapter Thirty-one

"Opals are fragile, Justine. They crack and craze like broken hearts if they are not handled with care. I know. I'm an expert on both," Philip Carpenter said kindly.

He had hurried after Justine when she'd left the house for one of her early morning walks. With gloved hands jammed deep into the pockets of a sheepskin coat, Philip's Christmas gift to her, she had tried to slip away, as she'd done every morning since her return to Silver Hill, to wander the bayshore and the woods, sobbing her heart out before she washed her face in the icy water of a brook and returned for breakfast. Then she became her usual chatty self, all high spirits and full of eager plans for the day ahead, though mostly she cooked and baked and there were more tomatoes and plums and gooseberries "put up" at Silver Hill that autumn than ever before.

Rambling lonely walks and afternoons passed in the kitchen had become a pattern she'd followed for months now, all through the flaming fall when in misty dawns she listened to the distant barking of dogs and the long plaintive whistle of the early train.

She wandered in the dry leaf-rattle of December trees, and walked through dim snowstorms and early dusks, desolate with despair and nearly overcome by remorse and regrets though she'd so confidently told Olympe d'Erlanger she'd never be. And all the while, Justine hoped no one at Silver Hill would ask any questions, at least not until she'd come to grips with herself and fallen out of love with Nicholas Jones.

Of course, the others were all too aware of Justine's troubled state. Her mother and father, Martha and Grandmother Elizabeth, Levi and her brothers had for months been exchanging worried looks and conducting whispered secret consultations, every one of them at a loss as to how to help, though each had managed to give her a bit of gratuitous advice about love. This morning, the last day of the year, it was Philip's turn, it seemed. He slipped his arm through hers and her hand into his own pocket.

"What have you there?" he asked as she withdrew her hand from its warm refuge and uncurled her gloved fingers to reveal a small perfect shell.

"It looks ordinary but it's very . . . special," she half smiled. "It's from France. Philip . . . I've something to tell you. I've done an awful thing, bet my beautiful opals—*your* opals—on a horse race that I suppose I can't possibly win

. . . now."

"That doesn't sound like you. Why can't you win?" he asked. "You've been training Georgie Boy, haven't you?" He helped her over a small wind-sculpted cliff of snow.

"The horse is fast but only a fair fencer, and he'd be going up against the best jumpers in the world. I've resigned myself to losing." Justine looked up at Philip's weathered, craggy face. It was and was thin and narrow with sad, kind eyes.

"I'll get you more opals, all you want. Don't worry so," he said in a tight voice. "Justine, there's a place in the outback of Australia that only I know of. It's called Lightning Ridge. It's where I found those black opals that are more rare and more beautiful than diamonds. There are more—many more—and they're waiting . . . only for you. Look," he said, extending his own hand, on the palm a tiny reptilian skeleton opalized in perfect detail and incredible color.

"Thousands of years ago, this little creature left its bones outlined in sand or lava, perhaps a mixture of both, that became rock, a perfect mold that over eons of time was filled by precious opal. Here, take him. I brought him for you." Philip placed the opal lizard in Justine's hand, beside the scallop shell, and for thanks, she gave him a smile, a rare gift during the past weeks. "Opals are like you, Justine, dazzling, full of color and life, and there's a lovely soft fire in them . . . in you. It saddens me to see it dimmed. Justine, listen! I found other marvels in

283

Australia, orchids that bloom underground. Their flowers never reach the surface, and there're thousands of miles of reef off Queensland, in clear blue water teeming with life, and . . . So much more I can't begin to describe it all," he declared with schoolboy gusto and enthusiasm. "Come to Australia with me. Start a new life. I can help you forget the sadness that's been clinging to you since you came to Silver Hill." Philip put his hands on her shoulders and turned her to him. "You bring back my youth, you see. I'm asking you to marry me, Justine, and give me a son and heir," he said, and she rested a hand on his cheek, not completely surprised by his proposal.

"I'm sorry," she answered.

"You know, your mother turned me down, too, standing just about in this same spot, I think. Can't blame a fellow for trying, can you?" He sighed deeply.

"Can't," she agreed, slipping her arm through his.

They finished their walk in friendly silence before turning back to the house, now snowcapped and snowbanked, closed in upon itself, secure against the cold, a haven, home. "I don't know yet exactly where I'll go," Justine said, "but day after tomorrow I'm leaving here."

"And so am I, Justine," Philip answered. "I'm sorry we won't be leaving together, but it's been the best Christmas I've had in a very long time, exactly like the ones I remembered at Silver Hill all those years ago."

The Christmas of 1898 had been a difficult one for Justine, not one of her best, but she had been determined, as she'd baked and cooked and wrapped gifts, not to let a shadow of her own sadness dim this time for anyone else.

The very house itself, set on the cliff above the bay, was like an immense giftbox with a great wreath of holly and apples and persimmon on the front door that opened repeatedly as family and friends gathered for the celebration. There was a candle in every window. Juniper garlands or swags of balsam decorated every mantel, and mistletoe was strategically hung in alcoves, window seats, and doorways.

The fir tree that Slade Hawkes had cut in his own woods, with the help of most of his grandchildren and various dogs, had been brought home on a sled, then set up to nearly touch the ceiling in the drawing room. Its scent wafted through the house, blending with the fragrance of woodfires and the rosemary Brigida had placed about, and it was decorated with ropes of cranberries and bright red apples brought from the root cellar, and lacquered wooden ornaments in the shapes of trains and boats and drums and sleds and gingerbread men. The real gingerbread men Justine had baked also adorned it, as did glass ornaments, hand-painted bells and globes and crocheted snowflakes in great numbers.

Gifts lay piled beneath the tree as four generations of the Hawkes family gathered, the newest baby to occupy the nursery just a few months old, all dressed up in antique lace and grasping the wooden rattle—three rings on a narrow shaft—carved for him from a single piece of fine hardwood by his grandfather.

Little boys in sailor suits, their hair slicked back, played hide and seek up and down the stairs, chased by little girls in red velvet or green with matching satin hair ribbons, who ran, laughing, from beneath the mistletoe whenever they were caught, more often by uncles than boy cousins who disdained such sissy stuff. Once, Philip found Justine curled in a window seat with her favorite cat, an orange tabby with a green bow. As she gazed out into the thickening dusk, he kissed her in a way that wasn't altogether avuncular. She kept even busier after that, and she actually was able to lose herself, for a time, in the pleasures of the season.

On Christmas day, her plaid taffeta skirt rustled as she hurried from kitchen to parlor with trays of sweets, and her pretty laugh could be heard as she helped her niece, Maud, decorate a dollhouse that was a perfectly detailed miniature of Silver Hill. There were tiny Tiffany lamps and gilded mirrors, little lace doilies, and wall sconces with miniature milk-glass globes. The double staircase, its railing spindles copied exactly from the larger ones, met at the first landing where a scaled-down, tall case clock actually kept perfect time.

"When I grow up and am married," Maud told Justine, as she placed a small punch bowl on a parlor table of the dollhouse, "I want a real house like this one. Do you?" She tucked a little blanket over the tiny doll in the miniature pendulum cradle.

"I don't know. I may never marry, Maud," Justine said with such harsh vehemence the girl was taken aback.

"But we've always talked about what we'd do when we fell in love and what sort of wedding to have and how many babies and—"

"Let's put the little red velvet settee against the wall here," Justine said quickly, "so there'll be room for the Christmas tree. Where's the snow globe and the carriage sled?"

"On the front porch," Maud answered walking around to the front of the dollhouse that was half as tall as she. "But Justine, I don't understand. I thought you were looking for your shining knight. That's what you wrote to me from that castle in France and now you say—"

"I found him and lost him, so now . . ." Justine placed the tiny coffee grinder on the kitchen table, then looked up at the girl's stricken face. "Oh, Maud, don't worry so. You know me." She forced a laugh, "Always in and out of love. Like that!" Justine snapped her fingers and Maud laughed, relieved. "Now, help me set this little table and then help me set the real one. It's Christmas eve and we don't want to be still dining when Santa Claus is circling Silver Hill. You know how long it takes *this* family, with all its talk, to get through a meal." Justine winked as she got to her feet, smoothing her gown.

"Do you know what Cousin Elliot told me?" Maud asked, with an indignant tilt of her dark head. "He said that the Puritans thought Christmas was a wild pagan festival and a menace to proper behavior. Anyone who took the day off at Plymouth was fined five shillings."

"Well, we celebrate Christmas in the German way. It was the German father of my friend, Bertie, the Prince, who first had a tree at Windsor Palace. It wasn't until years later, 1889, I think, there was a Christmas tree at the White House."

"Do you know what else Elliot said?" Maud persisted. "He said that Santa Claus was a Russian saint, the saint of sailors and thieves, and that he saved some poor innocent girls from a dreadful fate by dropping bags of gold, not toys, down their chimneys. Isn't Elliot *awful?*" Maud and Justine had stopped in the nursery for at least the tenth time that day to admire the baby sleeping there, and his nurse put a finger to her lips in caution.

"Cousin Elliot," Justine whispered, "is all of seventeen and fancies himself very knowledgeable and worldly wise, I dare say. Pay him no mind, that's my advice. But *do* keep him away from the little children. There's no point in spoiling their fun, is there? Elliot and Roweena . . . they do make a fine pair of killjoys, don't they?"

They had reached the staircase landing and stood giggling together as the front door opened to a sleighful of carolers and the McGlory family who'd arrived at the same time in a swirl of snow. There was much commotion and stamping of feet and shaking out of wraps.

"Oh, just look at that Roweena!" Maud rolled her eyes. "She's all airs and fluff now that she's Lady Molesworth. The last time I saw her, at Thanksgiving, she was *impossible*."

"Mm." Justine leaned on the balustrade and watched the scene below. Roweena was admonishing the valet about some infraction that only she seemed to be aware of. The landing clock's triple chime struck four.

"I was telling the little children a story and Roweena said I had too active an imagination. What she'd do if I were her child, she said, was make me wear a sign on my back saying Liar just to warn other people away." Maud's dark eyes were thoughtful. "People don't really do such dreadful things to children, do they?"

"I'm afraid they do," Justine replied. "My friend Daisy Havelock told me of a governess who locked her in a dark cupboard for the least offense, and when I go to Children's Aid in New York, I hear of even worse. Well . . . you're not Roweena's child, so don't pay any mind to her," Justine said softly as the woman looked up at them and offered a false smile. Her father, Billy, was rocking on his heels, his back to the roaring hall fire, when he saw Justine and Maud.

"Merry Christmas, girlies," he called up to them. "But where's my great-nephews you promised would be here. I've been waitin' to make their acquaintance. I thought you invited those Jones twins for Christmas dinner, Justine."

289

"I did, Billy," she answered, not explaining that each knock at the door had raised her hopes, or that she longed for Nicholas every second of every day. "I guess they . . . just had other plans, that's all."

Chapter Thirty-two

Gifts were opened early the next snowy morning, boxes spilled out toy trains and Noah's arks and dolls and books and frocks and silk flowers. Most exclaimed over were the gifts Philip had brought for everyone, Sheepskin wraps and capes from Australia.

Justine gave her mother a gold elephant pin with trappings of rubies and diamonds and pearls. For her father, she had found a brass captain's lamp, its bulbous globular glass chimney etched with a map of the world. And Slade gave his daughter the most spectacular gift of all, a real carousel horse on a pole. It was a golden mustang with a roached mane, all four hoofs off the ground, its flowing muscles detailed, starburst-etched jewels on its trappings.

"He was made by Charles Loof, an old friend," Slade smiled and took Justine's hand, wishing she were happier.

"We used to carve duck decoys together until Loof went over to carousels. I hope you like your gift, Justine. We all knew you needed a fine jumper to win your steeplechase," he added, giving her an affectionate hug that almost made her break down and cry.

There was foamy eggnog before dinner, claret after, the meal itself the traditional one at Silver Hill, oyster stew and standing roast with Yorkshire pudding, suckling pig and mince pie, stuffed turkey, venison, root vegetables whipped up with butter and cream, and the final course, plum pudding, brandy-flamed to great applause and served with hard sauce.

It was after that sumptuous meal that Roweena, still wearing black for "poor dear Eustace" as she so often said, approached Justine who was reading beside the library fire.

"You're going to forfeit the opals, I assume," Roweena said abruptly. Justine looked up from her book but said nothing. "I'll take them off your hands now if you like. I wrote to James Bennett. He says if you're willing, he doesn't object."

"I'm not willing. The race is some months away. Whether I forfeit or not, I'm not giving up my opals until I absolutely must."

"I'll *pay* you. I can afford to now," Roweena pressed, her voice a querulous whine.

"Can you really pay what they're worth? Eustace left you so well off then?" Justine flung back her golden mane of curls and stared into the fire.

"Yes, I can, and you can't win the steeplechase

now that Jones has deserted you. You couldn't have held him anyway, a man like that, a wild man like him. He'll never be trapped and tamed by you or anyone. Try to tie him down and he'd turn savage and murderous like a caged wolf. And his brother? . . ." Roweena crowed, clasping her hands with delight. "I learned from those two wretched Bohemian women who hung about him that he'd often gone 'round the bend. He was once actually incarcerated at Bloomingdale Asylum near New York. He was no one to win a horse race with." She laughed slyly.

"How dreadful," Justine said, her face ashen suddenly. "And I probably made things even worse for him."

"Never mind about that now. Given my suspicions, it's best you're rid of both of them."

"What exactly do you suspect, Lady Molesworth?" Justine asked angrily. She closed her book with a snap.

"Well . . ." Roweena moved closer and dropped her voice as if taking Justine into her confidence. "I never believed that Eustace just stumbled off the edge of the Jodhpur fortress or that he robbed the treasury of the royal jewels. I think Tony did, and Eustace caught him at it. Why else would Jones and his brother have run away as they did?"

"What more do you know about . . . either of them?" Justine demanded through clenched teeth, and Roweena pressed her thin lips tight for a moment, then looked away.

"Nothing, nothing at all," she protested, except

that Anthony is an opium addict and a drinker and . . . not to be trusted. But now, Justine, this is all irrelevant. What you'd best take note of and think carefully about is that I am the sole owner of the Molesworth stud and I intend to win the steeplechase. I will have those opals, now or later," she said with a sneer. "Now, I'll pay you for them. Later, you'll get nothing. Be sensible."

"But I could still win the race." As she glared at Roweena, Justine knew she'd be compelled to try.

"Just don't expect Nick Jones to come back and help you. That wild devil is beyond redemption and is on his way to perdition."

"There are some who doom others to the fate they fear themselves, perdition, for example," Justine retorted. "If you want my opals so desperately, you could try thievery yourself, Roweena. I wouldn't be surprised if you had a real talent for it but . . ." Justine left the sentence hanging, the accusation not lost on her unpleasant companion who sniffed and strode off, passing her own mother in the doorway without saying a word.

"Some people are not blessed in their children." Anne McGlory sighed and took a chair near the fire. "I am one of those people. My daughter seems to be full of spleen tonight, but it *is* Christmas and anyone else's pleasure diminishes her own. Roweena is corroded with jealousy, even of little children, of anyone who is happy." Anne lit a ready-made cigarette and blew a smoke ring that drifted toward the fireplace and up the chimney.

"Then I wonder why I'm her target tonight. I just can't imagine." Justine opened her book, though she'd no intention of reading. "I'm anything but—"

"Happy?" Anne's weary eyes went over Justine's face knowingly. "I can see that. I suppose it was a love affair?" Justine nodded. "And he left you?" Justine nodded again. "Good. Just be glad you had this overwhelming experience now while you're young. It will save you from making a terrible mistake later."

"What mistake?" Justine asked with amazement.

"Marrying for love. Love is not a foundation on which to build a marriage. Well, good night, dear. Sleep well." Anne glided from the room.

"Don't go choosing a husband at whim. And don't choose one for yourself alone. You must pick the right man to father your children, Justine," Elizabeth stated authoritatively.

On the day after Christmas, Justine had gone to her grandparents' suite to inquire after Del who was suffering with a touch of catarrh. Ignoring her grandmother's admonitions, she turned to him.

"How do you feel, Grandfather," she asked very loudly, taking his hand.

Elizabeth, seated in a chair by the fire and wearing a frilled tulle cap and a black dress with a white collar, was surrounded by a new litter of Pekingese puppies.

"She won't promise," the old man said, glaring at his wife.

"Oh, don't mind him. He's just being crochety and demanding," Elizabeth scoffed, and made a dismissing gesture with her hand.

"Promise what, Grandfather?" Justine asked again loudly.

"To open the window and let my soul go free when I die, that's what."

"Oh, Grandfather!" Justine exclaimed with a note of exasperation, smoothing his sheets. "*I'll* promise if you want but you've only got a little chill after all."

"Never mind him, I said. Listen to what I'm telling you, Justine. I see you pining. You may be able to fool the others, but you can't fool me," Elizabeth insisted. "Pick well or you'll rue the day you didn't. Put your fate in the wrong hands and you'll regret it."

"My fate's in my own hands," Justine answered snappishly.

"A woman's fate is always determined by the man she loves and that's that," Elizabeth declared, and Justine left the room in a flounce to return to the kitchen, sorry she'd ever left it.

"It appears I can't hide my feelings from anyone in this house. Every one of you has had something to say about my life," Justine exclaimed with affectionate dismay, looking about her. On the afternoon of the last day of 1898, all those in residence at Silver Hill had gathered around the library fire to toast each other before guests began arriving for the New Year's ball later in the evening. "Well, out with it, the rest of you, those who haven't already offered advice. Come on, don't hold back. Tell me what you think of my liaison with a wastrel, a reckless, gambling, brawling horseman from the Wild West. Shall I really forget him?"

"Here's to him," said Uncle Billy raising his glass. "You'd not have a dull life with such a man as that."

"But not an easy one either," Gray interjected.

"What's life for if not to run wild a little when you're young, risk all . . . fall in love and make it work?" Brigida asked. "Your father was something of a hellion himself and now . . ." She smiled.

"Father, what have you to say?" Justine was perched on the arm of Slade's chair, her hand resting on his shoulder.

"The man's reputation be damned! I never saw Nicholas Jones as anything but a perfect gentleman," he said, and Justine almost laughed aloud, remembering how very ungentlemanly Nick could be at times. "But that's not the issue now," Slade added. "He's gone and *you're* bereft so you'd better forget him; that's the issue."

"I offered to help her forget him. I wanted to marry her and take her away to the opal mines of Australia, but she turned me down." Philip laughed, making light of his very serious proposal.

"The father of those twins—it sounds as if they are like him," old Martha said. "I remember the man—wild and driven by the wanderlust, taking that slip of a girl out there to that rough mountain country. It was too hard on her, I've always thought."

"But Caitlin did love him so," Billy said sadly. "She'd have followed him through hell on Sunday. I've never seen any two people so madly in love, and when she passed on, it was near the death of him, too. I was told that by a fella who come into my saloon one night. He knew Quinn in California. This fella didn't know how it happened. And I myself never heard a word from the father of those twins in all these years, except for his note telling me my niece was gone."

"What I wanted—I told you all that day last spring—was a true, overpowering love like theirs, like Caitlin's and Quinn's, just a little thing like that," Justine said after a long silence. "I thought it would be easy to find and keep . . . but now I see that when love is so strong, when it flares that way, it can't last very long. It must burn itself out."

"Your own mother and father have given the lie to that theory," Philip told her. "And love changes, with time. I learned that myself."

"I don't believe I shall ever know true love again," Justine insisted, "not after—"

"No one can ever tell how the future will unfold," Levi Phillips said, speaking on the subject for the first time. He stood in the doorway, his gaunt face in shadow, his deep voice commanding attention. "Sometimes you can take hold of destiny. Sometimes you must just wait and be patient until fate reveals what it has in store. If you can do something good and useful while you're waiting, so much the better."

"I think I'll just take your advice, Levi" — Justine sighed — "and let time and destiny take their course."

Gray rose, smiling at his sister, and proposed a toast to the New Year, 1899, that was by then just hours away.

"To love and luck," he said, and raised his glass.

Chapter Thirty-three

And so on a wet, late-January evening, Justine found herself walking alone along Madison Avenue, hands sunk deep in her pockets, lost in thought. She was on her way home from the Charities Building on Twenty-second Street, where, on Friday afternoons, she taught cooking classes to little girls from the poor sections of the city — from Mulberry Street and Third Avenue, Harlem and Hell's Kitchen.

They were such serious, polite little things, Justine mused, in their rustling seersucker gowns and white aprons and caps, and they went about their lessons very diligently. They were being taught not only cooking but pot scrubbing and sweeping and shopping and the like. It was good preparation, the volunteer ladies said, for a position in some fine house or for running their own homes, those few who would be fortune enough to marry well. But Justine's thoughts did not long dwell upon her students, not on that wintry day. They turned to a boy of nine or ten, she supposed, a vagabond, a "Street Arab" as these homeless children were called. She'd come upon him for the first time soon after she'd taken up residence in New York, found him sleeping in the doorway of her father's house near Central Park, but when she'd tried to ask him in, he'd run like a thief. She'd seen the lad again, shivering in the cold, selling newspapers on the corner of Third Avenue under the elevated train, a cigarette dangling from one corner of his mouth; and she'd approached him once more, with the same result. He'd run like a wild thing afraid of being snared.

She looked for the boy every day after that, and on the occasions she spotted him, she kept her distance, just stood and observed. She'd followed him more than once, and after a time, a pattern began to emerge in what had at first seemed to her his random wanderings through the crowded, pushcart-lined streets of the Upper East Side.

Even in winter, the teeming streets of the Italian section of Harlem were noisy and crowded with itinerant vendors and hucksters. Men who warmed their hands over ash-can fires and chased off pilfering gangs of roaming boys. These boys sold newspapers and polished shoes, then gambled with the coins they'd earned. Beneath gray laundry strung across alleyways to dry, stiffening in the cold, these children would roll dice, smoke cigarettes, eat apples stolen from fruit wagons, squabble, fight, and wander off to see what lay around the next corner. They lived a lawless life free of ties or attachments, and the ones who survived on the streets were bright, sharp, and fiercely independent. The city was full of such abandoned children. The Children's Aid Society tried to collect them and send them West on the orphan trains, to a better life on farms and ranches. But it wasn't easy to befriend a "Street Arab," and Justine worked hard to win the trust of the child who had caught her attention.

One day, she bought all his papers. He looked at her with his canny, gray calculating eyes, as though she were daft, but he took the coins and ran. On another day, she brought him a jacket that she'd found in the attic, one that Gray had long outgrown. The child's own coat was threadbare and far too small, his thin wrists protruding awkwardly from it, but he never did wear the one that she gave him. He'd sold it for cigarette money, Justine decided, and after that she brought only gifts of food that eventually won the boy over. She took him an apple one day, a bit of candy the next, some bread and butter on the third, and soon he began to remind her of a lean, stray cat who hung about, knowing exactly where his next scrap was coming from. She got into the habit of taking a bottle of milk and a sandwich to the boy every morning on her way to Children's Aid, and on Friday afternoons brought him the nourishing, if inexpertly prepared, creations of her cooking class, enough food to feed a dozen boys which she was certain it did.

And finally, one afternoon, he told her his

name—Jim—and agreed to accompany her to a small coffee shop under the shadow of the El, where they talked for some time, the trains rattling above.

"I only had but the one sister, no one else," Jim told Justine as he picked up a bowl of soup with both hands. "She got sick and they took her away to Blackwell's Island there, in the middle of the river. For a long time after, I used to go down to the shore and look over, kinda waiting for her, I guess. But I never saw her again. She never did come back from that island, and I've been on my own ever since. I done all right. . . . Good soup." He winked and drank down the whole bowl without pausing for breath. "That your house, where I was sleeping that time?" he asked, wiping his mouth with the back of a hand.

"My father's," Justine said, ordering him another bowl and a plate of beef stew. "And you're welcome there anytime you need to get in out of the cold."

"Thanks, I'll remember that," the boy said with a quick grin, but when they left the coffee shop he darted off before Justine could stop him. "See you tomorrow, maybe," he called, then disappeared around a corner.

That had been two days ago, and Justine hadn't seen him since.

Now, as the rain that had been falling all day turned, at dusk, to snow, she worried about that child, wondering where he was and where he would go to get out of the wet and the cold.

303

Passing carriages threw up sprays of gray slush and left ankle-deep pools in wheel ruts as Justine turned a corner and walked toward the park, gathering her fur collar closer around her throat. On pleasant afternoons on this street she saw other sorts of children than Jim, babies resting on lace and satin pillows, swathed in sealskin wraps as they were trundled in Brewster-built perambulators of polished white wood with gilt trim. Wondering about the vagaries of fate as she was often inclined to do these days, Justine lowered her head against the wind, and walked more quickly toward the sheltering warmth of home.

At midblock, a figure that had been standing in a doorway stepped out onto the sidewalk and followed Justine for a few steps. Then he took longer strides and proceeded in silence for a time on a course parallel to hers. She never looked up until he slipped his arm through hers, and when she did, she spoke not one word, just kept on walking.

"You know I love you," Nicholas said. She nodded. "You knew I'd come back to you, didn't you?" She shrugged. "Well, I have, so will you look at me and smile?" he asked.

She didn't, just hurried right past her father's house on Millionaire's Row, past Mr. Frick's house and Mrs. Vanderbilt's, too — kept right on walking south now along Fifth Avenue which was busy with evening traffic. After another few blocks, Justine glanced at Nicholas as they passed through a pool of light from a street lamp. He wore a caped greatcoat and a soft hat pulled low so she couldn't see his eyes. Still she said nothing, just felt how right it was, having him beside her.

"I'd gotten over you," she finally managed to tell him, holding her emotions in fierce check. "I'd gotten on with my life." They paused at a corner to let a hansom turn in front of them, snow swirling around its lanterns.

"I thought it would have been easier than it has been, getting over you," he said. "But you've been . . . crowding my dreams. It's only right you should know."

By the time they reached the Plaza Hotel, an uncharacteristic calm had taken hold of Justine, and when they sat across from each other in the Palm Court over a little round doily-covered marble-topped table, she was very quiet and observant, her eyes darting over him. She feared that if she gazed too long or too directly at him, she'd lose her detachment. There, amidst the potted palms and lace, while waiters in little white jackets pushed about carts of fancy pastries and tea sandwiches, Nicholas seemed extraordinarily handsome in his vested Saville Row suit with its fine stripe, the tip of a red handkerchief showing at his pocket. But for all his dark glamour, there was a lean, almost sinister look about him, a fierce, feral animal elegance. He's just a wolf in shark's clothing, she thought, not meeting his eyes, just watching his fine, shapely hand that rested on his knee.

"Why are we here?" he muttered deep in his

throat, once a waiter had taken their order and brought it, and violins, three of them, had begun to play.

"For the Friday tea dancing." She smiled, aloof and remote, extending her hand to him as other couples stepped out onto the floor.

Her hand was soft and cool and even smaller than Nick remembered when he grasped it and leaned toward her over the little table.

"You don't think I could actually take you in my arms in front of all these people?" he asked in a soft, husky undertone. "You know what would happen." He recaptured her hand when she tried to withdraw it, and brought it to his lips. But he didn't say anything else, not for a while. He just watched her as she daintily sipped her tea, not touching his own. And as he watched, Nick barely restrained a strong urge to clear the table, to sweep everything onto the floor and carry her out of there, away from all the polite, old ladies and the proper young ones innocently dancing with their tame, proper escorts. He glowered as he glanced about the room, noting that, as always, Justine was attracting a disproportionate share of furtive, and not so furtive, admiring stares. He leaned over and whispered something in her ear, then flashed his most outrageous, rascally smile.

"No, thank you," she replied coolly, as though he'd asked if she wanted another crumpet with her tea. He is just a civilized savage, Justine thought, glancing at him. A wild man in a genteel setting. Of all the people in the room, only she knew what was really beneath the fine suit and the white-on-white shirt displaying flashes of silver and turquoise.

It was then Nicholas saw on Justine's cheeks the faint watercolor blush he so loved, and her eyes did meet his for the first time, briefly.

"You're looking exceptionally beautiful," he said in a controlled voice, studying her carefully and with obvious intent. Her golden hair was swept up in a softly caught swirl, and a prim but pretty, pink and ivory cameo decorated the throat of her lace blouse. His eyes followed a row of pearl buttons to her tiny waist, and up again. "It's a wicked shame, that blouse," he complained, leaning toward her, the scent of her rose perfume teasing his senses. "That openwork lace . . . it promises lovely sights that are concealed by . . . what? Silk beneath?" He was sorely tempted, as he'd always been, by the soft thrust of her breasts. He wanted to reach out and touch them, but Justine just stared boldly at him then as if she'd read his thoughts.

"I won't be alone with you," she said, lying. And he knew it. He stood, dropped a few bills on the table, and waited at her elbow towering over her.

"How did you know where—?"

"To find you? Levi Phillips told me the address on Fifth Avenue." Nicholas helped Justine with her coat, letting his hands rest on her shoulders for a moment.

"I should have known. Of *course,* Levi," she said, turning up her collar as they stepped out

307

into the swirling snow.

"I'm promising nothing," she said.

"Of course not," he answered.

Chapter Thirty-four

"Mother's redecorating again so she and Father are at Silver Hill. There's no one here. There won't be until Monday morning when the painters return." Justine pulled the dust sheets from a pair of chairs and lit a candle in the half-painted parlor. The windows were stark and bare, the lights of passing carriages sliding in shadowed patterns along the walls and the ceilings. Nicholas knelt to start a fire. "Mother has a friend, an actress, who's trying her hand at decorating, a woman who does everything in white, very simply, with a touch of chintz here and there. This Miss de Wolfe is getting rid of all the Turkey carpets and fringe and clutter. Well," she hesitated nervously, "can I get you something?"

"A brandy, thanks." Nicholas said as he peeled off the well-cut jacket and just stood there in the satin-backed vest, loosening his tie.

Justine went out of the room, and returned to find him leaning, both hands on the mantel, his back to her.

"I saw him—saw Tony—falling in love with you, you know. That's why it took me so long to realize, to admit . . ." Nicholas turned to her and she handed him a snifter. "Twins are alike, so it's not really surprising—is it?—that it happened to us both, to Anthony and to me, at the same time?"

"That damned satanic pride of yours made you think you could simply serve me up to him on a silver platter, hand me over," she said, with clipped anger.

"And *your* naïve schoolgirl optimism made you think it would be easy to get exactly what you wanted with no complications, that happiness was your due. We were all three blinded by love, I think." He shrugged and sank into an armchair, long legs extended toward the fire, head in his hands.

"It was deliberate blindness, obstinate self-deception," she told him, beginning to pace. He looked up and nodded, his expression troubled, his dark eyes sliding over her.

"My brother trusted me. He's weak, you know, and I've always been there before to catch him when he fell. I'd kill for him. You should know that."

"What I know is that the weak can be tyrants in their own quiet way," Justine said, sitting opposite him, taking care not to brush his knee or his hand, "and I know also, now, after . . . you, that the possibilities of loss of life are endless and terrible. What must we do about it all?"

"Later, we'll talk about that—what we'll do,

310

but now . . ."

She sighed, turning away from him toward the fire, her false calm deserting her on the instant, her heart, as she stood, beginning to pound. "I was ready to risk everything for you once, Nicky. And I am again, you see, but . . . you'll have to lead me on," she said. She'd come face to face with her dreams she knew, and she was helpless to resist when he advanced on her swiftly and enveloped her completely, his lips on hers, cautious, testing; her response instantaneous and clear.

"Slow, love." He smiled, flinging back the hair that had fallen forward over his brow. "We've got all night long, at the very least," he added, his voice fire and honey.

Carrying a candle, she led him through the house, tightrope-walking along a great roll of carpet, past scaffolded rooms and leaning ladders, to an intact pantry where she collected bread and cheese and wine. Then she took him up the backstairs and along a corridor to her room, a feminine haven of calm in the chaos of disorder. There were chiffon and tinted mirrors, bits of lace and ribbon, pearls overflowing silver boxes, and a canopied bed deep in white, down quilts from which they didn't emerge for nearly two days.

"I remember just how to touch you," he said when she'd closed the door and then stood hesitating, trying to hold back, wondering what she might be getting herself into this time, because, of course, this time, like the last, he'd made no promises.

Drawing her into his arms, he kissed her, not cautiously, but devouringly, his fingers tracing the line of her cheek, the length of her throat, and coming to rest at the tips of her breasts, her own hands guiding him. She shivered and moved away a little.

"It's too cold for me to . . . take off things." She undid her hair, though, shaking it out in a fall of gold and he kindled a fire. When it was leaping, roaring up the chimney, but not before, he turned to her again.

"Well . . ." He grinned, dropping his jacket and wiping his brow. Very carefully, she placed her cameo on the dressing table, took off the lace blouse, and stepped out of her skirt. She waited, and he looked at her.

"No corsets?" he asked hoarsely as he peeled off his shirt, unable to take his eyes from Justine's long coltish legs and up-tipped breasts. She was an exotic, delicious confection in a camisole and pantalets of deep jade green trimmed in black lace.

"Haven't you heard?" she asked softly. "Modern women are being . . . released from stays and corsets and . . . other constraints."

"Scandalous!" He laughed, really laughed. "And, so . . . tantalizing. But you've always been a bold one, I think I knew that from the first time, when you hid like a thief in the dark and stole my heart."

"Do I really tempt you?" She laughed, too, but seductively, and for answer was denuded on

312

the spot, swept into bed, and taken with a fierce passion that left her limpid and luxuriously violated—sated, for a time, until he touched her again. But of course, that was the way it had always been with them.

"You're so lovely. Every time I see you . . . it's like the first time." The room was ablaze with candlelight and the newly fed fire was leaping again when Nicholas stood at the side of the bed and pulled back the quilts. "And even when I don't see you . . ." He knelt above her and closed his eyes, his hands sculpting Justine, beginning at her shoulder, tracing along breast and hip and thigh, then coming to rest on the flat of her stomach. "Even when I don't see you . . . I *want* you. I wanted you all the time we were apart." She brought a hand to his cheek then drew him down beside her.

"Yes, I know," she said, leaning on an elbow, looking directly at him. "And now? Will you promise me all your wild nights and lover's dawns—always? Say it won't end, ever."

"I can't," he answered in a tight voice, not looking at her. "It's nothing to do with wild nights. I lost interest in all that as soon as I found you. It's Tony. Seeing us together . . . he couldn't manage it. It would kill him. Damn!" Nicholas cursed and turned away from her, then got up, his muscled body tensed with anger. He pulled on his trousers and, after pouring himself a glass of wine, went to stare into the fire, his back to Justine.

"So. All you've brought me tonight is a tainted joy, then?" she asked in icy fury, now sitting bolt-upright in bed, her fists clenched, her eyes molten green. Her anger was like a lightning flare, very sudden, bright, and cold. "Damn you, Nicholas Jones," she hissed. "Couldn't you have lied to me and loved me tonight at least and said all this tomorrow?" She hurled a pillow at him, but it fell short. "You know, Nick," she went on, reclining again, her tone accusative, and chill, "I realized when I saw you today that until you, I wasn't living at all, just passing time and waiting for life—real life to begin. And when I saw you, I wanted everything with you, a home and children and a future. I thought you were my dream come true. But I was wrong, I see. I misjudged you. You're a faint-hearted weakling, afraid of love. No coward is going to father my children. You're hiding behind your brother. He's your excuse for behaving like . . . a fool!" Nick shattered his glass in the fireplace, the liquor hissing in the flames, and turned on her with a face so hard and closed she was afraid she'd gone too far. Knowing she'd struck a nerve, she was terrified, for him and for herself. But when he spoke, he took her by surprise.

"You're right. You *are* a clever one," he said, his eyes going over her, as he came toward her, his body tense when he stretched out beside her again, propping pillows under his head, then taking her hand. "You know me so well, Justine, better than anyone ever has, better even than

Tony. Sure, I'm afraid of you, because . . . I love you—and because it's so treacherous, my kind of love. I'd want too much, too hard, and if I ever lost you . . . I couldn't stand it." When Justine tried to speak he silenced her with a frown. "I saw my father lose the only one in the world he ever really cared about and I knew, watching him, that I'd never let anyone that close, never need anyone that much, or depend on anyone that way. I'm sorry Justine, but I can't love you the way you want, the way you should be loved, the way you deserve to be." When he turned to her, his look of anguish melted her heart and all her anger, on the instant. "For me, love just has to come and go so . . . sooner or later you're going to have to forget about me—again."

"Oh, Nicky!" Justine sighed, hiding her face in her hands. "Take a chance with me, please. It'll be worth it, I promise, and love will last, I'll see to that. I'd do anything for you, really I would so—"

"Anything?" he asked, with a terrible, chilling laugh, before he uncovered her tear-glazed eyes and looked into them hard. "Well, I think I'd best tell you now what happened to my mother. My father thought he killed her out there in the wilderness because he wanted another child, a girl-child. He'd had a daughter long before, one he hardly knew. My mother had already lost two babies, but she loved him so much she wanted to give him . . . everything, deny him nothing; and so she tried again. My father lost them both, his wife and his daughter. Since then, I've never let anything come between my brother and me because all I had was Tony and all he had was me."

"And now you've got me, too, for however long you want me, even if it's just for tonight. No, no! Don't interrupt. It's only right you should know." Justine put a finger to his lips as she echoed his words of the day before. "I was a mere child, a little girl when I met you and now . . . I'm not. What I am, whatever I've become, I owe to you, forever, even if you are breaking my heart. So would you like to love me now, madly, without reason or reserve and then—"

"I would like that, yes." He nodded, and she never got a chance to finish her sentence, not for a long time, not until Sunday morning, when, dressed for the first time since Friday evening, they went out into the garden and found untouched snow blue-white in the early dawn, the air gray and cold.

"This seems to be our time of day, winter or summer," Justine said a bit tensely. "For hellos and goodbyes. Will you go now? Can't I have one more night?"

"Well, there's a thing to be done before we say goodbye," Nicholas said, reaching up to a branch of a cherry tree and causing a little snow shower that powdered them both. "Win a race."

"I'd given up on that without you, and now we've so little time. Georgie Boy, the gelding I've started training, is not a great horse. He couldn't win." The snowdrops clung to her hair like crystal flowers.

"You've given up?" Nicholas asked. "What's happened to that terrier tenacity I've heard so much about?"

"Oh, I guess I've sort of outgrown all that childish nonsense, but . . . well, how could we win now?" She shrugged, then followed him along a garden path, stepping into his footprints.

"Since I last saw you, love, I've been on a quest of sorts, searching for myself in a way, and for my brother . . . mostly for my father. I went to see our half sister in Florida, Evangeline, in the hope she'd know something about the man, but she's not heard from him in years now. In the course of our visit, though, she did tell me about Geronimo, the Indian Chief, who was a prisoner at Pensacola, along with some of his braves. The ladies of the city paid charity visits, as you do here, to the fort where he was being held, and he once told Evangeline about a lost valley high in the Sierras and of the horses there, unlike any he'd ever seen. So, I thought we'd all go and have a look for ourselves." He turned to Justine with a questioning smile.

"We?" she asked, backing away from him.

"You and me. And Tony. I know he's somewhere here in the city, and I'm going to find him," Nick declared, and she turned away and ran toward the house.

"Justine! We can't win without you!" he called after her.

"I never took you for a quitter, Justine. For a lot of other things before I got to know you—a tease and a flirt—but not for a quitter," Nicholas

317

said with goading disdain when he found her in the kitchen, still wearing her coat, boiling water for tea. She wouldn't answer or even look at him. "Too bad," he went on, drumming his fingers on the table. "I can just see Roweena's malicious smile as she flaunts your opals all over New York." That struck home, he could tell. Justine's shoulders squared. "And think of the money we'll win, what it could do for your waifs and your strays," he added, and she turned to face him. "Levi told me what sort of work you were doing. Look, just come West with us for a little while and help me choose the right horse and train him. You needn't come to England for the actual race. I'll see to that."

"You just try to keep me away," Justine said, "and you'll rue the day you ever met me."

"It'll never happen." He laughed, lifting her off her feet and swinging her about.

"One thing," she said, after he had kissed her.

"Anything." He smiled.

"I refuse to go sneaking about like a thief, stealing your love and hiding from Tony. After today, it's strictly business with you and me. After today, I don't ever want you to touch me again because . . . knowing what I do, knowing it's going to end, I couldn't bear it. Promise!" she insisted, and he looked at her, perplexed and incredulous and angry all at once.

"But Justine, why? How can I keep away from you when you'll be so close . . . and my need is so strong. Come on," he coaxed. "I'm everything you ever dreamed of. You told me so yourself."

"I don't care if you're the grandest man ever put on this earth," she said. "Don't ever touch me again."

"That wouldn't include today, would it?" He laughed lecherously.

"Well, okay. Today, I'm yours to do with as you like but after—"

"As *I* like?" He laughed.

"Promise or its no deal," she urged. And he did, lying. She suspected as much, but that was just fine with her. She had no intention of giving up this man without a fight, and a double deception might suit her purposes admirably.

Chapter Thirty-five

They sat at the kitchen table and talked about their shared past, short as it had been, and their future, short as it promised to be. Determined though Justine had been not to cherish him in her mind or heart, her body, as he well knew, hadn't let her forget. It was only her work, she admitted, that had saved her from her memories of him.

"I've been helping the Settlement House volunteers and some missionaries, too, in the Tenderloin and Italian Harlem. The work in the crowded tenements, the missionaries say, is as important as what they do in very distant places," she told Nicholas as the winter storm held sway again. Outside, wind whistled about the chimney, and the snow, which had stopped for a few hours, came down more heavily than before. "There are so many people crowded into places where there's no hot water or heat, where windows open onto dank airshafts and children grow up in shadows, like twisted plants starved

320

for light and air. Some of the youngest work twelve hours a day making cardboard boxes and paper flowers that they sell on the streets for cigarette money. And there's a little boy I see almost every day. He's thin as a matchstick, and living all on his own. I'd take them all in if I could," Justine declared. "But I do what I can. Now, tell me, what you have been doing."

"I went West to see Geronimo when I left Florida," he said, rolling a cigarette. "I took the train out to Omaha where they had the old man on display, in October, at the Trans-Mississippi Exposition, as they call it. He's always being mobbed wherever he goes by curiosity seekers. The government took him out of the Fort Sill stockade, where he's being held with some other Apaches, and they had him selling pictures of himself and the buttons right off his coat. As fast as he sells them, he sews on new ones and sells them too." Nick frowned. "It's sad, you know, to see an old warrior so powerless. His guards call him Gerry and it makes him very angry. All Geronimo really wants is to go home to the mountains that he misses, but, you know, people are still afraid of him?"

"He wasn't always an old man, and the stories one hears about him are still frightening," Justine replied. "When he was caught, I heard, he was wearing a blanket made completely of human scalps. What did you think of him?"

"That's just a story about the scalps," Nick said. "When I met the man, he was dressed in a dusty, three-piece suit and a plains hat he'd sell you for twenty-five dollars. He's still impressive, intimidating to some; with heavy black hair to his shoulders, thin lips, strong chin." Nick sent a smoke ring toward the kitchen ceiling and lamplight danced on the walls. "We've something in common, that old Indian man and me, we've both seen the mountains . . . seen the sun and the moon in the Western sky and we've both breathed that free air. I will, again, but not Geronimo, I'm afraid. The soldiers say he's a real unlovely character, but I think you'd like him, Justine. And I know he'd like you."

"Me?" she asked, pleased. "Why?" She went to the oven to look at a crock of pork and beans that had baking all day.

"Because he's a gambler, like you. He deals three-card monte at these Western shows, shouting at the top of his lungs and rakes in his winnings. He's got quick small hands like yours," Nicholas said, reaching to Justine. "He's a great shot, too, like you, and he believes in the special power of luck, a little like you, too, wouldn't you say?" Nicholas smiled. "But what Geronimo likes most is a horse race. Small as he is, he's too heavy to ride in a race, and always was, so his wife's often been his racing jockey.

"I told him about you and our steeplechase, and he told me about a high valley in the Sierras and a herd of horses that's been pretty isolated. They're a breed apart, a little Spanish Barb, a little Arab, a touch of thoroughbred, and a lot of mustang, in other words, pure American mongrel, and we, Miss Hawkes, are going to that high valley and catch us one of those wild horses and win a steeplechase against the finest jumpers Europe can produce. But now" — he looked at her in that way that meant only one thing — "now you'd better just get back to bed because I intend to make the very most of what little time's left before our new . . . arrangement goes into effect."

Justine blushed in that way of hers, like a watercolor picture, so delicate and pretty, and was starting toward him when they heard a sound at the pantry door. With some irritation, she flung it open, and there was the boy, Jim, trapped in a shaft of light from the kitchen lamp, coughing and shivering and soaked to the skin.

"You look like a half-drowned cat I once found," Justine said and the boy, a cigarette stuck in the corner of his mouth, grinned.

"I didn't mean to bother you none. I was just gonna use your doorway here 'til morning, if it's all right with you, miss." Justine instantly drew him into the room and over to the fire, and he extended his hands, red and cracked with cold, toward the warmth.

"Meet Nick, and take off your clothes," she said, turning her back.

Jim was still shaking violently even after he'd had a warm bath, and been wrapped in a quilt and put to bed in the only room of the house that could be used, Justine's.

Almost at once, he fell into a dream-disturbed

sleep and his befrienders sat up with him until morning. By then, Jim was burning with fever, and a doctor was summoned.

"The boy's underfed and so rundown it would be disastrous, putting him back on the street," the physician said. An old friend of the Hawkes family, he stood on the doorstep, bag and hat in hand, his expression one of concern. "The child needs building up, Justine, and good food . . . fresh air. After he's well, he should be placed in an orphanage or sent West on an orphan train. I'll look into it."

"No need. I'll take care of all that, Dr. Wells," Justine said, and as the doctor turned away she closed the door against a blast of icy winter air. She went right to the kitchen to prepare a tray of food.

"He couldn't have fallen into better hands than yours, could he?" Nick asked as he followed Justine upstairs. Jim's fever-glazed eyes lit up when she entered the room, and Nick couldn't help but notice the guarded adoration in them.

And Justine, Nick could see, returned Jim's affection as, over the next few days, she waited on the half-starved alley cat of a child hand and foot. Nick himself, though he came and went on his own business, also began to develop an attachment to the boy as Jim's health improved and his independent spirit began to reassert itself.

While painters worked in other parts of the house and Justine went off once or twice to Children's Aid, Jim and Nick played cards—for

matches. The boy wore Gray's old but very fine
clothes, pajamas at first, then sweaters and
shirts, that were a little too big in the shoulder
for him and, to his delight, too long in the
sleeve. The fortuitous misfit combined with his
own manual dexterity enabled Jim to cheat
through several games without getting caught, or
so it seemed.

He would expertly stack the deck when he
thought Nick wasn't looking. He could crimp the
cards — bend them in such a way that the deck
would cut exactly where he wanted it to as he
palmed some cards and slipped them up his
sleeve. Jim's gray eyes would shine, and he'd
smile angelically every time he won, which was
always, for he dealt himself one flush or full
house after the other and his mound of matches
grew.

But even though his shirt cuffs covered his
hands almost completely, it was an attempt at a
very obvious false riffle that finally exhausted his
opponent's patience.

"I saw you," Nick roared, directing at Jim the
fierce stare that had terrified full-grown men.
But the boy just gazed back at him serenely, and
blinked once or twice.

"What say?" he asked Nick, all innocence.

"I saw you cheating, sonny. I've been watching
you since the first deal, just waiting to see how
far you'd go. You've gone too far."

"I don't know what you're talkin' about, mister." Jim shrugged, replacing the deck of cards in
the middle of the table and beginning to edge

325

out of his chair.

"Do you know what they do to card sharks where I come from? They shoot 'em . . . or hang 'em . . . or worse." Nick bestowed his most lethal smile on Jim.

"Takes one to know one, mister," Jim replied with a worried scowl. "I gave you the mechanic's signal before the first deal. I put my left hand flat on this tabletop. How come you didn't respond or nothing? Oh, and 'mechanic' is the word in the trade, not cheat. Mulraney says so. He's been teaching me . . . things. I've been practicing by the hour, until my hands get too cold like they done the day I first come by here. Say, want me to learn you a few sleights of hand Jack Mulraney's been showing me?" Jim asked, and Nick roared with laughter.

"I noticed your so-called mechanic's signal, sonny. I just wanted to see how good you were. You're not bad, but your hands are too small for the false shuffle. Here, I'll show you," Nick said, taking the deck and performing the maneuver expertly. "I have seen the best card sharks in the world, and won my money back from some of them at Monte Carlo and St. Moritz. Who's this Mulraney who's been coaching you?"

"Happy Jack Mulraney, one of the Gopher Gang that hangs out on the West Side," Jim said, his expression indicating Nick's ignorance was abysmal. "Happy Jack is one of the gang that runs Hell's Kitchen. He's trainin' me for a good profession, he says, so I can go to Saratoga when I grow up, and on some of those ocean liners, to gamble and get *rich*."

"That what he does, Happy Jack, cheat at cards for a living?" Nick sat back and looked at the boy, hands locked behind his head, eyes thoughtful. "What else does he do in Hell's Kitchen?"

"Mulraney just about runs that part of town. He works out of Murphy's Bar on Thirty-ninth Street near Tenth Avenue. Nothin' goes on there Jack don't know about. Listen, I got these dice, see? Want to shoot craps?" Jim asked. "Happy Jack and me play for smokes. Got any smokes?" Jim asked, as Nick set up the boy's dinner tray, as a backstop for the tumbling dice, against the foot of the bed.

"The doctor said no more smokes for you, sonny, but I'll tell you what. Tomorrow, if you're feeling okay, we'll go see your friend, Mulraney. I'm trying to find someone who's probably lost in Hell's Kitchen, and I think Happy Jack just might be able to help me find him. Now"—Nick grinned—"I bet two buttons. Will you fade me?" he asked.

"Buttons?" the boy asked with disgust and then sighed. "Yeh. Two buttons. I'll fade you, but don't ever tell Mulraney about buttons. He'd never stop laughing."

"I'm jealous as hell of that little friend of yours," Nicholas whispered to Justine a few nights later as he was taking his leave of the Fifth Avenue house.

327

"How can you be jealous of a little boy, especially one you've been spending so much time with? Where did you two go today?"

"To meet some of his best friends — Happy Jack Mulraney and 'One Lung' Curran. Very interesting fellows. But I'm jealous of Jim because he stole my last night with you," Nick answered, reaching for Justine. She fended him off.

"That's all over," she said firmly. "It's strictly business with you and me from now on. You gave your word and you are a man of honor, are you not?"

"I'm not," Nick snarled, turning up the collar of his coat. "I want to renegotiate the deal. As long as we're going to be together, close, going West and all . . . it's going to be . . . difficult."

"No need to worry about temptation. I can't come with you now. I'm going to care for Jim." Justine gestured at the staircase, and Nick glowered at her for a long moment.

"Bring him, damn it," he snapped, pulling his hat low and stepping out the front door onto a Fifth Avenue deep in snow. "The mountain air is just what he needs. Sure, bring him and any other strays you happen to find on your doorstep. But remember one thing. You owe me a night and I'm going to claim it, sooner or later. Don't you forget." He grinned, fast and hard.

Chapter Thirty-six

A week later, Nick and Justine went to rescue Tony. That was the way they'd always think of what they did. They took Dr. Wells with them to that shabby furnished room on the lower West Side that was a terrible mess of empty bottles and stale food, unwashed linen and overflowing ashtrays.

"I probably passed this house a dozen times at least in the past month or so," Justine said as they entered the decaying red brick building and, in silence, climbed to the top floor to knock on Anthony's door.

"What is it?" a furry voice responded. Nick stepped into the dim, malodorous room and went at once to throw open the window and shade, and there was Tony, blinking and cowering like an animal at bay. Half-drunk on cheap gin and deathly pale, he kept his eyes on a spider making its laborious way across the cracked ceiling.

"We've come to take you home," Nick said sadly.

Dr. Wells quickly checked him out, then said, "You're to have nothing, not a drop ever again, once you've gotten over it this time. Understood?" He looked sharply at Tony as he folded his stethoscope. "You'll not make it to old age, young man, or even to middle, if you keep up this way."

"Okay. But just one more. To give me a little courage," Tony pleaded with a sheepish laugh, his pouched eyes little more than slits. "Bumpers, as the British say." He lifted the glass he'd filled to the brim and drained it in three swallows. "What do you mean, Nick, home?"

Nick didn't reply. He just helped him up and walked him out of that room, leaving everything behind: the soiled suits and stained shirts, the half-empty bottles—everything but the drawing pads Justine had gathered up as Dr. Wells and Nick helped Tony down the narrow, dim, foetid stairway and into the waiting hansom.

Five days of rantings, fevers, and horrible delusions followed before Anthony finally fell into the deep sleep that signaled the end of his alcoholic delirium. Nick had been warned.

"You can't do much for him now," the doctor had said. "All you can do is be there to keep him from hurting himself."

So Nick never left his brother once during the episode, but stayed at Tony's hospital bedside from the first signs of restless confusion through hallucinations and tremors and panics, and

330

through rantings and ravings about Justine and her treachery, about home and the hills and the mountains.

Sometimes Tony seemed like a child, sunk deep in the past, and at others, the past blended with the future that loomed before him, terrifying, as a cast of characters paraded through his nightmares. Larger than life, they crowded the room to torment him . . . Boni and Zou, Bet-A-Million Gates, and even Count Zenga. Most prominent were Eustace Molesworth and Roweena who, Tony tried to tell Nick again and again, were diabolical and dangerous and about to destroy them all. Listening but hardly hearing a word Tony spoke, Nicholas, man of action that he was, was enraged by his own inability to help his brother.

"You've got your work cut out for you this time, my dear," Dr. Wells told Justine, patting her gloved hand which rested on the carriage seat beside him. "What does your father have to say about all this, you going West with three dashing young men"—the doctor winked at Jim—"and no chaperone?"

"Well, Father doesn't know, not yet, but when you give him this letter"—Justine slipped an envelope into the doctor's pocket—"Father will have all the information he needs. There's just no time for family councils and lengthy considerations."

"So you're running off are you, young lady?"

Dr. Wells asked in his most authoritarian tone. "And I'm to be the bearer of that bit of startling news, it seems. It's a good thing Slade Hawkes isn't the sort to blame the messenger for the message."

"Father and Mother will understand this is something I must do without quibbling about social niceties. Besides"—Justine smiled—"I've got a valiant and devoted protector in Jim. Isn't that right?" She turned to the boy who nodded emphatically. He sat opposite her. Observant as always, he'd been glancing out the window at the familiar city streets he knew he'd not be seeing again for a long while. They were on their way to a hospital to pick up Nick and his brother, the boy had been told, and then they'd go straight to the train station.

"See you keep an eye on the lady, son, or you'll have her doting father to deal with besides myself," Dr. Wells teased, though the boy took him absolutely seriously and nodded again. "And as for you, young lady, since you insist on going through with this escapade, I'll tell you what I've already told Nicholas. The patient, Anthony, must be watched even more carefully now than when he was ranting. What can follow, in these things, is terrible remorse and melancholy. He must never be left alone because there's no telling what he might do. You understand?" Justine nodded. "One thing more," the doctor said. "You'll find Anthony to be suffering from a condition called Korsakoff's disease. It resembles amnesia, but it's peculiar to those who imbibe overly much as he has done for so long. Patients can recall the distant past quite well but not very recent occurrences. The illness is not well understood but we do know that with time, rest, good food, and . . . love, most of them pull out of it, sooner or later. So, my dear"—the doctor smiled—"you'll have two patients needing much the same sort of care while you're out there in the West chasing rainbows in your lost valley. I've no doubts about this young man, making a complete recovery. He's hardly coughed at all today." He ruffled Jim's hair. "He's practically cured already. You like horses, boy?" the doctor asked. Jim nodded.

"I've been hangin' out on Stable Row, doing errands for the auctioneer," he answered.

"Stable Row?" The doctor looked questioningly at Justine.

"Twenty-fourth Street that runs from Second Avenue to Lexington. It's all stables and a saddlery shop or two. The street's always full of hay and oats and very . . . pungent. They have horse pulls on auction days to demonstrate the strength of the draft animals."

"They also got Tom Thumb's tiny coach there, from Barnum's Circus, you know," Jim reported. "Hard to fathom, a person so little as that. I wish I could'a seen him—and I wish I had a smoke," he added, looking up pettishly from under beetled brows. Dressed in Gray's clothes, which had now been altered to fit him perfectly, the boy's very respectable appearance was in odd contrast to his New York street-urchin manner and speech.

"I've told you before. There'll be no more smokes," Justine said as sternly as she could, and Jim grinned.

"Happy Jack didn't give me this kind a trouble. He always give me all the smokes I wanted, especially when I done him a service. I helped you find this Tony Jones, didn't I?"

"Well, if you prefer Happy Jack's company to ours—" Justine began.

"I didn't say that or anything of the sort," Jim replied as the carriage pulled to the curb.

Tony came out of the hospital, gaunt and thin, his shirt collar too big and loose at the throat. He looked far older than his thirty-two years, far older than his twin brother whose own face was grim as the two climbed into the carriage. Anthony greeted Justine with a faint sign of recollection and a kiss on the cheek but not a word.

"You and me got the same sort of problem," Jim said when they were introduced. "They're making me give up my smokes." Though Tony smiled a little, he seemed to Justine merely a ghost of his former self, and a very quiet ghost at that. When she tried to draw him into conversation about India or France, he remembered nothing. It would be weeks later, after they'd found the high valley and had been camped there for a while, that his spirits began to lift and his memory to return.

Chapter Thirty-seven

"Meet Justine Hawkes," Nicholas said. "She's been with me a little while now. You'll like her."

"Pretty as an autumn apple, isn't she?" Rob Edwards commented. The manager of the Jones ranch in Sacramento, he had come east to Carson City in late winter, to meet the travelers as they detrained. A small, bandy-legged man, sturdy, solid, and friendly, Edwards had curly gray-threaded dark hair and a spray of white whiskers on his chin. He'd dressed for this momentous occasion in a high starched collar, a derby, and a tie pin with a silver nugget. At the first sight of Justine, he'd snatched off his hat and smiled, flashing a gold tooth. His accent, part Texan, part Irish, was completely captivating.

"Do we have the pleasure of meeting a future Mrs. Jones?" Rob's wife, standing beside him, looked at Justine with curiosity, and smiled.

"It's strictly business with Miss Hawkes and me," Nick said as they started toward the hotel where they would spend the night before heading off into the hills.

They left Carson City the next morning, Justine, Nick, and Rob, each well mounted, an extra horse and a pack horse on a lead, all the animals grain fed for the strength and stamina they'd need to run down a wild stallion.

Cath Edwards, with Jim and Tony for company, drove a covered spring wagon full of supplies. She was a pretty sprightly woman, much younger than her husband, who always dressed in bright colors and always sang, loudly or softly depending on the time and place and occasion. "The Pardon Came Too Late" and "The Picture That's Turned to the Wall," popular songs of a few years back, were her favorites, but over the weeks they were to spend together, Justine became certain the girl knew every mountain ballad and every Western tune ever sung by any cowboy anywhere, and that particularly delighted Jim.

When Cath produced a nickel-plated Höhner harmonica in a hinged wooden box with "Old Standby" on its cover, the boy found, to his own surprise and everyone else's, that he could pick out the notes of any song Cath hummed. And so, Jim and Cath became great friends during their travels west and south into the California mountains. In fact, they all became friends as they left the civilized, citified world behind them, like the wagon-train pioneers of old, and became part of the vast untouched wilderness. Only Tony was detached and sad and silent, as the doctor had predicted he might be.

"This country . . . it takes over your own self, doesn't it?" Cath asked Justine one day after they'd set up their first camp. "It's like you become part of it and you don't need a whole lot else to make you happy. Though there're some things you do need." Her voice trailed off as she and Justine looked over toward the men who were finishing building the small huts in which they'd sleep until the weather broke. Snow had been mounded several feet high in hive shapes, packed very solid, and then sprinkled with water that froze overnight, making a hard crust. Now, with shovels and picks, shirtless in the spring sun that was warm despite the snow still piled on the ground, Nick was hollowing out the last of the snug, snow domes, into each of which a smoke hole would be chipped.

"You and him been together like he said?" Cath asked. She and Justine were stacking supplies into the crook of a tree in case of a sudden meltoff anytime soon.

"Yes," Justine nodded, turning up the collar of her sheepskin coat and, with difficulty, taking her eyes from Nick who'd turned to look at her as if feeling her gaze on his bare skin.

"And now you are not . . . together. *That* way, I mean," Cath said, looking from one to the other.

"No, we're not. It's been a long time now since we were and it's . . . hard." Justine shrugged. "I mean, all those days and nights on the train and all. But, there are reasons we can't be . . . together."

"I never did suppose Nicholas was a marrying sort of man, all moods as he is sometimes, restless as a fire in the wind and looking like he's turned wild, his face lean with a kind of hunger, like a winter wolf. Of course, I wouldn't say anything to him, but it's love he's craving. Now I see you are inclined to the sunny side, not to the rain, and so, if you were to love him, you could balance him like. When the moods come on him, I mean."

"Can't. He won't have me, not in the way I want him to," Justine answered, knowing nonetheless she'd not turn Nick away if he came to her that night in her solitary igloo. All warm beneath fur blankets, she'd be yearning for him as she hadevery night since their last one together in New York. Taking note of Justine's expression, Cath didn't pursue the subject just then, but began singing "Down in the Valley." Before she got past "angels in heaven know I love you," Justine interrupted her.

"Well, Cath," she asked, "why don't you tell me how you met Rob."

"Met him at a hanging," Cath promptly replied. She and Justine had made a fire in a ring of stones under a sheltering outcrop of rock, and they were making a squirrel stew with salt pork and beans.

"At a . . . hanging?" Justine sat back on her booted heels and looked up, saucer-eyed, from what she'd been doing, stirring the kettle.

338

"Um," Cath nodded. "It was down to Fort Smith where they have a gallows the men call The Gates of Hell. That's because it can do twelve at a time, an even dozen. The day we were there, they were dispatching but six . . . horse thieves, I think. My, that was ten years ago almost, January of 1890. The hangman in that town, a gloomy person as you well might expect, was kept real busy because there was a hanging judge, Ike Parker, in the Oklahoma Territory then. Maybe he's still there for all I know."

"And what of Rob?" Justine prompted, consumed now with curiosity.

"I was working as a Harvey girl. You know about them?" Cath glanced at Justine who shook her head no.

"Mr. Harvey is a Scotsman who came over here to America and traveled west and couldn't get a decent bite to eat anywhere along the Atchison, Topeka and Santa Fe Railway. All the poor sodbusters and cowboys and train men were getting to eat in those days, in the 1870s, was rancid bacon and old eggs stored in lime to preserve them, such fare as that. They used to call the biscuits at the railway depots sinkers because they were so darned heavy. So Mr. Harvey came along and bought himself a run-down eating place in Topeka, scrubbed it up, and fixed it really nice with fine china and all. And after it was a success, he got to advertising for girls to be waitresses: 'Young women of good character . . . attractive and intelligent . . . eighteen to thirty . . . to work in the West.'

"When I was just near eighteen, in 1886 it was, I'll never forget, my sister sent me one of those advertisements from a Kansas City newspaper. It came just at the right time for me because at home then there were still ten of us, trying to scratch a living out the Georgia dust on a farm that couldn't grow enough of anything, not much at all, and . . . well, I wanted to get away from there and find me a husband of promise, not some poor farmboy sharecropper. The Harvey girls were the only women in some of the new Western towns, except for the bawdyhouse painted ladies and such." Cath blushed. "They were good places to look for a husband. So, I just up and went West with Mr. Harvey following the Santa Fe line across the country with the gandy dancers laying track, him opening new depot eateries — 'til my contract was up."

"Contract?" Justine questioned, carefully tasting the hot stew.

"You had to sign on for one full year, and promise not to marry in that time. They paid us seventeen dollars and fifty cents a month plus board and tips and uniforms, too. That was a plain black dress with a white collar and a little black bow. Gosh, after I quit being a Harvey girl, I never wore anything but beautiful Indian colors, orange and red and yellow and such." Cath laughed, peeking into her coat. "Anyway, we lived in big dormitories, all together, and there were matron ladies to watch over us and be sure we behaved properly. But they did let us have a dance in the courting parlor, as they called it, on a Friday night. A lot of the girls wed railroad men when their contracts were up, but I married Rob Edwards—after that hanging."

"Why a hanging, of all things?" Justine wanted to know, looking over to where the men were finishing work on the snow huts. Cath looked in that direction, too.

"Rob was a lawman then. He had to go to that hanging. I saw him pass on the street and he was so handsome, it was love at first sight. I just wanted to be with him, to find out who he was and all? So I followed him to the hanging and I fainted and he caught me up in his arms. After that, we were wed real quick and tried sodbusting . . . farming. 'No man would work for another if he could labor for himself,' Rob always said, but we had a bad winter and lost everything and so now we're working for the Joneses. Of course, you couldn't find a better boss than Nick. He's generous and fair, but someday . . . well, Rob and I have got each other until someday comes." Cath smiled, and Justine looked up to see Nick coming toward them.

"You'll be snug tonight, warm as toast," he told her, remote and polite and all smiling good humor. There wasn't the faintest suggestion in his voice or his eyes that he might consider joining her in her snow hut, and he chose not to see the disappointment written on Justine's face.

They rode out of camp every day searching for mustangs. Justine, Nick, and Rob traveled in ever-expanding circles through lost valleys and across pristine untouched snowmeadows, past spangled waterfalls, like living light, and over steep, bare gray protrusions of rock.

Justine and Nick rode knee to knee for days and days on end, and it was as if he changed before her eyes, became a new man, yet one she recognized, one she'd seen in unremembered dreams. In his long, leather duster coat and gauntlet gloves, a beaver hat shadowing his eyes, he became the hard, handsome cowboy with desert-haunted eyes, the mountain man of myth and legend. Knowing what to expect of the wild country, he'd made sure Justine had everything she'd need, too—peaked hats and warm gloves, buckskin leggings, and fur-lined boots, their tall shafts silver-studded and turquoise-trimmed. He'd even provided pure silk longjohns, caressing and soft and warm.

As the last winter days passed and spring came to the high hills, pulsing and fragrant, Justine found the first wild cyclamen and saw young deer nibble new grass on the edge of receding snow. She and Nick stood in admiring silence in the sliding shadow of a California condor, its wingspread nearly ten feet wide. They were almost always silent, the three of them, giving themselves up to the wild beauty of what they saw, which was exhilarating and beyond any need for words, until they camped far from home base under the night sky. Huddled beneath the same blanket at the camp fire, shoulder to shoulder with Nick, pristinely touching, Justine often thought how simple it would be to put an end to their agony of restraint and just place her hand on his muscled thigh, then turn her head ever so slightly . . . offering her lips.

One evening, she did just that, acquiescence in her smile, the soft, longing invitation in her eyes clear, she thought. Nick apparently didn't think so, or declined to accept. He merely smiled back and then spread his blanket roll as far from hers as it could be and still remain in sight of the camp fire. If it was strictly business she wanted, she'd have it. He'd decided that on the train coming West after she'd twice reminded him to keep his distance. Which was just what he'd been doing ever since.

"It's a good thing for Cath you came out here," Rob said on another evening as he and Justine sat sipping coffee. Nick had wandered off, a new habit he'd gotten into. "You and that city boy. Isn't he a shrewd one, though?" Justine nodded. "Well, she's certainly taken a liking to you both. We don't get many visitors to the ranch. Maybe once or twice a year someone wanders by."

"But it must be better than the Iowa plains where you came from, Justine responded.

"Well, I suppose. I would rather work for myself than for another but we lost everything one cold, winter. I should have known it would be

343

bad because we had a bad omen in the fall. Cath's last pair of lace gloves just fell to shreds when she tried puttin' them on. She'd do that, from time to time, slip on those gloves, the last real pretty thing she had left. Field mice got to them, I suppose, and it near broke her heart. I could see it, though she didn't say anything, just sat and watched the sunset, the long sunset before the harvest moon came up, and she not even singing a note.

"Then that mean winter came on us and we had to leave in the midst of it. There was nothing left, no wood, no food. . . ." Rob was shaving a stick with a pocket knife, exposing the green-white flesh of the sapling as he stripped it of bark. "We crossed these Sierras in a cruel season, and we were little more than skeletons, the pair of us, when we came down into the beautiful, gentle valley of the Sacramento River, all in a glow of spring. And then Nick did a golden deed. He hired us on and we've been with him ever since."

"You'll both come to England for the race. You must," Justine insisted.

"On the way, we'll stop for a bit in New York City." Rob nodded, now shaving the sapling to a sharp point. "Cath . . . she's always wanted to go there. Know why?"

Justine shook her head. "Why?" she asked.

"She's always wanted to see Lillian Russell and Diamond Jim Brady. She read about them in some magazine, about how he had twenty-six thousand diamonds in his collection and he *wears* them and lights up the Broadway night like a lantern. Have you ever seen him?"

"Him and Lillian Russell, yes. Their carriage is often tied at the hitching post in front of the Mark Cross Saddlery on Fifth Avenue." Justine emptied the dregs of her coffee into the fire. "He is an immense man, simply huge. His two passions, besides Lillian, are diamonds, of course, and eating."

"She keeps right up with him, does she?" Rob had stopped whittling to concentrate on what Justine was telling him.

"It would seem so. She gained so much weight dining with him, he bought her a gold-plated, diamond-studded bicycle. When you come east for the race, you and Cath might see her exercising right there on the streets of New York."

"There won't be any race if we don't soon find out we're after. It's April and you've got to be there to run the last of June."

Justine nodded.

"You're going to have to find a horse that's perfect, the right age about six or seven—and with the ideal confrontation. He'll have to be of a temperament to be easy broke to the saddle, and he's going to have to be smart as a Philadelphia lawyer. One in a thousand."

"Is there a horse that smart?" Justine said, pulling her blanket closer about her shoulders.

"If there is, we'll find him. Now you'd best turn in so we can get an early start in the morning."

The next day they finally came up on the hoofprints they'd been looking for.

Chapter Thirty-eight

Upwind from the snow-swollen brook where the horses had drunk, they lay side to side, the three of them, resting on their elbows, and watching and waiting, hidden in the underbrush most of the morning and into the afternoon. As they did, Nick began to sorely regret his cavalier rejection of Justine's offer of some nights before. Of course, she hadn't said anything, but her lovely eyes had been so willing, her hand so . . . suggestive that he'd almost succumbed and just swooped her up and ridden off with her into the wild hills and done what he'd been dreaming of for so long now.

Glancing at her lovely profile, he imagined taking her, as he'd done often before in reality, savagely and then, after a time, very slowly and with infinite attention to all those fine details he and she so enjoyed.

He rolled over onto his back and closed his eyes to stop himself from staring, but *still* saw her elegant body hovering in the air before him.

He felt silken skin beneath his fingers, and heard in his mind, her cries and catches of breath that meant only one thing. Nick opened his eyes and looked at Justine who was beside him, in the flesh; real, breathing, and beautiful. The sweet agony of it was almost more than he could stand. She was so close—kissing close—and she had been for hours. Sometimes she'd look through her brass spyglass and he'd be tempted to trace the line of her back and let his hand rest on the swell outlined by the buckskin trousers and leather chaps he'd given her, never anticipating these moments of smothered lechery.

She rolled onto her back and looked up at the sky, and that was worse for him because her jacket fell open and the compulsion to mold and caress what he'd not forgotten, what every nerve ending in his body remembered with electrifying clarity, was pure torment. Finally, she sat up, her back against a tree and just looked at him, her green eyes glowing with passion, pleading and teasing, threads of sunlight snared in her golden hair. She braided and unbraided it with a kind of irritable quickness, not fooling him in the least. But he'd waited this long and he was determined to win the round, play the hand to his own greatest advantage, have her agree to anything he wanted, accept any offer—marriage still no part of what he had in mind, but more of a sometime thing even though he was in love with her. He'd admitted to that already. It was just that he had to get her out of his system, that was all, because it was bound to end. No love

348

would last. But the tormenting desire for her lovely body, so slim and so close, was almost more than he could control. Only later would he realize it was Rob who'd gotten him through when he was about to promise her anything and claim the night of love he was owed . . . call in the debt. Rob talked him through it with that burred, lilted Texan-Irish drawl that was music to calm the wildest beast. . . .

"Now, you see that each stallion controls his own mares, and only one band at a time comes down to drink," Rob explained as, with wonder, they all watched the horses arrive at the river. "They come down in turn, and we got to see which stallion it is we want, which one of them is the best. Some's mean . . . vicious. There's outlaw horses. Like outlaw men, they'll kill their own kind. They'll fight each other to the death and you, too, if you should catch one. Others will just go and die on you before they'll accept anything you have to offer. And kill you in the bargain if they can. I lost my little finger to one wild stallion who bit it clean off," Rob said, flashing the four digits of his left hand. "And I've come in off the range more than once with a bootfull of blood from a horsebite.

Now, look at this lot coming to drink. You can see a little trace of nearly every horse that ever was in the world, if you look carefully, look right — Shetland and Connemara ponies, Irish hobbies, Arabian Barbs and Appaloosa paints, even a bit of thoroughbred, too."

"There's a fellow I heard about over to Arizona who is back breeding, getting beige and black mixed manes and zebra-striped legs, like the old horses here before the conquistadores' mounts got loose and went wild on the plains, before these wild stallions came stealing gentled mares off ranchers. Now . . . see." Rob's voice had changed suddenly. "There's *our* stallion, I should think."

"Look." Nick pointed, and Justine felt her heart jump in her throat at the sight of the band that came thundering across the meadow below them. These graceful, wild, beautiful horses, manes flowing and nostrils flared, were driven by a stallion of extraordinary size and beauty, a golden bay with a long white tail and mane. In the crystalline afternoon, with long purple shadows cast by Sierra mountain peaks falling across the land, he drove his mares with their colts and yearlings toward the meandering white river almost in flood.

In the first rush of spring, red-tailed hawks circled above and Western bluebirds were in the willows at the river's edge. Justine was quiet as she examined the stallion through her glass. He stood now, neck arched, head up, at least sixteen hands high, a tall, strong animal and a noble one.

"If beauty and ability go together as it's said they do, this is our one in a thousand, the horse we'll need to win our race," she said. "He's got superb head carriage . . . high, clear-cut, long withers. All great jumpers are built exactly that way."

"Yes, big and tall as he is, he'll make one hell of a jumper, if anyone can get a hand on him and live to say so." Rob already looked worried.

"The herd will summer here," Nick said. "The mustangs will come every day to drink at the river and that's how we'll get him. It's after that our real work will begin."

"There's two ways to go about this, my friends," Rob stated. "Stake out one of our gentled mares to attract him and lure him to us, then get a rope on him—or run that herd, as much of it as we can, into an enclosure at the end of the valley and hope he is among the catch."

"I'd want him penned," Nick said, "before I'd even try to put the rope on him."

It took time to build the large circular enclosure they needed. Nicholas and Rob, with Tony helping sometimes, cut greenwood saplings for days, the sounds of their axes echoing through the trees. They worked fast and hard, from dawn until past sundown, hardly pausing to eat the meals that Justine and Cath prepared and brought out to them. Jim fetched water in a pail for the men to drink and helped pile up the cut posts until there were enough. Then post holes had to be dug, and the saplings set, then lashed together with rawhide strips that were strong but elastic enough to give and not damage a fine animal who might plunge against the barrier. When that was done, an alleyway was built, almost a half-mile long, leading to the enclosure, and the pair of wings was well disguised with brush and dirt. The mustangs would be driven between them by Nick and Justine, while Cath and Rob waited at the gate to put up the bars once the animals were driven in.

"A mustang chase, that is truly a noble sport," Rob told Justine before they were about to begin and the two were walking about the enclosure, doing a final check of its strength. "Once the animals are caught, there is nothing in the world to compare to the thrill of taking your pick of the band while they are all circling and wild. After you have cut out the one you want from the rest of the herd and worked and worked at gentling him, then you'll be proud of the horse you've got and he will be loyal to you all his life long.

"You know, Justine, they must be kept circling in the pen once they are driven in or they will turn and tear into each other in fear and panic. Horses will imitate each other, follow each other's example, especially when they are afraid. Now, you and Nick must run them a long way, get them winded, as winded as you can, before they come in. They'll be easier to handle if you do. Also, let them drink their fill first. A horse full of water is a slower horse. But, I don't know why I'm nattering on this way. Nick knows all this," Rob said, putting a hand on Justine's shoulder, looking somber. "He is a man of real quality, Nicholas Jones. But then, you don't need me to tell you that. I suspect you know it already."

"I do," Justine said, testing a fence post by pulling on it with all her weight.

"He's got strength of character, and a shrewd brain."

"I know," Justine said again.

"He's the best mountain man I ever have met up with. This is where he belongs. He recalls the least detail of any terrain he's ever laid his eye on, even once. And he's a fine marksman, a great horseman—"

"I know," Justine said a bit shortly as she and Rob mounted up and headed back toward their camp, which had been moved higher into the hills in the warmer weather, the spring air fragrant with the scents of damp earth and pine. The days were fair and getting longer, but even so, the nights were still cool.

"To meet up with Nick Jones is truly deemed a pleasure by all save those who come in contact with his fists. I've seen him use them in defense of Anthony mostly. His brother would always rather compromise than fight."

"I know that, too," Justine said. "Do you think he's getting better? It's terrible for Nick, having him so closed off and silent."

"I'm no doctor, though I wish I was to help that boy. He's never been strong since I first took up with the Joneses. He often had these nerve storms as he calls them though this time it's different, him forgetting as he has. It's hard on Nick, and you could be a comfort to him." Justine looked away and didn't answer. "I can see how it is with you and Nick, so I'll ask, though perhaps I shouldn't, what is holding you two apart?" Rob took off his hat and wiped his brow with the back of his hand.

"You'll have to ask him that," Justine answered, putting her horse into a quick trot and leaving Rob behind.

They didn't get the golden stallion on the first drive. After they'd watched him wheeling and thundering away across the meadow, his dew-spattered mane flying, they were afraid they never would, now that he'd seen them and seemed to understand their intent—to steal his freedom. They did get most of his mares and young though, who came terrified, nostrils flaring, into the fenced space, the first those animals had ever seen. While Cath, Tony, and Jim shouted to keep the horses circling, Rob got the gate posts up and a blanket thrown over them to keep the horses from trying to charge right through to freedom.

Though they didn't get the stallion on that first run, they did get most of his mares and started in at once to rope them out and set them free until just one, a fine-boned young beauty, and her little white colt, were left in the pen. And that night, just as Nicholas predicted, the stallion came down from the mountains to try to claim what was his. They heard him calling softly to the mare in the moonlight, and then saw him pace along the fence, the mare and colt

354

following him on their own side of it, whinnying and calling to him. When he found no way in, the stallion tried to tear down the fence with a great drum roll of hooves and a scream of rage.

"Lord!" Cath whispered to Justine as they crouched, hidden, and watched that stallion. "Why, he's so wild and free, he's more like a raging tiger than any horse I've ever seen. Who on earth is ever going to put leather on that wild thing?"

Nicholas did. He got his lariat on the stallion when the great horse came again the next night to visit his imprisoned mare and colt, and the battle of wills that began between man and animal was awesome.

The horse, ears flat back, eyes rolling and blazing fire, screamed in rage and plunged and pawed the damp earth. The man, holding hard and fast, the rope coiled around his hand and arm, went down as his right leg doubled beneath him and his left extended as a brace against the plunging, furious horse.

The struggle went on for a long time as Nicholas, inch by inch, moved the great animal toward an opening that had been made in the post fence, and when the stallion saw—realized finally—that a way had been cleared for him to get to his terrified mare, he turned and ran to her, the rope that Nicholas released still dangling from him.

Breathing deeply, Nicholas, sweat-soaked in the

cool night, rope burns on his arm where the lariat had cut right through his leather jacket, helped Rob replace the fence posts and then turned to the others. "Keep out of there," he said, speaking more to Justine than to anyone else, knowing she was the only one who'd even consider trying anything so reckless as entering the pen now that the stallion was in it. She looked at Nick with respect but with something else in her eyes, too, resentment and anger.

"I'm not sure we should be doing this," she said, troubled, before she turned and walked away into the darkness.

Chapter Thirty-nine

For days after, Jim sat on the rail fence from morning till night and watched that beautiful mare and her fine little colt, who were calmer now that their stallion was there with them, even though that great beast plunged and raged if anyone approached them. As time passed and the penned animals refused all food and water, Justine began to wonder aloud if that stallion could ever be tamed, and Jim grew ever more agitated and pained at what he was seeing.

"It ain't fair," he said to her one day. "That horse—he loves that mama and her baby and he is trying to care for them. And if we take him away or if we hurt him, well then, that little horse will be an orphan like . . ." The boy choked back his words and pursed his lips, scowling. Justine put an arm about his shoulder and drew him against her.

"Look" she whispered into his ear, "we'll give them one more day. If the stallion's not on his way to being gentled by tomorrow night, we'll let him run," she said, and the boy looked at her quickly. "We won't tell anyone else, okay, Jim? It's our secret."

"And the race ... the bet ... your opals?" he asked.

"All that doesn't seem so important now, here, watching this beautiful, stubborn horse that's worth more than any race or bet or jewel." She smiled. "One more day."

"You really think we should let him free? ... I'm *going* to let him free," Jim said as he and Justine sat side by side on the rail fence in the dark the next night. "He's hungry, that's for sure, and thirsty. I can't abide seeing anything hungry like that." Justine, saying nothing, took an apple from her pocket and, with her pen knife, cut off a section that she handed to Jim before she took a slice herself. And the next thing she knew, the boy was down off the fence and right in the pen with those wild horses, walking straight at the stallion whose ears worked this way and that, while his eyes rolled back in his head as he snorted, getting the mare and colt protectively behind him.

Justine's scream brought the others running and it was Nicholas who scaled the fence, pistol in hand, to sit astride it, taking precise aim as that stallion screamed, reared, and plunged. Jim didn't even flinch. He just stood there and held out his hand, the piece of apple resting on his palm. The stallion came down on all four hoofs,

358

tossed his head, and reached forward, then took that piece of apple and chewed it and swallowed it; and the boy patted the velvet nose before he took up the end of the lariat that was still dangling from the animal's neck. Then something unexpected and wonderful occurred. The fierce and towering animal, now docile as a kitten, followed that very small boy back and forth across the pen, then around in circles and in figure eights, Jim's small smile turning into an ear to ear grin as the others watched in tense excitement. It was a wondrous moment on that clear spring night, on that ribbon of high mountain meadow, a moment none of them would ever forget. It was as if everything fell into place all at once.

"Hey! Justine," Jim called, "got another apple?"

"Apple, nothing, kid," Rob said, "you run and get him a big pail of oats, quick. We've got to put some weight on that horse and feed him up. Get him strong enough to run the toughest steeplechase in the world!"

Everything went quickly after that. Nicholas and Justine, with Jim always close by, worked together all day every day with the wonderful intensity of shared purpose and pleasure, and a sense of rightness in everything they did, though neither said a word about it.

Nicholas took pleasure in watching Justine bring the great horse under her sway, taming him to her hand and voice. He admired her handling of Jim, too, as she drew the boy into the work they were doing, explaining every step of the training as she went about her business with calm control and confidence.

Justine was happy, having Nicholas with her all the time, seeing him deeply pleased and obviously doing what he loved. He knew as much, even more, about horses than she did, and probably about children as well, little boys at least. She came to that realization as she watched Nick teach Jim to braid a lariat one day, guiding the boy's small hands on the rawhide strips again and again until Jim had mastered the skill and looked up worshipfully, quietly proud, at Nick who nodded in approval. With the boy and the horse, he was generous, even tempered, and kind, though he took no nonsense from either as he and Justine took turns working, varying the stallion's regimen so the animal didn't grow bored with his schooling and become rebellious.

"A thorough grooming is as good as a feed, it's often said," Nick told Jim, who was given charge of both. They started the groomings by just caressing the stallion with a soft rag, slowly and carefully and with great patience. Then, when he'd gotten used to that, a soft brush was used and finally a good stiff one that the animal grew to enjoy as his golden coat gleamed. The stallion was more difficult and sensitive about his unshod hoofs that had to be leveled and rounded with a rasp. Eventually, he accepted that, too, though never with very good grace.

"You must check his legs and feet every day without fail," Nick instructed. "And at any sign of puffiness in the fetlocks, rest him."

"For how long?" Jim questioned, running a hand along the horse's leg.

"Until any sign of tenderness is gone. I've seen many a good horse ruined because the owner wasn't patient enough."

Justine watched and listened and offered her own suggestions, and she longed, with increasing urgency as the days passed, to be in Nick's arms. If he wouldn't love her on her terms, it was getting so she was almost willing to take whatever he would give, any way at all. But she held back and so did he, and the days passed.

They named the horse Gavilan—hawk—and he was the one in a thousand they'd been looking for. Everything he had to know came almost naturally to him as—with an almost arrogant pride, Justine swore—he performed exactly as she wished, progressing from lead to snaffle to longe. A long rope was attached to a headpiece with a noseband but no bit, and the animal was led by one trainer, followed by another, and taught gaits and commands—walk, trot, gallop and whoa. Gavilan was an agile, well-balanced "daisy cutter" and when the time came, he took the bit well.

"He is a horse of moods," Rob said, leaning at the rail one day, three weeks into the training.

"Yes." Justine laughed. "As long as we follow

his routine he's fine, but if we don't . . . watch out. He won't do anything at all if Jim's not standing by, right, Jim?"

The boy, who had to come to love the training routine, was watching Nick put Gavilan through his paces. He nodded, his canny gray eyes smiling.

"He's eatin' up a storm," Jim told Rob. "Twenty quarts of oats, cracked corn, bran, and molasses every day, like you said, Rob, and twenty pounds of clover hay besides. You know what he does? He comes running at me full tilt when I sit up on the fence and whistle for him and clap my hands. He comes running so fast it looks like he'll go through that fence, but he pulls up short just in time. He gives me a scare every morning."

"Well, he'll give the other horses in the steeplechase a good scare, too. You'll see." Rob laughed. "You ready to start in jumping? When is he gonna be ready to be mounted? I'm gonna be here to watch *that*."

"Tomorrow," Nicholas answered, leading the horse to the rail. "Gavilan took the blanket with no trouble at all, and he's been carrying this little Virginia postage-stamp saddle for a few days now. "Tomorrow, I'll mount him. He's already felt a foot in the stirrup."

"Will it be like a Wild West Show, bucking and pitching?" Jim asked.

"None of that. The horse has to know who's boss. As soon as he's learned that, you're going to mount up, young man. You and Gavilan might as well learn the racing game at the same time."

Chapter Forty

Jim, it turned out, was as much a natural as Gavilan, ninety pounds of instinctive jockey atop the tall, powerful stallion. To the boy's intense, unending pride, he was made head rider, and he and the horse honed their skills at the same time as the training jumps—fence posts padded with saddle blankets—were put up higher and higher. Jim had good horseman's hands, a secure seat, and a kind of gutter-snipe scrappiness that made him a fine competitor. On Gavilan, he raced against Justine and Nicholas, not nearly as well mounted, across valleys and meadows fragrant with spring in the last week of May when it was almost time to leave for England.

On their final night in the mountain camp, there was a party. Justine, for the first time in weeks, put up her hair and put on a dress that was lacefrothed and pretty, if not exactly a ballgown. Cath wore a red skirt, a bright yellow blouse, and a blue neckerchief while she and Justine cooked the final celebratory meal—venison stew and blue cornmeal dumplings. She hummed happily.

Jim, proudly wearing a grown-up pair of galluses, a gift from Nick, played his harmonica; and there was a lot of talk and mutual congratulations over their success with Gavilan. There was also some excited, very optimistic speculation about the upcoming steeplechase, and Justine spoke of putting the stallion to stud after, at Silver Hill. But mostly there was an already nostalgic reliving of the weeks they'd just passed in the high Sierras, a rare time out of time, of closeness and shared dreams, a time now at an end.

The mood of the evening seemed to touch Anthony, and as the meal progressed, he, too, began to remember all sorts of things, bits and pieces at first, random recollections.

"How Jim would have laughed at Aimery d'Erlanger, wouldn't he?" Tony asked with a warm smile as he drank a glass of goat's milk and the others sipped a homemade wine that Rob had brought up from Sacramento for this special occasion. Tony had followed the doctor's orders, and he was looking himself again, exactly like Nicholas, well filled out and strong.

"Who would I have laughed at?" the boy asked eagerly.

"A very tall, very thin, very lazy duke who went to the beach at Deauville with two footmen, one to walk ahead and brush pebbles from his path, the other to carry his towel. All three of them were dressed up in long-legged, long-sleeved, red bathing costumes with yellow stripes.

It was a scene to behold," Anthony remembered.

"I'd like to see your duke and his foot people, skinny-dipping off a pier in the Hudson River like I've always done." Jim guffawed and Justine laughed, too, imagining the lad, thin as a matchstick and tough as a water rat, floating in the New York river.

"Oh, Aimery would tiptoe into the water like a sea bird and fall forward like a toppling tree," she recalled. "Then, he'd swim three strokes. Wasn't it three, Nicky?" she asked, turning to him and laughing again. After her eyes met his, her voice changed, softened, as she continued. "Well . . . Aimery was a sight. Tony did sketches of the man, didn't you?" she asked.

"I don't remember really, but you brought my portfolio from the furnished room in New York, didn't you, Justine? Let's see if old Aimery is in there." It was the first time Anthony had mentioned his drawings, and she got up very quickly to get them.

"I brought your pencils and watercolors, too! I'll be right back," Justine called excitedly to him.

Tony turned through the pages of his sketch pad very slowly as the dinner things were being cleared away, while Cath sang and Jim played his harmonica. The song now was "Molly Carew," an old English ballad, one not chosen at all by accident.

"Sure my love is all crost,

Like a bud in the frost,
And there's no use at all in my going to
bed
For 'tis dreams and not sleep that comes
into my head."

Cath wasn't one to pry into other people's affairs, but she used songs to say exactly what she
wouldn't think of uttering. Justine and Nick,
hearing the words of that well-chosen ballad,
avoided each other's glances until he laughed
suddenly—at Cath, at Justine, at himself. He
stood and bowed.

"May I have this dance?" Nicholas asked, and
Justine nodded, going into his arms as
the song, a waltz, was extended for their
benefit. Then, both laughing and looking into
each other's eyes, they whirled in firelight, at the
edge of a wilderness, to the sweet song of a
mountain girl and the music of a little boy's harmonica. Soon, they no longer laughed and suddenly, in midstride, they stopped before the
music did. Then it stopped, too, and there was
only the sound of the spring wind in the trees as
they stood together, not touching now, not even
smiling.

The others, gathered round the campfire,
watched them in silence, each with his own
thoughts, and if there had been any doubt in
anyone's mind about how things were with Nicholas and Justine, there was now none at all.

"I . . . remember! I burned all my pictures except the ones of you, Justine," Anthony said in

a low choked voice, and she and Nick, holding hands, carefully it seemed, came to look over his shoulder as he went on turning pages. What had just been so obvious as they'd danced together had already been there for anyone to see in those drawings done months before—love and pulsing desire that was almost palpable.

There were also many drawings—page after page—of intricate ornate woodcarvings, stone finials, elephant pediments, and Indian motifs. Then Tony, who had been flipping through the pad hurriedly, turned one last page and stopped cold.

"It's the woman, your friend, Justine. What's her name?" he asked, looking up as if at a complete loss. "She's the one who married Molesworth."

"Oh, yes. Roweena." Justine placed a hand on his shoulder as he flipped the pages again, nervously and very quickly. "I never realized you did so many sketches of her, and in so many different gowns. You must have spent days and days with her. But . . . where?" Justine asked, stopping his hand. "Not in India, surely, because the backgrounds are all wrong. It's New York!" she said with surprise. "Did you see Roweena in New York? Tony, do you remember about Eustace, that he met with . . . an unfortunate end?"

"No!" Anthony said emphatically. "I know nothing of Eustace but this woman—Roweena—she brought me . . . things. She brought them to my furnished room, drink mostly, I think," he added, going ashen and standing suddenly. "And

368

I promised her something in exchange."

"What?" Nicholas asked sharply.

"I can't remember," Tony answered, closing his eyes and bringing a fist to his brow. "I'll try, but . . . Does it really matter?"

"I'm not sure," Nicholas answered. "Anyway, don't worry and upset yourself. It doesn't matter now. Now you're with us."

"I'm going to retire." Anthony smiled faintly. "We've got an early morning, haven't we?"

The others stayed at the fire a long while, until just ash and low red coals were left, making a very small glow in the vast darkness under an immense starry sky. Jim, resting his head against Justine's shoulder, had fallen asleep as the adults around him talked into the small hours, everyone reluctant, it seemed, to end this last night in the wilderness. When they ran out of talk, finally, Cath just kept on singing and singing, one ballad and story song after another, about lost love and cowboys alone on the range, longing . . . yearning for a love and home.

"Do 'Cowboys' Meditation,' will you Cath?" Rob asked. "And then we must be getting to sleep, much as I resist it. We've a long way to go, darlin', across the country and over the sea to that place that was once home to me and now is a foreign land. Do 'Cowboys' Meditation.' "

And Cath sang, her voice so pure and high and touching that Justine recalled the myth of the wandering musician Indira had narrated in another time and place that now seemed no more than a figment of her imagination.

"At midnight when cattle are sleeping
On my saddle I pillow my head,
And up at the heavens lie peeping . . ."

The story Cath's song told reached them all, especially when she sang:

"Often and often I wonder,
At night when I'm lying alone,
If every bright star up yonder
Is a big peopled world like our own."

Although the musical tale went on for several more verses, about ranges and cattle on faraway stars, about broncos and riders and more, it was the idea of peopled stars that caught Justine's imagination.

"We're on the edge of a new country and a new world," she said with wonder when Cath had done. "Tomorrow we must leave these mountains where nothing has changed in a hundred years . . . in thousands, and go back to that new world in the making, out there."

"You can't cling to the past forever," Rob said, "though you must not ever forget it. I remember when I saw Buffalo Bill Cody at the World's Columbian Exposition in Chicago. It was in the year of eighteen hundred and ninety-three. Cath was with me. Remember Cath? Cody had a lot of men riding with him in that show, Arabian horsemen, Russian Cossacks, Mexican vaqueros,

South American gauchos, German uhlans, French chasseurs à cheval . . . and I recall thinking, back then, watching that great extravaganza, how varied and vast is the world, and how it is changing and getting smaller, somehow. But Mr. Cody will go on keeping the past alive for us all."

"I have seen Mr. Edison's kineoscope of Cody—flickering pictures that *move* before your very eyes," Justine said. "Mr. Edison is a friend of Father's. Father has always supported inventors, even foolish ones, like the man who made something called an 'early rising machine,' a bed that tipped the sleeper onto the floor, and also a 'loafer's chair' that fired a blank shot under anyone who stayed in it too long. But lately, all Father has talked of is a young Italian, Guglielmo Marconi and his black box that talks. Marconi and his brother signal to each other across fields with white handkerchiefs when these black boxes carry their spoken words. Father says we shall soon be talking to each other from ship to ship and so on. Mr. Gordon Bennett of the *Herald* will bring Marconi to New York and Father will invest in an American wireless company. There is a new and astonishing world unfurling all about us," she stated, gazing up at the unchanging stars.

"I don't for the life of me, understand why anyone needs a wireless talking machine when people who are right side by side don't speak the truth to each other." Cath shrugged, looking pointedly from Nicholas, who'd been grim and silent, to Justine and extending a hand to Rob. "We'll put the boy in his bedroll," she added, as Rob hefted the sleeping Jim in his arms. " 'Night, you all," she called over her shoulder, leaving Justine and Nick alone. In silence. It lasted *forever*, until the embers of the fire had faded completely, until Justine, too, finally stood.

"Well, good night," she said reluctantly. Getting no response, just a fast glare, she hurried away to her own shelter.

It was almost dawn when Justine awoke, the words of Cath's song, the one about dreams and buds wilting in the frost, ringing in her head. She knew at once what she must do, spend the time that remained in Nick's arms, here in the wild mountains where he belonged, where he was home. Tomorrow they'd have to go back to the intruding world, and now that their time together was almost gone, she had to have the memory of one perfect night of love in this perfect place to keep forever. Rising, she stepped into her jeweled boots and slipped on her lambskin coat. It was warm against her bare skin, and chafed at the tips of breasts that had risen and firmed during dreams of longing. She stepped out of her bent-pole shelter and started up the forest path that Nick had taken every night after the evening meal, as if trying to get as far from temptation—from *her*—as he could.

She walked with determination, head down so

she wouldn't fall over any roots and rocks, until, all at once, a figure loomed in front of her. She gasped, frightened, and looked up into Nick's eyes, glowing dark as she'd seen them before, as if fires had been kindled behind them. And there they stood, face to face, close, hearts hammering.

"I was coming to you," she said, a faint smile lurking about her lips, "to pay my debt."

"I've met you halfway to claim what I'm owed." The words were a rasp deep in his throat, and she lifted her arms to him with a little cry and let the coat fall open. She felt moonlight sculpting her body as his hands had so often done and then she was in his arms, and felt his lips and his hands, where she most wanted them and had so often dreamed they were.

He went into her standing right there in the moonlight, their joining as elemental and untamed as the night and the hills and the star-swirled sky above.

Somewhere, off in the distance, a mockingbird sang.

He'd built himself a treehouse that was cantilevered out over a waterfall and the rushing torrent sang in their ears—their words, their sighs, carried away into the darkness. After their first taste of passion in so long, Nicholas and Justine, though still love-starved and lustful, drew apart a little. In awe and delight they explored each other anew, almost as if for the first time. White radiant moonlight dropped through the pines and brightened the shelter in which they lay as Justine's wondrous, smiling eyes slid over Nick's wide shoulders and muscle-knotted chest. When she knelt at his side, her hand followed the ridged, sinewy line of his tensed arm, resting at his slim waist as her lips brushed his brow and then moved to the hollow of his throat. When her caress slid down from his hip, she heard his breath catch.

"I've waited so long to touch you," she whispered, "and I wanted you so, I almost—"

"I know," he said hoarsely, as he swept aside the silken curtain of her forward-flowing hair and kissed her lips. He reached to touch the tips of her breasts, hard as new little rose buds, and when she went still and quiet and her eyes drifted closed, he drew her down beside him again. Leaning on one elbow, it was his turn to investigate and explore her, to touch and caress with his hands and eyes what he'd so long been seeing only in dreams.

And when he was, for the moment at least, nearly sated with sight of Justine, Nick lovingly went about satisfying his other senses, inhaling the fragrance of her rose perfume and of her brook-washed curls, his hands molding and delineating her elegant body from throat to breast to waist to thigh. The sounds of her soft deep breaths changed, became low gasps and urgent little cries, as he kissed and tasted and mouthed her most delicate, responsive tips and clefts.

"I've been hungering for you so. I've been craven with the need of you," he said roughly. He knelt between her parted thighs, and she lifted her arms and he went into her again and it was like breaking open a velvet-soft, full-blown rose, the petals unfurling to expose its deepest, most treasured secrets. . . .

In what was left of that night, there was another moontide surrender, total and complete. Long-distilled passion flowed like a fiery, heady liqueur, and the taste of it was still sharp and hot when a bluebird broke into its exuberant morning song.

"Don't ask me to go, not yet," Justine implored as she felt Nick begin to draw away from her. They'd been pressed together, still and close for some time, their bodies joined, legs entwined; and when Justine spoke they began to move together again without ever having broken the bond of their last coupling.

"Go slow, love, and easy if you'd have it last a while longer," Nick said, shifting Justine above him. "You're so beautiful," he sighed, encircling her waist and bringing his lips to each breast tip before he rolled above her, taking control, moving with languid strength, the passionate, loving undulations going on and on and on.

It was full bright dawn when Nicholas finally moved away from Justine and offered her his hand. As she stood gazing at him with love-soft eyes, he placed about her waist a belt made of linked silver conches, each centered with a polished, pastel turquoise stone.

"Is this the turquoise at the end of my rainbow?" she asked, smiling. "Just like in the Apache myth you told me of?" Her eyes searched his face until he turned away.

"If I had a castle, you know, you'd be my chatelaine, the keeper of the keys of my kingdom and of my heart for always," he said gently. "And after all this time of keeping you away from me, though I could see the need in your eyes, it's as if I can't get close enough now, in this moment. I want to know every thought you have . . . I want to feel what you feel, even beyond words — always. Justine, I want this to last, but . . . whatever happens, remember this single moment. Now, this time, is true."

"The rightness . . . the completeness of this night in this place . . . how could I forget?" she replied curling beside him again.

"It's as if time doesn't move in these mountains, and when you're here, the land takes you over and strips you bare of all pretense. I can't lie to you here, Justine, and make promises I may not be able to keep, but . . . I have to say I love you. And whatever happens . . . if I should lose you, I'll miss you forever."

"There's no way of knowing how the future will unfold," Justine said, repeating Levi Phillip's words. "You're still afraid to take a chance on me, aren't you?"

"Justine . . . I want to take care of you, to *be* with you always, but . . . don't ever stand in starlight with anyone but me. Promise?" he asked, with heart-twisting desperation.

"No promises, not here, not now, at least none that we can't be certain to keep. And I want you to remember something, too, Nick. Whatever does happen, you're not to worry about me. I'll be fine no matter how it all comes out. I always am. I can take care of myself, and if you don't know that about me by now, you don't really know me at all." Justine looked down, not able to meet his searching, troubled eyes because she'd just betrayed their perfect moment with a lie. "Damn you!" she burst out. "Why can't you just . . . just love me? What are you afraid will happen when we leave here tomorrow . . . today?" She traced a hand along his muscled shoulder.

"Anthony — you saw him tonight — he's just starting to get better. I can't chance hurting him now, again. When he's strong, then I'll tell him about you and me and then . . ." He shrugged.

"Don't underestimate him. He'll never get strong if you do. Perhaps he won't ever remember that he loved me . . . once," Justine said rising from the rope bed that was piled with soft blankets, a warm nest she had no desire to leave. She draped her coat over her shoulders.

"No man who has loved you could ever forget, Justine. I think he's just beginning to remember. There's no way of knowing what he'll do when it all comes back to him." Nick stood also, his hard, lean body washed in first dawnlight, and took Justine in his arms again and kissed her before he helped her descend from the treehouse.

377

"We'll just have to wait and see — and help him, if we can."

Chapter Forty-one

"Oh, Anthony, really!" Roweena Molesworth exclaimed with a strained laugh. "Don't give it a moment's thought. Our little plot wasn't serious. I mean, you don't really think *I* could expect *you* to betray your own brother? I mean, how could I have just given Justine over to you anyway to do with as you wished, even if you did pretend to be your brother? You *silly* boy!"

"I am very relieved, Roweena," Anthony said, "because I was afraid I'd done something . . . evil. But what was it that you said in New York? I'm still rather muddled." He looked about the smoking room at Castle Rising near Sandringham, where Roweena and Count Zenga were guests of Lord and Lady Farquar.

"She said she'd provide poison for the horse that you could administer—aconite or hyoscine bromide. You were to give it to him the night before the race. In exchange, she was to have had the girl carried off to a tower in some castle somewhere, and then you could have done whatever you wanted with the twit." Count Zenga laughed, though his eyes glittered in anticipation of doing himself exactly what he'd just described with such skeptical amusement to Anthony. "Sounds like the plot of a melodrama, eh?" Zenga poured himself a brandy. "Let's just forget about all that nonsense, shall we, and have a friendly chat and a drink?"

Anthony nodded agreeably and looked about the room that was done in the Indian style, with silk plush curtains at the windows and a gathered tapestry ceiling. Bet-A-Million Gates took a gin and hot water from Zenga and strode over to thump Tony on the back and demand, with his usual swaggering vulgarity, to know all about this horse they'd brought over from America for the race.

"I hear there's never been anything like him — your stallion — in this country. I hear he's a big, fine fencer, with a long white mane who snorts fire like a dragon! Is it true?" Tony's eyes lit up with pleasure at the thought of Gavilan.

"Gavilan can't be beaten." He smiled. "He *is* full of fire and courage. He jumps neat as a stag deer and soars like a hare. How is your own horse doing, Gates?"

"Champion, thanks." Gates scowled. "He's Irish-bred, leggy, and very powerful in the quarters. But tell me more about this stallion from the Sierras. I hear he's fifteen hands and a thousand pounds. How did he travel?"

"More than sixteen hands and twelve hundred pounds, I think. We put a hundred pounds on him ourselves, with oats, since we took him out of the hills," Tony answered. "And he did the trip as well as could be expected. We had a stock car all to ourselves coming east to New York. Even so, he was snorting and fearful of the passing landscape until we covered the windows. We stayed with him the whole time and the boy, Jim, fed him. Gavilan will eat only if the boy feeds him."

"That so?" Gates asked with wide-eyed friendly interest.

"Yes," Tony nodded. "They're that close, the boy and the horse. The stallion was a little stiff and muscle bound when we reached England. That's from keeping his balance all that time in the swaying railroad car and then aboard ship, but he's fine now. He's going to win, I know it."

"We shall see. As dear Eustace used to say, I've never yet heard of a great thing done by any but a thoroughbred horse," Roweena scowled. "Your Atlantic Ocean crossing was smooth, I trust?" She and her companions had taken seats in a half-circle with Tony at the center and they were watching him intently.

"Yes. Smooth and fast. Justine's father provided us with passage on one of the modern, new ships of his merchant fleet." Tony picked up his glass of brandy and inhaled the sharp scent of the liquor. "Of course, when we finally got here, it was cold and damp as it always is in this country, even in June, and Gavilan's not used to this sort of climate. Also, he had to be shoed for the first time, coming out of the wilderness and all. But Justine's been exercising him for the past two weeks. She took him over the course yesterday. It was a magnificent performance. He's got a great heart and terrific staminas, and I can't tell you how beautiful he is. And smart. He can lift down a fence rail . . . open a door latch . . . come when he's signaled—by the boy, Jim, anyway. But you'll all see him for yourselves the day after tomorrow."

"Come when he's called?" Gates exclaimed, slapping Tony's knee. "Go on!"

"Sure. Jim has a special way of whistling and then he claps, and that makes the stallion come running like a puppy dog right to him, so fast you'd think he was going to trample the child into the dirt. But Gavilan stops, on a dime, and then he just rests his head on that lad's shoulder. It's a fine sight and it touches the heart every time." When Tony reached for his glass, it tipped and the contents poured over an inlaid table.

"Oh, never mind! I'll refill that for you." Roweena jumped to her feet, and returned moments later with a brimming glass of brandy. "Such an exciting occasion, don't you agree?" she asked, resettling herself in her chair. "The Erlangers are here, the Worth brothers, North, Barnato and all of them most anxious to see this great American stallion they'll be going up against. Who's sporting silk for you?" Roweena's conniving eyes narrowed noticeably.

"It hasn't yet been decided. If we want to keep the load light, it will be Justine or the boy who'll jockey. The only other person Gavilan will allow to mount him is Nick so . . . we'll see.

Now, I must go." Tony stood, looking very fit and handsome in a dove-gray waistcoat and dark suit, and Roweena slipped her arm through his.

"So soon? I thought we could enjoy an afternoon's outing," she suggested. Though still in widow's weeds, her complexion pasty and pale against the black gown, Roweena made it clear that she was completely available to Anthony.

"If the man has other commitments, Lady Molesworth, you shouldn't detain him," Count Zenga said, offering Tony his hand. "Good to see you again, sir. I look forward to seeing your brother *and* the beautiful Miss Hawkes."

"Mauro, you evil man!" Monica Matti said. She had swept into the room in a hiss of satin, just in time to hear the count's last remark. Her slim, elegant hand snaked out and rested on Tony's shoulder. "You'd better have a care, Mr. Jones, or Mauro will steal your girl." She laughed. "But if he does, I'll be more than delighted to amuse you in her place."

"She's not my girl," Tony answered, distancing himself from the pair of vulturous women.

"Say there, son," Gates bellowed as Tony reached the door, "your jockey going to run it in long or short leather?"

"Short. Justine prefers to stand over the withers. She always sits high," he answered.

"Like that American jock, Todd Sloane. He brought the short stirrup to England just two seasons ago." Gates nodded. "They all laughed. They said he looked like a 'monkey up a stick,' but you see how they are all racing now, like

Todd Sloane and he . . . But where are you off in such a hurry?" he called after Tony who couldn't get away quickly enough now that he'd learned what he'd come to find out. He'd finally put to rest the vague fear that had been nagging at him since that last night in California when he'd looked at his drawings and found the pale-eyed malicious stare of Roweena Molesworth looking back at him. He knew now that he'd made no deals with this crowd, done nothing to jeopardize the race or betray his brother and Justine.

"Mauro, really, What are you plotters up to?" Monica asked as soon as Tony had gone. "This is not Palio, remember. There are to be no underhanded tricks in this race . . . or are there?" she asked with a low laugh.

"Monica!" Roweena chided with a wicked smile. "We were just having a bit of a visit with Mr. Jones. Such a nice, friendly, *open* young man, and so chatty, too."

"Were you really going to poison that beautiful stallion?" Gates asked with a twisted grin. "I've done a lot of things in my time to win a bet but nothing like that."

"I was going to do exactly that, but now young Mr. Jones has given me a much better idea." Roweena rubbed her hands in glee.

"So much *rain!* Even the dawns are gray in

this country," Justine complained irritably. "Do you think it's affecting Gavilan? It's certainly not doing me any good."

"I think it will clear in time for the race, Justine," Nick said. "Relax. You're upsetting the stallion. Yesterday, you worried that something would happen to him, that that gang of thieves would tamper with him. So I sat up all night with my pistol, guarding Gavilan, and Jim slept right in the box stall with him; but there wasn't a sign of trouble."

"Roweena was plotting something when she visited Tony in New York. He told us so. You know that," Justine insisted. "And you mustn't forget, I saw Mauro Zenga on his home ground, at Sienna. He told me all about the Palio and how that race was won by cunning and cheating and sabotage. I can't believe he or Roweena or that Bet-A-Million Gates, who dopes his own horses, are going to run this steeplechase fairly."

And something else was bothering Justine, though she chose not to mention it to Nick because, like most jockeys before a race, she envisioned all sorts of signs and portents that could mean triumph . . . or disaster.

The Gypsy woman who had told her fortune before had been at the gates of Sandringham Park this morning, and Justine had been unable to resist ducking into the small, dark tent once more. As she'd sat across from the fortune-teller, the old woman's dark-ringed eyes had fixed intently on her crystal ball and her callused hand had gripped Justine's.

385

"Today, you will win," the woman said in a cracking, sandpaper voice, and Justine began to smile. "Today, you will win and . . . you will lose." Justine snatched her hand away and stood, furious at herself for tempting fate by trafficking with a silly old carnival crone. But the woman had been right before. "You'll win a race and lose your heart to a tall, dark handsome stranger," she had prophesied, and Justine had won at Ainscot that day and then . . . there was Nicholas Jones. Now, she was to win . . . and lose—again.

"Tell me more," she implored. "I'll cross your palm again with silver—with gold—if only . . ." But the Gypsy woman had folded her hands and closed her eyes, and after a moment's hesitation, Justine had left the tent and hurried to the stable.

"There're only a few hours now to starting time. Not much can happen with all of us right here in this stall with Gavilan, can it?" Nick asked with a note of vexation. Justine's unexpected nervousness was very unlike her, and it was affecting not only the stallion but everyone else as well. Gavilan was kicking at his stall and flinging his head, and no one but Jim could get near him.

"Just stay with him every minute. I'm going to walk the course one more time," she said, ducking out of the stall and leaving Nick and Jim to amuse each other.

There was a larger crowd at Sandringham than she'd expected, but Gordon Bennett had publicized the race and Bertie had been besieged for invitations. In the packed stands built for this private race, scattered amongst strangers, were her father and mother, Justine knew, and Gray, the Erlangers, Mauro Zenga and Monica, and Roweena. Rob and Cath Edwards were there, she in the new bonnet and lace gloves Justine had given her. And many lights of the racing world would be watching this extraordinary field of competitors that included the Prince's own entry, Ambush II, who had run the real Grand National some months ago, in March, but had only come in seventh.

Justine left the crowds behind and followed the narrow, four-and-a-half-mile track that would be circled twice. The course perfectly duplicated the one at Aintree down to the last detail. There were rails on both sides, and fifteen jumps, each to be taken twice, some of them gorse hedge, some thistle, others rail fence. The highest of the jumps was about six feet and that would be no problem at all for Gavilan. No problem either would be the notorious Becher's Brook, where many horses always went down. Taking a thorn fence just before the nine-foot-wide ditch was the undoing of some of the best. Farther along the track, there was a sharp right turn after a five-foot fence and later, two more wet spots, Valentine's Brook and the infamous Water Jump, twelve feet wide, immediately after a two-foot fence on the take-off side. But Justine had seen

Gavilan running free, leaping wider obstacles and deeper and colder ones, too.

Steeplechase competition had begun as cross-country, one-on-one match races years and years ago, Justine had learned. The riders tore along over fields and meadows and brooks, from one church steeple to another, in the little Irish towns and villages where the sport had originated. But no Irish horse had ever run in the kind of wild country Gavilan knew. For him, this steeplechase would be a romp, colt's play, a picnic; and he'd do it faster than it had ever been done, much faster than the nine-plus minutes that were the usual winning speed at Aintree. If only the noise and the bustle didn't upset him, if other horses didn't back on him too closely or go down and trip him up ... If ... so many ifs, Justine worried as she made her way back to the stable, through the crowd of vendors and conjurers and clowns, of bookmakers hard at work and Gypsy fortune-tellers gazing into their crystal balls.

Off in the grass field beyond the race course, towering above the trees and rocking slightly in the wind, was a bouquet of brilliantly-colored balloons, some hot air propelled, some hydrogen filled. Once the steeplechase was over and the winning horse crowned, another race was to begin, James Gordon Bennett's first cross-Channel balloon event. It would be a spectacle like no other ever seen in the history of the universe, or so Bennett had promised in that morning's edition of his *International Herald Tribune*.

Chapter Forty-two

"You're magnificent, the pair of you," Nicholas said. On their way from the paddock to the track, he had stepped back to look Justine over once more as she perched up on Gavilan's withers, practically sitting on his neck. The golden stallion pawed and pranced, almost as eager as his rider, it seemed, to get into this race and win.

Still anticipating trouble, Justine had insisted on riding, though Jim had protested, and as Nick brought Gavilan to the starting line, she was sharp-eyed and observant, looking for any indication of something not quite right.

She got a cheer from the crowd as she fell in among the other riders, all dressed in the bright racing silks of their stables' colors. She wore buff leggings, leather chaps, and a fringed jacket. She and Gavilan both wore silver and turquoise, she on boots and belt and on the rings on her fingers, the horse on several amulets glinting on its bridle.

"If a little turquoise works, why not a little

more, for luck and easy jumps?" Nick had grinned as he'd decked out horse and rider before they'd left the stable. Though he hadn't shown it, he had his own concerns about what might happen. In fact, he'd almost insisted on riding the race himself, but had decided, at the last minute, to give Gavilan the advantage, of a lighter jockey with subtle hands and the best seat in town.

And so Gavilan, in high spirits, danced out onto the track at Sandringham, his long white mane, well brushed by Jim, flowing like silk to his knees and his tail held high, a waving white flag all the others would follow from start to finish . . . right to the very end.

Once the field was off in a burst of applause, Gavilan cleared every hurdle cleanly, perfectly, and no other jockey, not even the most experienced, sat the jumps better than Justine until, going over the very last one, with the finish line in sight . . . all was lost.

Already in midair taking that last jump, Gavilan veered sharply to the right as if a hand on his reins had pulled him off course, and he missed the soft spot in the hedge that Justine had picked out on her walk. He cleared the jump anyway and crossed the finish line first, where he went down, a stream of blood pouring from a wound in his side.

In less than two minutes, the golden bay stallion lay dead, of a pierced artery, and Justine was kneeling beside him, weeping openly like a child.

She wouldn't let them touch him, not a single hair of his mane or tail. When the crowd surged from the stands and across the track toward her and the felled champion, Justine warned them off, brandishing the bloodied, double-pointed stake that had been set with several others in the gorse hedge, all tilted at angles perfect for piercing the side of a jumper.

"It's what they always do here, take souvenir threads of the mane, when a popular horse goes down," Nick told Justine, as he gathered her in his arms and tried to stop her sobs and trembling. "How . . . did it happen?" he asked in a strangled voice.

"I heard the whistle — Jim's signal — and then Gavilan lurched toward the inside rail. I . . . Listen!" she said, looking about as the familiar high-pitched two-note whistle sounded again. "Where *is* Jim?"

"There!" Nick pointed, and then he was on the run toward a man and a woman dragging a struggling boy off toward a stand of trees.

"Hurry, hurry, you damned fool!" Roweena Molesworth hissed at Mauro Zenga who had hoisted Jim under one arm and was attempting to fend off the boy's wild, fist-clenched blows with the other.

"Little urchin!" he roared as Jim's fists landed full on his nose and blood began to flow. Zenga hurried after Roweena, stumbling through the trees and across a meadow toward the anchored balloons.

With inelegant disregard for propriety, Roweena hauled herself into the gondola of one, then took Jim from Zenga, her long nails digging into the boy's arms. She waited impatiently as the count cut the anchor ropes and loosed the grapnel hook before he, too, climbed in and at once began to throw the ballast—sandbags—over the side.

"They are getting close—very close. What are you doing? Why doesn't it go *up?*" Roweena's eyes were so wide and glaring the whites showed all around their pale blue, protuberant pupils, and her hands were white knuckled as she clutched the side of the gondola now, not Jim, who was whistling as loudly as he could. As the balloon's basket bumped along the ground, Roweena turned on the boy with such ferocity Zenga had to restrain her.

"You get the opals and I get the girl, that's our deal, but if you throttle our little hostage, my sweet," he said with heavy sarcasm, "we'll have nothing to bargain with. Idiot, you've made a shambles of everything so far," he hissed at her, forcing a handkerchief into Jim's mouth and cuffing the child to the floor of the gondola.

"If you had done as I wanted and just poisoned the damned horse, none of this would have happened," Roweena shrieked, but the count only smiled sourly and glanced about, looking for something else to jettison. He'd even thrown out their cork life jackets.

"It was you, remember, who changed the plan after Anthony Jones provided such *useful* information," he snarled at Roweena, as he began to hoist a small steamer trunk from the bottom of the gondola to his shoulder.

"What are you doing? No!" Roweena shrieked as the heavy object was set on the gondola rail, then toppled over the side to land on the field below with a thud. That done, the balloon began to lift slightly.

"There's thirty-seven thousand cubic feet of gas in this monstrous contraption. The only thing that was holding it down was that object. You're not going on a transatlantic cruise, just crossing the Channel. You needn't have brought your entire wardrobe. Well, now what is it?" Zenga asked the dumbstruck woman.

"My dresses . . . my dresses!" she choked out, gasping for breath.

"But how can you care about dresses at a time like this?" he demanded, throwing up his hands.

"The jewels—the royal jewels of Jodhpur—they're sewn into my dresses, you bloody fool!" Roweena wailed. She covered her face and sank to her knees, and the count, his eyes wild now, climbed over the side of the gondola and stood on a narrow ledge. As the balloon drifted up more quickly he held on to it with one hand and reached out with the other toward the heavy trunk that was disappearing in the distance.

It was then Nicholas grasped the count's ankles and held fast.

393

The added weight was just enough to keep the balloon from rising any higher, though it continued to skim along the ground in the stiff breeze.

"Jump! Jump *now*, boy!" Nick ordered Jim, who was peeking over the side. Roweena was crouched beside him, rendered so helpless by rage she no longer was able to comprehend what was happening.

"My jewels . . . my jewels," she repeated over and over, wringing her hands, her witchy eyes glazed.

Jim didn't have to be told again. Flinging one leg over the side of the gondola, he sat poised for a moment like a small sparrow, then, closing his eyes, he jumped. Nick let go of Zenga at the same moment, and man and boy landed safely together in Becher's Brook on the race course. The furious Count Zenga, now dangling from the balloon, was violently dashed against a high-rail jump, the impact shattering his right leg, as the balloon lifted aloft, but with an excruciating effort, he managed to haul himself back into the car and to shake his fists at the roaring crowd below.

"My jewels, oh, my lovely jewels!" Roweena was sobbing uncontrollably, tearing at her heavy hair that had come loose and was flying in the wind.

"After what you've done — destroy that magnificent stallion — you should be glad you're getting out alive, skipping away into cloudland with me." Zenga laughed madly, his face contorted with pain. "Perhaps . . ."—he began to punctuate his words with deep breaths—"you and I . . . will pay a visit to Jodhpur . . . with a *new* carpetbag," he said. Roweena stopped weeping and looked up at him with interest.

"Yes. What worked once will work again," she agreed.

"After my leg heals. That will take some time, I'm afraid. But now, come here and help me." He took a cigar from his case and set it between his teeth. Then Count Mauro Zenga handed Lady Roweena Molesworth a box of matches.

The loud detonation was heard about the countryside for miles as a spark from the match struck by Roweena ignited the flammable gases swirling above her head. The crowd at Sandringham, including the Prince, watched the balloon explode into flying fragments, in stunned silent amazement, and Justine looked from the falling flaming wreckage to the small wide-eyed child beside her.

"Oh, Jim!" she said, going down on her knees and pressing him to her. "If anything had happened to you . . ." Overcome by emotion, she couldn't say any more.

"They *made* me," the boy whispered harshly. "They said if I didn't whistle, they'd shoot . . ."

"Shoot who?" Nick asked, leading Justine, who was now carrying the boy, away from the crowd a little, his arms about them both.

"Her. Kill Justine. The man had the gun aimed. And I whistled and . . . Gavilan heard. They knew he'd come if I called," Jim said in a barely audible voice.

"They knew?" Nick's face was suddenly dark with anger. "How?"

"That man said . . . he said Tony told them." Jim sobbed now, and Nick, eyes slitted, said nothing. He just took his pistol from its holster, aimed, and fired at the figure running toward them. Justine screamed when she saw Tony go down, and then Nick turned on her, his eyes sinister and wild.

"You!" he rasped in a terrible voice. "All this . . . it's about *you*." He hurled the gun away with all his strength, then turned away and walked off.

Nick abandoned Justine on that terrible day, in the midst of the milling, shouting crowd as, tears flowing, she ran toward Anthony, though desperately wanting to go after Nicholas. In her shattered heart, she felt she'd never really see either of them again. Nick was right, it was all her fault, and now one brother lay dying, and at the other's hand. She'd come between them, as nothing or no one ever had, to loose passion, jealousy, deceit, and murder.

Chapter Forty-three

Early on a June morning in 1900, in the first year of the new century, on the first day of summer when the air was weighted with the salt scent of the sea and the perfume of roses, a solitary figure rode one horse and led another up a drive overhung by branches of aged oak, young again in spring-green leaf.

As he crested the rise at Silver Hill, the rambling house, set on a bluff above a sparkling blue bay, came into view, and when he reached it, he dismounted to knock at the door and then knock again at once, lacking patience to wait, having come so far, not merely in miles but on a journey of the heart.

The door swung open and Slade Hawkes stood looking at the man on his doorstep for a long, hard moment. Then words were exchanged, and some five minutes later, the visitor tipped his hat and strode off to stand on the crest of the bluff. He looked in both directions, along the strip of bay beach, and then he saw Justine, perched on a driftwood log, wild flowers overflowing the large basket beside her. She was looking out over the water, and there was a lovely calm about her that he hesitated to disturb. But as the man stared, a faint breeze lifted her hair and tugged at the hem of her skirt, and she turned as if she felt the pull of his heartstrings. Then she rose and started toward him, hesitantly.

Digging in his heels, Nicholas slid down the long bluff, and was running toward her as soon as his feet hit the sand. When they were a few feet apart, he stopped and waited for her, and when she came into his widespread arms, he crushed her against his hard body and his mouth, desperate, bruising, sought hers. He held her as though he'd never let her go.

But he finally did, though he kept a firm hold on her hand as they paced the sand and he talked.

"I went to lose myself in Montmartre, after the race, with Boni and Zou. No, no! It wasn't what you're supposing," he said quickly, seeing Justine's expression. "Those two were always more Tony's 'friends' than mine. He was their amusing American errand boy; he got them drugs and wine and picked up their bonnets at the milliner's—that sort of thing. My interest in them ended . . . well, you know when—when my mystery lover first came to me in the dark. But Zou did take care of me when I thought I'd killed my brother, and that was no easy thing to do because . . ." He sighed. "It was six months before I worked up the courage to find out, one

398

way or another." Nick's eyes were fierce but pained.

"I know," Justine said, resting a hand on his cheek. "And I also know he didn't betray us to Roweena, not with intent. He went to her to say the deal between them was off, whatever it was, and he talked more than he should have."

"Have you seen him?" Nicholas asked.

"Oh, yes," she answered. "He's been here for months. We've had some talks. He told me . . . some things."

"Such as?" Nicholas kept his eyes on Justine, but she didn't answer at first, just watched a flock of jays chase a black and white kitten across the beach, then perch in their oak tree complaining.

"He told me you were afraid of love . . . but of course I already knew that. And he also told me that every awful thing I'd ever heard about you—that you were reckless and profligate and wild and contentious—"

"Come on, Justine!" Nicholas flashed his rascally grin, and she laughed.

"Well, that was always him, not you, Tony said, or else you playing the bad boy to cover for him. You took the blame for his misdeeds to shield him. You were so good at everything, he said, he'd always felt a failure. Even when he tried to be a villain and make us lose the race, he couldn't do it. He failed even at that. He was self-deluded, he told me, and he'd decided that a man who turns a blind eye to the truth of things can't be much of an artist. After he told me all that . . . he offered to marry me."

"And did you accept?" Nicholas asked hesitantly. "Are you already Mrs. Jones, because if so—"

"No, I'm not Mrs. Jones, not yet," Justine said quickly, relieving Nick of his immediate misery. "But I expect to be quite soon now," she added. "What have you to say about that?"

"You love me, not Tony, you know you do, and Justine . . . I love you. You know that, too," Nick said quietly. He freed her hand and stepped in front of her, and when he lifted her chin, she couldn't break the hold of his black velvet stare. "I want to be with you forever . . . give you the first snowdrop that blooms on the stream bank each spring, the last sunflower of every fall. We belong together in that wild valley wilderness where there can be no deceptions, no games, just simple truth and true love. What I want is to see the mountains in your eyes again." He smiled, his tone soft with longing. "I've built you a house in the pines and red clover, near our rushing river. Now I've come for you. Will you come home with me?"

She didn't answer at once and his eyes that had been full of hope and promise became imperious and fierce, almost threatening. For a moment, she glimpsed the man he'd been the first time she'd ever seen him.

"It's been a year," she said. "I'm different, Nicky. I've changed. I'm not the impetuous child I was when we met. I've grown up. I've had to."

"You look the same—dewy fresh and beautiful.

And you feel the same in my arms," he said, mildly teasing her now.

"Don't you dare laugh at me, damn you!" she implored. "I took a wild gamble on you and . . . in a way . . . I lost."

"It was a bold, reckless thing you did, an innocent virgin slipping into a stranger's arms that way." His voice, burred with desire, caressed her.

"You were never a stranger."

"And you were always an optimist. Have you lost your courage?" he asked, his hands on his hips as she looked directly at him.

"I'm more cautious now, that's all."

"I asked your father for your hand in marriage, Miss Hawkes." Nick took a step toward her, his intent obvious, and she backed away.

"I'm surprised he didn't brandish his horsewhip. What did he say?" They had come to a place where a low branch overhung the beach and a wooden swing descended from it. Justine lighted on the swing like a bird and, digging her bare toes into the sand, pushed back and let go.

"Your father said you had an infinite capacity for loyalty and love," Nick called, watching her pass in front of him, his eyes following her as her hair streamed in the breeze and her petticoats flared. "Your father also said that he'd always tried to see to it your path was strewn with flowers, but that . . ." He reached up and grabbed the rope of the swing, bringing it to a stop. "He said you're entirely free to make your own mistakes. Well? . . ."

"Did he also tell you that there is going to be

a wedding here soon?" she asked.

Nick looked stunned. "So you really are going to marry my brother," he said, turning away. "Well, I've no right to blame you because it has been a year, as you said. But somehow, Justine, I never expected—"

"That I'd not wait for you forever?" she asked, and he nodded.

"Could you . . . reconsider?" he asked.

"If I do, you'll accuse me of being a tease and a heartbreaker, I'm afraid. You might even call me a wicked wanton for leaving yet another man standing at the altar. Besides, there are other reasons why I must think about this very carefully. Will you give me a little time?" she rose, toying with a small object, a shell, that she'd taken from her pocket.

"Very little time, about five minutes. I've never been a patient man," he said, noting the glint of mischief in her lovely eyes. "Is there anything I could do to help you come to a decision?" he asked, resting a hand on her shoulder and lowering his mouth to hers, tasting it lightly again and again until he felt her body soften and bend to his. "Now is this any way to come to a reasoned decision?" he asked hoarsely.

"No," she sighed, "but impetuosity has its attractions, hasn't it?" He stepped away from her and grinned.

"I don't want to be accused of unfairly influencing you, so while you're considering, I'll go and get the surprise I brought."

"Oh, I've a surprise for you, too," she declared. "But . . . yours first."

Justine was facing away from him when Nicholas came striding back along the sand.

"Now!" he called out when he was within a few feet of her, and she peeked over her shoulder at a golden yearling stallion with a beautiful, long white mane and flowing tail.

"He's Gavilan's!" Nick laughed. "And there are others."

"She's yours," Justine said, "and there'll be more." She turned to him then, so that he could see the infant energetically sucking at her breast, tiny fists clenched, dark eyes, big and curious, settling on Nick. "She's four months old and perfectly beautiful, isn't she?" Justine looked up with tear-bright, smiling eyes. "Knowing how terribly I loved you, your brother offered to give your daughter a name."

"Well . . . it would have been the right one," he declared softly, going down on one knee and extending a finger that the baby reached for.

"Oh, Nicky! Did you really think I'd not have come after you? If so, you're a man of little faith. I'd have found you there in the high valley. I've always known exactly where you were, I never had a doubt, but it wasn't time . . . not yet. I was waiting for her."

"The wedding?" he asked. "Who? . . ."

"Not mine, love." She smiled, stepping into his arms. "It's Gray and Marie-Laure who are to be wed."

They walked along together in silence, at the edge of the bay that was a blue-green mirror, reeds and marsh grass surrounding it, pale green against pale sand. And in the evening sea air, gulls soared and called just as they had on that long-ago morning when love first began for Justine Hawkes and Nicholas Jones.

"Your father said another thing," Nicholas began after a time. "He said that the love of a man and a woman . . . the children born of that love . . . are links in the endless chain of life — that's all that really matters."

On the fourth day of July in the year 1900, there was a very large, very grand double wedding at Silver Hill. The brides wore yards and yards of tulle and Alençon lace strewn with seed pearls and paillettes, Marie-Laure's of crystal, Justine's turquoise-dotted silver. Anthony Jones was best man for his brother and Gray's father stood up for him.

There were fireworks. The party lasted a week. Then, Justine and Nicholas, with one half-grown boy and an infant in arms, went West as so many had done before them, part of the flow of history as they stepped together into a new century. They left Gavilan's colt at Silver Hill, and took in exchange a cutting of a great silver linden tree to plant in the wilderness.

"As you told me once, Mrs. Jones, there's no way of knowing how the future will unfold." Nicholas smiled as he lifted Justine over their threshold. "But I think ours is going to be long and filled with love."

"I'll surely bet on that, Mr. Jones," she answered, smiling too.

Epilogue

The Royal Palace of Jodhpur
October 3, 1900

Dear Justine,

That I was not able to come across the
sea to attend your wedding at Silver Hill is
a great regret to me, but I am writing now
to extend a traditional Hindu wish to you
and Nicholas: May you be blessed with
eight sons.

By the time you receive this letter you
will have been Mrs. Jones for some time
and I will have become a Maharani of
Baroda. My own wedding . . .

"Do tell me, Justine, what does she say?"
Brigida Hawkes eagerly asked her daughter. The
two were chatting in the shade of the pretty ga-
zebo Nicholas had just finished building at the
edge of the white water river. It was a gift to

his wife on the occasion of their third anniversary. Justine, absorbed in the letter, hardly looked up.

"Indira says she will soon become, by now has become, the wife of her Prince. Tommy Gordon left India for good and she's heard only rumors of him since, but she'll never forget him, she says."

Justine turned a page and read a few lines aloud to Brigida, who was knitting as usual, this time a bunting for Justine's next baby, expected in early winter. " 'The stolen royal jewels you had returned to us were not replaced in the treasury but were sold to help feed our people during this terrible time of famine that has gripped India for the past two years. Though your mother and I have never met, I will always feel close to her, and eternally grateful to her and to the other ladies of New York who have raised money to help us in our time of despair. Of course, the arrival of your father's ship at Bombay in September, heavily loaded with a life-giving cargo of corn and seed, touched us all most profoundly,' " Justine read on. " 'It is such acts of generosity that make me feel, as I told you before, that we are all connected, one to the other.' "

"The monsoon rains finally did come thank heaven," Brigida interjected. "The Indian famine is at an end, and now your friend has begun a new life, as you have." She looked up from her knitting to see Jim riding toward them across the meadow, holding a little girl in the saddle in front of him. Her granddaughter, Nicolette, was, at three, as comfortable on a horse as her mother had been at the same age. "When you answer Indira's letter, you will tell her all about the children, of course," Brigida requested.

"Of course, Mother." Justine took up her pen and placed a sheet of paper on her small lap desk.

Wild River Ranch
July 4, 1903

My Friend Indira,

Far removed from the world as we are, your letter, tucked into some mountain man's back pack, just reached us today. Your wish—that we be blessed with eight sons—is on its way to coming true. As I've told Mother, who is here on her first visit, I've a feeling our next baby will be a boy. Our little girl already has three brothers, twins born a year and a half ago and our adopted son, Jim, who's teaching her to ride. At thirteen, Jim's one of the best rodeo riders in the West. He'd like to play polo against your father's team one day when we all visit Jodhpur again as I promised we would.

I, too, am sad that you could not be at Silver Hill for my wedding and that I was not there to see you a bride, but though we are on opposite sides of the world, the distance is never great between friends who have shared the deepest secrets of their hearts as you and I have. My brother-in-law . . .

"Are you telling her everything?" Brigida asked. "About Anthony and? . . ." Justine nodded.

Nick's brother, Tony, has become a very important architect here by designing a family home that is similar to the Indian *bungalla* he saw in your country. The deep, overhanging eaves provide shade, and the open airy rooms flow together without the restriction of hallways and corridors. The layout is ideal for the warm climate enjoyed by much of this state. The population is growing very quickly and Tony is getting very rich with his California bungalow, though he slips away from work whenever he can, into the wilds to draw, birds mostly and other . . .

"Are you writing that you have friends living near, that you're not entirely isolated in your love nest?"

"Yes, I am telling her that, Mother." Justine laughed as she dipped her pen into a silver inkwell.

We have neighbors just five miles from us — Rob and Cath Edwards, who have a ranch of their own here in the Sierras. Though never blessed with children of their own, they are raising four youngsters taken from the orphan trains that regularly pass through Carson City. . . .

"She'll want to know about Gray, Justine. Be sure to tell Indira how happily married he is, and how Marie-Laurel's *pâtisserie* in New York is a great success?"

Justine didn't answer this time, just kept on writing as Brigida put down her knitting needles and waved at three men approaching on horseback.

I will write to our friend, Philip Carpenter, in Australia, asking that he send you and the Prince a wedding gift, the most beautiful and perfect black opal he can find. My own opals are rarely worn now, perhaps once a year at most, when Nicholas and I make our annual visit to San Francisco for . . .

Justine looked up then, as if, as always, she could feel Nick's dark eyes fixed on her. He was riding in now with her father and, amazingly, his father, too.

"He's still such a nice-appearing man, isn't

he?" Brigida asked, meaning Quinn Jones. Justine nodded. "Almost as handsome as your father, I'd say."

"Very nice-appearing," Justine said, "and his young wife is quite a beauty, isn't she? She seems to have cured him of the wanderlust that's driven him all these years."

"When Quinn appeared at your wedding, Justine, with a young woman not half his age, the granddaughter of a Hawaiian missionary, well . . . I was amazed. And pleased. It's good that he was able to come to terms with his sons after so long."

"Quinn Jones has a habit of turning up at weddings every twenty years or so. Nick's half sister, Evangeline, told me the last time she saw their father it was at her own wedding. He seems very happy, doesn't he?" Justine stood and smoothed her skirt, then smiled as Nick dismounted and came toward her quickly, his turquoise-and-silver spurs jingling.

"You must be talking about me." He grinned, having caught Justine's last few words.

"You are so vain and cocky!" she teased, stepping into his arms. "Do you suppose you're the only man I ever think about?"

"I'd better be," he answered, looking into eyes bubbling with mischief and mirth . . . and love.

LOVE'S BRIGHTEST STARS SHINE
WITH ZEBRA BOOKS!

CATALINA'S CARESS   (2202, $3.95)
by Sylvie F. Sommerfield
Catalina Carrington was determined to buy her riverboat
back from the handsome gambler who'd beaten her brother
at cards. But when dashing Marc Copeland named his
price—three days as his mistress—Catalina swore she'd
never meet his terms . . . even as she imagined the rapture a
night in his arms would bring!

BELOVED EMBRACE   (2135, $3.95)
by Cassie Edwards
Leana Rutherford was terrified when the ship carrying her
family from New York to Texas was attacked by savage pi-
rates. But when she gazed upon the bold sea-bandit Bran-
don Seton, Leana longed to share the ecstasy she was sure
sure his passionate caress would ignite!

ELUSIVE SWAN   (2061, $3.95)
by Sylvie F. Sommerfield
Just one glance from the handsome stranger in the dockside
tavern in boisterous St. Augustine made Arianne tremble
with excitement. But the innocent young woman was already running from one man . . . and no matter how fiercely
the flames of desire burned within her, Arianne dared not
submit to another!

MOONLIT MAGIC   (1941, $3.95)
by Sylvie F. Sommerfield
When she found the slick railroad negotiator Trace Cord
trespassing on her property and bathing in her river, innocent Jenny Graham could barely contain her rage. But when
she saw how the setting sun gilded Trace's magnificent physique, Jenny's seething fury was transformed into burning
desire!

*Available wherever paperbacks are sold, or order direct from the
Publisher. Send cover price plus 50¢ per copy for mailing and handling to Zebra Books, Dept. 2525, 475 Park Avenue South, New
York, N.Y. 10016. Residents of New York, New Jersey and Pennsylvania must include sales tax. DO NOT SEND CASH.*

ZEBRA ROMANCES FOR ALL SEASONS
From Bobbi Smith

ARIZONA TEMPTRESS (1785, $3.95)

Rick Peralta found the freedom he craved only in his disguise as El Cazador. Then he saw the exquisitely alluring Jennie among his compadres and the hotblooded male swore she'd belong just to him.

CAPTIVE PRIDE (2160, $3.95)

Committed to the Colonial cause, the gorgeous and independent Cecelia Demorest swore she'd divert Captain Noah Kincade's weapons to help out the American rebels. But the moment that the womanizing British privateer first touched her, her scheming thoughts gave way to burning need.

DESERT HEART (2010, $3.95)

Rancher Rand McAllister was furious when he became the guardian of a scrawny girl from Arizona's mining country. But when he finds that the pig-tailed brat is really a voluptuous beauty, his resentment turns to intense interest; Laura Lee knew it would be the biggest mistake in her life to succumb to the cowboy — but she can't fight against giving him her wild DESERT HEART.

Available wherever paperbacks are sold, or order direct from the Publisher. Send cover price plus 50¢ per copy for mailing and handling to Zebra Books, Dept. 2525, 475 Park Avenue South, New York, N.Y. 10016. Residents of New York, New Jersey and Pennsylvania must include sales tax. DO NOT SEND CASH.

ZEBRA HAS THE SUPERSTARS
OF PASSIONATE ROMANCE!

CRIMSON OBSESSION   (2272, $3.95)
by Deana James

Cassandra MacDaermond was determined to make the handsome gambling hall owner Edward Sandron pay for the fortune he had stolen from her father. But she never counted on being struck speechless by his seductive gaze. And soon Cassandra was sneaking into Sandron's room, more intent on sharing his rapture than causing his ruin!

TEXAS CAPTIVE   (2251, $3.95)
by Wanda Owen

Ever since two outlaws had killed her ma, Talleha had been suspicious of all men. But one glimpse of virile Victor Maurier standing by the lake in the Texas Blacklands and the half-Indian princess was helpless before the sensual tide that swept her in its wake!

TEXAS STAR   (2088, $3.95)
by Deana James

Star Garner was a wanted woman—and Chris Gillard was determined to collect the generous bounty being offered for her capture. But when the beautiful outlaw made love to him as if her life depended on it, Gillard's firm resolve melted away, replaced with a raging obsession for his fiery TEXAS STAR.

MOONLIT SPLENDOR   (2008, $3.95)
by Wanda Owen

When the handsome stranger emerged from the shadows and pulled Charmaine Lamoureux into his strong embrace, she sighed with pleasure at his seductive caresses. Tomorrow she would be wed against her will—so tonight she would take whatever exhilarating happiness she could!

Available wherever paperbacks are sold, or order direct from the Publisher. Send cover price plus 50¢ per copy for mailing and handling to Zebra Books, Dept. 2525, 475 Park Avenue South, New York, N.Y. 10016. Residents of New York, New Jersey and Pennsylvania must include sales tax. DO NOT SEND CASH.